Also by Colin Meloy and Carson Ellis

The Wildwood Chronicles

Wildwood

Under Wildwood

Wildwood Imperium

the
WHIZ MOB
and the
GRENADINE KID

Colin Meloy

Illustrations by
Carson Ellis

BALZER + BRAY
An Imprint of HarperCollins Publishers

Balzer + Bray is an imprint of HarperCollins Publishers.

The Whiz Mob and the Grenadine Kid

Library of Congress Control Number: 2017943134
ISBN 978-0-06-234245-4

The artist used graphite pencil to create the illustrations for this book.
Typography by Dana Fritts
17 18 19 20 21 PC/LSCH 10 9 8 7 6 5 4 3 2 1

First Edition

To Felix and Titine

Chapter
ONE

Before I tell you what Charlie Fisher saw, the incredible and beautiful thing he witnessed, and how it would set into motion a
series of events that would change his life in a very dramatic way for
a very long time, I should first explain to you who Charlie was and
how he came to be sitting there in the Place Jean Jaurès in Marseille,
France, on a warm Tuesday morning in April 1961.

To start with, Charlie was on vacation. At least, that was how his
father had suggested he view his current predicament. To that end,
the last few years of his life were a kind of series of vacations. To
you this might seem like a very good deal for a twelve-year-old boy,
which Charlie was. However: if your life was just a series of vacations,

one after another, you'd probably find the prospect of yet one more vacation pretty boring, which was how Charlie felt about the whole situation.

You see, Charlie's father was Charles Fisher, Senior. You are forgiven if you don't recognize the name; this all happened well before your time. No doubt your grandparents would be very familiar with Charles Erasmus Fisher Sr., the noted American diplomat, the one who had married the young German heiress Sieglinde Dührer in a well-publicized ceremony on the veranda of the Neuschwanstein Castle in Bavaria. The same Fisher who brokered the Reykjavík Accords and settled, once and for all, the long and bloody Greco-Hungarian War. But, sadly, it is his marriage that overshadows his great accomplishments as a warrior for peace. Charlie's mother, Sieglinde, was a beautiful woman, a stage actress of some renown, and Charles Sr. had fallen for her while on a trip to Vienna a few years after the end of World War II. Their marriage was short and spectacular and managed to produce a good deal of ink for the Washington gossip rags, not to mention Charlie Jr. himself, but by the time of Charlie's seventh birthday, they'd been separated long enough that the divorce, when it came, was a mere formality. Charlie had barely known his father, a man who had spent a fraction of his married life at the family's brick town house in Georgetown, Washington, DC. The boy received regular postcards, written in his father's impeccable hand, from such exotic locales as Moscow, Buenos Aires, and Yokohama, but Charlie could count on one hand the number of nights he'd actually had his father read at his bedside. Sieglinde, along with a host of assistants, nannies, and governesses, was Charlie's only real family. So it was a great surprise to Charlie when his mother told him one morning, in no uncertain terms, that she had grown very tired of being a mother and that Charlie was to live with his father from here on out. Sieglinde would be happy to consider herself a kind of "cool aunt" to Charlie, should he ever need one.

What could Charlie do? Being a boy of nine years at the time, very little. The housemaid, Penny, helped him pack his most prized and portable possessions (which amounted to: seven books, a suitcase of clothes, and a box of green army men) and kissed his forehead as she saw him seated in the backseat of a Lincoln Continental. He was driven to the airport and there put on a plane to Morocco, where his father (or someone) would be waiting to receive him. He was to live the life of a professional diplomat's child from this point forward, forever passing from one world to another, Toronto to Bombay to Vladivostok, his weeks and months a seemingly never-ending parade of vacations.

And he couldn't have been more bored.

Which was precisely what he was feeling when he was sitting in Place Jean Jaurès in Marseille, on that warm Tuesday morning in April. If you were as world-wise and world-weary as Charlie was, you would know that Marseille is a very famous French port town on the Mediterranean Sea. And if you'd spent as much time as Charlie had on airplanes, hacking through a reading list that had been prescribed by your tagalong tutor, you'd know that Edmond Dantès, the hero of Dumas's *The Count of Monte Cristo*, had lived out his imprisonment in the Château d'If, which sat on a small island off the coast of Marseille. *And* if you'd received as many lectures on safety as Charlie had by his stern father and his small army of assistants and secretaries, you'd know that many consider Marseille to be something of a thieves' paradise.

The idea excited Charlie—a haven for the criminal underbelly of the world, here in his own backyard. It was a welcome change from Zurich's sterile and modern avenues, from Hong Kong's restricted zones. It was the sort of thing that got Charlie's twelve-year-old imagination firing on all cylinders. However, once he'd spent a few weeks at his new home, he soon realized that if there was one epidemic currently endangering the lifeblood of Marseille, it was this: tourists.

Noisy, complaining tourists.

Charlie used this discovery, however, to good effect. He'd made a deal with his tutor, a perpetually cranky twenty-five-year-old man named Simon, that writing five-hundred-word stories based on people he'd seen on the street would count toward his English composition credits. A deal was struck; a short story writer was born. Charlie most enjoyed reimagining the interior world of the huddled masses of tourists, recently disgorged from some waiting cruise ship, who wandered the streets and squares of the city. And that was how he came to be sitting on a wooden bench, observing and recording the wayward sightseers in Marseille's bustling market at the Place Jean Jaurès on that Tuesday morning.

A frowning young woman in sunglasses trailed listlessly after a middle-aged man as he inspected the market's many wares. Charlie's fountain pen—a silver Sheaffer Imperial given to him by his father for his eleventh birthday—hovered above the lined paper of his composition notebook briefly before beginning the following passage: *She was an heiress to a sugar beet fortune. He was a traveling snake oil salesman. They met on a yacht. He promised her eternal youth. She had to follow him around the world as he collected the necessary ingredients for the potion. Little did she know, it was a search that would last a lifetime.*

He cocked his head sideways as he reread what he'd written. A smile bloomed across his face. He ironed out the next page with the palm of his hand.

"What are you doing?" came a voice, speaking slightly accented English.

"Pardon me?" Charlie looked over and saw a young boy, dressed in drainpipe blue jeans and a white T-shirt, sitting next to him on the bench. His light brown skin and dark hair suggested he was of Middle Eastern descent. This is the first time you've heard Charlie speak, so you should know that he spoke in a low, quiet

voice that over the last year had throttled about two steps lower. He was understandably a little shy about the change. At the behest of his mother, he'd seen a speech pathologist when he was eight, addressing a slight stutter he'd adopted during his kindergarten year. He managed to shake the impediment, but in the meantime developed a habit of, as his father called it, "speaking into his chin"—whatever that meant. But we must trust the elder Fisher's observation, and so you are instructed to read Charlie's dialogue in such a fashion. Keep in mind, however, that this rule will apply only to the first twelve chapters. After that point, you will find that Charlie begins speaking in an altogether different way. It is advised that you change your reading accordingly. For now, however, Charlie is speaking into his chin.

The boy responded, "I said: What are you doing? You writing poems or something?"

"Nah," said Charlie warily. "Just writing stories."

"Stories." The boy picked up a small stick and began scratching the tip absently against the wood of the bench. "Nice. Like that old bearded man?"

"The old bearded man?"

The boy winced, as if the act of remembering was some sort of physical strain. "What's his name. Writes stories. Heming . . . ford."

"Hemingway," Charlie corrected. "Ernest Hemingway."

"That's the one," said the boy, with a smile.

"Well, I wouldn't compare myself to him, but I guess the general idea is the same."

"Please, carry on," said the boy. "Maybe I'll watch for a tick."

Charlie smiled politely; he turned and surveyed the plaza for his next subject. His thoughts were interrupted when the boy spoke again: "Oh, I see."

"What's that?"

"You're writing what's going on. In the square."

"In a way, yes."

"Got it. Continue."

Charlie was preparing to do just this, when he was interrupted again.

"What about him?"

"Who?" asked Charlie, feeling a first twinge of annoyance.

"That fellow there. With the white hat." The boy pointed toward the market crowd.

Charlie followed the boy's finger. A heavyset man in a loose seersucker suit and a white panama hat was wandering the stalls. Every five steps or so, the man would raise his wrist and shake back the sleeve of his jacket to check his watch.

"Oh, right," said Charlie. He could feel the boy's attention over his shoulders, waiting for him to begin writing. He felt self-conscious at the boy's scrutiny. The boy must've guessed at Charlie's insecurity, because he turned his attention back toward the stick in his hand.

Charlie began to write: *Would he arrive? The man with the robotic arm had said he should be at La Plaine at two o'clock. He only had so much time before the Martian sentries would arrive, demanding their ransom.*

He'd just finished penning this last imagined observation when he noticed something that struck him as a little strange. There seemed to be a girl following the man as he wove between the vendors' carts, a girl who clearly was not connected to the man in any concrete way.

He wrote: *Unbeknownst to Radcliffe, the Martian sentry had arrived, cleverly in the guise of a little girl.*

Charlie's attention went back to the scene playing out: With every lazy pivot the man in the blue-and-white suit took, now snaking between a line of iron bollards like a slalom skier, the young girl seemed to ape his every move, several steps back. When the man occasioned to look at his watch, the girl would inch closer. Charlie tapped his pen against his cheek. He'd now spent enough time in this square, on this Tuesday morning, to have a kind of heightened awareness of the goings-on in the market, of the interplay between its occupants. The girl following the man seemed to somehow operate *outside* of that system, like she was a shadow or a ghost, existing somewhere *beyond* or *above* the bustle of the real-world market. Much like a Martian sentry would, he supposed.

Just then, he saw there was a boy in front of the man who exhibited the same disposition, the same disconnectedness. What's more, the longer Charlie watched, the more he realized that the boy was actually somehow *guiding* the man—slowing him down, blocking his exits. He began to almost control the man's movements: stepping to his left when the man began to go left, slowing down when the man began to speed up—all without the man's awareness. Before long, the girl behind the man was shadowing him perfectly, as if she were just an extension of his body.

And then it happened. The thing. The thing that would prove to put a ninety-degree kink in the straight line that was Charlie Fisher's life.

The man was robbed.

More to the point: he was pickpocketed.

But it wasn't just a quick grab in a moment of distraction; no, it was an orchestrated thing, a smooth tumbling of choreographed movements, one action cascading into the other. Charlie barely saw the crime happen—it was like catching a hummingbird in your peripheral vision, briefly, before it flitted away. The boy in front of the man stopped suddenly, bringing the man up short only inches from his back. And then: from seemingly nowhere, a third child—a boy Charlie's age—appeared from the crowd and casually batted the back of the man's hat so it tipped, ever so slightly, down on his forehead. The man, under the impression that he'd merely been brushed in the crowd, removed his hand from his pants pocket and righted the brim of his cap. That's when the girl who'd been shadowing the man, now perfectly positioned, gracefully smoothed her hand along the side of the man's trouser leg as you would wipe a piece of lint from your sleeve and abruptly began to walk away. A fourth child—another boy—materialized from the crowd and the two passed shoulder to shoulder. A thin brown object was transferred, one to the other. Charlie suddenly realized it was the man's wallet.

But the fleecing of the man did not stop there: the boy who'd forced the man into position turned around and made to apologize for his clumsy behavior: he reached his hand out in an offer of a handshake. The man, still ignorant of the fact that he no longer was in possession of his wallet, took the boy's hand with a reluctant smile and shook it. The boy smiled, bowed, and disappeared into the crowd.

The man's perambulations resumed as he stepped around the barking sellers in the market, waiting for his expected visitor. When he stopped, once again, to glance at his wristwatch, he froze in place. Even from Charlie's remove, he could see what the man saw: his wrist was naked. His watch was gone.

And Charlie stifled a laugh. He couldn't help it. He was awestruck. And while he knew that he was a bystander to an extraordinary theft, it had been done with such fluidity and art that it seemed to barely count as an illegal act. It seemed like magic to Charlie.

"Did you see . . ." He looked to his right to see if the boy in the blue jeans had witnessed the same thing, but he was alone on the bench; the boy had left. He then began scanning the crowd for the four children—the perpetrators of the incredible operation. They'd melted away, but now he was aware of several more figures in the busy market who appeared to be casing their victims with equal finesse. Prior to the crime, the plaza had appeared to Charlie like a field of clover: placid, unexceptional. But now his vision had focused and he could see the legion of bees that were harvesting that clover of its rich nectar. It was like he'd discovered the secret hive itself—the Place Jean Jaurès, on a busy Tuesday morning, was the domain of the pickpockets.

Floored, Charlie lifted his pen to absently scratch his nose—yet something wasn't right. He looked down to see what was in his hand.

The pen was gone.

He was holding a stick.

Chapter TWO

For a moment, Charlie entertained the notion that he'd never actually owned a Sheaffer Imperial fountain pen—that all along, he'd been using the piece of wood that was now in his hand. He imagined his father and his traveling entourage humoring the poor, addled boy and his beloved stick until such time as he could safely be committed to a sanitarium. Thankfully, this brief fantasy passed and Charlie returned to his senses.

One thing was certain: his pen was gone. Like the man's wallet and watch, it had been stolen. But how?

A new thrum of activity in the square startled him from his shocked contemplation; several market-goers were shouting in French at a few policemen who were milling about the plaza. *"AU*

VOLEUR!" was the refrain. Charlie had paid enough attention during his rudimentary French exercises to know this meant *thief*. His eyes skirted the now-chaotic plaza, the multitudes of market-goers whose attention had turned from casually perusing the sellers' booths to desperately checking their pockets and purses. A flash of blue and white, just off to Charlie's left, alerted him to a skirmish that was happening on the margin of the square. There, he saw the boy who'd just moments before been observing his writing. The boy in the white shirt and the blue jeans. The boy who had been absently scratching at the bench with a stick.

Charlie stammered a few words to no one in particular as the synapses of his brain busily pieced together the events that had transpired: pen, boy with stick, pen gone, stick remains, boy gone. The images flooded at him like flash cards presented by a particularly impatient teacher.

By the time he'd managed to get back on firm mental footing, the boy had escaped, having tussled with a heavyset policeman and come out the victor. He could be seen scampering off down one of the many arterial avenues that branched off the plaza like petals from a flower. He'd caught the attention of most of the law officers in the square, who were all desperate for some suspect to collar. A mad dash of black-clad policemen poured out of the Place Jean Jaurès, after the blue-jeaned pen thief.

Charlie leapt up and, his composition notebook tucked under his arm, gave quick pursuit after the stampede of police. He felt weirdly possessive of the young boy. That was *his* thief they were after.

"Wait!" he shouted. No one seemed to hear. Or if they did, they didn't feel like heeding him.

The thief was momentarily delayed on Rue Sibie when he upended a stall in front of a bookshop. It gave Charlie a moment to catch up to the action. A tempest of books fell sideways into the street and the boy scrabbled to stay afoot; two of the four police were not so agile— they tripped, fell on each other, and were out of the chase. Charlie nimbly navigated the obstacle, keeping pace with the two policemen in front of him. A woman illicitly selling pistachios on the sidewalk, seeing the police, scrambled to collect and hide her wares.

The street intersected with Rue des trois Mages, just a few yards beyond the bookshop, and a hectic flow of traffic made for a tricky crossing. The white-shirted boy managed it expertly, threading the buzzing scooters and Peugeot Coupes like a toreador dodging through a stampede of bulls. His pursuers had neither his agility nor his size, and one policeman collided noisily with a pair of boys on a Vespa. The machine went clattering across the pavement, and the air was awash with the sound of squealing brakes as the traffic came to a stuttering halt.

"*Pardon, pardon,*" said Charlie politely, as he braved the crossing. A consul general's son, he did have a kind of reputation to uphold. For his troubles, he received a barrage of abuse so loud and frenetic he was thankful his knowledge of French was as limited as it was. Reaching the safety of the sidewalk, he saw that the two policemen had managed to catch the boy. One officer had him by the collar of his shirt; the other was busy patting down his pockets.

The police were yelling angrily in French; the boy was waving his hands and saying, "*No parlez français!*" over and over. They'd just produced a pen, Charlie's pen, from the thief's front pants pocket and were waving it in the boy's face when Charlie arrived at the scene.

"Where are zee billfolds?" demanded one of the policemen in heavily accented English. "What else do yoo have?"

"Nothing, I swear!" shouted the boy. "I just nicked the pen, that's all."

Breathless and excited, Charlie put in, "It's my pen!"

The tableau froze and all three of the people in front of Charlie swiveled their heads to look at the newcomer.

"Verry good," said one of the policemen with an air of stuffy pride. "We have zee victim."

This was when Charlie said something that he himself did not fully see coming. He said, "He's not a thief."

"'E's what?" asked one of the policemen.

"I said, he's not a thief," responded Charlie.

"'E most certainly is," said the other policeman.

Charlie took a deep breath and said, "I gave it to him. I gave him the pen."

The other officer, still holding the boy by his shirt, sneered at Charlie and said, "Yoo gave it to 'eem?" His upper lip was marked by a thin splash of mustache.

"It was a gift," said Charlie. "Please let him go."

The policemen kept hold of the boy, though their attention was now entirely devoted to Charlie.

"'Oo are yoo?" asked one of the officers.

This might be a good place to pause for a moment and assure the reader that in every instance in which English is spoken in a French accent in this story, it will not be in the kind of ham-fisted attempt at portraying a French accent like the preceding few lines of dialogue. That is the last instance in which it will occur. Let us assume that when the text states that a person speaks English in a French accent, it is done as it might be by someone who is really doing his level best to speak a tongue that is not his own. I believe your imagination is ample enough to supply that detail.

Charlie answered, "I'm Charlie Fisher." He then pointed to the barrel of the pen, where his name was etched in a tasteful cursive script.

Slowly, reluctantly, the policemen relaxed their grips on the boy's shirt collar. The boy fell away and took a few steps backward, shaking his shoulders. He, too, was staring at Charlie in disbelief. He was so stunned, in fact, that he had a hard time coming up with an answer when one of the policemen asked him, "Is that true?"

"Y-yeah," the boy stammered. "Sure enough. That's the truth." He looked down at the pen, as if seeing it for the first time. "Thank you very much. For this pen."

Charlie smiled. "My pleasure. I hope you use it well." He then looked at the two officers and, steeling himself, said, "You can go. Everything's just fine here."

The two policemen exchanged a long, confused look. One of them began to say something, but Charlie waved away his objection. "Honestly, officers," he said. "Surely you have better things to do."

"Very well," one of the policemen said, finally. "If that is the truth."

"It is," confirmed Charlie.

"Well, then . . . ," said the other officer.

"Good day, gentlemen!" said Charlie loudly.

The policemen each stood for a moment, studying the two children as if committing their every freckle to memory. One grumbled something in French, the other laughed under his breath, and the two together strode off.

Once they'd gone, the boy in the white shirt looked at Charlie from between the strands of his brown hair, which had fallen over his eyes during the commotion. He glanced down at the pen, which he still had clutched in his hand. "Can I really have it?" was the first thing he said.

Charlie laughed. "You can. On one condition," he said.

"What's that?"

"You show me how you did it."

The boy's name was Amir and he hailed from Lebanon—or that was how he introduced himself. He'd announced his name and birthplace with the kind of confidence that only invited suspicion. He did not give his last name, and Charlie didn't press him for it. He said he hadn't meant to take the pen, that he figured Charlie didn't deserve to have his pen taken from him, but after he'd seen Charlie use it and he'd seen the words it'd created, he was suddenly very desirous of it. As if it, the pen, were the source of the strange stories that Charlie was creating out of thin air.

"So I took it. Simple as that."

They'd walked some blocks off and found the curb of a fountain a welcome place to sit. Charlie eyed his companion in disbelief, saying, "It doesn't seem very simple. I mean, I had the pen in my hand."

"I don't know how to tell you. You did have the pen in your hand, yeah. But you were looking off, weren't you? You weren't paying no attention to the pen."

"But I don't have to be looking at it to know that it's in my hand."

The boy made a face, one that suggested that further contradiction would only be impolite.

Charlie smiled. "Here, give me the pen."

"The pen?" The boy frowned and looked down his chin at the tip of the Sheaffer Imperial. It was sticking out of his shirt pocket.

"I'll give it back, don't worry."

The pen and the stick (which Charlie had kept as a souvenir of the theft) transferred possession for the second time that day. Charlie held the pen in his right hand, gripping it as if he were writing.

"Do it again," he said, nodding down at the stick in the boy's hand.

Amir laughed. "Well, I can't now, can I?"

"And why not?"

"Well, you're rumbled, so to speak."

"Rumbled?" asked Charlie.

"It means you're onto me. You know I'm fixing to pinch it." The boy licked his lips; he had the slightest trace of a beard on his chin, and his two front teeth hung slightly askew in their gums.

"Very well," said Charlie. "I shall act like I don't know."

The boy seemed to be open to the idea. He said, "Do as you were. Like, when you was writing."

"Oh, right," said Charlie, producing his notebook from beneath his arm. "I'll do that." He opened the book to a clean page and held the pen over it as if he were about to write. He waited, his eye straying occasionally to the boy who sat by his side. The boy hadn't moved.

"Well, you've got to write something," said Amir.

"Oh," said Charlie. "Okay."

He began to write his name: *Charles Fish*—

SCRITCH! A gash of ink scarred the page as Amir reached over and inelegantly yanked the pen out of Charlie's hand. Charlie flinched and glared at his companion. "Not like that," he protested.

Amir laughed, deeply, heartily. "That's the easiest way," he said, twisting the pen through his fingers playfully. "The clout and lam, like a proper rough tool."

"Do it for real, the way you did, with the stick."

"Okay, okay," said Amir as he handed the pen back. "For real this time."

The pen nib hovered over the paper once again, and Charlie began to write his name. To his great surprise, no ink appeared on the page. The nib scratched against the paper noisily but left no mark. Charlie studied the pen to confirm that it was not a stick, which it clearly was not. He then glanced over at Amir.

Amir was holding the ink cartridge.

"How did you . . . ," gasped Charlie, now speaking into his chin more than ever. "I don't believe it."

The boy shrugged, as if he could take or leave Charlie's statement. "Then don't," he said. "Can I have my pen back?"

Charlie wordlessly handed over the emptied pen shaft. Taking it, Amir unscrewed it and slid the cartridge back in place.

"Did you know the others? The pickpockets in the market?" asked Charlie, after a moment.

"Maybe," responded the boy.

"You can tell me. I won't say anything."

The boy fiddled with the pen before saying, "Maybe I ask you a question first."

"Fair enough," said Charlie.

"Why didn't you throw me?" asked Amir.

"Why didn't I what?"

The boy clarified: "Why'd you cover for me, back there, with the police?"

"I was curious," Charlie replied. "And you seem like a nice kid. You didn't deserve to be arrested."

"You didn't know that then."

"I had a hunch," said Charlie, smiling.

"Maybe you are too nice, Charlie Fisher," said Amir. "Maybe you don't read people that good."

"I think I'm a pretty decent judge."

"I stole from you. That makes me a criminal."

"But you're a different kind. You can do something that not a lot of people can do."

Amir shrugged indifferently.

"Teach me," said Charlie. "Teach me to do what you do."

The boy whistled between his teeth and shook his head. "I cannot, Charlie Fisher Jr., I am very sorry to say. We're from two different places, you and me. You're from the straight world. I'm a tool. It don't mix."

"A tool?"

"A cannon. A tout. On the whiz."

"Still not following."

"A pickpocket, Charlie. I'm a thief. You? You are a good American kid. A writer of stories. I think you should stay that way."

Charlie was undeterred. "Then maybe," he said, puffing out his chest, "maybe that *is* my pen after all. *Perhaps* I got my story mixed up with the police back there."

"You wouldn't," said Amir.

"I would," said Charlie. Two policemen could be seen, some yards away, directing traffic on a busy avenue. "Those two seem like they might be sympathetic."

Silence reigned between them for a brief moment as the two boys locked eyes. The clatter of the Marseillais streets dinned around them. Amir continued to flip the pen between his agile fingers.

"You put me in a tight spot," said Amir finally. He licked his lips and winced. "Very tight spot."

Charlie shrugged. "C'mon," he said.

"I'll think about it," said the boy in blue jeans, after a moment longer.

"Where? When?" chirped Charlie, barely letting Amir finish.

Amir shook his head disapprovingly. "This isn't a usual thing. I have to see, I have to make sure. How 'bout this: tomorrow, I'll come to your house. I'll show you then. Okay?"

"Okay," said Charlie, and he stuck out his hand to solemnize the deal. Amir shook it gamely. He then stood up and slipped his new pen into the pocket of his jeans.

"Thank you again for the gift, Charlie Fisher," he said, bowing formally. "Till we meet again." A streetcar, bursting with riders, clattered down its tracks on Cours Belsunce, and Amir ran to catch it. Leaping onto the sideboards and locking an arm around the railing, the boy turned and gave a final wave to Charlie before the tram rolled out of view.

Charlie watched him go, awed at the deftness of his every movement. If only he, Charlie, was gifted with such grace, he thought, if only he could enjoy that sort of easy confidence. What would such a life be like? But no: he was Charlie Fisher Jr., the friendless American. The scribbler of Avenue du Prado. Which made Charlie realize something:

"Wait!" he called after the long-gone streetcar. "You don't know where I live!"

Chapter
THREE

So Charlie had been duped a second time. Served him right, he supposed, having attempted to curry favor from a seasoned thief. His father said he'd always looked for companionship in the wrong places; he'd warned his son that if he kept it up, he would likely be forever alone. His experience with the pickpocket only seemed to prove this theory. His father would be incensed that he'd given away the pen, something that had been gifted to him with the hope that it would be some generation-spanning heirloom. He'd barely had it for a year and now it was gone.

And so he sulked his way down Cours Belsunce to La Canebière and from there to where the busy street let out on the Vieux Port—the Old Port—where a virtual pine forest of boat masts floated over the sun-dappled water and the tourists huddled on the quays in the sun, waiting on interminable lines for the ferries to the islands. Charlie was late for his lunch date with his father; they'd agreed to meet at the Miramar, a quayside restaurant, at half past one. He instinctively kept his hands in his pockets, now that he'd had firsthand experience with that dark trade of the Marseille squares. Everyone was suddenly suspect. A woman with a plume of balloons that reached to the streetlights solicited Charlie as he walked by and he jumped, his hands crushing lower into his khaki pants. Even the harmless soap peddler, dressed as if he'd leapt from a Manet painting in his Breton stripes and a Phrygian cap, seemed suspicious to poor Charlie. His nerves were thoroughly rattled once he'd reached the outdoor tables of the restaurant, so much so that he had an especially difficult time pronouncing *"Je cherche mon père"* to the stuffy maître d'. Thankfully, the Fishers were known at the Miramar, and Charlie was waved inside with a brisk gesture midsentence. He was directed to a corner table where his father, the elder Fisher, was laying careful siege to a tower of seafood. As he walked, he made a silent resolution to simply not tell his father about the pen theft. It was better to risk the discovery, some months hence, than suffer the elder Fisher's castigation.

"Sorry I'm late," said Charlie, edging into the chair opposite his father. "I got held up." He nervously grabbed his napkin and shoved it into his lap, nearly upsetting his water glass.

"Hmm," said Charles Fisher Sr., who had, at that moment, slid a particularly large oyster into his gullet and was indisposed. He daubed the brine from his mustache with his napkin and was about to speak when his son abruptly interrupted him:

"I gave away my pen. The Sheaffer Imperial. I gave it away." The words rushed out of Charlie like a cataract. So much for the plan of not telling. The confession, though, felt powerfully relieving.

Charles Sr. had forgotten what he was going to say. "You what?" he said, in its place.

"I gave away the pen. The one you gave to me."

"The Sheaffer Imperial?"

"The one," said Charlie.

"With your name on it."

"Yes," said Charlie.

"Well, in heaven's name, why?" asked Charles Sr., in clear disbelief.

Charlie grabbed a prawn from the tower and popped it in his mouth, an activity that bought him enough time to consider the implications of either telling his father the whole truth or just keeping his mouth shut. By the time he'd swallowed his bite and had chased it with a drink of bubbly water, he'd made up his mind. "I gave it to someone who seemed like he needed it," he said.

"Someone who needed it."

"Badly."

"Needed it for what? To receive dictation? A phone number or something?"

"That was exactly what happened," said Charlie, shoving another prawn in his mouth.

Charles Sr. was naturally skeptical. "Couldn't you have just lent it to him?" he pressed.

A different tack was braved, once the second prawn had been chewed and swallowed: "You always told me to be charitable to the people not as good off."

"Well," began Charles Sr., aware of the cul-de-sac he'd just entered. "Well." He, too, used a bivalve from the seafood tower to forestall his answer. "Well, I didn't mean a fifty-dollar fountain pen. With one's name engraved on it." He gave a great sigh and said, "Charlie, that was a gift from me. Of great value. Who did you give it to?"

"A boy on the street. At the Place Jean Jaurès."

"A boy on the street," repeated his father. "And this boy needed it to write down a telephone number."

"Yes."

"And presumably many more telephone numbers. A lifetime of telephone numbers, in fact."

Charlie Jr. grabbed another prawn, drowned it in cocktail sauce, and put it in his mouth. "Mmmr-rmmm," was his answer.

"I'll hazard a guess," said Charles Sr. "This was a boy with whom you desired friendship."

Charlie felt himself blush. Had that been the reason? "I suppose so, sir," he said.

"I can tell you, you won't get anywhere bribing people for their companionship. True friendship must be earned." He was gesturing at Charlie with the tines of his cocktail fork. As you now know, Charles Sr. had a mustache. You should also know that his mustache was brown and steadily growing gray, as was his impeccably trimmed and pomaded hair. He was wearing a worsted gray suit jacket, his daily uniform, and a napkin, which he'd stuffed into his collar. His fifty-two years were showing at the corners of his eyes and the edges of his mouth, though the Mediterranean had done wonders for his complexion—a complexion that had suffered so long in his prior engagement as special consul to Dublin, Ireland. "Listen," the elder Fisher continued. "There's an event—"

"I don't want to go," said Charlie.

"Hear me out," said his father.

Charlie grabbed the last prawn, ate it, and said, "I don't want to go."

"There is an event, Saturday night, that I'm sure you'd enjoy. There will be a lot of children your age there." Charlie's father gestured to the waiter, who gracefully swooped by the table and whisked away the emptied seafood tower. "The Viscount of Falmouth's son is in the city, and he's having his ninth birthday party. I will be going at the behest of his father. You are invited as well."

"No, thank you," said Charlie.

Charles Sr. continued as if he hadn't been given an answer. "I seem to recall them saying there will be pony rides there. And clowns."

These temptations did not deserve a response from Charlie, who was, you remember, twelve. Pony rides had never really been his thing, anyway.

"And children. Around your age. Many of them. I will personally introduce you. They will all speak English, it's assured."

"No, thank you," said Charlie.

"Charlie, at some point you will have to relent. You do have somewhat of an obligation to attend various functions in your role as the son of the American consul general to Marseille." The waiter had arrived again. He set a bowl of bouillabaisse in front of Charlie Sr., an omelet and *frites* in front of Charlie *fils*. Charles explained, "You were late. I took the liberty of ordering for you."

It was just as well that the lunch had arrived, because Charlie didn't have an answer for his father. Why didn't he want to attend? Who wouldn't want to be a guest at a party for visiting royalty? It might go back to his mother's betrayal or maybe his life of incessant vacationing that led to an aversion to these kinds of social gatherings. And it wasn't like Charlie rejected them out of ignorance or fear: no, he'd been to plenty of them. Black-tie bar mitzvahs in Tel Aviv, garden parties on sunny Delhi terraces. Grand galas hosted by Argentine royalty. No expense was ever spared for the food and entertainment at these events. The attendants were impeccably dressed and impeccably behaved. Which was fine and radiant and exciting, but Charlie was never grouped with the well-behaved and well-dressed adults; instead, he was shunted to the kids' tables, where the grossest forms of humanity alive would all be present: the offspring of the aristocracy.

Having met more actual princesses than might appear in your typical storybook, Charlie would assure you that they bore very little resemblance to their Walt Disney counterparts: they were spiteful and spoiled, to the last. They spoke in a kind of haughty, nasal way and they threw temper tantrums as if it were a competition. Their names were things like Eugenia and Lavinia and Elsinore. They rarely deigned to speak to Charlie for long, and when they did, it was always a very brief interaction in which they held their heads as if Charlie had just arrived freshly rolled in some rotting carcass. As for the princes—the Harrys, the Henris, the Heinrich van Spackleburgers—they were as far from Charming as you could imagine. They drove expensive sports cars, which they invariably wrecked as if they were Matchbox miniatures and, like die-cast toys, were immediately replaced with newer, shinier ones. They burped and slouched at dinner, and they were always carrying on about their various girlfriends in various places, counting them as if they were trifles they collected and threw away. They were savage to Charlie and his shyness; he was a commoner to them, the son of an American diplomat. A hanger-on.

Charles Sr. read his son's silence well. This was not the first time Charlie's antisocial tendencies had come up. "I know," he said. "I know it's hard for you. But you have to make an effort. You're a very likable boy, Charlie. You just haven't met the right kids yet."

"Right," said Charlie.

"And how will you meet the right ones, if you've just sworn off meeting anyone?"

"I know, Father," said Charlie. "I just need a bit of time, maybe."

His father nodded and quietly tucked into his fish soup. Charlie ate his lunch. The blithe hum of restaurant chatter filled the space between them, that particular brand of chatter that populates French restaurants, particularly in the south, during those late lunches of fish and shellfish and glasses of rosé, when the air is hot and the cool of the wooden interior is so welcome. The two Fishers ate without saying another word, apart from Charlie ordering a grenadine from a passing waiter. It arrived; he drank it. Charles Sr. took a last sip of his bouillabaisse, set his spoon down, and removed the napkin from the front of his shirt.

"Back to work," he said. "There are papers to be signed, passports to be cleared, hands to be shaken, and backs to be scratched." He gestured to the waiter. The check was brought and Charles Sr. laid out the correct cash on the tray. He then removed a pen from the inside pocket of his jacket and handed it to his son. "It's a hotel pen," he said. "No replacement for a Sheaffer, I'm afraid, but it'll have to do in a pinch. Try not to give it away."

Charlie smiled and accepted the pen. His father gave him a wink and patted him on the back. Charlie watched his father leave and then motioned for the waiter.

"*Oui, monsieur?*" asked the waiter.

"*Une autre grenadine, s'il vous plaît.*"

When it came, he drank it in silence, toying with the new pen. He tried to spin it between his fingers as Amir had, but found that he dropped it with every flick.

Let's keep Charlie seated there, elbows (rudely) on the table, the little plastic pen leaping out of his fingers like an escapee from an island prison. Let's keep Charlie like that, but let's move him. Now the scenery has changed. It is the next day, the next afternoon, and we are in a district of Marseille some ways south of the Vieux Port called the Prado. Ask directions: you will either be recommended to follow Rue Paradis away from the tangle of the port's pleasure boats and fishing skiffs until the street T-intersects with that wide, tree-lined Avenue du Prado; or, alternately, you will be told to climb the hill overlooking the Fort Saint-Jean and the Palais du Pharo, with that noble, zebra-striped basilica of Notre-Dame de la Garde standing like a birthday candle on the cake that is the great city of Marseille some many, many feet above you, and from there to follow the length of the Corniche, along the great Mediterranean Sea itself, a broad glassy

35

green only interrupted, from your perspective, by the treeless islands of If and Frioul, and then southward until you've reached a giant replica of Michelangelo's *David*, having been reassigned to the job of directing traffic on a dizzy roundabout where the Prado begins and the ocean ends.

Or maybe it would be best to take a taxi.

The Prado, during this time, was the most distinctive address to be had in all of Marseille. The wide avenue was lined with leafy plane trees, casting dappled shade on the stream of buzzing cars—only the finest makes and models—that cruised its length. On either side of the great thoroughfare was a parade of opulent stone villas, their baroque facades draped in blankets of hanging ivy and honeysuckle, their grounds protected by tall, wrought-iron fences. In one such home, the Fishers had taken up residence.

And there you would find Charlie, as if transported from his previous position in the restaurant Miramar to here, in one of the (several) drawing rooms of his immense three-story home. He still has his elbows (rudely) on a table and he is still fiddling with the pen. However: he has gotten a bit better at twining the pen through his fingers, you should know, owing perhaps to the amount of time he has spent practicing in the intervening moments between yesterday and today. Time he should be devoting to his schoolwork, something that his tutor, Simon, who is also here in this room, was trying to remind him.

"Can you put the pen down and focus for a moment, Charlie?" asked Simon.

"Yes," said Charlie, navigating the plastic pen (*Bienvenue! Hôtel Lutetia, Paris, FR*) from his ring finger to his pinkie. It was the most difficult of the finger exchanges.

"You have not put it down," said Simon, which was true.

Charlie didn't manage the transition from finger to finger; the pen fell with a clatter to the tabletop.

"Thank you," said Simon, misreading Charlie's clumsiness as obedience. "Now, I would like to point out one of the common mistakes you seem to make." Charlie's composition notebook was laid out in front of them, and Simon was busily dissecting one of Charlie's short stories as if it were a frog on a lab tray. "You remember what a dangling modifier is?"

"Someone who modifies, hanging from a cliff?" asked Charlie with a grin.

Simon didn't return the smile. Simon didn't smile very much at all, actually. It was surprising to Charlie, this fact, because to Charlie, Simon seemed to be living the very lush life. He was a grad student—and to twelve-year-old boys, University Students, with their newfound independence and lack of *real* responsibility, were in the ideal situation. He was enjoying an extended gap year from his studies and was living, free of charge, under the Fishers' roof while he gave thrice-daily lessons in English, French, and geography to Charlie.

For this, Simon was given a healthy stipend and three-day weekends off. He wore a goatee and heavy black glasses, in the beatnik style. On top of this, he was from Manhattan, played the nylon-string guitar, and had recently been seen in the company of a young French woman named Cécile. Why he should be such a stick-in-the-mud was anyone's guess.

"A dangling modifier is a phrase, a descriptive phrase, that is describing the wrong object in a sentence," explained Simon dryly. He gazed out the large picture window. "For example: 'Having climbed the fence, the distance to the ground was too far for the boy to jump.' The phrase 'having climbed the fence' is wrongly modifying the word 'the distance,' instead of . . ." Simon paused and said, "There is a boy climbing the fence."

Charlie followed Simon's gaze and saw that the tutor's clause, modified or no, was right: there was a boy climbing the fence. Or he had finished climbing the fence—a wrought-iron wall some ten feet high, crowded by a thick hedgerow that blocked the view from the busy avenue—and was now hanging from the top of it with his arm crooked around one of the fence's decorative finials. Some forty feet of the Fishers' manicured lawn separated the boy from the window to the drawing room, but even from that distance Charlie recognized the boy as none other than Amir, the pickpocket.

Before Charlie could say anything, Simon had already marched to the french doors that let out onto the lawn and shouted, "Hey you!

What do you suppose you're doing there?"

"Wait!" shouted Charlie, leaping from his chair.

"This is a private residence!" Simon continued, waving an accusatory finger in the air as only a professional tutor could.

Amir, hanging from the fence, was unthreatened. Seeing Charlie, he broke into a smile. "Hey there," he said. He waved his free arm.

Simon was about to alert the security detail when Charlie ran up to his side and said, "Hold on, Simon. I know him."

"You do?" the tutor sputtered incredulously. He looked back at Amir: unruly brown hair, dirty chinos, faded pink shirt, toothy smile. Somehow, despite this, his doubt was overcome. "Okay," he said. "But what is he doing on the fence? Couldn't he have just called at the gate?"

"He's strange that way," replied Charlie, and he ran across the lawn toward his friend.

"Wait!" shouted Simon from the open french doors. "Your lesson!"

"Having climbed the fence," Charlie replied over his shoulder, "the boy realized the distance to the ground was too far! Modifier undangled!"

"It's not too far," said Amir, once Charlie had arrived at the spot below him. As if to prove this, he neatly undid his arm from the fence and leapt to the ground with the ease of a tree squirrel. He landed, crouched, and sprang upright, presenting his hand to Charlie in greeting. "Hiya, Charlie," he said. "Nice place."

"How did you know how to get here?"

Amir brushed at his arms, as if tidying himself, and gave a whistle. "I'm among the gentry here. You come from—what do you call it—good stock, Charlie Fisher."

"Thanks. I mean, I guess." Suddenly Charlie felt very sheepish about his social standing. "It's my dad's, really. It's somewhat overly big for just us. I'd prefer something smaller or . . . But seriously: How did you know where to find me?"

"There are no secrets from Amir. Not in Marseille."

Charlie studied the boy for a moment before saying, "Well, welcome to my house."

"Thank you," said Amir, but his eyes strayed over Charlie's shoulder. "I think I have interrupted you."

Simon appeared at Charlie's side. "Oh, him?" said Charlie. "He's my tutor. We were just finishing up."

"Oh, were we?" said Simon. He introduced himself to Amir, who, in turn, eyed him suspiciously.

"Can we please be done?" Charlie asked Simon. "I told Amir we would meet up."

Simon placed his hands on his hips and breathed in deeply, as if suddenly becoming aware of the warm afternoon and that he was outside in it. The cries of seabirds could be heard, not too far off, and the air smelled faintly of the ocean and jasmine vines. His resistance quickly dissipated. He checked his watch. "We do have only ten minutes remaining," the tutor said. He looked squarely at his student. "You'll finish up your reading for next week?"

"Fifty pages, yes, sir."

"And start your essay. We need something to show for our work here, Charlie."

"Not a problem."

"That's the spirit, Simon," threw in Amir.

Simon smiled thinly. "Charming friend," said the tutor. "Your father approves?"

"Better that Father doesn't know."

A breeze rustled the leaves of the hedgerow; music could be heard from an open window in a neighboring house. "Very well," said Simon. "It *is* a beautiful day. You might be best out enjoying it. One mustn't lose oneself entirely to study."

"This one's schooling has just begun," said Amir, winking at Charlie.

Simon raised an eyebrow at the boy. Charlie quickly interjected, "What a card you are, Amir. Come on, let's . . ." He was at a loss for words. "Let's shoot some marbles."

"Marbles," said Simon. He turned and ambled back to the house, saying while he walked, "While shooting marbles in the *boules* court, the afternoon slowly turned to evening."

"Dangling modifier!" shouted Charlie. "The afternoon slowly

turned to evening while the boys shot marbles in the *boules* court!"

Simon waved an approving finger as he left their view.

The two boys watched the tutor disappear into the house. Amir then said, "You ready for a real lesson?"

"Let me get my things," replied Charlie.

Chapter
FOUR

Following Amir through the streets of Marseille was like tracking a frightened snake through tall grass. Charlie did his best impression of an intrepid field zoologist, but it was all he could do to keep up with the pickpocket as the boy dove across streets awash with traffic congestion, shot down hidden alleyways, and leapt over guardrails. There were so many near misses with pedestrians and motorists alike that the two of them trailed a sizable wake of hollered epithets along the way, with Charlie, the responsible one, unfortunately tasked with shouting loud apologies as they went. Amir clearly cared very little what other people thought of him or what sort of consequence his actions might have to his environment. He seemed to Charlie to live like a bright spark. And Charlie could only be a kind of mirror, reflecting this luminescence.

"Keep up!" yelled Amir, after having nearly lost Charlie in the mayhem of a small street market. A group of Algerian women, wearing dark headscarves, watched the two boys disinterestedly. Amir had just passed the last stall and was standing at the intersection of several small streets, waiting on Charlie.

"I'm trying," said Charlie when he finally reached Amir. The boy was about to spring away again when Charlie grabbed his arm. "Hold up," he said. "I need to catch my breath."

"Charlie Fisher," said Amir, who, it should be noted, was not in the least bit winded by this race through the warrens of Marseille, "you couldn't catch a turtle in a mud puddle. How are you going to catch your breath?"

"I don't get much opportunity to do this," said Charlie defensively. "I'm not in the habit of running from people."

Amir put his arm on Charlie's shoulder. "This is your most important lesson. Running from people."

"Right," said Charlie, inhaling quickly through his nose.

"But you will only have to run from people when you're made."

"Made?"

"Means to be found out. Funny word, that, 'made.' Like, you don't exist before. You are nothing till you're made."

The city rumbled about them, a weave of activity that seemed, while they stood still, to take absolutely no notice of them. "And that's exactly what you are. You are nothing, Charlie, in Marseille. Nothing."

Charlie shifted a little, uncomfortably.

"Ooh, yes," continued Amir, "I forget. You are the son of the consul general, yeah? Big shot. No, no, no. Right here, right now, you are nothing. We are nothing. We are just part of the scenery." Amir gave an all-encompassing gesture to their surroundings. A red car stopped briefly next to them and then, hugging the curb, disappeared down an alleyway that seemed scarcely wider than it. Two bicyclists on rickety black Gitanes clattered down the cobbled street, one chatting merrily to the other; their lunch, a pair of baguettes and a sausage, sprouted from their wicker panniers. A group of children, some yards up, in matching school uniforms, tussled over a comic book. "We are as good as wallpaper," Amir said.

A man in a clean, pressed, three-piece suit walked by them, carrying a briefcase. His eyes were intent on some point in the distance. Abruptly, Amir shoved Charlie into the man's path.

"Hey!" shouted Charlie.

The man careered around the obstacle. He shot Charlie a scowl and said, in French, "Watch where you're going, boy." Brushing the front of his suit jacket, the man continued on his way.

"*Pardon, monsieur,*" said Amir after him. He looked at Charlie. "There, you were someone. Something. To that man. Until you weren't anymore. It's a fine line, between nothing and something. But this is where you want to be, on this side, with the nothings. Because when you're someone, something, that's when you have to run."

Charlie smiled. "Got it," he said.

"No, you don't," said Amir. "But it's a start."

They caught the number three tram where Rue de Rome began, there at the roundabout that circled the magnificent Jules Cantini fountain, with its enormous column, and found a seat next to two shopgirls. The girls inched away from Amir, as if instinctively sensing the danger of his presence, but the boy was immediately able to put them at ease by his bright smile and the telling of a joke. Charlie, for his part, immediately felt a paralyzing discomfort whenever he was in the presence of girls. He let Amir's ease radiate over him and gave the girls a smile; one of them smiled back. He felt his face flush and looked at his shoes.

Amir slapped Charlie in the thigh. "Okay," he said. "Look at this."

A man had just climbed on board the tram—he was perhaps forty years old and looked to be one of the earlier travelers in Marseille's afternoon commute. His hair was neatly pomaded back and he wore a fine gabardine suit. In his hand was a wadded-up newspaper, which he unfurled with a flick of his wrist and, leaning against one of the vertical tram bars, began to read.

"Left britch kick, right britch kick, keister kick," Amir whispered to Charlie. His finger danced, pointing at various parts of the air in front of him.

"Excuse me?" asked Charlie.

The man glanced over at the two boys; Amir looked out the window. Once the man's attention had returned to the paper, Amir shot Charlie a glare. "Left britch, right britch, keister kick," he repeated in a hushed voice. "Pockets."

"Oh," whispered Charlie.

Amir said the mysterious words again, this time patting places on his body: right pants pocket, left pants pocket, rear pocket. "Coat pit," he added, and his hand mimed slipping into the inside of a jacket breast. The tram had stopped, and like the surge of a tide, one crowd of passengers heaved off the car to be replaced by another. The man in the gabardine suit, jostled, remained where he stood. Charlie looked down the aisle and saw that a conductor had boarded the tram and was calling for tickets.

"Amir," he whispered. He nodded to the prow of the tramcar. They hadn't purchased tickets. When Charlie rode the tram, which he rarely did, he always bought a ticket, even though he knew many people didn't. This time, however, he'd been swept up in Amir's gravitational force and was, heaven forfend, riding illegally.

Without a word, Amir stood up, and timing his movements with the initial jerk of the car leaving the stop, he bumped up against the man in the gabardine suit.

"*Pardon*," he said, which did not elicit any response from the man. He then sat back down next to Charlie, and, sliding something along

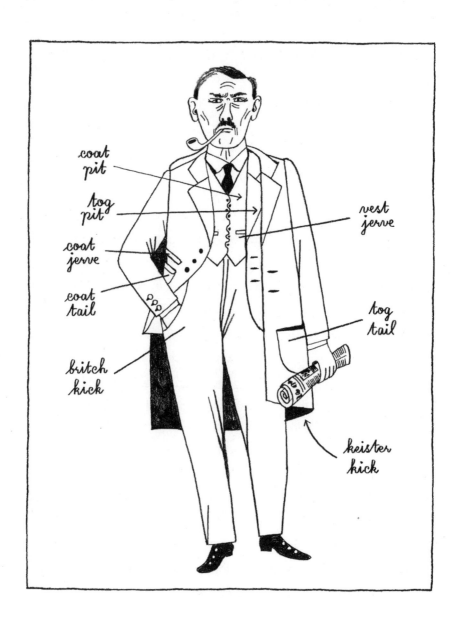

coat
pit

tog
pit

vest
jerve

coat
jerve

coat
tail

tog
tail

britch
kick

keister
kick

the wood of the bench between them, he said, "Coat jerve. Ticket pocket."

Charlie looked down and saw that Amir had procured a ticket for them.

It all happened very quickly: the conductor approached the man in the gabardine suit and casually asked for his ticket. Gabardine (we shall call him) reached into the small pocket on his suit coat—the one that was just above the larger pocket—and found it empty. He then began searching his jacket with increasing alarm. He spoke apologetically in quick-clipped French as he did this.

The ticket taker behaved as all ticket takers do when they are faced with a ticketless passenger: he told Gabardine in a tone that married complete boredom and a total, black-hole-like lack of sympathy, that he would be forced to leave the tram at the next stop. He then pulled out a small writing pad, and licking the end of his pencil like a butcher prepping his knife, he began writing the man a fine. His victim could only look on in despair.

Charlie couldn't stand it. He grabbed the stolen ticket that Amir had handed him and stood up. Amir hissed an objection, which Charlie ignored. "He can use mine," said Charlie, offering up the yellow piece of paper.

The conductor raised his eyebrow and lifted the pencil from his pad. Charlie, taking a moment to formulate the words, repeated the declaration in French. The conductor grabbed Charlie's ticket and, producing a hole punch, punched two dots into it.

"And one more for my friend," said Charlie, pointing to Amir.

"*Merci,*" said Gabardine once the conductor had left them.

"You can have the rest," said Charlie, handing the well-worn ticket back to the man. "Just a few punches left."

"Very kind of you," the man said, in English. "I do not know what happened to mine."

Amir grabbed Charlie by his shirt and led him to the back of the tram. "What did you do there?"

"I felt bad for the guy," responded Charlie.

"Why do you feel bad for him? So he's off the tram a few stops early."

"He was about to get fined. That's not nice."

"Pah," said Amir. "He'll never pay that fine. No one pays the fine."

"Well, still . . ."

"Still nothing, Charlie Fisher. Don't feel sorry for the mark. The mark is a sucker. What you did, you gave up your kisser. A class cannon don't kick the okus back unless he's rumbled, yeah?"

"I didn't understand a word of that."

The tram shook as it noisily handled a corner. The tram riders shifted in unison with the movement. Amir heaved a sigh.

"Why am I doing this?" he asked, to no one in particular.

"Sorry, was that a rhetorical question?" asked Charlie.

"Shh, Charlie," said Amir. "I'm doing this because you helped me. If you don't learn, fine. But you helped me and you asked me to do this, so I'm gonna do it."

"Thanks?" said Charlie uncertainly. "But maybe you could speak clear English while you do."

"I'm speaking English," said Amir.

"But with all the pits and the jerves and the cannons and such?"

"Ah, yes," said Amir. "The talk. You're going to have to learn that too."

Just then, the tram rolled beyond the canyon of shop windows and wheat-paste-postered walls into the wide, stony playa of the Quai des Belges. The sky was pristine blue, as only Mediterranean skies can be, and the comings and goings of the Frioul ferries in the port created a perpetual hubbub amid the crowded sailboat slips. A long line of ferry-goers curled its way from the ticket window to the street, attracting a swarm of buskers and panhandlers. Charlie watched it all through the dirty windows, rapt. The tram came to a wheezing stop.

"So what's the first plan of action?" asked Charlie. "This seems like a pretty good . . ." He suddenly realized he was speaking to no one. Amir had gone. He looked out the window and saw the boy standing by a cement bollard, looking somewhat miffed at Charlie.

With a jolt, the car began moving again, and Charlie dashed for the doors as they began to accordion closed. He managed to get one arm free of the tram and tried to mash the rest of his body through the gap it created. Amir looked on bemusedly.

"Wait—stop!" Charlie moaned. The tram driver began opening and closing the door, assuming some foreign object was in the way—which one was—and only these repeated motions could dislodge it. *Bang, bang* went the doors on Charlie's forearm. During one of the doors' in-breaths, Charlie managed an escape and tumbled out into the street. The tram moved on.

"Graceful," observed Amir.

"Well, you could've told me you were getting off."

"Observation," said Amir, tapping his temple. "Observation is the thing, yeah?"

"Is this how this is going to go, all day? Is *everything* going to be a lesson in how bad I am at this?"

"Everything *is* a . . ."

"Oh, *come* on!" protested Charlie.

Amir hit him, playfully, in the shoulder. "I'm joking. Let's go." He then jogged off toward the loitering crowds on the quay square.

"Ouch," Charlie muttered, rubbing his arm.

A trolley bus briefly blocked Charlie's view, but once it had passed, he could see the square laid out before him. The Quai des Belges.

For those of you wondering, you are free to pronounce the word "*quai*"—or, in English, "quay"—in one of the three following ways: *kway, kay,* or *key.* The word, which means "a structure built parallel to the bank of a waterway for use as a landing place," is descended from Middle English and Middle French, which is appropriate in this context. It is assumed that whoever decided to spell it with a *Q* was just having a joke. This quay is one of three such structures that are built on a port that dates back to prehistory, having been treasured by Greek sailors for its location and ease of use. It has not, in the intervening years, lost its luster. Now the water is populated by pleasure yachts and fishing boats and walled in on three sides by the facades of restaurants, bars, and hotels. Charlie and Amir stood on the gray paving stones of the square at the head of the port, farthest from the sea. They were two among many: a group of schoolchildren in maroon uniforms traversed the square; a small gang of soldiers in khaki stood in a circle, chatting and smoking. There was a woman selling balloons, as there was most days. Tourists and natives alike, whether they want to or not, must cross the square at the Quai des Belges, and, as a consequence, it enjoys all the activity of a beehive abuzz with bees.

"I figured it would be better to show you in the place where it is best," said Amir, gesturing to the scene around him. "This is, as they say, good training ground. Easy marks—maybe not the fattest touches, but still good. As good a place to turn you out as any." He saw Charlie's confused expression and appended: "Teach you to pick-pocket."

"Okay," said Charlie. "So show me."

"The whiz is sleight of hand, it's a ten-a-penny magic trick. Just we don't give back what we lift. But the same stuff applies. It's all about *manipulating* attention. Distraction. Misdirection. Everybody wants to see something special." While Amir talked, his hands began moving in a graceful, fluid way. If Charlie didn't know that he was receiving his first lesson on picking pockets, he would maybe think it was a little strange the way the boy's hands were moving, but certainly nothing out of the ordinary. To the casual viewer, Amir might seem to have simply an eccentric way of using his hands as he spoke.

"Look at that," he said. Amir had shifted to stand alongside Charlie. He held out his hand as if he were holding a newspaper or a brochure.

Charlie looked. He didn't see anything.

"What am I supposed to be looking at?" he asked.

"Look closer," said Amir.

Charlie squinted, but all he could see were the crinkly lines in Amir's open palm.

"Nothing," said Charlie.

Amir's other hand appeared at that moment, just below his outstretched one, holding Charlie's wallet.

"Exactly," said Amir. "Everybody wants to see something. Even if it's nothing." Amir quickly sidestepped back to face Charlie.

"Okay, give me that back," said Charlie.

"Check your coat pit."

Charlie sucked his teeth. "Which one is that again?"

Amir stood in front of Charlie and, like a gypsy busker playing spoons, slapped various parts of Charlie's clothing in quick succession. "Left and right britch kicks. Keister kicks. Coat tails." He pointed to the inside pocket of Charlie's jacket, saying, "Coat pit." Charlie slipped his hand there and found the reassuring lump of his leather wallet.

"You're supposed to be teaching me how to pick pockets, not just stand there and pick my own."

Amir smiled. "People become comfortable in their surroundings, yeah? They don't expect an invasion. Surprise, in this case, is your enemy." Suddenly, he leaned forward and slapped Charlie lightly on the side of the head. "No knives," he said.

"What?"

Something glinted in Amir's hand. It was the Opinel pocketknife that Charlie had stuffed in his pants pocket—his right britch—before they'd left. Amir had nabbed it without Charlie knowing.

"Well," began Charlie, "I—"

"We ain't working rough," said Amir. "No cannon with the know carries steel. That's for the heavy rackets." As he spoke, he managed a neat pirouette to Charlie's left side, giving a nod to a young woman passing by. "The beauty of the pickpocket, yeah? Is that he only needs these." Amir held up his left hand, palm out. It was, as you might expect, empty. "To do this," he continued, lifting his right hand up from his side. Charlie's silver Rolex watch was dangling from his fingers.

"Hey," said Charlie.

"You want your watch back?" he asked.

"Um, yes," said Charlie. It, too, had been a gift from his father. Losing the pen had been one thing—he couldn't imagine explaining away the watch.

With a lithe move, Amir slipped it into his own front pants pocket. "Okay," he said. "Steal it from me."

"Right," Charlie said, sizing up the challenge. He kept his eyes intent on the small bulge at the bottom of Amir's pocket.

"Eyes up," said Amir, waving his hands. "When you're fanning the mark, don't just stare at the touch—at the thing you're gonna steal. 'Cause I'm looking where *you're* looking, yeah? You're fronting me, the mark, and now I'm rumbled—I'm onto you. I see what you're going to do."

"But you know what I'm going to do."

Amir rolled his eyes. "This is a lesson, Charlie. Besides, with a real class cannon, it don't matter. I could tell you I'm going to pinch the glasses off your face and you wouldn't know till you was seeing fuzzy." He gestured forward with his fingers. "C'mon."

"Eyes up," repeated Charlie, looking at Amir directly.

"Good," said Amir. "You've got my attention. You've fanned me. You're making the frame. You're planning your move. Now misdirect."

"How do I do that?"

"You've got to make me change my attention. Away from you."

"Ah," said Charlie. He thought a moment. "Hey! Look over there!"

Amir winced a little, annoyed, but did as he was told. He looked off in the direction of a ferryboat that was idling into its slip. Charlie jammed his fingers into Amir's pocket and tried to grab the watch. His fingers hadn't even made contact with the metallic band before Amir had grabbed his wrist.

"What are you trying to do, tear my pockets out?" chided Amir. "No, no. You've fanned the ticker, the watch, right? I got deep pockets here and it's at the bottom. You know you ain't just grabbing it without rumbling me."

"So what do I do?"

"Move the watch *to you*. With your other hand."

"But how do I do that when you're right in front of me?"

"Step to my side."

Charlie did as Amir said and they both, elbow to elbow, watched the ferry hands lash the bollards on the quay with coils of thick hemp rope. Charlie's fingers found their way to the jangling weight of the watch and, through the trouser fabric, began to push it toward the top of Amir's pocket.

"Good, good," said Amir. "Imagine the mark's eyes got spotlights in 'em, yeah? Two bright white spotlights. And wherever they're looking, there's like a big white circle of light. Your job is to work in the darkness around that light."

But Charlie had frozen. His fingers had managed to creep the watch about halfway up Amir's pocket; any farther and he knew that he would be giving himself away. "Now what?" he whispered.

"You got another hand, right?" Amir whispered back.

"Yeah."

"So . . . use it. Turn away, let your other hand take the weight."

Charlie turned his body slightly to the right as if he were looking back over Amir's shoulder and exchanged the lump of watch into his left hand.

Amir continued to instruct: "Good. Now get your right fingers in the kick, easy like. Yep, just so. Feel that watchband?"

"Yes," said Charlie, scarcely able to hide his excitement. He had the band carefully pinched between his index and middle fingers. "I've got it."

"Now, this is the tricky part. Don't just yank the okus, you'll rumble me. You got to make it natural. Shade your touch, yeah?"

"Which means . . . ?"

"Cut into me, it's called. Walk away and give me a brush-by as you do. Like you're finished looking at whatever it was we was looking at, yeah? Just walk."

Charlie did as Amir instructed, stepping away toward the street and letting his shoulder make contact with the fabric of Amir's pink shirt as he went. The watch tumbled easily out of the boy's pocket, snagged between Charlie's fingers. He took a few steps and turned around, grinning triumphantly. "I did it!" he shouted.

"Shhh!" chided Amir. "Keep it down, Charlie."

"I did it!" repeated Charlie, this time in a whisper.

Amir smiled, apparently won over by the American's enthusiasm. "You're safe as kelsey, Charlie. Nice work." He then mimed a bout of proud sobbing, rubbing his eyes with his balled fists. "My boy's first touch! I'm under the moon!"

"The phrase is 'over the moon,' actually," said Charlie. He went to strap the watch back on his wrist when he realized he'd been holding a simple piece of chain all along. He looked up at Amir. "Are you serious?"

Amir grinned and flashed the shiny silver Rolex that hung on his wrist. "You don't think I'd give it up, do you?"

"Can you just give the pocket picking a break for a moment?"

"It's my job, I can't help it."

Charlie walked back to Amir and reached out his hand. "Just give it back, please."

"No, no. This is a good lesson. No one keeps a watch in their britch kick anyway. I'll teach you the easiest ticker score in the books."

With the elegant Rolex strapped to his wrist, Amir reached out for a handshake. Charlie took his hand.

"Again," said Amir, "imagine the chump's eyes are like spotlights, yeah? Always work in the dark around that light."

"Sure, but what if he looks down?"

"Don't let him look down. Steer his attention. It's a push and pull, yeah? You have to ease into any touch. It's like . . . it's like . . ." Here Amir was searching for an apt metaphor. "It's like when you're trying to make it, you know, with a girl."

Charlie blushed. "I wouldn't know much about that," he admitted.

"What, you never kissed a girl, Charlie?"

"I gave Alice Grundel a peck on the cheek at her coming-out party."

"That don't count." Amir took an exasperated breath before continuing, "But you got an imagination. So imagine you're going to make a move on old Alice Grundel, yeah?"

"Okay," replied Charlie sheepishly. He'd always had a thing for Alice.

"And all the while, you're, like, measuring your chances, yeah? Gauging her response. Waiting for the moment. Stepping back when she's giving you the cold shoulder. Warming her up again. And then when you get the green light, you go for it. No hesitation, yeah?"

"Maybe there's another analogy that might apply?"

Amir glared at Charlie. "Seems like pickpocketing ain't the only lesson you need. But okay, here goes. Like, you're sneaking up on someone. You watch them, you wait till they ain't looking, yeah? You move closer. Patience is key. Always patience. And watching. So here." His hand still gripped in Charlie's, he twisted his wrist so that the clasp of the watch was visible. "Pinch the band so that it stays tight against my wrist. Always keep the pressure, so I won't feel it coming loose. Now, with the two fingers, quickly undo the clasp."

Charlie did this; the silver band clicked open. With his thumb and his ring finger, he managed to keep the heavy watch face pressed to Amir's skin.

"Now," continued Amir, "misdirect."

Thinking spontaneously, Charlie reached with his left hand and tugged at the lapel of Amir's shirt. The boy took the bait and glanced down at Charlie's fingers. While Amir's attention was thus diverted, Charlie nimbly flipped the unclasped watch over into his hand and stepped back, shoving the timepiece into his pants pocket. Amir smiled. "Well done," he said.

"That felt good," said Charlie.

Amir put his arm around Charlie's shoulder. "That ain't the half of it, my flash companion. Wait till you're on a big score, working three- or four-handed with a real class cannon and a proper tool running duke. Pulling in the fattest marks this city'll give you. That, my friend, is living."

"So, let's do it," said Charlie.

"Let's do what?"

"Let's do a real 'score.'" He waved to his surroundings. "You didn't bring me all the way down here just to have me steal my own watch from you."

"Maybe I was just seeing how you'd fare first."

"And . . . ?"

"C'mon, Charlie. I taught you a couple easy touches. You ain't ready for the big time."

"How did you learn, huh? I bet there was a time when you were just thrown out there. A fellow has to start somewhere, right?"

Amir stared at Charlie for a moment before replying, "Okay. Say I let you play center field a bit. Turn you out as a stall man. You won't mess that up too much."

"Oh, this is grand. Real grand!" Charlie exclaimed, and he clapped his hands enthusiastically.

"Besides, you might be the perfect stall. No one's gonna suspect a well-dressed American kid." Amir winked gamely at his new friend. "This might be a gas, after all."

Chapter
FIVE

The two boys made their way up La Canebière, that wide boulevard where the action of the quay funneled eastward and which the American soldiers, during World War II, affectionately renamed "The Can o' Beer." The shop fronts were open from their shuttered afternoon siestas and the cafés began to overflow with locals enjoying their post-work pastis and glasses of rosé wine, fogged by condensate and rimmed with lipstick marks. The smell of tobacco smoke and freshly brewed coffee was everywhere. Amir had slowed his pace to a casual stroll, his hands in his pockets, and this time Charlie had no trouble keeping up. The flood of pedestrians on the crowded sidewalk sometimes felt like a rushing river current, which the two boys were either swimming against or being carried along by.

"Hey," hissed Charlie. "What about him?"

He was pointing to a young man, aged about twenty-five, standing alone by a newspaper box. The man was counting out change in the palm of his hand, his brow furrowed. He was so distracted by this task that he seemed to Charlie to be the ideal mark.

"That egg? No way," replied Amir. "Prat diggers looking for smash, maybe. But that is no job for a class mob."

"You'll have to translate," said Charlie.

"There are three kinds of marks, Charlie. Eggs, bateses, and pappies. An egg is a younger guy. Probably not carrying much of interest. Starting out in life, yeah? Like that guy, counting his ridge, his smash—his change. He's down on the knuckle, that one. Poor. A fat mark never counts his smash. Wouldn't want to deprive this one of his life savings, know what I mean? So that is off-limits. Then there's a pappy. Your typical elderly gentleman. A pensioner. Someone's grandpapa, no doubt. A class cannon don't go in for that. What we want is a good, solid bates. A well-off guy in his forties. Thinks he's the cock of the walk, yeah? He could lose a leather full of dough and he wouldn't care one way or the other."

"Got it," said Charlie, renewing his search.

"Way I see it, we're evening the score a bit, yeah?" said Amir. "Bringing folks down a peg or two. You find a real loaded mark with an okus the size of St. Peter's, and you trim the fat a bit. Give some other guy or gal a chance in life. Like these chumps over here."

Charlie's eyes followed Amir's nod toward a group of men in well-pressed black suits standing in front of the colonnaded entrance to what looked to be a law office. "Lawyers. Parasites on society. In fact . . ." Here Amir ran over to a nearby waste bin and returned with a half-crumpled sheet from the morning's newspaper. "Why don't you put your hump up for me, Charlie?"

"Pardon?"

Amir shoved the newspaper in Charlie's hands. "I'm gonna lighten their load a bit. And I need you to shade the duke. Go on and ask 'em if they can read this blute for you. Really get it in their faces."

Charlie's heart started racing. "What if they—"

"There's no what if. Just believe in yourself." Amir gave Charlie a reassuring slap on the shoulder. "I'll be right behind you."

The men were smoking cigars, holding them out at arm's length and then bringing them back to their mouths as if they were playing imaginary trombones, and a perpetual cloud of smoke overcast their heads. They were indeed affluent; they reeked of wealth and privilege. Charlie immediately recognized them as the types one might see at the gala fund-raisers his father sometimes made him attend, the ones who sat smugly at their tables while neighbors glad-handed them at frequent intervals. Surely, as Amir had said, they wouldn't miss a few francs.

"*Excusez-moi*," said Charlie. "*Parlez-vous anglais?*" Charlie's French was awfully rudimentary, but he was mostly certain he'd

asked them if they spoke English.

"Hrrm," began one of the men, "Yes, I do."

"Oh, good," said Charlie. "Do you mind telling me what this says?" He then unfurled the newspaper and brought it up in front of the men in such a way that the ground below them was completely covered. It was a little awkward but didn't seem to invite immediate suspicion.

"Why, it says a Russian man has been launched into space," said one of the men, his English smooth but heavily accented. He wore thick black glasses and a short-shorn beard. He spoke around the stalk of his cigar. "*Un homme dans l'espace.* Man in space. What do you say to that?" He then turned to his compatriots and began speaking in French; the men all expressed wonder and craned in to look at the photo of the cosmonaut that was printed below the headline. Charlie himself was won over to this remarkable news and began to decipher the lede of the article when he felt a sharp tug on his shirt, just at the waist, and was reminded of his task.

"Thank you, gentlemen," he said. "*Merci.*"

"*De rien,*" responded the men.

Charlie left the newspaper blute, as Amir had called it, with the lawyers, who continued to discuss the incredible story long after Charlie had left them. When he saw Amir standing some feet away in the sanctuary of a doorway, he smiled and waved. "Did you see that?" he asked. "The Russians put a man into space." When he saw that Amir seemed unimpressed, he repeated the most important bit: "Into space!"

"Charlie, you don't shade yourself," said Amir. "I could've picked your pocket ten times over those fellows."

Charlie's heart was racing. "Did you get out okay?"

"Easy queasy," said Amir.

"It's easy peasy, actually," said Charlie. "What'd you get?"

"A handful of cordeens," said Amir, holding up what appeared to Charlie to be three accordion-folded wallets. He handed one to Charlie and proceeded to dump the contents of the other ill-gotten billfolds into his palm. "Five hundred francs in mine. Very nice haul."

"I've got three fives and a tenner," said Charlie, displaying his emptied wallet.

"A pocket watch, a handful of ridge, and a pipe," said Amir, removing more treasures from his pockets. "All in all, not bad."

"Huh," said Charlie. He chewed on his lower lip a bit, glancing down the street as he did. "I feel a bit conflicted about all this."

"That's natural," said Amir, putting his arm over Charlie's shoulder. He had thrust the pipe between his lips and was mouthing it like a real grown-up. "But to men of their means, this is a drop in a very large bucket, yeah? Your first real score, Charlie. Let's ding the dead ones and go celebrate." With these words, he grabbed the wallet from Charlie and threw it, along with his, into a nearby waste bin.

Charlie was still mulling over the moral implications of his "stalling" when Amir guided him through the doors of a café.

"I mean," said Charlie, pushing himself onto one of the stools at the counter, "I didn't actually do the stealing."

"Tell yourself whatever you like, Charlie," said Amir. "What are you drinking?"

"Grenadine," replied Charlie.

Amir then turned to the young waitress behind the bar and said, "*Deux grenadines, s'il vous plaît!*" The waitress, her eyes blackened with mascara and her blond hair coiled into a beehive, grumpily acknowledged the order.

Charlie thought for a moment, his fingers making little swirls in the Formica countertop. "They were lawyers, you said?"

"The worst kind," responded Amir. He chomped comically on his newfound pipe.

"Say they just finished trying some suit," said Charlie. "Some inno-cent young man, about to get married. A man who was about to get a promotion over one his coworkers—this coworker was passed over."

"Good, good," said Amir.

Charlie continued, "And so the coworker sets up the man, maybe falsely accusing him of some great espionage. And this man is arrested and is tried before the assize court—for which the coworker gives false testimony."

The story was briefly interrupted as the waitress set down two glasses of atomic-red syrup on the countertop in front of the boys.

Two bottles of Lorina soda appeared alongside the glasses and the boys poured them, fizzing, into the grenadine. The waitress eyed the two boys, the way their heads were bent together as if they were crafting some elaborate plot. Rolling her eyes, she walked away.

"The guy is put away for decades," said Charlie, taking a sip, "and those lawyers, those marks, were out celebrating just another day of settling justice. A bent justice."

"Well told, Charlie," said Amir.

"That works, a bit," said Charlie. "I don't feel so bad."

"That's good, real good," said Amir. "Storytelling will suit you well in this business. You know, now that I think on it, it occurs to me that the best cannons are the best storytellers. But they're also good story listeners. They're always on the lookout for a tale." He paused and took a slurp off the brim of his glass. "Stories sort of come out at you, yeah? A real good storyteller follows a story like he's hustling a chump, like he's on the whiz. He figures out who the bad guy is, who the good guys are. He listens and pieces together the information that he doesn't have, like Sherlock Holmes. Then he follows those leads. In the pickpocket racket, it's called the grift know."

"The grift know," repeated Charlie, ever the studious learner.

"Uh-huh." Amir wiped a red soda mustache from his upper lip and surveyed the café. In many ways, it was a typical Marseillais café. A bench upholstered in Naugahyde ran the length of the wall opposite the bar, and a generous splay of tables and chairs hosted a healthy post-work crowd. The afternoon being mild, the patrons spilled out into the street-side seating; a multitude of conversations made a pleasant racket between the wood-paneled walls. Several dressed-down waiters (this being a run-of-the-mill café) sauntered disinterestedly among the clientele, neatly defying physics with their overfilled trays of emptied glasses balanced on the palm of one hand. A young man in a brown khaki uniform sat a few stools down from Amir and Charlie, busily tearing his cocktail napkin into little shreds.

"For instance," said Amir, gesturing to the soldier, "what do you suppose his story is?"

"A soldier, obviously," responded Charlie, eyeing the man carefully. "Maybe he's a new recruit. He's nervous about shipping out. That's why he's tearing up the napkin."

"Good, Charlie. You're finding the story. Though I don't think he's new. I think he's on leave. That's a deep tan for a new recruit. Most of those guys are coming from all over the country, and you can't get a tan like that in March in France. My guess would be Algiers."

"Oh," said Charlie, "I'd say you're right."

Amir squinted over his glass of grenadine, studying their subject. "He's definitely worried about something. Anxious. What do you suppose it is, Charlie?"

"Isn't going to war anxiety-inducing enough?"

"But he's drinking alone. A guy all broke to pieces about war would be surrounding himself with his brothers-in-arms, yeah? No, something else is up here."

The man called for the waitress. He spoke a few words to her and she replied shortly, gesturing to the clock behind the bar. He studied the clock and then looked nervously at the front door to the café.

"He's waiting for someone," Amir and Charlie said in perfect unison.

Amir then shifted in his seat and watched the bartender as she retrieved a bottle of pastis from the shelf and refilled the soldier's glass. The man knocked the cloudy yellow liquid back with all the intent of someone who was steeling his nerves against the hardiest of challenges.

"Whoo," said Charlie, giving an impressed whistle. "So he's obviously *very* nervous about meeting this whoever-he-is."

"Or 'she is,' more likely." Amir had now turned to Charlie and, his back to the soldier, began speaking in a hushed voice. "He's got something in his pocket."

"He does?" said Charlie. He must have said it inordinately loudly, because he was immediately shushed by Amir.

"Yes," hissed his friend. "Coat pit."

"How can you tell?"

"It's pushing out the fabric. You can see the outline. Plus, he keeps touching it. Watch."

Charlie, half-hidden behind Amir's shoulder, waited and watched. Sure enough, the soldier reached up to his right breast and patted something that was secured in his inside coat pocket. As if satisfying Charlie's curiosity, the soldier then slipped his hand into his jacket and pulled out a small black box.

"He's got it out," said Charlie.

Amir, his back still to the soldier, said, "What is it?"

"A box of some kind. A clamshell box."

"I knew it," said Amir. "He's going to open it, huh?"

"He is, yes."

"And it's a necklace—no, a ring." Amir smiled cockily.

Charlie craned his neck for a better view. Just as Amir had guessed, the soldier was now holding a small golden ring and studying it like a pawnbroker. Even at Charlie's distance, he could see a small diamond sparkling on the ring.

"You're right," said Charlie. "So that means . . ."

"Our poor soldier is preparing himself for a big moment with his best gal, I'd say. That, precisely, is the grift know, my friend. That is following the story." Amir sat up straight and looked around the room. "Now let's have a little fun."

"You're not going to . . . ," began Charlie, before confirming his own suspicions by simply seeing the shifty look on Amir's face. "Isn't that against the code? I thought we were looking for a—what do you call it—a bates? An older, richer guy?"

"Oh, come on, Charlie. Just a little harmless fun is all. I'll be right back."

Before Charlie could object, Amir had lumped a pile of change—smash—on the counter of the bar, swiveled off his stool, and slipped out the front door. The bartender watched him go and then looked at Charlie, as if for an explanation. Charlie shrugged his shoulders.

"You are finished?" asked the woman, in English.

"I think so?" said Charlie. He phrased it as a question. The woman scraped the change across the counter and dumped it into her hand. Charlie smiled and shifted on his stool. He tapped his fingers impatiently on the counter and glanced down at the soldier. The man's date still hadn't arrived, and his nervousness seemed heightened with every minute that passed. Charlie tried not to stare too much, but it became apparent that the man was so preoccupied that Charlie could've thrown an ice cube at his forehead and he wouldn't have so much as blinked.

Finally, the door to the café swung open; both Charlie and the soldier turned expectantly to see who had arrived. The soldier frowned; it was only a boy wearing a pink shirt and a wry expression, the white antenna of a lollipop stick jutting from his lips. Some kind of exchange transpired between the soldier and Amir, though try as he might, Charlie could not make out their conversation. It ended happily with the soldier smiling and shaking Amir's hand. Amir, in turn, gave him a respectful salute and returned to the stool next to Charlie.

"What did you do?" asked Charlie, glaring at his compatriot.

Amir ignored the question. He handed Charlie a lollipop,

enshrouded in waxed paper. "I got one of these for you."

"You went to a candy shop?" asked Charlie incredulously.

"Mm-hmm," said Amir, from behind the lollipop. He took it out of his mouth and studied the sticky green globe at the end of the stick.

"What are you up to?" asked Charlie.

"A classic sneak job," said Amir. "Introductory, really." A glint of gold on Amir's pinkie finger just beneath the bar gave Charlie enough information to realize that the boy had stolen the soldier's ring.

"How did you—" began Charlie. "It was in a box, though."

"And now it's out."

Charlie glanced back at the soldier in time to see him, once again, pat the top left breast of his jacket, unaware of the heist. "What, you put the box back?"

"He'll never be the wiser. Oh—hold up. Here comes our gal." Amir indicated the front door with his lollipop stick. Charlie looked; the door had swung open again to reveal a young lady, perhaps eighteen years old, wearing a modest blue shift. She had her brown hair tied back with a ribbon that circled the crown of her head like a halo.

The soldier beamed when he saw her. He stood up abruptly from his place at the bar and ironed out his uniform with the palms of his hands. The two sweethearts greeted each other warmly, trading quick kisses on each cheek, and the soldier ushered the girl over to a nearby table. So engrossed were they with each other's company that they did not see Amir as he grabbed Charlie and dragged him over to sit at the neighboring table.

Charlie, caught up in the maelstrom, undid the waxed paper on his sucker and popped it in his mouth.

Amorous words were clearly being exchanged at the table next to Charlie and Amir's, as the two lovers, the soldier and the girl, had their heads lowered and were gazing fixedly into each other's eyes like two bulls about to charge. Their lips pronounced words, in French, that well outstripped Charlie's comprehension. A Johnny Hallyday song pealed from the jukebox in the corner of the café.

As if the music served as some sort of magnetizing force, the couple leaned in closer to each other. The soldier reached into his coat pit and retrieved the black jewelry box. The girl tittered and held her fingers to her lips. Amir winked at Charlie.

The soldier held the box outward and opened the clamshell hinge. The girl's face fell. The box clattered from the soldier's fingers; the box's contents spilled out onto the wooden tabletop: a plastic ring with a bright red candy ruby in place of a diamond.

Pop went Amir's sucker from between his lips.

The girl reached over and slapped the soldier soundly upside his cheek. She then shoved the table out from the bench, the edge hitting the soldier squarely in the chest, and stormed out of the café. Amir stifled a laugh; the soldier was too befuddled to notice. He stared in absolute disbelief at the candy ring on the table before him.

"*Qu-quelle* . . . ," he stuttered breathlessly, before overturning his chair and racing after his fleeing would-be fiancée. Amir burst into laughter.

"Did you see that?" cackled Amir. "Looks like he made a bad choice in jewelry. Girls can be so very picky, you know."

Charlie was stunned. "That was not right," he managed.

"Not right? That was brilliant! One of my better moves."

"That man's whole life was on the line. And you ruined it," said Charlie. He could feel the blood rising in his face.

"Oh, come on, Charlie. It was just a joke." Amir pulled the actual ring from his pocket and, setting it on the table, admired it. "He does have very good taste."

Charlie lunged out with his hand. He managed to grab the ring before Amir could steal it away. Amir grabbed Charlie's clenched hand; Charlie threw his other hand over Amir's. They sat there, hands locked together, as they stared at each other across the table.

"You'll have to learn to lighten up a bit, Charlie," said Amir, "if you're going to be on the whiz."

"Robbing lawyers is one thing," said Charlie. "This isn't right. You know it."

"I wasn't going to keep it," replied Amir.

"Oh?"

"There is more to the hustle. But you will have to trust me. You will have to give it to me."

Charlie held fast.

Amir persisted: "Charlie, time is running out if you wish me to finish this job." He arched his eyebrow.

Perhaps because the better angels of his nature were taking a typical Provençal siesta, Charlie let the ring fall to the wooden table-top. Amir snapped it back into his hand. "Really, Charlie," he said. "Leave this to the professionals." He snaked out of the bench, around the table, and headed for the door. Charlie followed.

Outside the café, the soldier had managed to collar his sweetheart at the busy intersection where the Canebière met Cours Belsunce. He was in the process of pleading his case. A few curious onlookers had stopped to spectate, watching this timeless drama unfold before their eyes. Charlie, arriving at the scene just behind Amir, managed to parse a few of the hurled accusations: the soldier, whose name apparently was Felix, was *un blagueur* and *un cochon*. He didn't, and never would, take their romance *sérieusement*. A few of the female spectators shouted encouragement to the wronged woman, while the few men who had stopped stroked their chins contemplatively and urged the soldier *courage*. Such a mob was an ideal cover for Amir and Charlie as they made their way through the crowd. Charlie saw Amir brush by the woman, notably the woman's pink leather purse, and continue on through the thicket of waving arms and gesticulating hands. Having crawled free, Amir and Charlie rendezvoused at the fringe of the crowd. Amir waved something in Charlie's face. It was a monogrammed tissue.

"You stole her pocket handkerchief," observed Charlie. "So you've added insult to injury. I just don't get—"

Amir was quick to interrupt him. "Quiet, Charlie. Watch." He pointed back to the crowd.

Through the tangle of spectators, Charlie could see the girl in the blue dress crying, her face buried in her hands, while the soldier continued to make his plea. She abruptly turned away from him and reached into her purse, presumably to retrieve her handkerchief. To her dismay, it was not there. While rummaging for the missing item, her face betrayed the fact that her hand had fallen on something else, something entirely unexpected, in the depths of her purse.

She pulled out her hand; she was holding the diamond ring.

The crowd instantly hushed. The soldier seemed as dumbfounded as any of the onlookers. Whether out of complete shock or some sort of well-honed military instinct, the soldier dropped down to one knee and, in a breaking voice, proposed marriage.

A wide smile spread across the girl's face and she punched the soldier angrily, once, in the chest, before throwing herself into his arms, laughing through her tears.

"*Oui!*" she cried. "*Oui, bien sûr, mon amour!*"

The soldier, shell-shocked and smiling, ran his hand through her hair and kissed her brow. The crowd gave a happy cheer, while the soldier gamely accepted the responsibility for what appeared to be, after all, a very clever and romantic ruse.

Charlie laughed and slapped Amir on the arm. "Brilliant!" he shouted. "That was the plan? All along? You're a crafty devil, Amir."

"Well," said Amir, hemming, "maybe not 'all along,' but it did serve a purpose. You see, Charlie? There is always a story. There is always a tale to follow." Amir put his arm around Charlie's shoulder and the two boys strolled away from the scene of their crime, laughing and reconstructing the day's events as they went.

Perhaps this would be the end of this story. Here, on this crowded afternoon thoroughfare, with that ever-present scent that perfumes the Marseillais air—a kind of mélange of sewage and soap—clinging to one's nostrils; with the roar of the street traffic and the chatter of the pedestrians and the barking of the street vendors, hawking scarves and trinkets and shoes. Here, between the high walls of the apartment blocks and storefronts, bleached white by the high Mediterranean sun. It would be a tidy story. But no. Here, it is just beginning.

"Amir!" came a girl's voice, cutting through the clutter of city noise, just as the boys were making their way back down to the Quai des Belges. The voice made Amir stop cold.

"Oh boy," he whispered.

Charlie looked at Amir, alarmed. "What?"

"Amir!" the voice called again. It was remarkable not only in its volume and authority, but also by the fact that Charlie could tell, with the one word uttered, that it was American. Charlie searched for its source.

"Who is that?" Charlie asked Amir.

"Jackie," said Amir. "It's Jackie."

"Who's Jackie?"

"Oh, you'll meet Jackie," said Amir, and the boy's spark, once so bright, seemed to Charlie to be extinguished for the first time that day.

Chapter
SIX

It didn't take long for the owner of the loud, commanding American voice to appear. She was a girl who looked to be just on the other side of puberty, a young teenager, and she was wearing a simple white blouse and a green skirt, printed with a cornucopia of tropical fruits. She had her dusty blond hair pulled back in a ponytail; it was tied with a white ribbon at the nape of her neck.

"Did you make a friend, Amir?" asked the girl. She smiled brightly, if somewhat archly. The sentence she'd spoken was long enough to give Charlie the idea that she was from the Southern states. Her voice sounded like honeysuckle.

"Hello, Jackie," said Amir. "This is Charlie. Charlie, Jackie. She's a cannon."

"Charlie," said Jackie, "are you straight?"

"Pardon?"

Amir began to answer, but Jackie shushed him. "Are you on the whiz or aren't you?" she pressed.

"Well . . ."

"He's straight," said Amir. "Though I was showing him a few touches. Just a few."

"Fascinating," said Jackie. "But why on earth are you teaching a chump anything, Amir? Chumps are to be hustled, not taught."

"I did a bit of hustling myself," Charlie said daringly. "I ran a stall. Put up my . . . my hump. Just a bit ago."

Jackie stared Charlie down as if he'd just crawled from the pit toilet of a public latrine. She was only a few inches taller than Charlie, and yet she seemed to tower above him. "Did it speak?" she asked Amir.

"Ah, c'mon, Jackie," said Amir. "We were just fooling about, yeah?"

Jackie seemed to ignore this. "You're late for the meet, Amir."

"Am I?" he asked. "What time is it?"

"Quarter of six," answered Charlie, looking at his watch. Considering present company, he was somewhat surprised it was still there.

"Oh yeah. Say, Charlie. I've got to scram, yeah? Been a good time."

"Wait, wait," said Jackie. "It's really darling that we've got a chump here who thinks he's a cannon. Come on, Charlie, show me a touch."

"A touch?"

"I've got something in my pit." She pointed to a small pocket in her skirt. "Take it from me."

Amir protested, "Jackie, c'mon. We've got to make the meet. We don't have time for this."

"No, they can wait," said Jackie. "You were turning out a real cannon. I want to see his work."

Charlie bit his lip and studied the girl's pocket. His heart was racing. It was one thing to perform these actions on an unsuspecting victim, quite another thing to attempt one on a professional. While under pressure, no less. He tried to remember Amir's instructions. Misdirection. Steering attention. The mark's eyes are two spotlights; work in the dark around their shine. Taking a deep breath, Charlie moved his left hand toward the girl's pocket.

But before he'd even reached the fabric of her skirt, Jackie slapped his hand down. "Never mind," she said, scowling. "I guess some folks just have the whiz know, some don't."

Charlie let his hand fall to his side, chastened. He could feel his shoulders sag as Amir gave him a pained look. "It's all right, Charlie," said Amir quietly. He patted Charlie on the arm. "Maybe see you around, yeah?"

The two pickpockets, Jackie and Amir, then swiftly turned heel and dissipated into the sea of passersby on La Canebière. Charlie remained where he was, staring at his shoes. He was wearing white leather loafers with tassels. He suddenly was overcome by a feeling of disgust for his shoes. He was deeply ashamed of them, these stupid white things. More to the point, he loathed the person inside those shoes, this stupid, naive American rich kid who thought he could run with the quick thinkers, the darers, and the riskers. That he could keep pace with that irrepressible stream of ingenuity that runs beneath everything, that subverts the phoniness of the world. No—instead, he was a part of that phoniness. He, Charlie Fisher, was a fraud. He could feel himself beginning to cry.

Before any tears fell, however, he quickly wiped his eyes with the sleeve of his shirt and began walking toward the tram stop on the Quai des Belges. He caught the five fifteen back to Avenue du Prado. This time, he paid for his ticket.

Arriving home, Charlie tried to quietly slink upstairs to his room without anyone noticing, but a voice rang out just as his feet touched the second riser of the grand staircase in the house's foyer. "Charlie!" The voice resounded off the marble tiles of the floor and the high vaulted ceiling. It was coming from the atrium, just off the foyer. It was, without a doubt, the sonorous voice of Charlie's father.

"Yes, sir?" asked Charlie.

"Come in here, please," replied Charles Sr.

Bathed in the evening's last winks of sunlight, Charles Sr. was standing on the tiled floor of the glassed atrium. He was wearing an apron over his work wear—his worsted three-piece suit—and was tending to a forest of ferns. The bridge of his reading glasses was clinging to the tip of his nose as he, with a red-handled pair of clippers, pruned away the dead or dying fronds. The air felt junglelike; Charlie stepped into the room like a tourist lost in some Malaysian rain forest. Charles Sr. didn't look up from his labors.

"Your mother called," said Charles Sr.

"Oh?"

"She's in Toronto. She wished you a happy birthday."

"My birthday was two weeks ago."

"Exactly," said Charles Sr., glancing up from the tomato vine he was currently inspecting. "I told her as much. Perhaps she'll get it right next year."

"Did she have anything else to say?"

"Not much," said Charles, snipping a grayish vine away from the otherwise healthy plant. "She's 'finding herself,' she said. She's even getting some film work up there. I wished her the best of luck. She said she'd try to phone back when you were home."

"Ah, okay." Charlie was familiar with this sort of promise; they would likely not hear from his mother for another six months.

"Yes," said Charles, guessing Charlie's thoughts. "We should not wait up for it." He set down his clippers and removed the bifocals from his eyes. "I am so sorry, Charlie," he said. "So very sorry. She's just—"

"No need, Father," said Charlie. Seeing his father become

emotional was always very uncomfortable for him. "I do like it here. With you. Instead." Somehow the words, as they came out, didn't sound very convincing.

"Do you?" asked Charles. "I'm glad of that."

Charlie nodded. The conversation seemed to have reached its logical end point for the two Fishers. He turned to leave.

"Oh, and Charlie. The Päffgens are coming for dinner tonight. Do you remember them? They have three boys. I think one may be your age. Nice fellows," Charlie Sr. said. "In any case, you'll want your dinner jacket and trousers."

"Very well. Thank you, Father," said Charlie.

Upstairs, in the safety of his room, Charlie threw himself onto his bed and buried his head in the pillows. He briefly tried to recall his mother's face to his mind's eye; he found the job to be exceedingly difficult. In its place, he saw a head shot she'd framed on their mantel in Georgetown, taken long before he was born. Defeated, he grabbed his book—*Treasure Island*—from his nightstand but it did not distract. He stood up and paced the floor, visualizing each touch that Amir had taught him. His fingers moved in front of him as he walked; he mimed Amir's easy gait and gestures. He was still stung by his failed test with the girl, Jackie. He knew that if he had a second chance, he could've succeeded. He just needed a little more practice. Finally, after some time had passed, a knock came at the door.

"Charlie, sir?" came a voice.

"Yes?"

"I have your dinner jacket and trousers, freshly cleaned and pressed."

"Okay, bring them in."

The door opened and in walked André, the assistant butler. He had Charlie's black jacket and pants folded neatly over his arm. André waited while Charlie undressed down to his underwear; he laid the outfit out on the bed before taking the clothes Charlie had shed. As he was leaving the room, however, he paused at the threshold.

"Will sir be needing this card?" asked André. He was a Frenchman, from Aix, but his English had a high polish to it.

Charlie looked at the servant, confused. "Card?"

"The card that was in sir's trouser pocket."

Charlie reached out his hand; André placed a small black cardboard square in his palm. Charlie inspected it. It was a business card, though its provenance was unknown. It was nothing Charlie had collected himself. A drawing of seven gold stars made a constellation above the printed words *Le Bar des 7 Coins*. Below that, in smaller script, was written the address: *46 Rue Sainte-Françoise*.

"Thank you, André," said Charlie. "You can go."

André gave a quick bow and exited the room.

Once he was alone, Charlie flipped the card over in his hand and studied it. Aside from the address and the name of the business, there was no other evident writing. He certainly didn't recall either picking up such a card or being handed one—he instantly flashed to his last interaction with Amir, just before he'd left with Jackie. Amir had given him a pat on the arm and perhaps had brushed against him as he'd turned to leave. The boy must've slipped the card into his pocket; but why?

"Le Bar des Sept Coins," murmured Charlie, as if it were an incantation. A flurry of activity in the courtyard below his window—the swing of car headlights turning into the driveway, the racket of doors being opened, the hum of titles announced and welcomes made—alerted Charlie to the fact that his father's dinner guests had arrived. He quickly got dressed, gave his hair a short tousle in the mirror, and slipped the card into his pants pocket before heading downstairs to greet the visitors.

The evening proceeded as so many previous evenings had: Charlie was introduced to a dizzying array of new and unfamiliar faces while he tried to play the role of a diplomat's son as well as he could, a performance that would likely get mixed reviews from most quarters. In this circumstance, the Fishers were playing host to the Päffgens, an aristocratic family from West Germany. Never was Charlie's relatively low upbringing brought into so much scrutiny; the Päffgens (mother, father, three sons) had been landed gentry since the time of the Hapsburgs, and their conversation, gait, and table manners seemed as genetic as their impeccably chiseled cheekbones. The table conversation turned to the politics of their homeland, of a wall about to be constructed to separate the eastern and western portions of Berlin, and to the various film stars they entertained at their manor outside Munich. Charlie made a few attempts to find common ground with the Päffgens' oldest son, Rudolph, a boy two years Charlie's elder, but the conversation tended to bottom out fairly quickly once Rudolph discovered that Charlie didn't own a sports car or have any interest in the success of the Bayern Football Club. Besides, Charlie was driven to distraction about the card that was currently sitting in his pocket and the business it purported to advertise: Le Bar des 7 Coins.

So driven to distraction, in fact, that he couldn't help pulling it out and studying it while he and the Päffgen boys played billiards in the manor's basement recreation room after dinner. The adults were smoking and drinking cognacs in the upstairs parlor. Charlie was just about to slide the card back into his pocket when Rudolph snatched it from his hand.

"Bar des Sept Coins, heh?" read the boy, his French inflected with a certain Bavarian glide. "What goes on there? You have a girl waiting for you?"

The other Päffgen boys giggled, leaning on their billiard cues. Apparently, they'd all decided that such a situation was ludicrous for poor Charlie.

"No," said Charlie defensively. He grabbed for the card, but Rudolph snapped it out of his reach. "A friend gave that to me."

"You've got some seedy friends, Charlie," replied Rudolph,

scoffing. He looked at the card one last time before mercifully returning it to its owner. "Rue Sainte-Françoise. That's up in the Panier. The old town. Only beggars and thieves hang about up there. What's left of it." The Päffgens had kept a summer home in the Prado long before Charlie and his father had arrived. Rudolph and his brothers knew the city as well as any native. The Panier was, indeed, the oldest neighborhood in town. It was a home to mostly poor immigrant families. The Nazis had dynamited a good section of it during the occupation; much of the southern part of the neighborhood was still in rubble. The remainder was a warren of mazelike streets and winding alleyways.

"Yeah, I know," said Charlie. "That's why I like it." He attempted a devious smile; he must've looked like he was suffering from gastric pain, because the Päffgen boys all looked at him uncomfortably.

"Sure, Charlie," said Rudolph, turning to the green felted table and settling the shaft of his billiard cue on the bridge of his index finger. He took a shot; the red nine caromed into the corner pocket. "Whatever you say."

Charlie hardly slept that night. He'd set the business card on his bedside table, leaning against his reading light, and it seemed to watch over him like an all-seeing eye. Even during his few moments of sleep, his dreams were haunted by those seven twinkling gold stars. He watched them flit in and out of the pockets of faceless strangers, always just out of his grasp. His mind barraged him with questions: Why had Amir given him the card? What was the Bar des 7 Coins?

When he finally awoke to the glint of dawn on his bedroom window, he leapt out of bed and picked up the card. His mind was decided: he would find this mysterious café. He would find out why Amir wanted him to go there. Perhaps it was all some kind of test; some kind of final lesson in his pickpocket tutorial. He opened his chest of drawers and rooted around in his clothes for his most low-key outfit. He intended to fit in, as best he could, with the residents of the Panier. He found an old pair of corduroys and pulled them on. The left knee was threadbare. He then threw on a red plaid flannel shirt, unbuttoned, over a white undershirt and surveyed himself in the mirror. It would have to do. He shoved the business card in his pocket and went downstairs to grab a bite of food before he left for his adventure.

His father was already at the breakfast table, a napkin folded into the undone collar of his shirt.

"Up early, aren't you?" asked Charles Sr., his eyes peering down the lenses of his bifocals at the day's *Le Figaro*. A spoonful of boiled egg was poised halfway between the white porcelain cup and his mouth.

"I need to get art supplies, by the Old Port," answered Charlie, scooting himself into a chair across the table from his father.

"By the Old Port? Well, why on earth don't you send André? Or

Guillaume in the car?" His eyes drifted up from the paper to take in Charlie and his outfit. "And why are you dressed like that?"

"Like what?"

"Like a . . . Like some kind of lumberjack." He indicated Charlie with his newspaper.

Charlie felt himself redden. "I'm not dressed like a lumberjack. I'm just dressed like me."

Charles Sr. had no response.

"And I really need to pick the art supplies out myself," said Charlie. "Simon insisted."

"Simon insisted, hmm?" said his father, snapping his newspaper flat with a flick of his wrist. "You know, you're the son of the American consul general. It may not be wise to have you just gallivanting around town like some drowsy tourist. Or a lumberjack, for that matter."

"I'll be fine, Father," said Charlie. He'd poured himself some cereal and was in the process of spooning it into his mouth.

"At least take the car," said Charles Sr. "I've got meetings in the afternoon, but Guillaume could be at your disposal till, say, one o'clock."

Charlie tried to imagine rolling through the Panier in the back of the silver Citroën DS, being driven by the house's black-capped chauffeur. It was unthinkable. However, refusing his father might seem too conspicuous. He had to accept. "Okay," he said. "Thanks."

Charles Sr. mumbled an approval and disappeared back behind

his newspaper. Charlie finished his breakfast, excused himself, and went off to find Guillaume.

Guillaume was enjoying a similar activity to Charlie's father: he was reading a newspaper in the passenger seat of the silver Citroën, only he was browsing *La Provence*, and his short-billed cap was set back on his head. His lips dangled a lit cigarette and the smoke was lazily drifting out of the open window. When he saw Charlie approach, he quickly flicked the cigarette out onto the driveway, adjusted his cap, and waved.

"Hello, Charlie!" he called.

"Hi, Guillaume," said Charlie. "I need a ride."

"Oh, very well," responded the driver. "Where to?"

"To the Old Port. The Quai du Port."

"Your wish is my command, Charlie," he said. He promptly climbed out of the car and opened the rear passenger-side door. "Please," he said, gesturing to the backseat. Charlie slid in.

As they pulled into the traffic of Avenue du Prado, Guillaume glanced in the rearview mirror and said, "Where are we visiting in the Vieux Port?"

"I'm getting art supplies. From the art supply store," responded Charlie, somewhat unconvincingly.

Guillaume didn't reply for a moment. Then he said, "There is no art supply store on the Vieux Port, Charlie." The car idled at a stop sign; a policeman was directing traffic. A gloved hand waved, and

Guillaume guided the car leftward onto the Rue Paradis.

"I think there is," was Charlie's feeble reply.

"No, there is not," said Guillaume. The Fishers' driver had grown up in Les Catalans, a very old neighborhood just north of the Prado; his was a seventh-generation Marseillais family. "There is one in the new shopping center by the Zoological Gardens. Shall I take you there?"

Charlie chewed on his thumbnail for a second before saying, "I'd rather go to the Vieux Port, please."

"Very well," said Guillaume. "This is something I can do. But you will not find an art supply store there."

Before too long, they had arrived at the Vieux Port. Guillaume expertly managed the logjam of traffic that always seemed to tangle the east end of the port at the Quai des Belges. They quickly rounded the northwest edge of the water and made their way along the Quai du Port. Charlie could see the spire of the Église Notre-Dame des Accoules, the church that marked the easternmost border of the Panier. He called out, "You can drop me here."

Guillaume braked hard and swerved to the curb. A pair of tourists looked up from the red cover of their Michelin travel guide just in time to leap out of the way. "This is where your art supply store is?" he said cheekily. "I see no art supply store." He offered to open Charlie's door, but Charlie demurred.

"I can do it, thanks," he said. He climbed out of the car and stood on the curb, taking in the gradual ascent of the winding streets, the smell of the ocean, the connective tissue of the laundry lines that linked the myriad windows of the tall stone buildings, one to another. Guillaume was standing by his side.

"Shall I wait here for you?" he asked.

"No, I'll find my way back home."

"I don't know what you're up to, Mr. Fisher," said Guillaume. "But I think if you're going in this direction, you be careful, okay? And be out of there by nightfall." Here he pointed just beyond the white bell tower of the Église Notre-Dame.

"Thanks, Guillaume," said Charlie. "I'll be careful. And please: not a word of this to Father."

Guillaume winked and walked back to the idling Citroën. "Out of there by dark, remember," said the chauffeur before sliding back into the driver's seat of the car.

Charlie turned and gave the man an enthusiastic thumbs-up. The gesture didn't seem to inspire any kind of confidence in the Catalan driver, because he frowned beneath his bristly mustache before gunning the engine of the silver car and pulling out into traffic.

Charlie watched the car disappear around the corner where the Quai du Port curved northward between the walls of the Fort Saint-Jean. Once it was gone, he turned and looked back up the hill toward the Panier. "Here we go," he whispered to himself, and began climbing the gentle slope of the street.

Chapter
SEVEN

Forget the broad, leafy avenues of the Canebière and the Prado, the straight-blazed lines of Cours Belsunce and Rue Paradis— each drawn out with the exacting eye of modern city engineering: the Panier was a wild labyrinth of an almost pagan design.

The neighborhood existed before the first stone was laid on the grand avenues of Marseille, and as such, the streets of the Panier appeared to wander as if they'd grown from primitive seed, tracing their own inexplicable paths like shoots from a tree. The buildings that lined these twisting thoroughfares seemed to be made of similarly organic stuff; they leaned in all directions, as if the wind had blown them into their current positions, looming precariously over the action on the streets below. Their facades were pockmarked with oddly shaped windows in strange places; wheat-pasted broadsides advertising amateur theatrical performances and political slogans of dubious merit checkered their walls. Never wider than a single lane of traffic, these streets wove a knotty thread through the buskers and Laundromats and cafés and laborers and wild-haired children and wizened women that were the lifeblood of this ancient neighborhood.

Charlie had never before ventured into the Panier; he did so now like Hercules hunting the Cretan Bull. However, unlike Hercules, he hadn't been walking fifteen minutes before he realized he was hopelessly lost. He'd tried to keep the white bell tower of the *église* in sight as a sort of guiding star, but the spire had quickly disappeared behind the buildings' walls. Indeed, he found it surprising that even the sun managed to make its way into this warren of humanity.

"Excusez-moi," he entreated two young girls in white pinafores loitering by the stoop of a dilapidated apartment. He'd found them drawing on the pavement with chalk. *"Où est la rue Sainte-Françoise?"*

They looked up from their project and stared at him blankly. A woman appeared at the doorway and fixed Charlie with an intense glare. She said something quick and sharp in French, something Charlie couldn't understand.

"I'm just looking . . . ," Charlie began in English before quickly switching to French: *"Je cherche . . ."* At a loss for further words, Charlie fished the business card from his pocket and showed it to the woman.

Her eyes widened to read what was printed on the card; she immediately shouted something to the two girls, and they ran inside the building. The woman gave Charlie one final, withering look before shutting a bright green wooden door in his face.

"And a very good afternoon to you, too," Charlie said quietly.

A horse and cart rattled up the street, led by an old rag-and-bone man in a tattered plaid suit. Charlie stepped aside to let him pass and was rewarded by the doff of a dirty fedora for his consideration. The cart was loaded to the brim with an odd assortment of bric-a-brac: piles of old clothes, washtubs, toasters, and a single coatrack. Kicking at the cobblestones, Charlie followed the cart until it stopped again and its owner began to collect a pile of tin cans that had amassed on the side of the street. Charlie screwed up the courage to ask the old man for directions to the Bar des 7 Coins.

"*Excusez-moi*," said Charlie. He held out the business card. "*Où est ce café?*"

The man looked at the card and said something, though it was neither French nor English.

"*Pardon?*" asked Charlie.

The man spoke again, and this time Charlie could hear the lilt of Italian in the man's cadence, though a variety of impediments including a grill lacking several teeth made it difficult to understand. The man must have sensed Charlie's frustration, because he suddenly stopped talking, tapped his finger on the card, and shook his head gravely.

"No," he said. "No go." He then doffed his cap again and said something to his horse, who clearly had no trouble deciphering his master's words; the cart jerked back into motion and the man and his horse continued onward up the street.

Charlie watched the cart disappear around a bend; he puzzled over the man's answer. He began to feel as if he would never find this strange café that inspired such a reaction from the neighborhood's residents. Several more passersby reacted similarly to his call for help, and he began to wonder if it was not entirely safe to be advertising himself in such a way. He finally answered the demands of his aching feet and seated himself at one of the two outdoor tables in front of a small, decrepit *boulangerie*. The proprietor, a middle-aged woman, all but acted as if Charlie wasn't there as she took his order for a *pain au chocolat* and a Coca-Cola—admittedly, hers was a welcome reprieve to the sorts of looks he'd been getting all morning long. He considered asking her about the café, but didn't want to jeopardize their winning relationship.

Charlie sighed and sipped at the bottle of soda; he looked down the rambling street to where a small square could be seen. Something caught his eye: there, mostly covered by a neighboring building, was the edge of a sign. On the sign was a painted golden star.

He quickly slapped a two-franc coin on the table and leapt up, near running down the street toward the square. As he'd hoped, he rounded a corner and saw the gold star joined by several others on a broad sign above the storefront of a café. The words *Le Bar des 7 Coins* were written there.

Involuntarily, Charlie clapped his hands together and shouted, "There it is!" He caught himself just as the words escaped his lips and looked around to see if anyone had heard him. The square was empty; several tables were laid out in the midmorning sun, but they were all unoccupied. The square sat on a low terrace; beyond the railing, a woman could be seen sweeping the stoop of her apartment building. A bird whistled from the branches of a nearby tree. Charlie tried to dampen his enthusiasm as he walked toward the doors of the café.

A casual onlooker might assume that the café was closed; there seemed to be no light emanating from inside, and the door was firmly shut. The outside tables were layered in dust, and several of their accompanying chairs were upended, as if no one had sat in them for ages. Charlie cautiously approached the door and peered in. The glow of a few lamps shone through the glass. He tried the door. It was unlocked and opened with a loud creak.

Those few lamps visible from the outside illuminated a shabby dining room inside the café, a tiled floor covered in grimy tables, and a long wooden bar littered with a smattering of dirty glasses. Someone, at some point, had tried to pair a few dozen chairs to the café tables, but it was as if the chairs had all, over the course of time, migrated to strange and far-flung places in the room. Several of them looked as if they'd drunk too much pastis themselves and were lying,

dozing, on their sides. Charlie walked slowly up to the bar and craned his neck to see if there was any other human soul in the Bar des 7 Coins other than himself.

"Hello?" he called. "*Bonjour!*" he added, for good measure. No one answered. He thought he saw a mouse scurrying along the back side of the bar. Several bottles of unknown vintage had accumulated on the shelves behind the bar; they were all covered in a healthy layer of dust. Charlie walked back into the center of the café and, righting one of the chairs, took a seat at a table and puzzled.

He puzzled for several minutes this way.

He removed the business card from his pocket and flipped it over in his fingers. There was no doubt: it was the same café. But why had Amir given him the business card for a derelict café, for a business that seemed long defunct? He was getting ready to leave when he heard a sound coming from some distant room.

It was whistling.

Charlie froze in his chair as the whistling grew louder, accompanied by the sound of heavy footsteps. They were coming from somewhere behind him. Unbidden, his mind identified the song being whistled as "Les Enfants du Pirée," a song that had been inescapable on the radio for the last year. It was something about the state of the café that led Charlie to believe that whoever was whistling and walking must be a ghost. He swiveled his body quietly in his chair, looking to see what kind of apparition was about to appear.

If it was a ghost, it was a very fat ghost. And when it material-ized, stepping through a swinging door behind the bar, it seemed as shocked to see Charlie as he was to see it. The "it" in question was, no doubt, a very large man in a floral-printed shirt that enveloped his body like a muumuu. The shirt looked like it hadn't been washed in several weeks. The man wore a short beard, and his black hair was thinning in strange patterns on his head. His eyes widened to see Charlie, then darted around the room nervously.

"*On est fermé*," he said in a voice that sounded strangely flutelike, coming from such a large body. He was informing Charlie that the café was closed, though a quick look at Charlie's watch confirmed that it was almost noon. What café in their right mind would be closed at Thursday lunch?

"But—" began Charlie.

"You are English?" asked the man.

"American, actually," said Charlie. "And I think I'm looking for—"

"We are closed," said the man. His English wormed from beneath a heavy accent.

"On a Thursday at lunchtime?" Charlie could not hide his dis-belief.

The man seemed to appraise the situation. He scratched his beard thoughtfully. "Okay," he said. "We are open."

That was easy, thought Charlie. "Oh," he said. "Good."

"Yes," said the man. He was still standing, somewhat frozen, behind the bar. "What would you have?"

Charlie was so confused by this interaction that he'd forgotten that he'd meant to ask after Amir. "What—" he stammered. "Are there any daily specials?"

"No," said the man.

"Okay," said Charlie.

"Yes," rebutted the man. "There are daily specials."

"Oh," said Charlie. "Okay. And what are they?"

The man seemed suddenly stumped by the question, and he frowned as if he considered it unfair that Charlie should press him this way. "They are . . . ," he began. His eyes scanned the restaurant, as if trying to conjure the words. "Hhhhhh," he said, after a time, which mostly sounded as if the man were trying to expel something from his throat.

"Pardon?"

"Hhhhhh," the man repeated. Finally, the sound more or less transfigured into an understandable word: "Horse."

Charlie grimaced. "Horse?"

"Hare," corrected the man. "Rabbit. In a stew."

"You said horse, just before."

"Didn't. I said rabbit. In a stew."

Charlie figured it wasn't wise to press him. "Anything else?"

"That's it."

"Do you have a menu? Maybe I'd look at your menu."

The man ran his hand down the bar thoughtfully. He seemed to gaining a semblance of confidence in his role as waiter. "No menu today. Just the special."

Charlie was hungry. Besides, he thought that maybe ordering from the gentleman would go some way to make him more at ease. "I'll take the rabbit stew, then," he said.

"You will?" The man seemed surprised.

"Well, if it's the only thing for lunch, I guess so. Yes."

The man abruptly lifted his hand from the bar and walked back through the swinging door. It had barely swung back in place before he appeared again. "Would you like something to drink while you wait?"

"Sure," said Charlie. "A grenadine?"

The man winked and smiled, pointing a chubby finger in Charlie's direction. "Good choice, my friend." He walked the length of the bar, stopping only once he was in front of the shelves of dusty and disordered bottles. He managed a dramatic pirouette to face them. Charlie, from where he sat, could hear the man whisper, "Grenadine. Grenadine. Grenadine," as he searched the bottles' labels for the right one.

"Is that it, there?" called Charlie. "The one with the red stuff in it?"

The man gave Charlie another wink over his shoulder as he reached out and grabbed the bottle Charlie had identified. He picked up a glass from the bar, spat in it, and wiped it clean with the hem of his shirt. Charlie winced and looked away, trying to turn his attention to the decor of the café. Several oil paintings were hung on the walls, which were covered in a faded patterned paper; one of the paintings was mysteriously of a coat without a body inside it. Another was of some fortress, piled high on top of a mountain peak. The café itself seemed as if it once had been a fine establishment, but it had long fallen into disuse and disrepair. Newspapers cluttered the corners, and muddy scuffs covered the old tile of the floor.

"Here you are," came the man's voice, directly over Charlie's shoulder. A tall glass filled to the brim with a reddish liquid appeared in front of Charlie. "*Une grenadine.*"

"*Merci*," said Charlie. He eyed the glass suspiciously. As if postponing drinking it, he looked up at the man and said, "Do you know someone named Amir?"

"Amir?" asked the man. "No. No Amir."

"Kid my age, maybe. Lebanese, I think. Brown hair? I think he might've given me this card." He reached into his pocket and showed the business card to his waiter. The man looked at it blankly.

"I don't know this card," he said. "I don't know Amir." With a whistle, he began walking back to the bar.

"This is the Bar des Sept Coins, correct?"

"It is," said the man.

"But you've never seen a brown-haired kid named Amir."

"Never," said the man emphatically. Maybe—just maybe—too

emphatically, Charlie decided.

Charlie, mystified, picked up the glass in front of him and absently took a sip. A sudden burning sensation ripped through his throat as he gulped down the drink. He looked back at the man, shocked. "This . . . ," he sputtered, "what is in this?"

"Grenadine."

"And . . . ?"

"And gin, of course," said the man. He'd returned to his place behind the bar.

"You put gin in my grenadine?"

The man seemed genuinely offended by Charlie's critique. "Is there any other way to drink it?"

"I'm twelve years old, sir," said Charlie. "Do I look like I take gin in my grenadine?"

The man gave a disinterested shrug. He disappeared back behind the swinging door, leaving Charlie alone with his thoughts. He stared out the front door of the café, wondering for a second time whether he should just give up his search for the boy pickpocket and get on with his life. This thought was interrupted when the swinging door behind the bar swung again and the man in the muumuu appeared, holding a plate.

He sashayed proudly over to where Charlie was seated and, with a loud *"Bon appétit!"* laid the dish in front of his only customer.

"This is the rabbit?" asked Charlie.

The thing on the plate was, without a doubt, not a stew. Instead, it was definitely a sandwich. And one that looked as if a few bites had been taken out of it.

"*À la Marseillaise*," said the man, smiling toothily.

Charlie peeled back the top slice of the bread; a gooey layer of what appeared to be some kind of chocolate spread adhered it to its downstairs neighbor. He could not find it in his heart to quibble. "Looks delicious," he said. He was about to pick it up and take a bite when he thought better of it. "Listen," he said, scooting his chair away from the table. "If you do see someone named—"

"I do not know this Amir," the man interrupted.

"I know," said Charlie impatiently. "But if you do—"

"It is very unlikely that—"

Charlie countered loudly, "BUT IF YOU DO." He waited to see if the man would interrupt again. When he didn't, Charlie continued calmly: "If you do see him, will you tell him Charlie Fisher stopped by?"

"Charlie Fisher," repeated the man. "Yes."

"Tell him . . ." Charlie searched for the words. "Tell him he dropped this and I was just returning it." He set the business card on the table with a resigned sigh.

"Very well, monsieur," said the man, whose sudden shift in tone gave away his eagerness to be done with Charlie altogether.

Charlie began to ask for the check when he was interrupted by the most sudden and abrasive change in atmosphere he'd ever, in his short life, experienced. In a matter of moments, the once-placid café was transformed into a whirlwind of absolute chaos.

The café door swung open with a tremendous crash, and in ran a horde of kids. They moved too fast for Charlie to count them, but his embattled mind managed to guess there were six or seven. His heart felt like it was leaping out of his chest. Two of them dove toward him as one, only separating inches before his table; his glass of gin-and-grenadine (mostly gin) flew violently sideways and splashed to the ground in a most spectacular manner. Charlie himself fell over backward in his chair, spilling comically to the dirty tiled floor. He scrambled to his feet just in time to see his waiter, suddenly looking very alert, standing in front of the mirrored wall behind the bar, corralling the children toward him. Charlie saw him reach behind one of the bottles, and much to Charlie's surprise, the entire wall of shelves opened to reveal a secret passageway behind it. One by one, the kids disappeared behind the shelves; the waiter counted each of them, like a mama duckling numbering her young. Apparently one was missing, because he looked quizzically out into the room; he seemed surprised to see Charlie still standing there.

"Charlie!" came a voice from the far end of the café.

It was Amir, breathless, having just dashed into the dining room. Both of the boys faced off, seeming equally shocked to see each other. Finally, a smile broke across Amir's face.

"C'mon!" he cried, running and grabbing Charlie's hand. He dragged Charlie across the room, sending chairs flying as he did so. Charlie, at that point, began to hear the encroaching wail of sirens, somewhere out in the street. The heavyset waiter impatiently waved them toward him; when they arrived at the doorway, the waiter put his hand on Charlie's chest, stopping him.

"You know the chump?" the man asked.

"The chump's with me," said Amir.

Apparently, that was enough explanation for the waiter. Charlie and Amir dashed under the man's arm just as he let go of the strange door and it closed behind them. Together, they entered the darkness.

Chapter
EIGHT

"**W**atch your step!" someone instructed Charlie, though he could not say who. The way was pitch-black on the other side of the secret door. It was also very cramped, which Charlie discovered by simultaneously scraping both elbows on the opposing walls of a passageway that seemed to be slowly angling downward. The air became cool and slightly wet. A flicker of electric light could be seen somewhere off in the distance ahead of him, illuminating the parade of figures he was following in silhouette. The cry of sirens was all but silenced by the closed door behind them. He reached out to touch the shoulder of the kid nearest him. The bare glow of the corridor's light showed that it was Amir.

"Where are we?" whispered Charlie.

"Shhh," warned Amir. "Just follow."

Charlie could hear some sort of hushed argument occurring at the front end of the line as they arrived at an abrupt end to the corridor. Curiously enough, the file of bodies began suddenly corkscrewing downward and out of sight. It didn't take long for Charlie to arrive at a spiral staircase that had been built into an ancient-looking stone well. Grasping the wrought-iron banister, he carefully followed the wooden steps; they seemed to multiply endlessly as he traveled. After some time, the stairs let out on a stone surface and Charlie looked up. His breath caught in his throat.

The glow of the electric lamps revealed that he was standing in the midst of a massive catacomb.

Charlie struggled to date this strange subterranean burrow—but he'd have to guess that, like many European catacombs, it likely dated to Roman times. The stones were darkened with soot and age, and wide cavities had been constructed into the walls of what amounted to a long, low corridor. Presumably, bodies had once been interred in these cavities, but there was now little evidence of them. Instead, fine Persian rugs and tasseled pillows had been thrown about, giving the appearance of a kind of exotic salon. In the center of the room was a large table, surrounded by chairs. Its surface was piled high with what appeared to be paper money, coins, and treasure of every metallic hue.

The argument that Charlie had overheard in the corridor above had continued in this new environment, though it had grown in intensity. It was between two boys, roughly Charlie's age. One was a boy with deep-ebony-colored skin; the other was a mop-topped white kid of almost comically large proportions for his apparent age. The former spoke in a rich accent that Charlie couldn't place, the latter in some kind of Slavic dialect. Their English, though, was strangely similar in its alienness.

"That chump had a dipsy, Bear," said the first boy. "I felt it. He came down on me before I knew what was happening!"

"That weren't no dipsy," said the second. "That was some old Iowa tweezer poke. You spooked, that's all. Almost throwed the mob."

A girl interjected, "He was a whiz copper, boys. Didn't you see that fuzzy tail?"

The two boys stopped and stared at the girl. Charlie, squinting his eyes against the low light of the torches, recognized her as Jackie, the girl he'd met with Amir the day before.

"No," said the boy they called the Bear, in disbelief.

Jackie pulled something from her purse and threw it on the table. It was a silver badge. Everyone in the room ran to look at it, including Charlie.

"Look at that," said the girl. "Whiskers got whiskers." She removed several more items from her purse and threw them on the table: a wallet, a watch, a laminated credential card, and what looked to be a much beloved photograph of a cat.

The argument was immediately forgotten; the entire room erupted into laughter. Charlie found himself joining in, though he wasn't entirely sure what he was laughing about. Apparently Charlie's contribution was conspicuous in some way, because as soon as he began, the entire room stopped.

Everyone's attention was suddenly turned to the newcomer. Charlie's laughter dwindled away awkwardly. "Hi," he said, after a beat.

Jackie pushed through the crowd of kids, all of them struck speechless by Charlie's presence, and fixed Charlie with an unholy glare. "Who in God's name are you and how did you get here?" she asked in a tone of voice that Charlie, had he written about it in one of his stories, would have described as "it could disintegrate hard steel."

Amir, thankfully, stepped in. "This is Charlie. You remember Charlie Fisher, right, Jackie?"

"What, the chump you were turning out yesterday?" asked Jackie.

"That's him," said Amir.

Jackie, by this time, had turned to face Amir squarely. "And how, pray tell, did he come to find our scatter?" Before Amir could offer a reply, she corrected herself, saying, "How did he come to *be actually inside* our scatter?"

Charlie scanned the crowd that was now surrounding him. There were eight kids in total, including Amir and Jackie, of varying ages, heights, and ethnicity. Of the pack, three were girls. One of the girls approached Charlie—she was certainly the youngest of them all and decidedly the smallest. She wore her brown hair boyishly short; she spoke to Charlie in the most hardened London Cockney accent he thought he'd ever heard.

"Shall I stick this britch?" she asked. She'd reached into her pants pocket and retrieved a knife, which she waved threateningly in front of his face.

Charlie assumed it had been a question asked of someone else, but he figured it wouldn't hurt to offer his own opinion: "I don't think you should," he said.

"I didn't ask you," said the girl menacingly, now inches from his face.

"Mouse," said Jackie. "Back off."

"Yeah, Molly," said Amir. "We don't work rough."

"This ain't workin' rough when you've got a chump in your hideaway. Steps need to be taken, Amir."

"He's my friend," said Amir. "He's on the whiz."

Jackie let out an exasperated puff of air. "He's on the whiz? Didn't *he* graduate awful quickly from prat to tool."

The boy who'd been arguing with the loutish Russian, the ebony-skinned one, walked over to Charlie's side and inspected him. Much to Charlie's surprise, a second boy, nearly identical to this one, emerged and stood on Charlie's other flank. They appeared to be twins. The first spoke loudly into his left ear: "He passed the test?"

"The seven bells?" asked the one on his right.

"What?" asked Charlie, confused.

"Seven bells," said the boy on his right.

"For seven coins," said the boy on his left. They'd spoken in quick succession, and the effect was dizzying on poor Charlie.

"What do you think?" asked Amir. "Of course he ain't been to the school. He's from here. But since we lost—"

"Don't," interrupted Jackie angrily.

Amir turned on Jackie. "What, we can't talk about it? Can't talk about Munan?"

"Don't say that name in my presence," hissed Jackie.

"Fine," said Amir. "Ever since we lost the-boy-whose-name-must-not-be-spoken, we've been down a man. We need fresh blood."

"And this chump is your idear of fresh blood?" asked the younger girl, Mouse.

The third girl spoke from where she stood: "Why don't we call the Headmaster? Why doesn't he send us someone?" This girl had fine black hair, cut to her shoulders, and seemed to be of East Asian descent. Charlie, even having traveled the world as extensively as he had, had never seen such a diverse band of children assembled in one place. It was like looking at a United Nations assembly made up entirely of professional child thieves.

"Who are you all?" Charlie asked without really meaning to. It just came out.

"Your worst nightmare," said Mouse, the little Brit. She was still brandishing the knife in her hand.

"No one you want to know," added the Asian girl.

"We're nothing," said the boy to his right.

"We're not really even here," said the boy to his left.

("Please don't do that," said Charlie when this rejoinder came in disorienting stereo.)

"We're the Whiz Mob of Marseille, Charlie," said Amir. "And we're down a tool. That's why I invited you here. I'm glad you got the hint." He gave Charlie a wink before turning to his compatriots. "You think the Headmaster's going to get us a replacement cannon? You're nuts. He'd want us to work down a man."

"Or woman," added the black-haired girl.

"Or woman. Sorry, Michiko, Jackie, Mouse."

"That's true," said the Bear.

"Or," continued Amir, "he'd want us to improvise. So that's what I'm doing. Charlie Fisher here"—he gestured back to Charlie—"for whatever reason, this kid saved my hide. He fronted for me with the fuzz. When we were working the Jean Jaurès. So I owed him one, didn't I?"

The entire room murmured its assent, as if an agreement had long ago been struck and Amir was merely adhering to it.

"Didn't I, Jackie?" he repeated, looking at the teen girl.

"Sure enough, Amir," she replied.

"So we did a few jobs, him and me, y'know, working two-handed. Dug through a few prats." Amir paused and looked back at Charlie. "And he did all right. I think there's a bit of the know in him."

"This chump's got the *know*?" asked a boy who Charlie hadn't yet heard speak. He was of middling height with mussed black hair and carried the slightest spackle of a mustache on his upper lip. He also wore an eye patch over his right eye, which might've borne mentioning earlier.

"I don't see it," said the Asian girl, who Charlie guessed to be Michiko. She squinted a bit at him for good measure. "Nope," she said.

"If you are confident, let us see you do a touch," said the lumbering Russian boy.

"Well . . . ," demurred Charlie, remembering all too well his last trial by fire with Jackie. "I'm not quite—"

But Amir interrupted him: "He can do it."

"I can do it," parroted Charlie, giving Amir a surprised and slightly terrified look.

"Okay, then," said the boy with the eye patch. "Here, Bear. Gimme that tweezer poke."

The Russian did as he was asked. Charlie saw a leather wallet, snapped closed with a small metal clasp, exchange hands. The boy with the eye patch, who we'll refer to as Eye Patch until such time as his name is revealed to Charlie, pulled a single centime coin from

119

his pocket, deposited it in the wallet, and snapped it closed. He then placed it in the inside pocket of the worn blazer he was wearing.

"Get the smash from my coat pit," said Eye Patch. "Take the coin from the wallet."

"Oh, come on," said Amir. "Inside a tweezer? Give the boy a chance."

"No," said Jackie, stepping forward with a smile. "I think this is the perfect trial. If you're so sure he's got the know, this shouldn't be any trouble. Come on, Charlie Fisher: see if you can score a centime off Pluto here." She was referring to Eye Patch, who will no longer be called Eye Patch, but by his name, Pluto, instead.

Charlie took a deep, determined breath and began running through everything Amir had taught him. Over the last twenty-four hours, he'd mentally prepared for such an encounter, wanting nothing more than to have a second chance at the test he'd failed the day before. His dreams had been rife with touches, prats, and pokes; his waking life since yesterday had been filled with imaginings of smooth, accurate sleight of hand. He'd been visualizing success since the moment he'd climbed out of bed. He felt the energy of the room swell around him as the kids began animatedly discussing his prospects; as he sized up eye-patched Pluto and his encasing blazer, he began to hear side bets being taken up by the spectating crowd. "Five francs on Pluto," said one of the twins. "I'll take ten on the chump," said the other.

"What are you waiting for, then?" Pluto asked Charlie.

"For the record, this isn't a very fair environment," said Charlie, beginning to pace nervously. "I mean, ideally we'd be in some sort of square or plaza, correct?"

(The girl Mouse, playing the bookie, began collecting the kids' bets. "Charlie Fisher at twenty-five to one," she said.)

"A cannon with the know can make it happen anywheres," said Pluto.

"Oh, I have the know," said Charlie, gaining confidence. He rooted himself in the spot directly in front of the boy.

("Make that thirty to one," said Mouse. A few of the onlookers grumbled disappointedly at the announcement.)

"You don't have the know. You don't have nothing," said Pluto.

"Well . . . ," began Charlie.

"Well, what?"

"At least I got two eyes," said Charlie. For the record: Charlie had never before made fun of, or called attention to, someone's perceived impairment or disability. It was just not something he did. In school, when he'd been in school, he often found himself siding with the outcasts and the marginalized of his peer group. Using someone's particular challenge as a way to unman them was contemptible to Charlie—but he knew that in this situation, he had to surprise himself as much as anyone else.

The boy Pluto did not seem so much offended as amazed that

this was the tack Charlie was taking. He stared at Charlie for a few moments before he began laughing. He began laughing loudly, nearly howling, and he had to set his arm on Charlie's shoulder to support himself.

"Oh, this one," he said between laughing fits. "This one's a joker, not a cannon."

And that was when Charlie moved in. With his right arm, he reached over and grabbed Pluto at his shoulder. The boy's attention went immediately to Charlie's hand. With his free left hand, Charlie made a grab for the inner jacket pocket of the boy's blazer. The boy immediately freed his hand from Charlie's shoulder and reached down, grabbing Charlie's wrist and preventing him from reaching the wallet. However: before you count Charlie out, assuming that he had made the unwise decision to simply muscle (*clout and lam*, as Amir had called it) the centime coin from the wallet in Pluto's jacket, you should know that this was all part of a larger, if somewhat hastily planned, ruse. With the boy's attention now diverted to Charlie's hand inside his jacket, Charlie was easily able to swing his foot between the boy's leg and around his knee.

They both, Pluto and Charlie, went tumbling to the ground in a heap of *boy*.

The entire room, having cast their lot with either party, sensed that their bet was at risk and so therefore tried to protect their investment as best they could by diving into the fray as well. Unprintable slurs were hollered; challenges leveled. A few punches were wildly thrown.

Charlie, for his part, was still earnestly trying to snatch the centime coin from inside the clasped wallet inside Pluto's jacket. With so many arms and elbows flying, he was able to innocuously crawl his hand around Pluto's chest while the boy was fighting off some bettor who had cast his lot with Charlie. He felt a sudden flush of excitement as his fingers found their way to the leather wallet and its clasp. He'd barely begun to fumble with the simple catch when he felt a tremendous pain in his stomach; Pluto, in the turmoil, had fought off his attacker and elbowed Charlie out of the way. Charlie let out a terrible groan. His fingers let go of the wallet and he rolled away from the writhing pile of bodies.

Pluto shook himself free of his confederates and, standing, looked down at Charlie, smiling.

"See?" he said, giving one his assailants a bit of a kick. "He's playing the rough tool. He's got no knowledge." As if to settle the argument once and for all, Pluto reached into his jacket pocket and retrieved the wallet. Undoing the clasp, he upended it in order to dramatically let the centime fall to the floor.

However, no centime fell to the floor.

The wallet was empty.

Pluto's face went flat, and he mouthed something in disbelief. Every kid in the room slowly and silently clambered to their feet.

Charlie was as shocked as any of them. As much as he would've like to take credit, he hadn't even been able to undo the tweezer—the clasp—on the poke before he'd been pushed away. He began to recover himself; his gut still radiated pain from the place where Pluto's elbow had made contact. He pulled himself up on to his knees. That was when he felt some object rub against his thigh. Something was there that hadn't been before. Reaching into his pocket, he pulled out a single, dull-gray centime coin and held it out in his fingers.

Everyone in the room let out a collective gasp.

"Well, well," said Jackie, who was busy returning the ponytail to her hair. "A natural-born talent."

The crowd around Charlie murmured their appreciation for what they'd witnessed; those who'd bet on the long shot and put their money on Charlie's success enjoyed a brief celebration. Mouse begrudgingly paid them out at the rate she'd quoted. Pluto, having dusted himself off, eyed Charlie perhaps more suspiciously than the rest, but, like his compatriots, soon forgot about the episode entirely.

"But we have to get approval from the Headmaster," continued Jackie, speaking to Amir. "This is . . . irregular."

Amir nodded.

"And he ain't no cannon," she continued. "So he managed a tricky touch. We're not bringing a greenhorn straight into the grift rackets. He'll throw us. He needs experience."

"Sure, Jackie," said Amir. "We'll let him play center field till he's proper turned out, yeah?"

Jackie nodded. She looked at Charlie and frowned. "C'mon, fellas," she said. "Enough horseplay. We got a knockup to divvy. Let's skin the pokes and ding the dead ones." At her instruction, everyone moved to congregate around the long table and began picking through their ill-gotten gains.

Charlie was left where he stood, still holding the centime coin in the palm of his hand. Amir walked over and grabbed it from him. "Ace work, Charlie," he said, smiling archly. He turned the coin around in his fingers, studying it.

"Thanks," Charlie said. "Though I didn't—"

"Shhh," warned Amir, his finger to his lips. "A secret. Between me and you, yeah?" He then slipped the coin into the front pocket of Charlie's flannel shirt and gave it a congenial pat.

"Did you . . . ?"

"Shhh," Amir repeated. "Secret." He threw his arm over Charlie's shoulder and led him over to the table, where everyone had gathered. "Welcome to the Whiz Mob, Charlie Fisher," he said.

Chapter
NINE

Michiko hailed from Hiroshima; she'd been born one year after the bomb had fallen. She had been raised by her parents in the rubble of the city.

"I don't like Americans," she said, when Amir introduced her.

"Right," said Amir, looking at Charlie. "She doesn't like Americans."

Borra "the Bear" was twelve and was from Soviet Leningrad by way of Zurich. His family had been a storied aristocratic one, friends of the Romanovs. They, like most of their social strata, had a cataclysmic fall from grace during the Russian Revolution. Borra and his extended family had managed to live quietly in the country for decades before they'd been rooted out by Stalinist agents and were forced to escape to Europe.

"And that's Sembene. He's a stall," began Amir, pointing to one of the twins.

"*I'm* Sembene," said the other.

"And I'm Fatour," said the one Amir had pointed to. He winked at Charlie. "Or am I?"

"We can only take their word for it, really," said Amir. "Senegalese. Identical twins. Surprisingly helpful on the job."

Charlie gave a friendly wave to each of the kids as he was introduced. They each, in their turn, looked up and acknowledged the introduction. They were busy organizing all the loot that lay scattered across the table. Coins were being gathered in one pile, cash bills in another. Valuables—necklaces, watches, rings—were being arranged in different piles, while emptied wallets (*dead ones*) were thrown to the floor in a heap. Charlie had never seen such an amassing of treasure in one place. It was like a pirates' hoard come to life.

It must've been a sizable haul, because the mood in the room, since the discovery of their infiltrator, had lightened considerably. The pickpockets laughed and chided one another as they divvied the loot.

"Jackie here you've met," continued Amir. "She's our top tool. Chattanooga, Tennessee, girl. Am I right, Jackie?"

Jackie looked up from the table. She flashed her eyelashes at Charlie and gave him a plastic smile. "A good Southern belle," she said. She picked up one of the gold rings and gave it a vicious bite of assessment.

"She's been on the whiz longer than any of us," said Amir. "Headmaster had her turned out when she was six."

"A class cannon," said Jackie, "is what you'd call that."

"She's also the 'umblest of the lot," said the young British girl. Jackie, standing next to her, gave her a push.

Amir smiled. "And that's Molly the Mouse. She can hook, she can stall. She's our little nine-year-old whiz moll. East End of London, born and raised. Real Dickens stuff there."

"Pleased to meet ya, me flash companion," hammed the girl.

Amir continued to round the table with Charlie at his side. "And of course you're acquainted with Pluto here. Our folder man. He plans the jobs. Buenos Aires born. Came up in the circus, right? Lost his eye in the knife-throwing show."

Charlie shivered. "You took a knife to the eye?" he asked.

Pluto replied, "No, I was the one throwing knives. Nicked the shoulder of the girl I was throwing at. She came at me with a six-inch heel." He hooked a finger into the inside of his cheek and pulled it out, making a sickening *pop*.

Charlie put his hand to his mouth.

"And that's our charming brigade," said Amir. "The waiter, Bertuccio, you met upstairs. He's a Corsican. Runs the goulash joint. Keeps us safe as kelsey."

"Goulash joint?"

"The scatter. The hangout. The Bar des Sept Coins."

"Oh," said Charlie. "Got it."

Having made a complete circle of the table and met everyone who'd assembled around it, Charlie felt as if he'd been spun on the swing carousel. He tried to hide his admiration for the kids; he didn't want to appear overly fawning. He edged closer to the table and watched as the pickpockets haggled over their pile, assaying its worth and talking up the work they'd done to get it. Molly the Mouse was holding up what looked to be a tie clip and was studying it with a somewhat derisive look on her face.

"'Oo's nicking stickpins?" she asked the table.

"That would be Borra," replied Sembene—or was it Fatour? A quick aside here, gentle reader: we shall continue assigning dialogue to either Sembene or Fatour with the understanding that no one is entirely sure which is who and who is which, least of all their compatriots. Of course, this is a quality that they have long relished and cultivated. We will not deprive them of their fun.

"In Moscow," the Bear replied, defending himself, "stickpins fetch very good price in market."

"Nah, nah," said Molly. "That's the old rackets, mate. You ain't some flat jointer. A stickpin prop ain't nothing but shag if it's not got ice in it."

(Charlie, at this moment, cast a curious glance at Amir, who gave his quiet translation: "A tiepin is worthless without a diamond in it.")

"You might as well be binging braces, Borra," said Pluto. "Now there's a class racket."

The entire crowd laughed at this joke, though its meaning was lost on Charlie. Amir saw his confusion and explained, "Binging—stealing. There was a cannon some of us ran with who made it a habit to steal chumps' suspenders after each job."

"Tate the Great," put in Molly. "One of the best."

Amir had to stifle an urge to laugh as he recounted, "See, Tate, he'd work lone wolf, yeah?—on his own. And he'd fan some party like a ballroom dance. He'd work the floor, binging pokes, ridge, slum—whatever they had—but before he was done, he'd bing all the fellas' suspenders and stand off, watching all of 'em running off to the bandstand, holding up their britches like this." He grasped his pants' waist with both hands and comically ran across the room as if his trousers were about to drop to his ankles. Everyone laughed, even Charlie. "Tate'd ding the suspenders—he'd dump 'em all—outside the ballroom, and the gents would spend the next hour tryin' to figure whose was whose, all the while their pants falling down."

"He was a classic," said Borra, his laugh a husky guffaw. "Not many of his kind anymore."

"Where is he now?" ventured Charlie.

"Some layoff spot somewhere," said Amir, somewhat mournfully. "He's off the whiz these days."

"You can do that?" asked Charlie. "Just . . . be off the whiz?"

"Yeah," said Amir. "Anyone can do it. Declare yourself out, it's called."

"But why would you want to?" put in Michiko, fanning out a multicolored stack of crisp franc bills like a peacock's tail.

"Exactly," said Amir, smiling at Charlie.

"We're on the whiz," said Pluto, "because we want to."

"Because we're good at it," added Michiko.

"The Headmaster doesn't force the rackets on anyone," said Jackie, herself now holding a gold watch and admiring it. "We're here because we're drawn to it. And because we can do our little part to wage war on the rich in a way that no army could."

Charlie squinted and pointed a finger at the crowd around the table. "Wait," he said. "Are you guys Communists?"

Jackie laughed. Borra spat derisively on the ground. Michiko shook her head and said, "We are not anything. We are the Whiz Mob *du Marseille*."

"Binged a few okuses off commies, though," said Sembene.

"Not particularly fat marks, them," added Molly.

"Tools follow no particular political persuasion, Charlie," said Amir. "We follow the prats."

"How does this— How did you—" Charlie paused, trying to arrange the flood of questions he had into one succinct thought. He asked, "How do you all know each other?"

This question caused everyone at the table to look up at Charlie. They exchanged a few furtive glances. Jackie shot a look at Amir. Sembene said, "Can we tell him?"

"We'll have to kill him," said Michiko, giving a mischievous smile.

"Can I do it?" asked Pluto. He sneered at Charlie. Clearly, the boy was still harboring ill will toward Charlie for having binged the centime.

"Shush, Pluto. Amir?" asked Jackie.

"We can tell him," said Amir. "He should know."

"We might as well," added the Bear. "He has seen everything else."

"What?" asked Charlie, confused, looking around the room. "What's the secret?"

"We're a whiz mob, Charlie," said Amir. "One of lots. All over the world."

"Every major city's got one," said Jackie. "We're not the first you've run into. Not that you would know."

"We work in secret," said Sembene.

"In the shadows," said Fatour.

"And that's all you need to know," said Michiko.

"Oh, come on," said Amir. "If he's going to run with us, even playing center field, we just gotta tell him."

"Please do," said Charlie.

Amir nodded to Jackie. "You tell him."

"The School of Seven Bells," said Jackie. "Ever heard of it?"

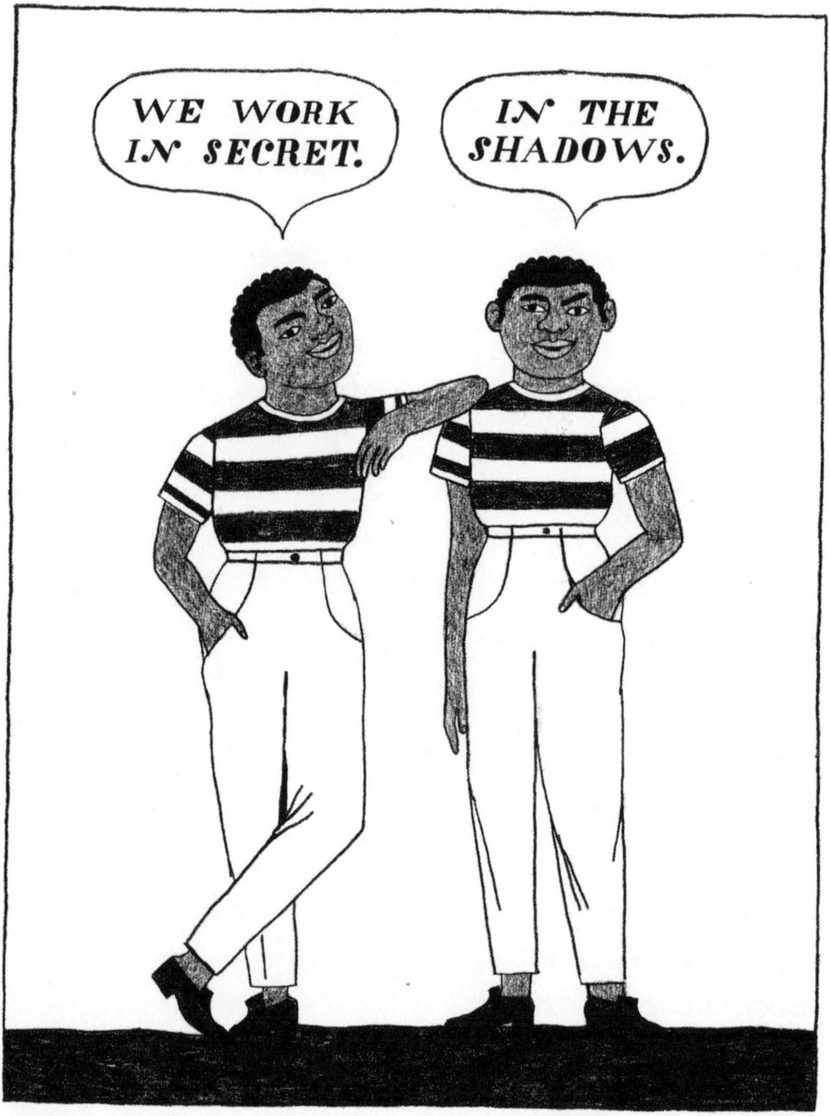
WE WORK IN SECRET.
IN THE SHADOWS.

"Can't say I have," said Charlie.

"Of course he hasn't," put in Pluto. "He's a chump. He's a—"

"Just tell him your story, Jackie," interrupted Amir.

Jackie paused before speaking again. She picked up a gold chain necklace and draped it between her fingers. "When I was a girl in Chattanooga—a very little girl—growing up on a plantation, I had a lot of time on my hands. I had a big family; every one of my brothers and sisters had to figure out how to stand out. I developed a . . ." She searched for the word. "A skill. Not only how to use my fingers in a crafty and secret way, but I figured out how to mess with folks', you know, understanding of where they were—and where I was. It was like I could manipulate time. I could totally change the way people were in the world. I found I could take my daddy's bifocals off his face without him even knowing it. I taught myself to pick locks, to steal candy. I could frame the gardener—or any one of my brothers or sisters—for anything I might've done wrong. You can imagine I was a bit of a handful. But I had a talent. Turns out, I had the *know*.

"The grift know. The grift sense. I wasn't aware at the time, but it was a thing that linked me with tons of other kids in the world, all over the world. One day I was playing in the garden of the big house when a man arrived. He was dressed real nice, had a suit on. He spoke in a strange accent. I remember him clear as day. He knelt down in front of me, held out a coin. He made it do magic things. He made it disappear, made it reappear in the pocket of my pinafore. He asked for my father and mother; I remember them speaking to him at quite some length. When they were done talking, my father came over to me and said that the man was there to take me somewhere. Somewhere incredible. Where kids like me could be taught, where a particular talent like mine could be refined and honed. Next thing I knew, my bags were packed and I was driven away. This guy's name was Nigel. He was a Finder. We traveled for many days—by car, by plane, by boat. We crossed countries and oceans. Until finally we arrived at the strangest place I'd ever seen. On top of a mountain in the middle of Colombia—in South America, we came to the school. The School of Seven Bells."

Charlie listened intently as the girl spoke. The room had quieted. All eyes were on Jackie.

She continued, "You probably can imagine how strange it all seemed, me just a six-year-old girl from Chattanooga. This castle-like building in some place on the other side of the world from where I was born. But that's where I learned to channel my talent into something useful. Something that can change the world. Me . . ." Here she gave a wave of the necklace still wound in her fingers to include the rest of the kids in the room. "And everyone you see. We were all brought together by our skills, our abilities. Under the instruction of the Headmaster, we honed those skills. We became a whiz mob. And we were sent out into the world to do our work."

"To pick pockets?" asked Charlie.

"To right the imbalances," interjected Michiko. "To take the rich folks down a peg."

"Also to get rich ourselves!" threw in the Bear with a wide smile.

"We take our little cut, the rest goes to the Headmaster," said Jackie. "What he keeps is kinda like tuition."

"Paying for the education of tomorrow's cannons," said Amir, his hand dramatically on his heart.

Charlie let out an astounded laugh. He looked at each of the kids in turn, waiting for them to break character, to reveal their elaborate joke. When they didn't, Charlie said, incredulously, "Do you know how crazy that sounds? A secret school for pickpockets? In South America?"

Amir shrugged his shoulders. "Craziness is relative, yeah?"

"And you're all sent out to work in groups like this? I mean, is there a whiz mob in, say, Washington, DC?"

"Yeah," said Amir.

"Tokyo?" asked Charlie.

"Uh-huh," said Molly.

"Moscow?"

"There is," responded the Bear. "*Konechna.*"

"Um . . ." Charlie searched his brain. "Sydney, Australia?"

"A very fine one, in fact," answered Jackie.

"Kiko's in that mob, right?" asked Amir. He gave an impressive whistle. "Now, there's a cannon."

"We are everywhere," Jackie reiterated. She spun the gold chain around her index finger a few times before flinging it onto the heap of gold on the table.

"Okay," said Charlie. "So why is it called that? The School of Seven Bells?"

"A very astute question, Charlie," said Amir, "with a very simple answer."

"It's named for the final test that every kid must take before he or she is declared a true cannon, before they're turned out on the whiz," explained Jackie. "We all have passed the Test of the Seven Bells."

Charlie scanned the room; everyone nodded in succession.

"So . . . ," he ventured. "What is the test?"

"Seven coins," said Sembene.

"For seven pockets," said Fatour.

"Let us demonstrate," said Jackie.

Jackie had grabbed Amir by the shoulders; she proceeded to lead him to the center of the crypt. An electric light in a black shroud hung over the place where he stood, casting ominous shadows over his body. She helped him don what looked to be a khaki-green soldier's coat that she'd retrieved from one of the catacomb's stone recesses. Several cargo pockets decorated the chest of the jacket.

"In the middle of a room called the arena," explained Jackie, "a big, open room in the center of the school, there's a dummy. A man-nequin. That's all that's there." She walked back over to the table and retrieved a handful of coins from a pile. Amir, hearing her description, did his best impression of a mannequin, though his rigid features drew laughs from his audience.

"Shhh!" chided Jackie. "You're a dummy."

"That should be an easy one for you, Amir," called Molly the Mouse.

Amir's face dropped as the room erupted in laughter. "Brilliant joke, Mouse," he said, deadpan.

Jackie continued, "And on this dummy is an outfit with a bunch of pockets with little bells attached to each of 'em. And inside each pocket is a coin." She proceeded to drop, in quick succession, the treasures in her hand into seven of Amir's pockets; she described each drop as she did so: "One in the coat jerve. One in the tog pit. One in the coat pit. One in the right chest kick and one in the left. One in the tog tail. And one in the top britch. Seven coins. Seven pockets. Seven bells."

She stepped away and looked at Amir where he stood. She waved Michiko over. "It is the student's job to make each touch without ringing the bells."

Michiko, rising to the challenge, rubbed her hands together excitedly and faced Amir's unmoving mannequin. Her fingers moved with fluid grace—while there were no bells hanging from Amir's pockets, Charlie could barely see the fabric of the pockets move as the girl managed the first and second touches in quick succession.

"She does it, she passes the test," said Jackie. "Ring a single bell, however, and it's a fail."

Michiko circled Amir like a lion stalking its prey. She studied each pocket briefly before—*zip*—her hand struck quickly and quietly, snagging the coin from its hiding place.

"There is problem, though," put in the Bear, walking toward the mock test in session. "Three pockets in—if you make it that far—Headmaster comes into the arena. Wants to see if you can still perform under pressure. You think you're in good shape because you are really swinging with it—you've nailed four of seven touches. But then all of sudden you've got Headmaster coming at you." Borra then took on the gait of an altogether different character than himself: he hunched his back slightly and, spitting on his palms, aggressively parted his hair into the semblance of a severe comb-over. He was applauded by his compatriots for his efforts—they began to hoot and jeer this new addition to the reenactment. The entire room had by now taken on the feel of a theatrical production. "Okay, so now—I'm middle-aged man with bad breath," said Borra, his voice pitched in a mock British accent, "and terrible teeth."

Michiko tried to keep a straight face as Borra began slouching around her, peeking up over her shoulder and whispering in her ear. A few of the onlooking pickpockets laughed; he might've been overdoing it a tad.

"Careful, Michiko," he hissed. "Don't rumble him. Mind those prats. Keep your composure, what."

Despite the pressure, the girl managed to coerce another coin from its pocket; Amir remained the steadfast mannequin, his eyes comically unblinking and his arms stiff. Michiko rounded Amir's shoulder and maneuvered her hand into his jacket's inside pocket. Borra followed her so as to be looming directly over her shoulder as she went for the prat.

"Some make it," said Jackie, giving a wink to Amir. With that signal, Amir let out a loud "DING!"

"Most don't," she continued.

Michiko, once so confident, was deflated. Borra-as-Headmaster leered and guffawed like a vaudeville villain. The entire room erupted into applause, as if some great stage production had finished. The three kids—Michiko, Amir, and Borra—snapped out of their individual characters, stood gamely in line and, smiling, took their bows.

Charlie couldn't help but clap along. "That's amazing," he said. "Simply amazing."

"You wouldn't make it very far with *your* technique," said Pluto, frowning at Charlie. "Wrestling the mannequin to the ground would not work."

"He does have a point, Charlie," said Amir, shedding the khaki jacket.

"Yeah, well," said Charlie. "I do need practice."

"Oh, you'll get practice," said Amir.

The Whiz Mob had returned to their winnings on the table and continued to sort. They gabbed and chided one another as they spoke with a winning camaraderie that was undeniably magnetic. It seemed to Charlie that there could not be kids on the entire globe who were more diametrically opposed to the financiers' and politicians' children he was likely to meet. His was a sanitized, guarded existence; his peers were all equally sheltered. These kids would undoubtedly mop the floor with the bullying Päffgen boys of the world, and likely make off with their wallets for good measure. This was a crowd Charlie could roll with, if only he could develop the skills. One day, perhaps, he could stand at this table in this mysterious catacomb as an equal, sorting the day's take and telling stories of old jobs ("punching gun," as they called it). After a time, the waiter Bertuccio returned from the café upstairs with a large cutting board covered in sliced salamis and baguettes.

"Oh, sing us a tune, Bertuccio," called out Molly to the waiter. The Whiz Mob all seemed equally enamored of this idea, and they began hammering their fists on the table, demanding song.

Bertuccio smiled, blushed, and wandered over to one of the catacomb's decorated nooks, where a Spanish guitar was waiting for him. Taking it up, he plucked a few of the strings, tinkered with the tuning pegs, and began singing.

Charlie, now sitting in a chair next to Amir, fell into a kind of reverie at the sound of the man's voice—it was a rich, gliding thing that echoed about the low stone ceilings of the catacomb like wisps of cloudy vapor. He sang in Italian, and Charlie could not recognize the song, but he fell under its spell nonetheless. When the waiter had finished, the entire room gave up their applause and demanded more; Bertuccio humbly obliged. Charlie began to lose track of time, here in this subterranean chamber, surrounded by the piles of treasure and food and otherworldly chatter of the Whiz Mob. Eventually, he moved to one of the recesses and, lounging against a large tasseled pillow, might've nodded off momentarily, lulled to sleep by the intoxicating world he'd found himself in.

After a time, Charlie came back to earth. He glanced at his watch, but he saw that he'd neglected winding it; the second hand was still. "Anyone have the correct time?" he asked, rubbing his eyes.

Jackie, reclining back in a chair at the table, looked at the face of a watch she'd been admiring. "Ten o'clock," she said, before holding it to her ear to assess its condition. "Nope," she added, and she threw it to the table. She began cycling through a pile of watches, seeking out the working specimens. "Five fifteen. Nine thirty-five. Four ten." She smiled at Charlie. "Take your pick."

"I should really get going," said Charlie, "whatever the time. My father—I'm expected home."

"Wait a second," said Pluto. He looked at Amir. "How do we know he's solid? How do we know he's not going to beef gun to the whiskers?"

Amir shrugged. "At this point, Pluto, we can only take his word."

"I'm solid," replied Charlie, hoping that would suffice. "I won't . . . beef gun. To the whiskers. Or anyone else, for that matter." He looked around the room, shifting uncomfortably. "What are the whiskers again?"

Someone laughed. Michiko let him off: "The cops, Charlie, the cops!"

"Right," said Charlie. "Definitely not the whiskers."

"If you're in, you're in," said Amir. "No backing out now."

"I'm in," said Charlie. "Very much so."

Amir pointed at Pluto. "Pluto, our folder man, has a job for us Sunday. If you want to come along. Ain't that right, Pluto?"

"What's he gonna—" began Pluto grumpily, before Jackie interrupted him.

"He's here now, ain't he?" she said. "We'll take him along. Let him play center field. He can't do any harm."

"C'mon, Pluto," said Amir. "We need our ninth tool."

Pluto kicked his shoe against the stone floor before saying: "Hippodrome Marseille Borély. Racecourse. It's the Prix de Saignon. Massive quarter horse stakes race." He gave Amir a sour look before adding, "Every fat mark in the south of France will be there."

"And I will be there too," said Charlie cheerily.

"Nine a.m. sharp," said Pluto, rolling his eyes. "Front gates. Don't be late."

"On my word," said Charlie. He held his hand up in a gesture that could only be described as a combination Boy Scout salute and taxi hail. Suddenly aware of the awkwardness of this motion, he quickly let his hand fall to his side.

"See you there, Charlie," said Amir. He turned to the waiter. "Bertuccio, will you show our cannon-in-training out to the straight world?"

"With pleasure," said Bertuccio. He and Charlie then made their way back up the spiral staircase, down the tight brick corridor, through the secret door, and back into the deserted dining room of the café. By now, the sun had started to set and the street outside the windows of the café was cast in long shadows. Bertuccio opened one of the doors, gave a quick scan of the area, and ushered Charlie outside. The waiter put his finger to his eye as if to say *keep safe*, then disappeared back into the café, leaving Charlie, bewildered and ecstatic, back out on the streets of the city.

Chapter
TEN

It was dark by the time Charlie returned home. The front gates were closed; he had to ring the doorman to have them opened. The tall windows of the Fisher mansion were lit bright, and Charlie could see his father's silhouette looking down over the grounds from his upstairs study window.

Charlie had barely walked into the main foyer when the butler appeared, saying, "Your father has asked for you. He is in his study."

It was a serious matter indeed when he was asked to visit his father's study, a place reserved for the most intimate of lectures and scoldings. Oak bookshelves, lined with leather-bound volumes, covered every inch of wall space that wasn't papered with the various awards, commendations, and diplomas that Charles Sr. had been awarded over his many years as a servant to his country. Photographs peppered the in-between spaces, photos of Charles Fisher Senior shaking hands amicably yet sternly with every head of state imaginable. A large desk was anchored to the center of the room. His father was standing just beyond the desk with his back to the door, still facing the window, when Charlie entered the room timidly. "Yes, Father?" he asked.

"Where were you? Are you aware what time it is?" His father's voice sounded strained; Charlie had never heard such concern there.

"Sorry," said Charlie. "I guess I just lost track of time."

"I spoke to Simon; he said that he hadn't told you to get art supplies. In fact, he didn't know what I was talking about." Charles Sr. still had his back to his son. "What is going on, Charlie?"

"I—" Charlie began. He was interrupted. His father had turned around to face him.

"This is unconscionable behavior, Charlie. It is nine thirty at night. You have missed dinner. You have not given a soul any mention of your whereabouts. Do not forget, Charlie, you are the son of the American consul general!"

"I'm sorry, Father," Charlie said. "I was out with friends. I'd lost track of time."

"There are considerations—you, a boy, in your position in life. You have to—" Charles Sr. stopped abruptly. "What did you say?"

"Which part?"

"You said you were out with friends?"

"I did," said Charlie. He didn't realize that the admission would stop his father so completely in his tracks. "Some kids I'd met," he added.

"Oh," said Charles. "Well."

"C'mon, Father," said Charlie. "Don't act so surprised."

"I'm not surprised at all," said Charles. His father's face, however, still betrayed a state of relative shock. Finally, a little smile broke across his face. "Good for you, Charlie. Who are they? Who are their families? Would I know them?"

"I doubt it," said Charlie, thinking fast. "Private-school kids. On foreign exchange." It wasn't technically a lie.

Thankfully, his father didn't press him. "Very well," he said. He seemed to tamp down his enthusiasm, remembering that he was playing the castigating parent. "I'm glad you've found some chums. But it still does not excuse your tardiness in returning home." Having finished, his attention was swayed to a book on his desk, which he casually opened with a flick of his finger; he seemed to trace the first few words of a chapter. Charlie remained in the room until his father looked up and, seeing he was still there, said, "That is all."

"Thank you, sir," said Charlie. "I won't do it again, promise."

"Mm-hmm," said Charles Sr., idly flipping a page in the book.

Charlie retreated into the hallway and, once he was out of sight of his father, dashed down the carpeted hall and into his room. There he threw himself on the bed, breathless, still awash in the sweet, incensed air of the pickpockets' subterranean catacomb. He fell asleep promptly and deeply.

The following morning, Charlie ate his breakfast in silence. Once he was finished, he cornered André outside the larder.

"Yes, sir?" asked the assistant butler.

"I was wondering if you had an extra—what do you call it—a valet?"

"You mean a gentleman's valet? A suit stand?"

"Exactly. Something I could hang a jacket on."

"Your father has several. Shall I fetch one for you?"

"Please do," said Charlie.

Later that morning, a wooden stand appeared in the corner of his room. You may not be acquainted with such a device, but it has served many fine-dressed men and women over the years. It is essentially a coat hanger, as one would find hanging in a closet, mounted on a wooden stand. Charlie studied the thing for a moment—it stood roughly as tall as Charlie was himself—before draping one of his navy blazers over the hanger. He adjusted the jacket at the shoulders before fastening the top and middle buttons. It made an admirable, if disembodied, man's torso. He then grabbed a handful of coins from a turtle-shell bowl on his dresser and began seeding each pocket on the jacket with them. He'd found an old emptied wallet in one of his father's drawers, and he slipped it into the jacket's inside pocket—its coat pit. For good measure, he folded up one of his handkerchiefs and slipped it into the breast pocket. He took a few steps back and admired the made-up dummy.

"How do you do?" he asked.

The coat stand did not respond.

"Well, if you're going to be that way . . . ," Charlie said, before he edged closer.

Charlie began to practice.

He practiced fronting the mark—working directly in front of the dummy. He practiced shading with a blute—holding a folded-up newspaper between himself and the dummy to cover his hand as it wormed its way around the fabric. He cautiously coaxed the smash from the jacket's pockets with his index and middle finger while his pinkie carefully opened the jacket's lapel like a shut-in parting his window curtains. He practiced unsloughing—undoing—the buttons on the jacket front to better get access to the coat pit; he practiced reefing the kick from that inside pocket, a move Amir had shown him that involved carefully making pleats in the fabric of the jacket with one's fingers so as to move the wallet up toward the opening of the pocket and there to fall into a waiting palm. By lunchtime, he'd even devised a move where he binged the handkerchief—the wipe—from the dummy's outside breast pocket—the tog tail—and used it to safely shade his hand as he banged a coin from the coat jerve, or the ticket pocket.

He did not do these things smoothly; he made many mistakes. He had no doubt that his amateur skill would not get him very far in the Test of the Seven Bells—but that was not really his aim. He merely wanted to *try*.

And so he practiced.

Sunday morning arrived. Charlie woke early and, after some deliberation, dressed in the jeans-and-flannel combo that had been so winning for him the day he'd first set foot in the pickpockets' scatter. He placed a cap on his head at a rakish angle and bid adieu to the dummy in the corner of his room, the one who'd been so cleanly picked over for the last few days. He thought he heard an audible groan of relief.

By the time Charlie was heading out the door, his father had already made his way to the atrium and was assiduously tending to his garden. He'd been apprised of Charlie's plans—a day trip to a *calanque* a few miles down the coast, where the family of one of his new friends had a yacht anchored—and had not hidden his appreciable pride in his son's newfound social life. He answered Charlie's quick "Good-bye!" with a fatherly wave over his shoulder.

It being Sunday, much of the house staff had been given the day off, and there was (thankfully) no Guillaume to expose his ruse; it was typical that Charlie should be responsible for his own transportation on weekends. He walked down Avenue du Prado to the imposing statue of David, forever standing guard between the ocean and the avenue, and there caught the number nineteen bus, jumping off a few stops down Avenue Pierre Mendès France to the front gate of Hippodrome Marseille Borély.

Now, the racecourse at the Borély is an extraordinary thing. It is not the destination of horse-racing pilgrims worldwide, like Pimlico or Churchill Downs; it does not carry the romance of Del Mar in California or Melbourne's Flemington—but it is certainly a sight to behold, nestled as it is smack up against the placid Mediterranean to one side, the stark white cliffs of the Vallon de l'Agneau to its south, and the fine mansions of the Prado to its north. On a sunny day, when the races are run and the stakes are high, there is no better place to be.

And, indeed, that was a sentiment clearly shared by a large slice of the Marseillais population this sunny Sunday in April. Charlie arrived at the front gates of the track to discover a veritable tide of people hovering around the entrance, waiting to make their way to the bettors' windows and the grandstands. He craned his neck, looking for his confederates—his Whiz Mob—but no familiar face leapt out at him among this sea of derby hats, ascots, sunglasses, and fedoras. He fell in line with the crowd and shuffled his way forward; in the meantime, he monitored the purses, handbags, and stuffed pockets of the race-going crowd. To Charlie's (admittedly untrained) eye, everyone here seemed moneyed enough to pass muster with the strictest interpretation of the so-called Code of the Whiz Mob—that no one facing financial hardship, marginalization, or oppression of any sort should be targeted. This was the upper crust of the upper crust of Marseille society, a fact that struck home when the following occurred:

"Charlie Fisher! Is that Charlie Fisher?"

The woman's voice came from behind him; it was no voice Charlie recognized from his time in the pickpockets' scatter. Whomever it belonged to was undeniably old, posh, and speaking in English. Charlie turned around to see a middle-aged man and woman, well dressed and wearing dark sunglasses, bearing down on him.

"Hello," said Charlie, smiling wanly.

The man turned to the woman, saying, "I told you it was him."

"Charlie Fisher," said the woman, reaching down and pinching his cheek with a gloved hand. "Don't you remember us?"

"I don't think so," said Charlie. The crowd jostled forward; a boy in a cap advertised racing programs for sale.

"We're the Monroes! Eddie and Carol!" said the woman.

When Charlie gave no indication of remembering, the woman—Carol—said in an exasperated tone, "We're friends of your father!"

"Put 'er there, Charlie," said the man. He stuck out his hand, and Charlie shook it. The man was clearly American, whereas his companion seemed to speak in an accent that hailed from the plummiest parts of Olde England. "Is your father around?"

"You haven't come to the racetrack by yourself, have you?" asked Carol.

"I'm meeting..." Charlie stammered, "I'm meeting some friends. And their parents. Some parents have brought their kids, and I'm friends with them. With their kids. So I've come to meet them. The parents and the kids."

"Oh," said Carol. She was momentarily thrown by Charlie's inability to communicate what would seem to be a pretty simple explanation. "Well, that's nice."

Eddie, on the other hand, took it in stride. "Sounds like good fun." He leaned in close; Charlie could smell the man's musky cologne as he spoke into Charlie's ear: "Hot tip. Number five in the sixth race. Grecian Dancer. She's a long shot, but she'll get there." He stood back upright and winked.

"Thanks," said Charlie. "Oh. There they are." He pointed in an indiscriminate direction and waved, as if at some distant person. "I should really go. Nice to see you both."

"Tell your father we said hi!" said Carol as Charlie walked away.

"And remember," said Eddie. "Number five horse! Sixth race!"

Charlie smiled and waved, desperately relieved when the crowd swallowed the Monroes whole and he was standing again on his own. Self-consciously, he began to button his plaid flannel shirt, suddenly aware of how poorly dressed he was for the event. He looked around for the Whiz Mob; he checked his watch. It was past nine. They'd have started by now, right?

"*Programmes!*" called the program seller. "*Demandez le programme!*" Apparently he'd spotted Charlie as a potential sale, because the boy began hovering around him, repeating his pitch.

"*Non, merci,*" said Charlie.

"*Demandez le programme!*" said the boy again, this time very loudly and in his face.

"*Non!*" repeated Charlie angrily.

"Just buy a program, Charlie," the boy said, in English.

Charlie looked at the boy; the boy lifted the brim of his houndstooth cap. It was Fatour.

"Oh, hi!" said Charlie. "I didn't know it was—"

"Shhh," hushed Fatour, annoyed. He cast his eyes about him as he handed a program to Charlie and mimed receiving payment. "Follow me."

Fatour walked away from the front gate and across the parking lot, toward what looked like an unused ticket kiosk. Charlie followed. "Who were those pappies you were talking to?" asked the pickpocket.

"Oh, them? Just a couple my father knows."

"They recognized you?"

"I guess so," said Charlie.

Fatour rolled his eyes. "You have to be invisible, Charlie. Blend in."

"I'm trying."

The boy stopped and, turning, surveyed Charlie's outfit. "Not dressed like a lumberjack, you're not." He continued walking.

"Why does everyone think I'm dressed like a lumberjack?" wondered Charlie aloud.

On the other side of the wooden kiosk, just out of sight from the horde of race-goers queuing at the gate, the Whiz Mob was gathered.

"Howdy, Charlie," said Amir. "Glad you could make the meet."

"You're late," said Jackie. Charlie, upon seeing her, was taken aback. She was dressed to the nines in a dashing canary-yellow shift dress and coat. She wore a wide-brimmed black straw hat that sat on her head at a dangerous angle, and her lipsticked lips burst red from beneath its shade. She was pulling on a pair of black polka-dot gloves as she spoke. "Pluto will fill you in."

"O-okay," stammered Charlie. He turned to the other pickpockets: Amir was leaning against the kiosk, wearing his customary pink shirt and drainpipe chinos. Sembene stood nearby, dressed in a short-sleeved patterned shirt and blue jeans. Michiko was there in a smart pastel skirt and a Peter Pan–collared shirt; the Bear stood by her side in a blue blazer and slacks—they both seemed dressed to fade into the crowd like ghosts.

Pluto, squaring himself up in front of Charlie, seemed to be ripped straight from the front windows of a Fifth Avenue men's clothing store: pastel-pink sports coat, neckerchief, and a sharp straw trilby hat. Even his eye patch seemed to contribute to the overall aura of a very cosmopolitan young man, intent on a lucrative day at the track.

"You're running with Amir and the twins. Center field, remember? Don't try anything. Your job is to watch and learn. Got it?"

"Got it," said Charlie.

"Bear's steering for Michiko, who's running cannon." Pluto whipped out a brochure for the track and, unfolding it, revealed a map of the racecourse itself. He pointed to one side of the track. "They're working over here, by the grandstand."

"But I will be going here first," said the Bear, indicating the bettors' parlor with a thick finger. He'd taken one of the racing programs from Fatour; he now snapped it open and began reading the schedule of races. "We are working the track. Might as well make some money on the side, okay?"

"Sure," said Pluto. "Just don't blow your okus on bad bets this time, huh, Bear?"

Borra mumbled something—probably disparaging—in Russian.

Pluto was undeterred. "Amir, Charlie, and the twins—you're working the crowd by the track. Jackie—"

He was interrupted by the girl. "That's Jacqueline to you," Jackie said in a lilting, high-society Southern drawl that could melt butter.

"*Jacqueline*," Pluto continued, "and I are working the Premier Club, in the suites above the grandstand."

"How are you going to get in there?" asked Charlie. The one time he'd been to the Marseille Borély had been with his father, at the invitation of some wealthy real estate baron from Chicago. They'd spent the entire time in the viewing suites that had been built at the top of the stands, where well-dressed waiters saw to your every need. A special pass had been required; the security, Charlie recalled, was very tight.

"Oh, we're credentialed," said Pluto, reaching into his coat pit and retrieving a laminated card. The flowery logo for *Le Club Premier* was printed there, above the name *Alejandro Escobar*.

Jackie snaked her wrist around the crook of Pluto's arm, saying, "I so *adore* the races, Alejandro."

"And where's Molly?" asked Charlie, taking in the motley group. "I mean, the Mouse."

"Ah," said Pluto. "The coup de grâce." He rapped his knuckles against the wooden wall of the kiosk.

"Coming!" came a girl's voice from inside the box.

"C'mon, Mouse!" said Pluto. "Charlie's here. Everyone's accounted for."

A door in the kiosk opened a crack, and Charlie could see Molly's face peer out. "This is ridiculous," she said.

"Come on, Mouse," said Amir, holding back his laughter. "Show us your stuff."

The door swung wide and the girl stepped sheepishly out into the light. She was dressed in an outfit made entirely of shimmering satin that looked as if it had been dipped indiscriminately in a series of colored paints: the breast of the jacket was purple and covered in orange diamonds; the sleeves were bright yellow. On her head was a goggle-topped helmet, which sported the same yellow-and-purple color scheme as the jacket but in a kind of beach-ball pattern. Her pants were white and puffed out like twin parachutes. Charlie immediately recognized this getup as something known in the racing world as jockey silks, the iconic outfit worn by all the riders. To add to the general rainbow hue of her attire, Molly's face was beet red.

"Happy?" she asked.

Pluto attempted a straight face. "Molly, Mouse," he chided genially, "it's a bit of genius, ain't it? You're going to hit more fat marks in the paddock, behind the scenes, than any of us could imagine. That's where the owners are. That's where the big spenders are, checking out the horses. That's where the real fat bateses hang. Trust me. I've put the bee on it."

"I better be swinging with jug pinches in there," said Molly, blowing an errant strand of brown hair from her eyes. She pushed her face up close to Pluto's, scowling. "Or there'll be hell to pay, flash." She gave his eye patch a flick of a finger.

"Okay, Mobbies," said Pluto, ignoring the threat, "you know what you're doing, you know where you're doing it. Back here at four p.m. sharp, got it?"

The gang all nodded and pledged to do so.

"And you," said Pluto, suddenly pressing his finger into Charlie's sternum. "You stay back, do you hear me?" He then scanned

Charlie's attire archly. "Unless we see some trees need cutting down."
With that, the mob began to disband into its smaller units, moving in the direction of the field in which they would work. Fatour punched Charlie in the shoulder as he walked by.

"He said that because you're dressed—" he began.

"Like a lumberjack," said Charlie. "Yeah, I know."

Chapter
ELEVEN

Inside the racecourse, the energy was a humming, thrumming hive. Charlie, along with Sembene, Fatour, and Amir, was funneled into the park with a tide of humans, each intent on their own prize and the means of acquiring it. The grandstands, white and gilded as a wedding cake, had been built on the east side of the track, there better to take in the majesty of the Mediterranean Sea over the loamy oval of the racetrack. By the time Charlie and the three pickpockets had pushed through the bottleneck of the entryway and into the concourse, a race had just begun. A trumpet blared its fanfare; the starting gate cracked open and the day's first round of horses leapt onto the track in a thunderous wave.

The crowd erupted when the horses passed the stands. The racers made a second and final round of the track, eliciting an even louder chorus of cheers and shouts, and were testily reined in after they'd stormed across the finish line. Some in the crowd celebrated their success; others tore up their tickets and scattered the pieces to the wind like a ticker-tape parade for their own failure. And then it was back to the bettors' stalls, to begin the whole cycle over again.

"Keep close," said Amir, as they made their way through the milling crowd. "But not too close. Let us work, yeah?"

"Got it," said Charlie.

"I'm gonna find us a nice bates," said Sembene. "A real jug touch."

A new race was being announced; at the center of the oval track, on the pitch, the number tiles on the scoreboard were being traded out to reflect the new odds. A group of spectators had gathered near the guardrail by the finish line and were scribbling in their programs. Sembene, playing steer, broke away and began to orbit this group in an action Charlie'd been told was called "fanning the mark." He was secretly gauging the prize among the huddled race-goers. Apparently he was unsatisfied, as he came back and shook his head, nearly imperceptibly, at Amir. They moved on.

The horses were being loaded into the starting gate; the pickpockets gravitated toward the crowd watching the animals as they bucked and snorted in their enclosure. Sembene scouted; a signal was given. Amir moved forward while the twins inserted themselves into the crowd.

And then it began to happen.

Quickly, quietly, with motions and actions that seemed both orchestrated and impromptu, the three pickpockets fell to their prey like mice picking over a plate of cheese. They slipped and darted between the milling race-goers as if they had an extraordinary under-standing of the pacing of time and space—it was as if they'd been given some sort of blueprint as to what exact steps each mark would take, each lift of an elbow or turn of a hip. And just as quickly as they'd descended on the crowd, they retreated, returning to the place where Charlie, transfixed, was standing.

"Take this," said Amir. He slipped two wallets into Charlie's pants pocket.

"And this," said Fatour. Another wallet and two gold chains were added to an opposite pocket.

"This too," said Sembene, packing both of Charlie's back pockets with loot.

"What am I supposed to do?" asked Charlie.

"You're the duke man," said Amir. "Stash all of it back at the kiosk. Then come back."

Happy to be in service, Charlie turned to run toward the front gate when he was stopped by Amir. "Slow, Charlie, slow," he said. "Remember, you're just having a day at the races, yeah?"

Charlie heeded this direction and began to saunter away. He tried to whistle a casual tune, though he could not whistle. He was particularly mindful of the number of wallets he was currently carrying. On his way across the parking lot, now filled with quiet Citroëns and Renaults relieved of their drivers, he even tried to jam his hands into his pockets, only to find the way blocked by the absurd amount of contraband that'd been stashed there. When he finally arrived at the kiosk, he breathed a sigh of relief. There, inside the door, was a large sack that had already accumulated a good portion of the day's take. Charlie added his contribution to the pile and hurried back to the track.

"Over here, Charlie," called Amir, once Charlie had returned. The pickpockets had moved up the concourse a few dozen yards.

"Okay," reported Charlie. "I stashed the pokes."

"Good, good," said Amir. He then gestured toward an older man in a sharp pin-striped suit, engrossed in the reading of his racing program. Sembene and Fatour had positioned themselves to flank him. "Watch this," said Amir. "This is what we call the Senegalese Spin."

Charlie watched as Sembene reached up and tugged at the sleeve of the man, effectively, in the argot, fronting the mark (facing the victim) and giving up his kisser (showing his face). They exchanged a few words; the man returned to his program. Sembene's hand remained positioned just above the man's right pocket. Then Fatour, on the other side of the man, pulled on a sleeve and the man's attention turned to his left side. The action of moving his hips to face Fatour caused the money clip that was in his right prat to fall into Sembene's hand. The man, confused at having confronted what appeared to be the *same* individual who had just earned his attention, engaged briefly with Fatour before looking back at his racing program. At which point Sembene, again, tugged at the man's right sleeve—causing the man to turn and allowing another item to fall into the fingers of Fatour, whose hand had been positioned at the man's left prat. This give-and-take happened several more times, with the man growing more bewildered with every turn, until he'd apparently been picked clean and the twins disappeared into the crowd.

"Wow," said Charlie.

"Twins," said Amir. He looked at his watch. "Let's move on."

As they walked away, Charlie looked back at the chump they'd just cleaned out. He'd taken his hat off and was waving it briskly in front of his face. His tie was comically undone. He looked as if he was trying to ward off a sudden onset of vertigo. The man was out of view before Charlie assumed he'd discovered he'd just been burgled.

"We've got two hours to pick this track clean," said Amir, "before the whole place is rumbled."

Farther down the concourse, they continued their work. Charlie watched. And marveled. And he began to see.

When each crashing line of horses pounded across the finish line, Charlie realized, the members of the crowd would effectively identify themselves as either winners or losers: those tossing their tickets to the ground in frustration and those enjoying a moment of celebration before cheerily turning heel and heading toward the bettors' stalls to collect their winnings. They were unwittingly sorting themselves into two columns: the fat marks and the empty pockets—and the Whiz Mob read these signals like antennae, picking up vibrations from distant stars.

The winners, having collected their cash, would inevitably return to the concourse, emboldened by their success and flush with their winnings. Sembene, the steer, would glide in front of them as they made their way, subtly guiding their movement. When Sembene stopped, so would the mark. Fatour would then approach and begin the score, handing the collected loot back to Amir. Amir would then return to Charlie, instructing him to bring the loot to the kiosk.

Their fingers worked like nimble machines; their feet danced on the pavement.

They binged ladies' hairpins in one motion and used them like chopsticks to retrieve rolls of cash hidden deep inside purses and clutches. They banged handkerchiefs to shade the sneaking fingers of a fellow tool, returning the wipe to a different owner altogether.

Once they'd started, there was no stopping them. They were like a basketball team that only got looser and more agile the more they played.

They binged watches, assayed their value, and sometimes, in the same motion, returned them to the owners' wrists if they were fake or faulty. The owner would not know that between the moments he'd lifted his wrist to check the time, the watch had briefly left his possession. Likewise, they were able to assess a chump's viability by binging his wallet and checking its contents—thereby getting a better understanding of his place in the social pecking order. Too low and the wallet was returned, unemptied.

Amir found a poem, a love poem, in a man's glasses case. He did not rob the man further.

The pickpockets watched the scoreboard change—they monitored the odds of each race. They binged winning tickets from the skilled or lucky gamblers, exchanging them with losing tickets to the chump's coat jerve or sometimes his very hand.

This was not just thievery. They did not steal money solely from wealthy congregants of the racecourse—they practiced an art that was by turns beautiful and graceful, by turns crafty and mischievous. The flow of wallets, watches, jewelry, and coins was like a tumbling Rube Goldberg machine of fingers and hands and elbows and arms, always ending in the ever more loaded pockets of Charlie Fisher Jr.

Charlie made several trips to the kiosk, each time feeling more and more sure of himself. He waved genially to passersby; he walked with a spring in his step. The sack in the kiosk grew heavier and heavier as the Whiz Mob quickly and quietly sapped the racecourse's chumps of their wealth.

Walking back for another load, Charlie crossed paths with Borra. The Bear was poring over the racing schedule; Charlie, feeling chipper, whispered the tip he'd been given by Eddie Monroe, the American who'd recognized him earlier in the day. "Grecian Dancer. She's your horse." He smiled and continued walking; he felt Borra's heavy hand land on his shoulder.

"What did you say?"

"I just had a tip," said Charlie. "Earlier. Grecian Dancer. Sixth race."

Borra looked down at his program. "Sixth race is next. What do you know of this horse?"

"Nothing, really," said Charlie, shrugging. "Just got a tip."

Borra smiled, revealing a gold tooth in place of his right canine. "I will bet on this horse. I have won nothing today, Charlie, but you have given me hope." He slung his arm over Charlie's neck and led him toward the bettors' stalls.

"I should really get back to Amir and Sembene and Fatour," said Charlie. "I'm their duke man."

"It can wait, Charlie," said Borra. "We have binged enough today. Now it is time to win. You come with me. You will bring me good luck."

"O-okay," said Charlie.

"When I was young boy, in Saint Petersburg, Leningrad, whatever you want to call it," said Borra, as they crossed the concourse, "my grandparents owned most beautiful Arabian Thoroughbred. Petushka was his name. He was beautiful, Charlie. Win many prizes in races. At our dacha in the country, I spend long summer days feeding Petushka ripest red apples, riding him through beautiful meadows."

"That must've been incredible," said Charlie.

"Then Soviets take him and put him on yoke, for plowing field of local collective," replied Borra, frowning. "It is what it is." They'd arrived at the bettors' window. Borra slammed a ten-franc note down on the counter. "Ten francs on Grecian Dancer to win, *s'il vous plaît!*" he near shouted.

The money was taken; a ticket was issued. Borra gave the ticket a lingering kiss before handing it to Charlie.

"You, too," he said.

"Do what?" asked Charlie.

"Kiss it," said Borra.

Charlie gave the ticket a modest peck.

"No, no, no," said Borra. "You must kiss it. With passion!"

Charlie felt himself blush, suddenly aware of the crowds of people around him. Under the watchful eye of the Bear, he brought the small piece of white paper to his lips and began kissing it. Having never actually kissed anyone aside from his mother (and Alice Grundel, which didn't really count), Charlie did his best impression of a John Wayne/Maureen O'Hara–style collision until Borra snatched the ticket away.

"That is maybe too much," said the Bear, annoyed.

"Charlie," came a voice. They turned around to see Michiko

running up. "What are you doing?"

"I'm, uh, being Borra's good luck charm," said Charlie.

"Borra shouldn't be betting," said the girl, eyeing her compatriot angrily. "Borra should be binging."

"You see my score," said Borra, defending himself. "I've banged plenty. Now is time for Grecian Dancer."

Michiko didn't bother finding out what he meant. "Molly needs a duke man."

"Charlie can do it," said Borra. "He dukes for Amir all morning."

Michiko looked at Charlie.

"Sure, I'll do it," he said. "Where is she?"

"In the paddock. You won't be able to get inside, but she can meet you at the fence."

"Okay," said Charlie. He looked at Borra. "Good luck."

"I hope you have not kissed it away!" Charlie heard Borra shout as the Bear slipped away into the crowd.

Between two sections of the grandstand, a channel led into the undersection of the bleachers. A sign on the wall indicated the direction to the paddock. A new race was announced over the loudspeakers, causing Charlie to fight against a current of race-goers issuing out of the tunnel. Beneath the stands, he began following a dark cement hallway, its floor littered with torn-up tickets and discarded racing programs. He soon arrived at the paddock: a cavernous room where a ring had been constructed around a dirt floor, hemmed in by a tall green fence and several dozen watchful wagerers. One by one, the horses for the upcoming race were led in by their trainers and walked in a slow, tidy circle inside the ring. The riders, dressed in their multicolored silks, kept the horses on a tight rein. The onlookers watched them intently, made notes in their programs, discussed the various merits of each horse with their neighbors, and sized up their viability. This was where the true gamblers congregated, away from the dilettantes who littered the concourse, those betting on horses merely because of whim or some arbitrary fondness for a name or number.

"Pssst—Charlie," came a whispered voice.

Charlie looked over to see Mouse gesturing to him between the bars of the fence. She was on the inside of the ring, perfectly camouflaged amid the pageantry of the horses' draped coverings and their riders' motley outfits.

"Oh, hey, Molly!" whispered Charlie. "Michiko said you needed a—"

"Quiet!" hushed Molly. "Down here."

The two walked to the end of the ring, where the fence met the wall. A long throw of shadow gave them a discreet meeting place.

"Come closer," said Molly, waving him forward.

Charlie stepped closer to the fence; abruptly, Molly grabbed him by his britch kicks and pulled him, hard, so that the two of them were pressed close together, with only the cold metal fencing separating them.

Charlie, somewhat scandalized by this sudden intimacy, stood frozen while Molly slipped the loot she'd binged into whatever pocket would fit it. When he was finally loaded down like a pack mule, she let go, giving Charlie a quick shove in the process.

"Go," she hissed. "And come back when—"

"*Vous!*" shouted a man suddenly, from across the ring. Weaving through the promenading racehorses, he began walking toward them. "*Garçon!*"

Fearing the man was speaking to him, Charlie instinctively leapt back from the fence line. The Mouse had already turned her back to Charlie and was preparing herself for the encounter, whatever it might be.

"*Garçon!*" the man repeated.

His pockets overflowing with stolen goods, Charlie breathed a sigh of relief when he saw that the man was speaking to Molly, not him, and it was Molly's gender-neutral jockey attire that had caused him to refer to her as *garçon*, not *fille*. Molly did not wish to correct him.

"*Oui?*" she answered.

Quick aside: you know by now that Charlie's comprehension of French, while being somewhat improved since his arrival in Marseille, was still dreadful. Molly's familiarity with the language, on the other hand, was near impeccable, owing to the mandatory language competency courses at the School of Seven Bells, where a turned-out tool is expected to be conversational in fifteen languages, fluent in eight, and masterly in three. Since we intend to make every attempt to accommodate the reader who has not also undergone the rigorous academic curriculum of the school, we will translate, into English, the following conversation, which Molly, on the spur of the moment, chose to speak in a common dialect that any native-born French speaker would recognize as hailing from the northern suburbs of Paris. Charlie picked up enough of the quickly spoken exchange to get the general gist. You, the reader, will not be kept in the dark merely because of Charlie's academic laziness—which is, really, nobody's fault but Charlie's.

You're welcome.

"Who are you riding? Who's your horse?" asked the man. He was speaking sideways around an enormous cigar that was clenched in his teeth.

Molly, impressively, did not miss a beat. "Sultan's Bride," she answered.

"She running . . . ?"

"In the tenth," answered Molly.

The man chomped on his cigar and studied her. "What are you, one ten? One twenty?"

"One hundred and fifteen centimeters tall," she replied.

"Perfect. You can ride Baron Moncerf's horse in the sixth. King-maker's jockey is out. Bad oysters, apparently. I've got silks for you behind the paddock."

This was the first time Charlie had seen Molly hesitate; she appeared thrown. "I . . ."

"Sixth race. They're moving them to the gate now."

"I should really . . . ," began Molly.

"You are a licensed jockey, aren't you?" asked the man, pulling the cigar from his mouth and letting a plume of smoke drift from his lips.

"Of course."

"Then follow me," said the man. "We need someone on that horse *now*."

Charlie waited for Molly to flash him what he imagined would be a quick, anguished look, but, to her credit, she did not. Whatever fear she might've been feeling, her only tell was a slight hiccup in her first step as she moved to follow the man before picking up a confident pace and striding out of the paddock.

"Molly!" hissed Charlie, alarmed. Why hadn't they foreseen this? Wouldn't putting one of the tools in jockey silks and installing her in the paddock have invited this? He looked around the room. He was afraid to draw attention—he was so loaded down with valuables stolen from every chump in the room that he was barely able to keep his pants up. Slowly, carefully, he turned around and walked out of the paddock. He made a slight jingling noise with every step, like he had bells on his feet. Once he was out of earshot, he began running, sounding like some sleigh escaped from a Christmas pageant, through the tunnel and out into the daylight.

"*Excusez-moi,*" said a woman, leaning up against the wall of the grandstand. "*Jeune homme!*" Charlie looked over at her; she pointed to his feet. He looked down. Someone's gold choker had made its way down his leg and was now emerging at the hem of his pants. He waved a thank-you and quickly reached down to grab it, stuffing the chain back into his pocket. He could feel the other items that Mouse had stashed on him beginning to travel around his person. He'd spent most of the day testing the capacity of all his pockets—it seemed as if the stitching was finally giving way. Grasping at the outside of his pants, he halted his quick pace and sauntered, awkwardly, toward the exit of the park. When the kiosk came into view and he was sure no one was looking, he began running across the pavement. Coins rattled from his pockets and jangled to the ground. Arriving at the sack of loot, he quickly emptied his pants of the plunder and made a mad dash back to the concourse.

"Amir!" he shouted, forcing his way through the crowds. "Amir!"

The boy was standing with Sembene and Fatour; they were eating ham sandwiches. Amir jolted at the sound of his name being shouted so loudly.

"Charlie, keep it down," said Amir. "This place is hopping with whiz coppers now."

"It's Molly," Charlie managed, sputtering breathlessly. "Molly. The Mouse. She's a jockey."

"I know," said Amir. "That was Pluto's idea."

"No. You don't understand. She's really jockeying. They've got her on a horse."

"Nah," put in Sembene. "Molly, she does not know how to ride a horse."

Charlie blanched. "She doesn't . . . ," he sputtered. "Don't they teach you that at your school?"

"Equestrianism?" said Fatour, taking a bite of his ham sandwich. "Wouldn't be necessary, I don't think."

"That doesn't matter. She's riding. In the race!"

Just then, a trumpet fanfare blared from the conical speakers mounted inside the grandstand. A voice announced the horses' procession to the starting gate. Amir, Sembene, Fatour, and Charlie all ran for the guardrail. Several horses and their jockeys were making their way along the thick dirt carpet of the track. One horse strayed behind, shying and snorting, clearly at odds with its rider. This was undoubtedly Molly's horse, Kingmaker. She'd shed her purple-and-orange silks for a green-and-white-checked outfit and was desperately trying to regain control of her unruly mount.

"Oh heavens," said Amir. "This will not be good."

A few of the jockeys watched their hapless fellow rider with curiosity. The trumpet rang again; the horses began loading into the starting gate. Molly was still wrestling with Kingmaker on the track. A few officials began to make their way over to her, but before they drew close, the horse apparently decided on its own that it was ready to race; it suddenly bolted toward the gate stalls. Molly was thrown backward against the horse's flanks, but she managed to keep one hand on the reins. This was not Kingmaker's first race; sensing his rider's cluelessness, he managed to kick and snort his way into the starting gate with very little guidance from Molly.

"*Les chevaux sont sous les ordres!*" sounded the announcer from the stands.

Charlie began biting his fingernails. Borra sidled up beside them. "What is happening?" he asked.

"Molly's on a horse," replied Amir.

"Seven horse," said Sembene.

"Kingmaker," said Charlie. "She got conscripted."

"Oh," said Borra. "She cannot ride a horse."

The four boys next to him all nodded their heads simultaneously in agreement.

"As long as she does not mess with Grecian Dancer, this is fine."

Charlie looked over at the Bear. Borra shrugged.

A bell rang; the starting gate made a loud metallic clang as the ten gates, in unison, slammed open.

"*Et ils sont partis!*" shouted the announcer. The crowd roared. The horses pummeled onto the track, an explosion of mud, muscle, and noise.

Molly and Kingmaker were still in the gate.

Charlie, even from his remove, could hear the girl cursing the horse. Kingmaker seemed to have a plan of his own—perhaps chagrined by the fact that his rider was so inept. Finally, after a few desperate kicks to his flanks from Molly, the horse leapt from the gate and onto the track. Molly let out a scream that could be heard from the farthest bleacher seat. She was immediately thrown backward. A single stirrup, her right foot affixed inside, saved her from toppling off her steed altogether. Charlie gasped.

"Hold on, Molly!" shouted Amir.

The *peloton* of horses was already rounding the first bend of the track's semicircle by the time Kingmaker was out of the gate and sprinting. Molly lolled on the horse's rump like a rag doll doing sit-ups as she tried to right herself. Her writhing must've gone some way to spook the horse, as he began to spring faster and faster with every movement she made.

The crowd, initially focused on the scrum of horses in the lead, suddenly caught sight of Kingmaker and his dangling jockey.

"*Regardez!*" shouted a man behind Charlie.

"*C'est dommage!*" shouted another. Charlie could only imagine the dismay of those who'd put their money on Kingmaker. A scattering of tickets showered over Charlie's head, proving this assumption right.

Miraculously, Molly had managed to get herself back in the saddle. She'd kicked her left foot into the stirrup and was reaching for

Kingmaker's reins as they whipped, noodle-like, across his neck. Sensing this, the horse seemed to lean into his sprint; he was now just a few strides from the pack. The onlookers in the stands picked up on this incredible recovery and began crowding toward the guardrails. Much to Charlie's amazement, Molly and Kingmaker had managed to insert themselves into the lead pack of horses and had, together, heaved into the second furlong of the race. Just then, he felt Amir whisper into his ear.

"Look, Charlie."

Amir was nodding to the surrounding crowd: they were all perfectly rapt, hypnotized by the incredible sight of the horse and his incompetent rider as they nosed into sixth, then fifth, then fourth place. Amir smiled at Charlie. "The perfect stall."

And with that, the pickpockets got back to work, fleecing whatever valuables remained from the moneyed race-goers—all those watches, wallets, and chains that had not yet found their way into the pickpockets' nimble fingers. Meanwhile, Molly and Kingmaker had improbably kicked into high gear and were coming around the corner and into the final furlong with gusto, running neck and neck with the front-runner—a horse that wore the number five, listed in the program as one Grecian Dancer. Those who'd torn up their tickets saw this change in fortune and began scrambling around on the ground, desperately trying to piece together the shreds of paper they'd so recently scattered to the pavement.

The final stretch arrived; the horses all leaned into their stride as their jockeys laid hard on their whips. Molly was clinging to the saddle for dear life, listing ever more off to the side like some trick rider. Molly and Kingmaker made a solid challenge to Grecian Dancer's dominance. Charlie moved to the guardrail and watched, captivated.

"Go, Molly!" he shouted. "Come on, Kingmaker!"

He felt a strong push at his side. It was Borra. "C'mon, Grecian Dancer! Get up there, number five!" he hollered. He had his ticket stub clenched in his thick fingers. In a flash, the horses all clambered across the finish line and the crowd exploded in cheers.

It would be said that Kingmaker, the Arabian quarter horse from the stables of Baron Moncerf of Paris, made his name that day. He would go on, of course, to prove his mettle in some of the most prestigious stakes races of the European circuit. From there, he would eventually conquer the Triple Crown in America, a feat not matched a full quarter century after his death. As the equestrian-minded reader will know, he would be retired with full honors to a grassy field in Brittany, there to live out his days feeding on ripe clover and frolicking in that unearthly Breton sunshine. When he died, he was eulogized by presidents and prime ministers alike; all the great European leaders strove to outdo one another in their remembrance of this incredible creature and the races he'd run and won. And no eulogy was complete without mention of that day in April 1961, at the Hippodrome Marseille Borély, where Kingmaker first tasted that sweet liquor of victory, ridden haphazardly by an unknown jockey who disappeared—melted into air, as it were—as soon as the horse and rider had crossed the finish line.

By the time the owner's entourage had gathered in the winner's circle and the wreath of red roses was being slung over Kingmaker's sinuous neck, the Whiz Mob had grabbed their stash from the ticket kiosk and were dashing for the bus stop, there to make the long ride to the Panier and the Bar des 7 Coins. Borra threw himself down heavily on the bench next to Charlie, grumbling, "Fine tip, Charlie. Fine tip."

The scraps of a torn ticket fluttered to the bus floor.

Chapter
TWELVE

Back at the scatter, the celebration was uproarious. Pluto and Jackie, having had the largest haul of the entire mob, regaled the pickpockets with their story of daring among the upper crust in the Premier Club. They did so without dropping their adopted personas of Alejandro and Jacqueline, he a leering South American oil tycoon and she his trophy bride. They spoke in hilariously mincing accents and sashayed around the room like the sort of cartoonish aristocrats one sees in the funny papers. A large emerald-encrusted brooch, binged from someone Pluto gathered to be a Swiss oligarch, claimed pride of place at the center of the large table in the catacomb. Michiko and Borra, like Charlie's section of the Whiz Mob, had had a differ-ent kind of success working the bettors' stalls, favoring quantity over quality. They'd watched the race standings closely and targeted the gamblers who were on hot streaks—those whose wallets and purses were bound to be the fattest.

Molly the Mouse fumed angrily the entire bus ride to the Panier and then again all the way through the warren of streets and alleyways to the doorway of the Bar des 7 Coins. She was still glowering under a dark cloud, tucked away in one of the catacomb's blanketed recesses, when they began distributing the score and, in the argot, dinging the dead ones.

"Come on, Mouse," said Pluto. "Haven't you suffered enough?"

"You have to admit," added Amir, "it was a brilliant ploy."

"Best stall I've ever seen," said Michiko. "Right when the whiz dicks were coming out and the whole tip was getting rumbled."

Borra, grumbling again, dissented: "I get fifteen francs of her share. She cost me that. Grecian Dancer should've won that race, fair and square."

This quip finally got the Mouse talking. "Oh ha, ha, ha," came the girl's voice from the little grotto. "It's all just a laugh to you lot. A fine bit of funny business. I ain't never ridden no horse afore, 'member? Coulda been killed up there. Nearly did so."

Amir, laughing, wandered over to where she sat. "Come on, Molly. You did the mob good. They'll be punching gun on this one for years back at the school. Wait till the Headmaster hears tell."

"I just want my clothes back," said Molly, her arms folded

defiantly across her chest. She was still wearing her garish jockey silks, the ones the gentleman in the paddock had given her.

Jackie stifled a laugh. "The green and white really suits you, dear," she said, in her best *Jacqueline* voice. "Don't you think so, Alejandro?"

Pluto leaned his shoulder against Jackie's and twirled a watch fob. "Oh, it does, *dahhhling*, it just does." They both fell together, laughing.

A frilly pillow was launched, cannonball-like, from the alcove. It hit Pluto squarely in the face. "And that's not the last of it, you keep that up!" shouted Molly, before turning away angrily and staring at the wall. Pluto gave his fellow pickpockets a kind of *who's the sore sport* look. They continued to gab over the table as they separated the wallets and purses from the cash they contained.

Charlie walked over to the alcove. "Hey, Molly?"

"Leave me alone."

"I feel like . . ." He struggled for the words a moment before saying, "Like maybe it was my fault? I should've said something to that man. I should've gotten us both out of there. That's what a real tool would've done." The girl's back was facing him. He couldn't tell if she was registering what he was saying. "Anyway, I'm sorry."

The girl didn't answer for a long time. Finally, just before Charlie was going to return to the table, he heard her say, "Don't think nothing on it. It weren't your fault."

Charlie paused, chewed on his lip a moment and, deciding on something, turned around. "Hey," he said, "I found this on the table. Figured you should have it." Molly turned around to face him as he reached into his pocket and pulled out a long metallic chain. On it, someone had attached a small silver pendant shaped like a mouse. He handed it to Molly. She took it, admiring it in the glow of the dim electric light.

"Aw, thanks, Charlie," the girl said, brightening. "That's real nice."

Back at the table, tall piles were being amassed, a taxonomical audit of everything the upper slice of society might carry with them to some public outing. Once the final watch had been appraised, the final coin spun across the table to join its fellows, the pickpockets were allotted their portion of the proceeds. A handful of cash and few bits of jewelry that might be easily pawned were handed out to each member of the Whiz Mob in kind, a sort of daily take or per diem in lieu of actual wages from their ringleader, the Headmaster of the School of Seven Bells. Jackie, as lead cannon, did the honors, singling out each pickpocket with a comment on their contribution.

"Pluto, ace work foldering a proper jug crush," she said as she slid a pile of cash and a gold watch over to where he stood.

"Michiko—solid pull, even if you were working lone wolf half the day." The girl glared at Borra as she received her share.

Before the Bear could defend himself, Jackie spoke: "Bear, next time keep focused on the job, not so much on the odds. Maybe you won't *lose* money instead of binging it."

"I would have come up very good if not for—"

Jackie hushed him, sliding him his portion of loot. "You can eat your losses. A bet's a bet." The Mouse had climbed sheepishly from her hiding place and was standing at the far end of the table. "I think Molly gets double share, considering that ace stall. And winning a stake race to boot." A sizable pile was collected and pushed toward the girl in the jockey silks. "Incredible job there, Mouse. You put your life on the line. We'll make sure the Headmaster hears."

Molly blushed and received her portion.

The doling out of the assessments and daily cut continued until each of the pickpockets had been recognized. When it was done, Amir stepped forward.

"What about Charlie?" he asked.

"Charlie? He was playing center field," was Jackie's reply.

"But he duked for Sembene and Fatour and me."

"And for me," put in Molly. "If he weren't been there, I'd've been stuck with a heap of okus."

Charlie, moved by these acknowledgments, remained quiet.

"He was on the job, so he gets his share. In with the pinches, in with the pokes," said Amir. The rest of the pickpockets lauded this statement with quiet murmurs of approval.

"Okay, Charlie," said Jackie. "You earned yourself a cut." She slid a stack of franc bills toward him. Reaching into the pile of assorted *slum*, or jewelry, she found a small, ornate pocketknife and tossed it to Charlie. He caught it in the air.

"Thanks, Jackie," he said. "Thanks, everyone."

At that moment, Bertuccio appeared, announcing that dinner was ready. He came into the catacomb with a large chopping block piled high with freshly grilled meats and vegetables. A bottle of grenadine was produced from one of the chamber's alcoves and placed on the table.

"May I?" asked Charlie, sliding a glass toward the bottle.

"Ah, yes," said Bertuccio. "I had not forgotten. Charlie Fisher, a true connoisseur of *soda à la grenadine*."

"No gin this time, please, Bertuccio," said Charlie.

"Of course," responded the waiter, smiling. He proceeded to fill Charlie's glass. "Anything for the Grenadine Kid."

Charlie felt a palm slap squarely in the middle of his back. It was Borra, who shouted, "Your nom de guerre, Charlie!" He, too, held up a glass of the bright red liquid. "To the Grenadine Kid. May his kicks be full and his marks fat!"

The pickpockets sounded their approval, leaning in to meet Borra's glass with theirs above the center of the table. Charlie beamed inwardly as he took the first sweet sip from his brimming glass. Everyone, at Bertuccio's insistence, then laid into the rich repast the waiter had supplied. Once the Whiz Mob had eaten their fill, Bertuccio pulled out his Spanish guitar and, like before, lulled the crowd into blissful silence with another lilting, soaring song. Borra, kicked back in his chair, dozed, snoring quietly. Sembene and Fatour curled together on a bench, back to back. Jackie watched the singer thoughtfully, her fingers toying with a stack of franc coins on the table. Charlie found himself sitting alongside Amir; they were both caught up in the spell of Bertuccio's strange and beautiful song. Amir seemed to shake this bewitchment, because he gave Charlie a quick swat on the arm.

"Hey, Charlie," he said.

"Yeah?"

"Follow me."

Together, they left the dozing pickpockets in the catacomb and wound their way up the spiral staircase, along the stone corridor, and out the secret door into the deserted main room of the Bar des 7 Coins. Charlie then followed Amir as he went through the swinging door behind the bar and into a kitchen thick with the scent of thyme and rosemary and garlic.

"This way," said Amir. He led Charlie up a cramped staircase that climbed several flights till it ended at a large wooden door. Opening it, Amir waved the way forward, and Charlie stepped out into the open air, finding himself standing on a tall rooftop that commanded a view of the city of Marseille the likes of which Charlie had never seen before.

"Wow," said Charlie.

"Beautiful, yeah?" said Amir.

The building stood some ways up the hill that defined the Panier's geography; from this vantage, there was very little to block one's view of the surrounding cityscape. Much of the Vieux Port could be seen, its waters forever crowded with fishing boats and little schooners. The port ferry, plying between the Quai du Port on the north side of the harbor and the Quai de Rive Neuve to the south, chugged unhurriedly across the rippling water. It being early evening, the port-side cafés were brimmed with their rosé-sipping clientele. Several brightly painted dory boats dotted the quays, from which fishmongers advertised their catch to the milling crowds of tourists: mussels, oysters, sardines, and herring, all laid out invitingly on beds of seaweed. Across the port, atop the high hill, the great black-and-white-striped basilica looked down on this gregarious city, a priest watching his congregation with some equal mix of admonishment and endearment. A boat blew its horn on its way out of the mouth of the port, passing just below the opulent Palais du Pharo; seagulls cried and whirled about in the evening air.

"Yeah," said Charlie. "Really beautiful."

"Wait," said Amir. "Smell."

"Smell?" Charlie took a long, lingering whiff.

"What do you smell?"

"I'm getting—ocean. A bit of fish, maybe?"

"Hold on," said Amir. He was leaning against the building's low plaster balustrade; he craned his neck out and surveyed the street below. "Try again."

Charlie did so; this time, his senses were assaulted by an incredible smell: the scent of freshly baked bread, intermingled with some kind of pungent herb Charlie could not identify. "What is that?"

"This woman, next door, she makes flatbread with olive oil and herbs every evening for dinner, for her family. She does this like clockwork, you know. I come up here just to catch the smell." He took another long inhale. "I've never met her, this woman, but I know she must be Lebanese. Or at least from somewhere around there. She makes *manakish* with the *za'atar* herbs, I can tell. That is how my mother made it." Inhaling again, he said, "That, Charlie, is the smell of my childhood. The smell of my home. There is nothing like it."

"Do you ever get home, to see your parents?"

"Me? Oh, no," said Amir. "Once you're on the whiz, that's it. The Whiz Mob is your family." He was quiet for a moment before saying, "I miss them, though. I had two sisters. I wonder what they are doing. They were very tough, smart girls, Charlie. Maybe you would've liked them. I think they would have liked you."

Charlie blushed at this mention. "Why don't you go back? Just to visit?"

"It is not so safe anymore, my home. Wars. Fighting. I worry for my mother, my father. But this is life, yeah? A boy must leave his mother, eventually."

"Or his mother leaves him," said Charlie quietly.

Amir turned his back to the cityscape and pushed himself up to sit on the balustrade. He looked squarely at Charlie. "Really?"

Charlie nodded.

"That's maybe worse, I think," said Amir.

"It's okay. I'm over it. She wasn't much of a mother to begin with."

"I'm sorry to hear it, Charlie," said Amir.

"That's life, yeah?" said Charlie, doing his best Amir impression.

Amir smiled. "But life is long, Charlie. And we don't know how it's all going to unfold. I won't be in Marseille forever. Headmaster'll call us away and we will be assigned to a new city, a new country. There are always new adventures on the horizon. New places, new people. It's always changing. We can't all be the lady making the *manakish* in her kitchen, every night."

"Maybe she gets tired of it," surmised Charlie. "Maybe it's the same dull routine, every day. She might not even notice that smell anymore."

Amir took this in, thoughtfully. "True. We're the sentimental ones, ain't we? Us on the outside. Though sometimes I come up here and I smell that smell—the baking bread, the *za'atar*—and I think, what if I just stopped? Just declared out? There's a Lebanese café in the Vallon des Auffes, just below the Corniche, that I've seen. I think a family from Beirut owns it. What if I just hopped off the mob, what if I just got a job in the kitchen, yeah? They could use a kid like me. And I'd have a little fishing boat in a slip there, a little bed inside."

"Sounds incredible," said Charlie. "But would you really give all this up?"

Amir waved his hand in the air in front of his face as if dispelling a momentary dream. "Nah, never." He smiled at Charlie. "Whiz Mob for life."

"I wish I could say the same," said Charlie.

"Keep working it at, maybe you will," said Amir.

The two were silent for a moment, before Charlie said, "Hey, Amir."

"Yeah, Charlie?"

"I just wanted to say thanks."

"What for?"

"For doing this. For helping me. For being a friend. I—" Charlie paused, gathering his thoughts. "I've never really been great at making them. Friends, I mean. I've moved around a lot. First with my mother, but then when she left and I was with my dad—we've just been everywhere without really stopping. Maybe if I was good at it, I could make friends in the places we go, but it just hasn't really happened. This is the first time I feel like I've found a home. That I've found my friends." He was suddenly embarrassed by this long admission. "I mean, I don't want to corner you. I can call you that, can't I?"

"What, a friend?"

"Yeah." He waited cautiously for Amir's answer.

"Of course, Charlie," said Amir. He smiled warmly at Charlie— though did Charlie detect some hint of sadness in his voice? Some sudden, heretofore unseen chink in Amir's emotional armor? "Of course you can."

"Oh, good," said Charlie, beaming. "To friendship, then," he said, putting out his hand.

Amir shook it. "To friendship."

Just then, a woman's voice called out from the street below, speaking in Arabic. The two boys on the rooftop looked over the edge to see a middle-aged woman, wearing an apron, standing in the doorway of the neighboring building. Charlie needed no translation from Amir; he could tell that the woman was calling her children in for dinner. Before too long, a scrabbling gang of kids appeared from around one of the corners and came dashing toward the woman, nearly bowling her over in their excitement. The woman laughed and chided the children before turning and following them inside.

"Come on," said Amir. "We should get back to our family. Our friends."

Charlie nodded and began to walk across the sun-bleached roof of the building. He'd only just arrived at the door to the stairway when he noticed Amir was not with him. He turned to see the boy still standing at the edge of the balustrade, looking out over the city, framed in a sort of gilded halo by the drifting sunlight.

"You coming?" called Charlie.

"Yeah, Charlie," said Amir. "Right behind you." He jogged across the rooftop to catch up with Charlie.

Chapter

THIRTEEN

Watch closely. You are looking down from the topmost spire of the basilica of Notre-Dame de la Garde; you are witnessing the passing of time in this ancient port city. It is early spring and the air is warm, even at your great height. The city below lays itself out before you as if it were a model landscape, a construction of foam and clay and balsa wood. It is teeming with people, some walking, some piloting small, puttering cars or riding clanging streetcars. From your vantage, you can see it all. Let's not spend too much time pondering how you got up to where you are, or more pressingly, how you expect to get down; let's instead marvel at your omniscience, your incredible perspective from that height as the world turns around you.

And there is Charlie Fisher—do you see him?—bicycling his

way home along the Corniche, the wind at his face and the sun over the Mediterranean Sea. It is an eclipsing sliver, just setting beyond those distant islands, little black mounds in the pitching green of the sea. Boats are splitting the waters, some ferrying homeward the many tourists who have braved the trip to Château d'If and witnessed the place of Edmond Dantès's brave, if fictional, escape. The light is a vibrant pink. But look at Charlie: he is the very picture of a self-satisfied boy as he sits upright in the saddle of his bike, a wayward grin arriving and departing from his lips as he replays in his mind's eye whatever whirlwind adventure he's just left.

It's all right if you don't immediately recognize the boy—this Charlie would appear very changed from the Charlie of a scant two weeks before. He has spent his time in the interim ferrying himself, much like those sunburned tourists out in the bay, between two distinct lives: one in which he was the obedient son of the American consul general to Marseille, and one in which he was the Grenadine Kid, the promising acolyte to a gang of pickpockets. As a consequence, a sort of glow had attached itself to Charlie, and it had not dissipated by the time he'd walked his bike up to the front gates of the Fisher residence. Pierre, the groundskeeper, let him in.

"You're looking very well today, Charlie," said Pierre.

"*Merci, Pierre*," replied Charlie. He strolled alongside the bicycle, letting it drop sidelong against a manicured row of boxwood shrubs.

Simon was at the front door, gesturing to the watch on his wrist.

"You're nearly late," he said.

"Nearly late," said Charlie, smiling, catching his breath. "But not quite."

His tutor grumbled something, but agreed.

"You were looking forward to a scolding, weren't you?" asked Charlie.

"Come on," said Simon, ignoring the comment. "The concert is in an hour. Get out of those *filthy* clothes."

Charlie was walking a fine line, living these two lives, but he was managing it with something almost like finesse. For example: he was still keeping pace with his studies, all the while spending half his days clambering about the more-trafficked squares, parks, and cafés of greater Marseille, playing duke man for the Whiz Mob. He'd had to drop out early from the day's divvy to make the eight o'clock curtain call for the Orchestre Philharmonique de Marseille, something Simon had arranged for his field studies in baroque composers. Tonight's concert was a Handel concerto, and Charlie had arrived home just in time to leap into his tuxedo, shove a ham-and-cheese croissant down his gullet, and catapult alongside Simon in the back-seat of the family Citroën.

"What were *you* doing today?" asked Simon archly, as Guillaume drove the car out of the gravel drive and out into the street.

"Oh, you know," replied Charlie. "Things."

"Perfect day for it, really. Things."

"Some things more than other things," replied Charlie.

"Well, a jack of all things . . . ," said Simon. He did not, however, press for specifics. It was a tacit agreement between the boy and his tutor: Charlie would show up on time for lessons and he would endeavor to finish his assignments. In return, Simon would not question Charlie's activities outside of his schooling, nor would he report anything unusual to Charlie's father. One could assume that Simon, thinking he knew Charlie as well as anyone, figured that the worst possible trouble that the boy could be getting into was perhaps testing the patience of the librarians at the Marseille Library by lingering too long after closing.

Cécile, Simon's paramour, was waiting for them by the bollards in front of the Opéra de Marseille. She had her brown hair pinned back and was wearing a pale chiffon gown. Simon's whole gait changed when he saw her, and it became clear to Charlie that his studies were not the only reason for their outing tonight.

"Hello, Charlie," said Cécile, giving him a quick peck on each cheek in greeting.

"Hi, Cécile," said Charlie.

Simon, after exchanging an amorous greeting with the girl, extended his arm. She took it, and the three of them walked toward the theater. This was not the first field study Cécile had accompanied them on; ever since it became clear that Charlie's time was occupied elsewhere, Simon had apparently decided there was room for indiscretions on his part as well. Again, Charlie, happy with his tutor's collusion, wasn't about to point it out to his father.

They followed the princely dressed crowds through the lush interior of the opera house; they found their way to the box that Charles Sr. had happily loaned them. The lights dimmed and the orchestra struck up a humming drone that filled the concert hall like a blanketing fog.

"Tuning," pointed out Simon, keen to find moments where he might fulfill his responsibilities as tutor.

The music began; Charlie fell into a reverie. Simon, his hand resting on Cécile's, watched his pupil proudly. Clearly, his instruction in music history had resonated with Charlie, as the boy was taking in the performance like a happy sponge. However, what Simon could not know was that Charlie was not watching the orchestra.

He was watching the crowd.

He was watching the purses and the pockets, laid out below him in the warm light of the hall. He was watching the men's black jackets, opened at the front, and the sliver of lining that suggested their coat pit, that most fertile inside jacket pocket where a man might carry things closest to heart, there, closest to his heart. He was watching the women's clutches, held closed by a tweezer or a button that could be undone, silently, with two fingers without ever alerting the owner. The clock faces of a hundred watches caught the glare of the stage lights and flashed, like little stars, all over the orchestra floor, a constellation of treasures just waiting to be teased away.

When the final note had been played and the lights came on full and the crowd meandered noisily from the concert hall, Simon tapped Charlie on the shoulder.

"What did you think?" asked the tutor.

"Very educational," replied Charlie.

Do you see them? From where you sit, from your vantage at the topmost spire of the Notre-Dame de la Garde, you can see everything unfold below you. Watch Charlie as he heads back home, back to his bedroom, back to the silent dummy in the corner. In the weeks that have transpired since he first set it up, Charlie has adopted a friendly camaraderie with his practice dummy, whom he's named Dennis. That night, he spoke to him as he shed his tuxedo jacket like a reptile's skin.

"What's that, Dennis? Oh, the concerto was positively *charming*. Just lovely, you know. Handel. Or was it Bach? Hard to keep those two straight. How was your night?"

The mannequin stared back, still wearing the jacket he'd worn for two weeks now.

"Oh, you don't say?" asked Charlie. "You lost a centime coin? How tragic."

Charlie rounded the mannequin, and, feigning to wipe a bit of lint from its shoulder, he appeared on the other side with a single coin in his fingers.

"Here it is," said Charlie. "It was right in your pocket. Try to keep it safe, why don't you?" With a quick movement, he tucked the coin back into the dummy's front pocket, giving it a loving pat as he did so. The boy then flopped onto his bed and fell quickly asleep, still wearing his formal shirt and trousers.

The dummy watched over him like a proud, protective parent.

And he had every right to be proud. You see, it had been a mere two weeks since he'd suited up the practice mannequin, since his first outing to the racetrack with the Whiz Mob; by now Charlie was binging the keys from Guillaume's belt clip and swapping the head butler Michel's handkerchiefs with the housekeeper Madame LaRouche's dusting cloths. And he did so unsuspected, never rumbling his victims. Only you can see him work his newfound trade, you up there on the basilica. Watch your step.

Even his father was not safe from his exploratory bings. One morning, using newspaper as a stall and tucking it under his father's chin in the pretense of showing him some news item, Charlie managed to sneak Charles Sr.'s block and tackle—his watch and chain—from his vest jerve and transfer it to the opposite pocket. Later, when he asked his father what time it was, it was a very befuddled Charles Fisher Sr. who searched his pocket—the same pocket he'd worn a watch in since he was a very young man—only to find the watch in an altogether different place.

"Nine fifteen," managed Charlie's father, once he'd found it.

"Thank you, Father," said Charlie. "That's all I needed to know."

Charlie's father studied the watch a moment curiously, before returning it to its customary place in his vest pocket. He then looked at his son suspiciously.

"What happened to your watch, Charlie?" he asked. "I don't suppose you've given that away to win some new friend."

"Oh, no, Father," said Charles. He gave his sleeve a shake, revealing his watch where it always was: on his wrist. "Just making sure I'm showing the correct time."

"Ah," said Charles, satisfied.

As you can see from your incredible vantage, Charlie and his father were in the elder Fisher's study. Charles Sr. had just returned his attention to the telex machine, which had abruptly begun clacking away. He cradled the unspooling paper as a baker would handle his phyllo dough, reading the contents through the lenses of his bifocals. "It appears," he said, "that the Lumiravian ambassador will be arriving Saturday. . . ." Here he trailed off, quietly reading the code to himself. He then turned to look at Charlie. "There will, no doubt, be a luncheon. Do you think you'll want to attend?"

"This Saturday?"

Charlie's father nodded, knowing his son's answer.

"I just can't, sir," said Charlie. "I'm meeting the gang."

Of course, "the gang" was the name he'd given the Whiz Mob, his newfound compatriots. A fairly elaborate story had grown up around this "gang," one that Charlie was constantly having to build upon, using every ounce of his storytelling chops. These foreign exchange students and their families that Charlie was palling about with, they had to be wealthy and respectable enough to avoid any concern on his father's part, yet not so prominent that it would be conspicuous that they'd never fallen into the consul general's social orbit. Their story must be simple enough so as not to inspire too much investigation, yet interesting enough so as not to sound invented. It was a true novelist's dilemma if ever there was one. Thankfully, Charlie's imagination had been, thus far, up to the task.

"It's Isobel's birthday Saturday," continued Charlie.

"Isobel—she's the Estonian?" asked his father.

"Mm-hmm."

"The one with the amputated leg."

"Sadly, yes," replied Charlie. Admittedly, it had been somewhat of a stretch, that detail, but there was one evening he'd arrived home so late that some kind of extraordinary tale had to be told.

"How's she faring? That was quite an injury."

"Doing very well," replied Charlie. "She's a real champ."

"Glad to hear it." The telex machine noisily disgorged a new length of paper, and Charles's attention was once again turned to its decoding. As you can no doubt infer, even from where you are standing, Charles Sr. was content to overlook the inconsistencies in Charlie's reportage of his day-to-day activities—he was mostly just thrilled that his son was not only engaged in a real way with this new and strange city, but had thrown in with what sounded like a pretty interesting flock of kids and their families. Was he being lax in his parenting? Knowing what we know (and we know quite a lot), that answer is a definite *yes*. However, if you had any experience navigating the complexities of parenting (and maybe you do), you would know that any parent is loath to question their child when that child is *happy*.

And Charlie was *happy*.

Watch him. You can see it, can't you? Even you, having only gotten to know Charlie a couple of weeks before, must see the change. His confidence in the sleight-of-hand trade of the pickpockets was spilling over into every other aspect of his life. He no longer found himself shrinking in the face of every social exchange he was forced to have; his periodic meetings with his father's friends' children were no longer torturous stretches of time. Even the boorish Päffgen boys, still in town, still loitering at the Fishers' residence on a bi-nightly basis for reasons Charlie couldn't fathom, seemed thrown by Charlie's renaissance.

"I get it," said Rudolph, wagging a finger in Charlie's face while his brothers threw billiard balls at each other. "I see what's happening."

"What?" Charlie said.

"You've done it, haven't you?"

"I really don't know what you're talking about." Charlie could feel himself shrinking, afraid the boy had somehow pieced together the disparate halves of his twin lives.

"Admit it: you've been kissed."

Charlie smiled, unsure of how to reply, but the smile was enough to win a hardy punch on the shoulder from the Bavarian boy. "I knew it. Nice work, Charlie."

But what had kissed him?

He'd been kissed by something the Whiz Mob called *the promise of the pocket.*

Granted, there were still some jobs that the Whiz Mob deemed too tricky for Charlie to work—these they called Big Tips. They were carefully planned affairs, many days in the preparation, which often involved Pluto and Michiko, the mob's two best steers, fanning the time and place of the job with an almost overdone attention to detail. The risk was too great even for Charlie to work center field, and the stakes too high.

These jobs often involved working directly within sight of the police—at some official convention or departmental get-together, or perhaps binging the winnings from a group of high-rolling casino gamblers with ties to organized crime. The sorts of jobs where the consequences of rumbling the mark and getting nabbed wouldn't likely be limited to a slap on the wrist or a night in the pokey—instead, a tool's life could be at stake. You will be too young to remember this, but Marseille, at this time, was still the sort of place where the criminal underworld held sway. For this reason, Charlie was all too amenable to declaring himself out for these jobs, in the argot of the mob. You might think, knowing Charlie as you do, that he would stay at home like some bedridden child on a school's field day, mooning at a rain-streaked window. Quite the contrary. He would use the time to further rehearse his pinches on Dennis, the pickpocketing practice dummy, banging centime coins from its pockets with ever-increasing grace and agility.

But please spin the world back a bit. Let's see him, now just over a week beyond his inaugural tip job at the Marseille Borély racecourse. The Whiz Mob was walking two abreast down Rue Saint-Michel. They were an imposing sight, even though the median age of the group was close to thirteen. That day, a Wednesday, with no tip formally fanned, the plan was to *drift*. It was something they did regularly, something that was common among whiz mobs of the Seven Bells. Also called, in French, the *dérive*, it was a time-honored whiz tradition of wandering, cloudlike, through the streets and avenues of the city, letting the winding thoroughfares guide your feet rather than any sense of direction or intended destination. It was an unconscious celebration of the tie between the city and its cannons. Chances were, you'd arrive at some kind of tip, be it a café crowd spilling into the street or a birthday party for a wealthy banker—it didn't really matter. The idea was to drift.

And so they were *drifting*, when Pluto made the following

observation after Borra suggested Charlie stall for him and Michiko:

"He's a sucker. And once a sucker, always a sucker."

Borra shrugged, replying, "He does not anymore seem like a sucker to me."

"Maybe you just don't have a nose for it," was the one-eyed boy's response. You see, while the rest of the Whiz Mob had taken to Charlie fairly quickly after his day at the races and subsequent rechristening as the Grenadine Kid, Pluto had held tight to his skepticism about Charlie's abilities.

"I'm right here," said Charlie, which he was.

"I know that," said Pluto. "It smells like chumps."

Admittedly, he was laying it on a bit thick. He hadn't made too much objection to Charlie's running duke a few days earlier, when they'd relieved a post-regatta luncheon crowd of their unneeded cash and jewelry.

This is important, so let's spin the world back again. Let's see that job unfold. We'll come back to the *dérive*, promise.

The regatta job was a greenhorn's tip, that's what Jackie had called it. A recipe for easy binging: wealthy men in loose-fitting clothing, sun-drenched and tipsy on rosé. Every spring, the Bar de la Marine would host the race, and every spring, every able-bodied yachtsman would throw in his hat to be the first to weave through the coastal isles and into the thronging Old Port. The winner, as always, was summarily showered in champagne on arrival back at the bar. A crowd of enthusiasts and bettors collected outside on the bar's quayside terrace; wine and spirits flowed. The pickings were so easy that Charlie, having been duke for the first fifteen minutes and given a moment's reprieve, began fanning the crush for—perhaps—an easy kick.

A man in a garishly striped boating jacket was fishing in his pants pocket for something, all the while holding an animated conversation with two young women; his other hand was occupied holding a champagne flute that was perhaps over capacity. When he removed his hand, his right, from his pocket, a corner of his money clip was revealed. Charlie, seeing it transpire, felt a nudge at his side. It was Sembene.

"There's an easy bang," the boy said. "A hanger."

"I see it," said Charlie.

"Make your frame. It may take a little reefing, but a kick out like that is easy."

"I won't get in trouble with the mob?"

"Why would you get in trouble, Charlie?"

"'Cause I'm supposed to be duking." He gave a quick look around their surroundings before half whispering, "I'm not a cannon."

Sembene gave him a wink. "Just between us."

Charlie took a deep breath and sized up the challenge once more—little had changed. Molière's wigged head could be seen peeking from the opening of the man's pocket, announcing the size of the score: at least five hundred French francs. Certainly, gauged Charlie, someone who was so careless with that amount of money would not miss it, should it go missing. He moved forward, his lips puckered in a mock whistle, and awaited his moment. The man began waving his hand, describing some facet of the race, or perhaps some other great conquest, and Charlie struck. Sembene was right: the clip was big and heavy enough that Charlie was forced to reef the kick—creating pleats in the fabric to push the okus toward the opening of the pit—but luckily it was a move he'd been practicing at home on his dummy. The man shifted his hip and the clip fell into Charlie's awaiting hand.

He nearly shouted in celebration. He turned to walk away when he saw that one of the girls the man had been talking to had left the conversation and had rounded on Charlie. She cleared her throat; Charlie looked up and saw that it was Jackie.

Charlie smiled. Jackie glared. She jerked her head angrily toward the bar, some twenty feet in the distance. The two walked silently to the open doors of the café.

"What are you doing, Charlie?" asked Jackie in an enraged whisper once they'd gotten out of earshot of the quayside crowd.

"Sorry, Jackie," replied Charlie. "I'm really sorry."

"That was *my* chump. That was *my* pit." Her face was flushed beyond the layer of blush she'd applied to her cheeks for the occasion.

"I—I . . . ," stammered Charlie.

"He beat you to it," came a voice. They both turned and saw Amir, leaning against the facade of the building, sipping at a bulbous

Orangina bottle with a bright yellow straw.

"I was making the frame, Amir," said Jackie. "I was fronting the mark, I had him steered already." Here she turned to Charlie, saying, "You think that okus was sitting there, half out his pit, by accident? You did, didn't you. Like God himself came down and just handed that kick to you, like you're some chosen cannon or something."

"Relax, Jackie," said Amir.

"Do your own jobs, Charlie," said Jackie. "Don't step in on someone else's."

"Got it," replied Charlie, shocked and scandalized.

The girl gave one last angry look at both of the boys and then stormed back to the crowd. Charlie stood silently, his mind thrown between the ecstasy of having managed his first bing—even if it had been assisted by Jackie's steer—and the shame of having been lectured so publicly by the mob's class cannon.

"Interesting," said Amir, pushing away from the wall. He gave another tug on his straw until the bottle sounded a resigned gurgle. He overturned it, gave it a few shakes, and dropped it to the pavement.

"What's interesting?" asked Charlie.

"What she said. 'Do your own jobs.' Seems, in some way, you've won over the Southern belle. You may have just graduated, Charlie Fisher." He slapped Charlie on the back and wandered, aimlessly, toward a huddle of stumbling sailors, falling in with them as if he were some long-lost comrade at arms.

"Do your own jobs," repeated Charlie, like a mantra.

But it was always Pluto who was the holdout, who'd always been the holdout, who grumbled anytime Charlie's name was volunteered for doing anything but center field or—at the very least—running duke. And so it was that day, just a week after the regatta tip, as they were walking through the Panier's dusty warren of streets like a pack of wild dogs on the prowl. If you remember, and you should, Pluto had just made mention that it smelled like chumps, referring, of course, to Charlie, who was walking just behind him.

"So what's a chump smell like, Pluto?" asked Molly.

"Expensive cologne. Freshly washed linens. Soap," was the boy's reply.

"Someone who has good hygiene, basically, is what you're saying," lobbed Amir.

"That would count you out, Pluto," put in Jackie.

"Ha!" This was ejected from Borra; it hurled from his chest like a pipe bomb, and it made Charlie jump.

Pluto ignored them. "All I'm saying is that we're putting the mob at risk when we put him up. Even running duke. But now he fancies himself a cannon?"

"I was gonna have him stall a bit is only, Pluto," said Borra.

"He'll throw the mob," said Pluto, unconvinced. "It ain't safe."

"I'm not going to throw the mob," said Charlie. He'd been hesitant to dive in; he didn't feel like he had much standing to argue. "If

I get caught—if I rumble someone, I'll take the blame. I wouldn't throw *anyone*."

"How can we know?" asked Pluto.

"Don't be a nag, Pluto," said Amir.

"I would never do that," replied Charlie, ignoring Amir's interjection. And then, quite unexpectedly, Charlie said something very brave—which might've surprised you, knowing the Charlie you once knew. But remember, a change was occurring, a transformation beginning. "Besides," he said, "I can't get caught."

"Can't?" asked Pluto.

"Can't. Won't."

"Prove it," said Pluto. He had stopped in the street and was now facing Charlie.

"Okay," said Charlie. "How?"

"Run lone wolf. We'll shadow you," said Pluto. "Drift us somewhere. See what your whiz know picks up."

These were two things Charlie had never done before: lead a drift and work alone, without the net of a stall and a duke. He hesitated in his response, painfully aware of the fact that the entire Whiz Mob had stopped in the street and were all watching him closely. He glanced at Amir; the boy's face was expressionless.

"Fine," said Charlie.

Molly and Sembene clapped their hands excitedly. Borra suppressed a laugh. Pluto stepped off to the side of the street and waved his hand forward, ushering Charlie into the lead position in the group. "Please, to begin," he said.

Charlie took in his surroundings. He was on a narrow street in the Panier; several streets careened off it in various haphazard directions—streets that might be indistinguishable from alleyways to the eye unaccustomed to the Panier's labyrinthine layout.

"I say . . . ," Charlie began. Something caught his eye at the elbow-jog of one of the side streets: a hastily drawn bit of graffiti on a wall that resembled an arrow. "That way."

And so the *dérive* began.

They climbed the lazy, winding slope of the street and clambered single file through a tight passageway between two looming buildings; they crossed a deserted playground and dodged the chairs and tables of an outdoor café. With every new direction Charlie guided them on, he gained new confidence in his lead of the drift. He was letting himself go, letting the streets and alleys decide his course, watching for small signs in the layout of the city and allowing his mind to interpret them. They dashed through private gardens and tightroped along the tops of walls. Before long, they hopped a retaining wall and landed, like creatures arriving from another planet, in the middle of simple city plaza, one that had attracted a large group of people to watch a magician who was setting up his show by a water fountain.

Landing by Charlie's side, Pluto gave him a strained look. "Lucky," he said.

Of course, by this time, Charlie knew a good press when he saw one. A spellbound crowd, their collective attentions all ensnared by a single preoccupation, a crowd that was more than likely made up of predominantly moneyed tourists—it had all the markings of a proper jug touch, in the parlance of the mob.

The Whiz Mob hung back by the wall; Jackie gave Charlie a little shove in the small of his back.

"Go get 'em," she said, "lone wolf."

Charlie stretched his shoulders and twisted his neck, as if prepping his body for the work to come. "All right," he said, as much to himself as anyone else. He walked toward the crush, trying to take on the persona of someone who had just happened on the scene, someone exploring the city for the first time and coming upon a charming street performance. It felt good; he felt like he was writing a story for himself, not unlike one that he would ascribe to the characters in his composition book. He wasn't Charlie the pickpocket anymore. He was Charlie the wandering tourist, the innocent child.

"Come on, then," said the magician by the fountain. "Come in close. I won't bite."

(He was speaking in French. Charlie was able to understand most of what he was saying by context. As always, you have the luxury of an interpreter.)

The crowd followed his instruction. Charlie moved with them. He felt his shoulder push up against the arm of a man in shirtsleeves and his hip against a woman's purse. He was surprised in both cases that neither audience member seemed in the least bit concerned about the close proximity of their neighbors. The environment was ideal.

The magician began his act. Charlie began his tip.

And in that sense, the two seemed almost coordinated in their work. While the magician wowed the onlookers with vanishing scarves and materializing coins, Charlie worked to do the very opposite—using purse flaps and handkerchiefs as cover, he disappeared coins and cash from the pockets and purses of the unsuspecting crowd. While the magician strove to direct their eyes to him and his show, Charlie worked to make sure the spectators' eyes were anywhere but on his covert movements. And yet they were essentially doing the same work: they were manipulating the fabric of what people thought was real and using it to their benefit.

Charlie's pockets were soon full; without a duke man, he would be unable to continue working. It happened that, just then, a pair of policemen appeared and began shooing away the gathered crowd, citing the magician for unlawful assembly and solicitation. The magician pleaded with the cops for clemency while the crowd wandered away, ignorant of their financial losses at Charlie's hand. Charlie, for his part, took his time returning to the Whiz Mob, who were all still standing against the wall on the far side of the square. Just as he was making his way back to announce his success, he felt someone grab the sleeve of his shirt.

"Hey, you," came the voice of a man. Charlie turned to see it was the magician.

"What?" asked Charlie, shaking his arm from the man's grasp.

"Give me half."

"What are you talking about?"

"Don't think you can fool me, Yankee Doodle Dandy," the man said in English. "You think I do not see what you are doing? Little prat digger, pinching skins from *my* audience, yes? Give me half and I let you go."

The police officers were no longer paying any mind to the magician, though they were still too close by for Charlie's comfort. "Fine," said Charlie. He reached into his pocket and pulled out a wad of franc bills. He shoved them into the magician's outstretched hand. The magician glanced at the pile and shook his head.

"Come on," he said, still holding out his hand.

Charlie frowned and pulled out a tweezer poke he'd pinched from a woman's silk purse. It was near to overflowing with bills. "Here," he said. "That's about half."

"*Merci,*" said the magician. He glanced over Charlie's shoulder. "You on the whiz, Yank?"

"I don't know," Charlie replied. "Maybe."

"Careful with them lot," said the magician, indicating with his eyes the group of kids standing by the wall. "If you know what's good for you."

With that, the magician leapt back a few steps and gave a stagey bow. "From one illusionist to another," he said. *"Adieu."* He then sauntered off, whistling a tune.

When Charlie returned to the Whiz Mob at the wall, they were bowled over in laughter. Borra threw his arm over Charlie's shoulder and snared him in a friendly headlock.

"Amazing," said the Bear. "You go up against wrong magic man, Charlie."

"Still, that was ace work. Up until the end there," said Molly. She was barely able to finish this sentence before she dissolved into fits of laughter.

"That magician's finest trick of the day," said Michiko. "Magically disappearing half of Charlie's pinches." She, too, was sputtering with laughter.

"Laugh all you want," said Charlie. "I still made a haul." He reached into his pockets and retrieved his takings: even with the magician taking part of the cut, it was an impressive bing.

Pluto pushed the wallets and cash back toward Charlie's chest. "Shhh," he said. "We've still got coppers about. Let's not count the knockup till we're safe as kelsey." Once Charlie had stashed the goods back in his pockets, Pluto said, "But still. Nice work, *Grenadine Kid*."

Everyone quieted to hear this admission. "Thanks," said Charlie.

Pluto smiled. "For a sucker, anyways. Now we oughta get back to the scatter before Monsieur Presto over here fleeces us some more."

Charlie, with Borra's arm still draped over his shoulder, fell in line with the rest of the Whiz Mob as they wandered away from the square, each of them rehashing and laughing good-naturedly at Charlie's tip. All, that is, save for Amir. Noticing this, Charlie ducked from underneath Borra's embrace and fell in line with Amir.

"What'd you think?" asked Charlie. "Pretty good drift, decent press, right?"

Amir didn't say anything at first. Charlie thought he hadn't heard him. He repeated, "Pretty decent press, right?"

"I heard you the first time, Charlie," said Amir, nearly cutting him off.

"Oh, I—"

"Yeah, decent press." Amir then abruptly stepped away, jogging to catch up with Jackie at the head of the gang. Charlie was left in the rear, puzzling over his friend's words. He soon found himself walking alongside Molly.

She apparently noticed his change in mood, because she said, "What's up, Charlie?"

"Nothing," said Charlie.

"Did Amir say something?"

Charlie was about to recount the entire exchange, but he thought better of it—perhaps it was nothing. A bit of sour mood, perhaps. Certainly nothing to be too thrown by. "Nah," he said. "It's really nothing."

But the feeling Amir had driven into him lasted the rest of the day and into the evening. It stuck in his gut like a stone.

FOURTEEN

And so the afternoons turned to long days and the long days turned to lazy weeks; April revolved into the depths of May, and the tourists began to descend from farther-flung reaches. The Whiz Mob's daily and weekly take began to expand with each new wave of foreign travelers. Just as Charlie began to adopt a larger role in the mob, he began to grow closer and closer to the strange clique—he began to learn their funny mannerisms and their little insecurities. He began to recognize Molly's little fits of stubbornness, born out of her being the runt of the gang; he could tell when one of Borra's grumpy spells was about to come along, usually due to that morning's or afternoon's nearness to one meal or another. He once even stashed an extra sticky bun from the gang's quick café breakfast and revealed it (much to the Whiz Mob's—and particularly Borra's—surprise) just when the giant Russian began to grumble about some chump he'd rumbled. He watched Pluto and Jackie spar, the two elder siblings of this large, strange family; Charlie often found himself in the role of mediator between the two of them, perhaps owing to whatever skill he'd gleaned from his father's work, and he grew in estimation with both of them.

Most impressively, he began to learn how to tell Sembene and Fatour apart from each other, even when they were dressed identically: Sembene was the more articulate of the two—Fatour the blunt one. For this, he was rewarded with the twins' admiration, even if they begrudged him his ability to see through their practiced grift. Michiko was a tough nut to crack, being somewhat quiet and introspective, but a respect was fostered between them as two kids, she and Charlie, who were perhaps more enigmatic than the world gave them credit for.

But as each member of the mob became more familiar and friendlier to Charlie, it was Amir who seemed to grow increasingly distant with every day that passed, with every tip they worked. The change seemed to emanate from their exchange on the roof of the scatter, those many weeks prior, when Amir had first pledged friendship to Charlie. There was a certain sorrow in Amir that Charlie had not seen, one that seemed to blossom as the weeks went by. One particular moment stuck in Charlie's head long after it had transpired.

They'd just been working the lunch crowds gathering along the esplanade of the hilltop basilica—you were JUST THERE—and were eating sandwiches, sitting in a long line on the stony rampart of the lower deck, despite the complaints of the church's volunteer staff. They were talking about what they planned on doing, once the Headmaster had called them home and they were allowed a respite before their next assignment. It was a topic of conversation that came up fairly often, and it always put a damper on Charlie's mood.

"I'm going to go to America," Borra was saying. "To New York City. I will go to the top of the Empire State Building and order the biggest steak you ever saw."

"Hate to break it to you, Bear," said Jackie. "There's no restaurant at the top of the Empire State."

"Who said anything about restaurant? I will have steak made for me, delivered while I sit at table on top of this building. I will buy out the whole top floor—it will become Borra's Restaurant. Maybe I put up big neon sign to advertise."

The rest of the Whiz Mob laughed at the suggestion.

"I'd eat there," put in Charlie. "Sounds delicious."

Borra, sitting next to Charlie, threw his arm over the American's shoulder. "You can make reservation, Charlie. You will have best table in the joint. Aside from me."

"Charlie's not going to your restaurant, Borra," said Amir suddenly. His tone was remarkably flat.

"Who says?" replied Borra.

"Charlie's going to be here, in Marseille."

"I am?" asked Charlie. He smiled at Amir, trying to gauge the boy's sudden seriousness, but Amir did not budge.

"And we're going to be right back on the whiz. We'll be lucky if we get a weekend off in Bogotá." Amir had finished his sandwich; he crumpled up the wax paper it had arrived in and threw it over the cliff edge.

Borra made a face at Michiko, who was sitting on the other side of him. The girl shrugged in response.

"Spoilsport," said Michiko.

"And you, Charlie," continued Amir, standing up to look down on Charlie, "you are going to stay here, be a good consul general's son. Who knows, your pop gets lucky enough, he might make ambassador. Live in a nice flat on the Left Bank in Paris, a view of the Eiffel Tower from every window."

"That doesn't appeal to me," grumbled Charlie. He'd suddenly lost his appetite; he looked down at his sandwich with something approaching disgust. He then glanced over at Jackie and saw her glaring at Amir.

"Don't burst his bubble, Amir," Jackie said.

"Yeah," put in Molly, from farther down the line. "I mean, what if . . . Suppose Charlie comes with us?"

There came a general murmur of approval from the ranks, apart from Amir, who'd remained silent.

"Suppose," continued the girl, "we take him along. He's got a good hand on things. I bet the Headmaster'd take a shine to the lad, show him a few tips, put him through his paces. Turn him out a real proper tool."

A shot of excitement pulsed through Charlie's chest, though he tried to imagine the implications—his forlorn parents, his lost youth. He didn't have to contemplate it long, however, because Amir had angrily stomped his feet to get the mob's attention.

"Are you kidding me?" he said. "We're a Whiz Mob, not some kind of press gang, recruiting kids for the Seven Bells. That ain't our job, yeah? 'Sides, the Headmaster would take one look at Charlie and laugh his head off."

Charlie flinched and looked down at his feet, shocked by this sudden appraisal from his friend.

"Quiet, Amir," said Jackie, annoyed.

"Yeah," said Pluto. "Go easy on him."

"Be thankful, Charlie," said Amir. "You get to be on the outside, looking in. At the end of the day, you go back to your mansion in the Prado, back to your father, your family. What do we do? Sleep in a tomb, surrounded by treasure that don't belong to us." He sniffed, once, and then said, "See you suckers back at the scatter." He then hopped down off the ledge. A clattering tour train was wheezing by just at that moment, and Amir hopped onto its running board, making the train's rear occupants start and shift away nervously. Amir, and the train, soon disappeared around a switchback on the road to the base of the hill.

"What's got into him?" asked Sembene, after he'd gone.

"One pea soup poke too many," said Fatour.

Charlie was silenced, wounded.

"Don't listen to him, Charlie," said Jackie. "He gets this way. You're good with us."

A group of clergy had amassed not far from where they sat, conferring quietly and looking over at the Whiz Mob; two local constables had joined them.

"Psst," hissed Molly. "Whiskers. Let's split."

As they each vaulted the balustrade and scurried from the premises, Charlie felt Borra nudge him. "Best steak you'll ever have, Charlie," said the Russian. "Borra's Restaurant. You'll be my first guest."

They made their way down the hill, knitted like a clutch of schoolyard ne'er-do-wells: balancing on curbs, throwing stones, and slapping fives. It didn't take long for Charlie's spirits to be lifted. The rest of the mob made an effort to bring him out. Amir's outburst was quickly pushed aside, and the afternoon was again filled with the easy joviality of Borra and Molly's antics, Jackie's quick wit, and Pluto's jibes. Michiko strutted at the head of the gang, cool as a Godard heroine in her black beret and striped shirt, while Sembene and Fatour traded piggybacks along the sidewalk.

When they got back to the scatter, Amir was sitting at the bar of the Bar des 7 Coins, sipping at a bottle of Coca-Cola. Bertuccio was standing near him, playing the sympathetic bartender and lending an ear to his sad-sack customer. When Amir saw Charlie enter the room, he quickly apologized and gave Charlie a good-natured slap on the back.

"Don't worry about it," said Charlie, but in truth, he could feel that the smallest fissure had appeared in their friendship, one that threatened to widen, one that he thought would be impossible to repair.

And that fissure broke wide open, some few nights after the day at the basilica.

It was a Thursday night. Charlie was sitting at the small desk in his room at home, working through his Latin conjugations, when he heard a clatter at the windowsill. Walking to the glass, he looked out at the darkened yard—not a soul could be seen. He returned to his desk, briefly, only to be brought back to the window when the noise, the sound of small stones hitting the glass, came again. He threw up the sash and stuck his head out. It was a warm evening and the scent of lavender perfumed the air, owing to the bushes Pierre painstakingly maintained on the ground floor below his window.

"Hey," hissed a voice. It was coming from a large plane tree, one that grew from the boulevard. Its long, thick limbs had managed to surpass the top of the wrought-iron fencing.

"Who are you?" asked Charlie.

"It's Amir!" came the voice. "I'm in the tree!"

"I see that. I don't think it's safe."

"Oh, I'll be . . ." What he would be was never made clear, because just then there came a loud crashing noise as Charlie watched a silhouetted human body tumble from the branches of the tree to the yard below. The figure of Amir hopped to his feet, maybe overselling the rebound a tad, and ran across the grass to the flimsy wooden trellis that had been nailed against the wall of the house. It supported the vines of a climbing rosebush and clearly could not manage much more. Before Amir could cause himself further harm, Charlie half shouted from the window, "I'll come let you in, Amir."

It was late; his father was long gone to bed, and Charlie knew the staff would be busy at their nightly activity, smoking cigarettes and playing cards in the kitchen. He was able to easily smuggle Amir up to his room without alerting a soul.

"What are you doing here?" Charlie asked Amir. They'd parted ways earlier that evening, at the scatter. It had been a quiet afternoon, with no one particularly moved to organize a tip, and the Whiz Mob had all lolled on the rooftop of the Bar des 7 Coins, playing dice and drinking grenadines. Like days prior to that one, Charlie had paid particular attention to Amir's quietness. It was a great surprise to see him here, in his home, in what appeared to be a bit of a lather.

"I've got to talk to you, Charlie," said the boy. His face was now streaked with a few small abrasions, and there were leaves clinging to his hair. He looked like some actor AWOL from a production of *A Midsummer Night's Dream*.

"Okay," said Charlie. "Talk."

"You've got to stop."

"Stop what?"

"You know what," said Amir. "Stop playing around, yeah? You need to get off the whiz."

Charlie laughed. "Why would I do that? Amir, what's going on?"

Amir began to speak, but stopped after taking a quick glance around the room. His eyes fell on Charlie's practice dummy. Charlie saw his attention drawn to the mannequin and said, "That's Dennis." He was trying to add a little levity to the conversation; it seemed to do little.

"Wow, Charlie," said Amir. "You are committed."

"Why wouldn't I be?" asked Charlie. "I haven't gone from playing center field to duking and binging by just sitting around on my hands."

Amir smiled. "You're an altogether different kid, Charlie. When I first met you, when I showed you the tips," he said. "Do you remember all that?"

"The lawyers in front of the courthouse. The soldier and the ring. Of course I remember. Those were a couple amazing days."

"Who would think that you would be here?"

"Not me, that's for sure," said Charlie.

"When I first met you, I had no idea . . ." He trailed off.

"No idea about what?"

Amir abruptly shifted his tone. "That day, when I stole your pen, and you shook the whiskers from me—you helped me."

"Amir, we've been through all this. . . ."

"Listen, Charlie. Now I'm gonna help you."

"And you did help me, Amir. You showed me the whiz. You gave me all this." Here, Charlie waved his arm around the room as if to indicate his new life now. His renewed self.

"Nonsense," said Amir.

"What do you mean?"

Amir looked at Charlie for what felt like a very long time before saying, "Think about it, Charlie. You had an amazing life before the whiz. You still have it. You don't want to mess it up, yeah?"

"Oh, that's rich," said Charlie, suddenly feeling his hackles rising. "What do you know about my life?"

"I know you have a house that's warm and a father who loves you. You have a man who teaches you music and books. You have a cook who makes food for you, a maid who cleans your room."

"Maybe I don't want all that stuff."

"Then you're a fool."

Charlie sputtered a laugh. "It's awful easy, on the outside looking in, to say that kind of thing. You don't know me. You don't know my life. It's my choice what I do with it."

"Now, Charlie . . . ," began Amir.

"Don't 'now, Charlie' me. How come it's okay for you to choose this, to go on the whiz, but I'm somehow not allowed? You think I'm too delicate a flower or something?"

Amir didn't respond.

"That's it, huh," continued Charlie. "That's what you 'had no idea' about. You didn't think I could do it. That I could cut it as a tool. Oh, Charlie Fisher, the consul general's son. He's too sheltered. He's too bourgeois. He's not Whiz Mob material. Well, guess what, Amir? I am. I've been accepted. Jackie and Borra. Mouse and Michiko. The twins. Even Pluto, for God's sake. They've all accepted me. They're my friends, too, now." Charlie peered at Amir, glaring. "What happened to you?"

"To me? Nothing has happened to me."

"What about all that stuff you've said to me? That stuff about me being a natural, having the grift know and all. I mean, why even say that?"

Amir was silent; Charlie pressed him. "Why show me the ropes, take me under your wing, only to turn around and tell me that I'm not fit? Why do that, huh?"

Amir paused, before saying, "I was trying to make you feel better."

The wind rattled at the window. Someone laughed downstairs.

Charlie could feel the tears welling in his eyes. "Trying to make me feel better?"

"Yeah," said Amir. "You were lost, had no friends. So I took pity on you, yeah?" His voice was rising, and the distinct tang of anger could be heard seeping in.

"Get out," said Charlie.

"You're no tool, Charlie. You're just a chump. A sucker—an American sucker."

"Get out!"

"Get off the whiz, Charlie, if you know what's good for you!"

Charlie, having finally reached his limit, punched Amir once, hard, in the arm. Amir winced and grabbed at Charlie's wrist. Charlie shook it free, dragging Amir forward. The two boys went tumbling to the ground, fists and feet flying. Before too much damage was done, Amir prized himself from Charlie's clutches and staggered backward to the window. He wiped a spot of blood from his lip and, glaring at Charlie, threw the window open.

"Dig your own grave, Charlie," said Amir. "I'm done with you. I came here to help you, but you can't be helped." He paused, glaring at Charlie. "I also came to give you this back." He reached into his pocket to retrieve something, but his hand came out empty.

"This?" asked Charlie. He was holding the Sheaffer Imperial pen in his hand, binged handily from the pickpocket's britch kick during the tussle. "Who's the chump again, Amir?"

Amir smiled wanly. "Bye, Charlie. Nice knowing you." With that, he straddled the windowsill and vaulted down the trellis.

Charlie woke the next morning still shaken by this altercation. The Sheaffer Imperial pen lay on his bedside table, reminding Charlie that it had not, after all, been some terrible dream. He pulled himself from bed, threw on his clothes, and shuffled downstairs. He greeted this Friday morning with all the deference of a funeral-goer; his father was already gone to work, and the servants were busily tucking into the docket of their daily responsibilities. Charlie satisfied himself with a bowl of cereal and a glass of juice.

He'd planned on heading to the scatter that morning—that was how he'd left it with the Whiz Mob the day before. They were going to drift that afternoon, and they'd all but insisted that Charlie come along. But now that Amir had so clearly spurned their friendship, would he still be welcome? Maybe Amir had only confronted Charlie out of a fit of pique, and that he'd be, again, waiting at a table in the Bar des 7 Coins with a bottle of Coke and an apology.

Knocking back the remainder of his orange juice, Charlie heard himself say, as if reciting a locker room pep speech, "I'm going to go."

The way he saw it, he'd taken his stand against Amir. He'd held his ground. He'd shown that he could go toe-to-toe with any of the cannons in the Whiz Mob. Were he to retreat now and "declare out," he would only further prove Amir's dismissal of him. No, he would

go to the scatter, and if Amir was there to confront him, so be it. Charlie's allegiance was to the Whiz Mob. He would not be intimidated.

His heart was racing the entire tram ride to the Old Port; it sounded in each step as he hiked the cobbled streets of the Panier, those streets that had seemed so alien mere weeks ago, which he now walked with the confidence of a native.

The café was empty when he arrived. He pressed the button behind the Pernod bottle that activated the secret door behind the bar and walked the long stone corridor to the spiral staircase. When he arrived in the catacomb, the mob appeared to be just finishing a late breakfast and were getting ready for the day's tip.

"Hey, Charlie," said Molly. "Just in time."

"You look like garbage, Charlie," said Pluto.

"I didn't sleep very well," replied Charlie. He was looking around the catacomb for Amir, who was nowhere to be seen.

"Well, you better sharpen up, kiddo," said Jackie as she walked to Pluto's side. "We need you."

"Need me?" asked Charlie.

"We've got a job, tomorrow night. We need another cannon."

"It's a Big Tip," said Borra, who was seated at the table, inscribing something in the wood with a knife.

Charlie, surprised at the sudden invitation, said, "Really?"

"Really," said Pluto. "We need you to work Amir's position."

"W-what . . . ," stammered Charlie. "What happened to Amir?"

No one opted to answer the question for some moments before Molly piped up, "He declared himself out."

"What?" asked Charlie, in disbelief.

Pluto nodded gravely. "Last night. Don't know what's got into him. He showed up here all bent out of shape. Couldn't get him to see sense. Said he was done. Said he was declaring out, that he couldn't do it no more."

"Blowed his moxie," said Molly. "Didn't see that coming at all."

"Coward," muttered Borra, from the table.

And suddenly, Charlie had won. There would be no final confrontation at the scatter between him and Amir. What's more, he'd been explicitly invited to replace a proper Seven Bells cannon. He had finally proven himself, despite Amir's attempts to sabotage his involvement, and yet he felt deeply conflicted, even sorrowful about it.

"Well?" asked Jackie, sensing Charlie's hesitation.

"I'm in," said Charlie.

Chapter
FIFTEEN

He would need a tuxedo. It happened that Charlie owned not one, but three of the uncomfortable getups, so that would not be a problem. He even offered to lend one to Pluto, who was his closest match, but they'd already managed monkey suits for all the Mobbies who needed one. The prat was to be some sort of gala function. It was to be held at the Palais du Pharo, that neoclassical edifice overlooking the south bank of the Old Port, and black-tie dress was required. Sembene and Fatour were going as part of the catering staff; Borra was connected with the local workforce of the building and would be going disguised as a coat-check boy. The rest of the mob would be coming as guests.

The job had required weeks of rigorous fanning on Pluto's part:

arranging appropriate outfits and credentials for everyone—but this was typical of a Big Tip.

"This is going to be the one, a real jug touch," said Pluto. "The upper crust, flaunting their diamonds and pearls. Trying to out-flash each other. We're going to be dripping in slum, boys."

"And girls," said Michiko.

"And girls," said Pluto. "That was implied."

"Whatever," said Michiko, rolling her eyes.

Charlie would be running with Michiko, working the ballroom two-handed while Pluto and Jackie worked the tented outdoor gardens. Sembene and Fatour would be binging from the buffet line while Borra harvested the ripe pickings of the coat closet.

"Like shooting apples in barrel," he said.

"That's not quite right," said Charlie. "But I get it."

And Amir—well, Amir was gone.

To Charlie, it felt like watching some well-known play or picture with the main character somehow erased from the stage. All the components were there—the set dressings, the costumes, the music—but the ensemble was lacking its main character. He decided that this was a temporary hang-up, and that once he'd gotten used to Amir's absence, all would feel perfectly normal again within the Whiz Mob. He would no longer feel like a boy invited to a party whose host has gone missing.

Perhaps Pluto had guessed his reservations when he cornered

him that night, just as Charlie was getting ready to leave the scatter. The plan was to meet the following evening at a café some few blocks down the hill from the Palais; from there, the Whiz Mob would wage their assault on the gala. Everyone was advised to have a quiet night, to get some rest, and Charlie was heading home to do just that. Pluto stopped him at the bottom step of the spiral staircase.

"What's up?" asked Charlie.

"I know it's weird," said Pluto, "Amir being gone. I know the two of you were tight."

Charlie nodded. "It's really no big deal. I'm not going to let it affect me."

"Good," said Pluto. "Because we need you tomorrow. We need cannon Charlie."

This gave Charlie a small lift; he'd never heard Pluto refer to him as a cannon. "He'll be there," he replied, smiling.

"That's what I like to hear," said Pluto.

Charlie turned to go, but paused again on the stair. "I saw him, you know," he said. "Amir." He hadn't admitted this to anyone. Amir's sudden dismissal of him still stung, and he was loath to inform anyone of it.

"You did?" asked Pluto. "Where?"

"At my house. He came by. Must've been around ten o'clock."

"What did he say?" Pluto looked genuinely concerned.

"He said . . . He said I should get off the whiz."

Pluto let out an exasperated noise. "That you should get off the whiz? That's ridiculous."

"Yeah," said Charlie. "He seemed really agitated. It was so strange. I know he's been kind of a pill lately, but I'd never seen him like that before. He was just really . . . mean."

"Well," said Pluto, "good riddance to him then. No one needs that. Between you and me, he was probably jealous. It's not often you turn someone out and they show you up within weeks of being on the whiz. Can crush a guy's confidence, you know. Promise me you won't let it get to you. He was always a bit of a wild card. To be honest, I'm glad you're taking his place."

"Yeah?"

"Yeah. Honest."

Charlie smiled shyly. Pluto gave him a good-natured pat on the arm and said, "We'll see you tomorrow, then."

"Till tomorrow."

Charlie arrived back at the Fisher residence in time for dinner. It was a rare quiet Friday evening, and two settings were laid out on the absurdly long table that commanded the center of the large dining room, two small cities shunted to one side of an uninhabitable desert. Charlie and his father sat perpendicular to each other, with Charles Sr. seated, as he always was, at the head of the table.

They sat in all but total silence through the first and second courses. Charlie found himself alternately consumed by thoughts of Amir and of the impending Big Tip the following evening. In his mind's eye, he conjured spectral prats and walked himself through the motions of emptying them. He undid virtual tweezers and dipsies, he reefed imaginary kicks from stubborn pits. Every few moments, however, the scrubby face of Amir appeared before him, whispering some denigrating comment about his chump-ness, and Charlie's calm composure was all but erased.

The cheese course came, and Charles Sr. took the liberty of selecting a few hunks for the table. It was only then that he spoke:

"André mentioned that you were having one of your tuxedos steamed and pressed," he said. "I don't suppose you've decided to join me for tomorrow night's function."

"What?" Charlie was lost to another reverie and had only caught the last few words.

"The queen of Lumiravia, in town for the weekend," said his father. "I must've mentioned it to you. Don't you remember? I supposed you were planning on joining me, considering you were having your suit readied."

"Oh," said Charlie, having to think fast. "No. There's a party in Toulon. The Edelweisses. Someone's birthday. I told them I'd go."

"Toulon? That's a bit of a drive."

"Yes," said Charlie. "I'll be gone most of the afternoon. Probably won't get back till late."

Charles Sr. seemed genuinely crestfallen. "You've come a long way in recent months, Charlie. Don't you suppose you've gotten over your shyness enough to participate in the consul's social schedule? I have no doubt that you would find it highly edifying." Charles paused to fork a bit of brie into his mouth. Once he'd finished chewing, he said, "What's more, I would enjoy your company."

"I will," said Charlie. "I promise. Just not tomorrow night."

"You could invite your friends, you know," said Charles. "Have them over to the house one of these nights. Or perhaps they could join you at one of these functions."

"Oh, no," said Charlie, perhaps too quickly. For a moment, he imagined the Whiz Mob wandering the halls of the Fisher residence, stripping the house of every valuable bauble that could fit into their pockets. The thought made him choke on his gruyère. "I've asked them, but they're always so busy. Maybe soon."

"Very well," said Charles. "I do wish to meet them. They sound a charming bunch. Particularly . . . what's his name again . . . Clark Kent? The one who managed to survive three weeks alone in the jungles of Cameroon. Fascinating stories, I imagine."

"I'll mention that to him," said Charlie, feeling himself blush. "You know, I should really finish my Cicero before bed. I've got my Latin final Monday morning." He pushed himself away from the table, dabbed his mouth with his napkin, and stood. "Good night, Father," he said.

"Good night," said Charles. "Sleep well. One last thing, Charlie.

Have André check the fit of that tuxedo. We should perhaps have you measured for a new one. You have grown, my boy."

"Very well, sir," said Charlie. He gave a little bow and left the room.

That night, he did not work on his Cicero. His Latin verbs remained unconjugated. Instead, he assaulted poor Dennis, the practice dummy, by loading him up with cash and jewelry and robbing him of every piece, coin, and bill till his pockets were again empty. A body double had arrived for Dennis, a kind of spruced-up version of himself, wearing Charlie's clean and pressed tuxedo. It stood beside its twin silently, enduring the other's misfortune. It was past midnight when Charlie fell asleep at the foot of his bed while he was flipping his Sheaffer Imperial pen between his fingers with the dexterity of a spider spinning its web. He awoke with the pen lying in his lap.

Charlie arrived at the café at the appointed hour, dressed in his formal wear. He must've grown a few inches since he'd last worn the outfit. The hem of his pants hung so high over the tops of his shoes, it was as if his pants and footwear were mortal enemies and were making a concerted effort to keep a safe distance from each other. He'd expected that he would be the best put together of the Whiz Mob when he saw them at the rendezvous point, but he was wrong: the pickpockets looked as if they'd been torn straight from the Parisian society pages.

Pluto was wearing a sharp bespoke tux and his hair was pomaded and combed back neatly. Jackie sat next to him at their table, wearing a gorgeous red ball gown with a plunging neckline. Her lips matched the fiery red of the dress, and her intensely blue eyes, highlighted as they were with an imperious amount of eyeshadow and mascara, caught Charlie as he walked into the café like two ice-cold spotlights. Michiko was reclining against the bar in a sea-green sleeveless gown embossed with flowers. She wore black sunglasses and was sipping at a Coca-Cola bottle through a zebra-striped straw. Molly sat near her, at the bar, wearing a shiny yellow ball gown, draped to the floor. Even Sembene and Fatour, dressed as they were in white bow ties and black jackets—the de facto uniform of the Palais du Pharo wait-staff—outshone Charlie's poorly fitting tuxedo.

"Hi, guys," said Charlie.

The door to the WC swung open and Borra lumbered into the café, his blue blazer and tie combo winningly askew enough to make Charlie feel somewhat better about his own high-water trousers and crooked bow tie.

"Right on time, Charlie," said the Russian. "You look . . ." He paused in his assessment once his eyes landed on the hem of Charlie's pants.

"Barely passable," said Jackie. "Really, Charlie. Aren't you the son of some important minister?"

"Consul general," said Charlie. "I think it shrunk."

"You're a growing boy," said Jackie.

"That," said Charlie, "is just what my dad said."

"We'll have to get you something tailored," said Pluto. He then made a mental count of his accomplices in the room. "We're all here. Shall we head to our party?"

A young couple in the corner watched them disinterestedly as they made their way out into the street. Molly caught Charlie's eye as they clustered near the door of the café.

"Amir ain't here," she said, guessing his thoughts.

"We don't want to wait just a little longer? See if he shows?"

"He's out, Charlie," said Molly. "And out is out."

"He ain't coming back," said Michiko.

Charlie nodded, trying to remain resolute in the face of his friend's defection.

Out on the avenue, Pluto and Jackie walked at the head of the gang, carefully cataloging every facet of the upcoming tip. They'd already planned the operation, back at the scatter, but at Pluto's insistence, they reviewed everything down to the smallest detail.

"Right," said Pluto. "Listen up. Organization is key. This place'll be crawling with fuzzy whiskers. If anyone gets a whiff, if a single soul is rumbled, we're out. First off: me, Charlie, Jackie, and Michiko go in as guests. Charlie, Michiko's your date. Jackie's mine."

"How romantic," said Jackie.

"Don't get any ideas," Michiko said to Charlie, winking.

Charlie felt his face redden. "How do we get in again?"

"Our impeccable charm," said Pluto.

"Wait," said Charlie. "You don't have invitations? I thought you said we had invitations." This struck Charlie as a pretty big oversight, if true. He'd been to enough high-level functions to know that lacking an invitation was tantamount to enjoying the party from the street. Charm, no matter how impeccable, would not get you far.

"Security's real tight on this one," was Pluto's answer. "They're taking names at the gate. I put the bee on this one through a fellow I know. We've got one name on the list, good for myself and three guests." He looked at his watch. "Once we're through, Jackie will get to the staff entrance door by seven fifteen, provided there are no holdups. Sembene, Fatour, Borra, and Molly, you guys know where to be?"

"North side gate, by the garbage bins," said Molly.

Jackie took up the story: "Good. From there, Sembene and Fatour, you boys head straight to the kitchen. Hopefully you'll be out on the floor quick. Borra, to the coat check. Molly . . . Just try to act regal."

"'Tis in my nature," said Molly, adopting a posh accent.

"What if we get hung up at the front gate?" asked Charlie.

"Relax," said Jackie. "We've been through this dozens of times. It always works out. There is *always* a way into a party."

At this point, Borra, Molly, Sembene, and Fatour bid their

colleagues good luck and broke away down a side street, presumably leading to the Palais's staff entrance—but not before Borra had gripped Charlie firmly on the shoulder and said, "To you, Charlie, I wish most luck."

Charlie accepted the Russian's well-wishes with a cringing smile (his grip was incredibly strong), while a wave of nervousness crashed over him. He adjusted the lapels to his tuxedo, straightened his tie, and thrust out his elbow to Michiko, who was walking at his side.

"Shall we?" he hammed.

Michiko smiled and took his arm.

The two couples fell into step on the avenue, and with each block they began radiating more confidence until they were all but indistinguishable from the flocking partygoers who were arriving, two by two, at the front gate to the color gardens that surrounded the Palais du Pharo like a leafy moat. Limousines and taxicabs birthed lavishly dressed men and women onto the sidewalk by the gate—two couples even arrived by horse and carriage—and the pickpockets were forced to take their place in the queue that was forming.

A quartet of tuxedoed giants, armed with clipboards and pencils, guarded the entrance to the grounds. Each couple was forced to announce their names, which the gatekeepers would locate and tick off their list with a scrawl of a pencil. They were scrupulous in their attention, and the flow of humanity into the Palais had slowed to a trickle. Charlie could feel his heart rate quicken. He looked at Pluto, who seemed unshaken. Michiko's grip tightened on his arm as they arrived at the head of the queue.

"*Comment vous appelez-vous?*" asked one of the men as Pluto stepped forward.

"Baron Marius d'Anton," answered Pluto, his voice dripping with what Charlie assumed to be some aristocratic dialect. "And three guests." He said this, of course, in French.

The man did not blink at the outrageous name—he'd been hearing similarly ostentatious titles all evening—and began searching the register for Monsieur Le Baron. He evidently came up empty-handed, because he looked at Pluto after a time and shook his head.

"No," was all he said.

Pluto laughed uncomfortably. "That's impossible. Please check again."

Out of what might be a reluctant deference to the upper classes, the man gave another survey of the neatly stacked paper on his clipboard. The answer, at the end of the search, was the same.

"No," said the man again.

Jackie leaned forward. "Dah-ling," she drawled, in Southern-soaked English. "What in heaven's name is the holdup? Certainly Father is expecting us inside. *Ah* haven't come all the way from *Nah'leans* to be held up at the *do-ah*. Or my name isn't *Peabody*." She glanced at the man after her recitation and was *shocked* to see it had no effect.

"This is an outrage," said Pluto. "I demand to see whoever is in charge here. I will not be treated like some common riffraff!"

Charlie felt Michiko pull on his arm; she led him closer to the fray, though for what purpose, he could not know. Seeing their attempt at gaining entry go so horribly awry, he was ready, in the argot, to nash it and nurse the Whiz Mob's failure over grenadines at the scatter. Several couples behind them began to grumble impatiently at the delay; Pluto and Jackie were holding their ground, their complaints growing louder with every moment. Several other similarly dressed security personnel began to gravitate toward the fracas; Charlie felt himself being pushed forward by the crowd.

"What's going on here?" shouted one of the elder gatekeepers. "What's the holdup?"

"These . . . kids, sir," said the man who'd been denying Pluto entrance. "They're not on the list."

The other man glanced at them; Charlie was surprised to see the man's attention alight on himself. The man peered closer and said, in English, "Is that you, Charlie Fisher?"

Pluto and Jackie fell away. Michiko remained clinging to Charlie's arm.

"Y-yes?" answered Charlie.

"Are these"—he paused, taking in Charlie's confederates—"your friends?"

Charlie did not know the man, nor how the man knew him, but

he knew well enough when to seize an opportunity. "Yes," he said. "And we're not being allowed in."

"Well, that would be a grave mistake," said the man, now looking at the clipboard-armed guard. He then switched to French, saying, "This is the son of the American consul general and his friends. Let them in."

Unperturbed by his mistake, the guard waved the four of them forward. Within moments, they were through the gate and into the gardens.

"Three cheers for Charlie Fisher," Pluto said.

"What just happened?" asked Jackie, her hand to her lips.

"I don't really know," said Charlie. "They must've recognized me."

"Why didn't we think of that before?" shouted Michiko, tugging on Charlie's arm. "It's ingenious."

"Nice work, Charlie," said Pluto. "You really came through."

Charlie smiled and said, "It was nothing, really. Benefits of my upbringing, I guess."

As if on cue, a servant appeared with a tray full of champagne glasses. Pluto gathered four of them, one for each of the pickpockets, and doled them out. Holding his glass out in front of him as if it were some holy relic, he said, "To quicken the pulse and quench the nerves."

The four glasses met in the center of their circle, making a melodious *ting*. "To the whiz, cannons," said Pluto.

"To the whiz," said Jackie.

"To the whiz," said Michiko.

"To the whiz," said Charlie. He waited till they'd thrown back their heads to ingest the bubbly stuff before he upturned his own glass and emptied its contents onto the grass. Say what you will about Charlie Fisher and the serial larceny he'd been accomplice to for the last several weeks, he wasn't about to go so delinquent as to drink alcohol. Besides, if he did, what librarian or bookseller would possibly order this book, let alone recommend it to a bright and studious reader such as yourself? Let's all be thankful he abstained and continue with our story. For now, the Big Tip was on.

Chapter SIXTEEN

But first, a quick aside.

You might be interested to know that the Palais du Pharo was built in 1858 by Napoléon III (not *that* Napoléon, but another) for his wife, Doña María Eugenia Ignacia Augustina de Palafox-Portocarrero de Guzmán y Kirkpatrick. The emperor and Doña María Eugenia Ignacia Augustina de Palafox-Portocarrero de Guzmán y Kirkpatrick did not live in the residence during the emperor's life, and Doña María Eugenia Ignacia Augustina de Palafox-Portocarrero de Guzmán y Kirkpatrick ended up donating the property to the city of Marseille after Doña María Eugenia Ignacia Augustina de Palafox-Portocarrero de Guzmán y Kirkpatrick's husband's death. The city, undoubtedly, was very thankful to Doña

María Eugenia Ignacia Augustina de Palafox-Portocarrero de Guzmán y Kirkpatrick, because the Palais was a fine neoclassical building with commanding views of the Old Port and the Mediterranean Sea. It is anyone's guess why Doña María Eugenia Ignacia Augustina de Palafox-Portocarrero de Guzmán y Kirkpatrick chose not to live in such a fine residence, but we can assume that, being an empress, Doña María Eugenia Ignacia Augustina de Palafox-Portocarrero de Guzmán y Kirkpatrick had her pick of the litter when it came to extraordinary addresses.

You might also be interested to know that Doña María Eugenia Ignacia Augustina de Palafox-Portocarrero de Guzmán y Kirkpatrick was commonly called Empress Eugénie, but it's a bit late for that information, since that is likely the last time she'll be mentioned in this book.

While Charlie had not lived the life of an empress, he had set foot on the grounds of many an exceptional house, those marvelous buildings at which we, the common folk, might only steal glances from between the chinks of the close-set trees and hedgerows that guard them from trespassers, through the bars of the wrought-iron fences that separate the haves from the have-nots of this world. Charlie, being the son of a well-respected career diplomat, was allowed passage.

And the Palais du Pharo put many of those houses to shame. Especially on that particular May evening, when the gardens surrounding the building were aflame with torches casting flickering light on the milling partygoers, each one decked out in the best finery of the day, and music from a distant bandstand drifted in the air like a wandering stream. The building itself looked like some great Greek edifice, the sort of place where one would expect to see philosophers, playwrights, and politicians, dressed in drapery, meandering about and engaging in high-minded conversation about the future of civilization. And while one might be tempted to loiter in the outside grounds the entire evening, the golden light shining from the Palais's many windows, the shadows that leapt about its ceilings, and the silhouettes on the balconies promised that the party indoors was an equal to anything the gardens had to offer.

Pluto rubbed his hands excitedly before sauntering off, refilled champagne glass in hand, to the rendezvous with the rest of the mob. Michiko wrapped her arm tightly in the crook of Charlie's. Jackie circled a group of chatting socialites with the temerity of a lioness.

The binging was beginning.

With a single look, Michiko was able to communicate to Charlie that she would run cannon to his duke on several older men who were standing near an ornate gazebo; Charlie fell in behind her as she approached. She wandered into the crowd like some kind of spirit or sprite, a figment of the viewer's imagination, so completely was she able to avoid detection. Charlie followed doggedly, pretending all the while to be some party guest, looking for his partner. Wallets tumbled like dice from a cup into Charlie's palm; watches flipped neatly from Michiko's hand into Charlie's. It took only one circumnavigation of the chattering push before the gentlemen had been neatly stripped of valuables and the two pickpockets were onto their next press.

Nearby, a pavilion had been assembled in the center of the gardens, and a sweeping tune was being played by a small orchestra on a bandstand, while a smattering of guests danced blithely on the grass.

"Care to?" asked Michiko.

"I'd be honored," replied Charlie.

And they were off, waltzing to some cheery melody the conductor had just ushered into life with a wave of his baton. A new crowd of dancers arrived, and soon the pavilion was abuzz with swaying bodies, clasped together in pairs.

"Well," said Michiko, her right hand lazing on Charlie's left, her left hand on his other arm. "Not bad, Charlie Fisher."

"Dance lessons," Charlie explained sheepishly, his right hand gently pressed against the small of Michiko's back. "My mother made me take them. You know, in order to be a good society brat." As if to punctuate the comment, he navigated them in a deft double turn that made Michiko shout.

"Don't whirl me away," she said, laughing.

"I'll try not to."

"You know, Charlie," said Michiko as their feet shuffled through the grass, "I don't typically care for Americans."

"So you've said."

"But for you, I think I may have to make an exception." She laid her head on his shoulder.

"Don't go soft on me now," said Charlie.

Michiko laughed before saying, "Say, Charlie. Why don't you waltz me a little closer to one of our neighbors?"

"Gladly, mam'selle," replied her partner.

It was a sneak job as old as the honored profession itself, the dance tip. Charlie guided his partner gracefully up to the nearest couple, allowing Michiko to make the slightest contact with the back of the woman's gown. Before this touch was even registered, Michiko's hand would drop from Charlie's arm and find its way to the sucker's purse. A squeeze of the leading hand let Charlie know the tip was won and he would spin her away, breathing a quiet apology to the suckers; they smiled, if somewhat annoyed. Charlie felt something heavy and undoubtedly valuable slide into his left hip kick.

"Older couple, two o'clock," whispered Michiko, her lips close to Charlie's ear.

And so it went, as the band segued into a loping Spanish melody, that Charlie and Michiko swayed and swung around the pavilion floor, casually brushing against each of their fellow dancers in turn, with every orbit filling Charlie's pockets with ill-gotten items lifted from their pockets and purses. At one point, an older gentleman with silver-streaked hair asked to step in and dance with the radiant

Michiko; Charlie could only oblige.

As she was spun away into the center of the floor, her right hand inconspicuously making its way down the gentleman's back, Charlie shoved his hands in his pockets and strolled off the dance floor.

"Hey there, sailor," he heard someone say. He turned to see Molly.

"Oh, hi," he said, smiling. "You made it in."

"Easy peasy," replied the Mouse. "You swinging?"

It took Charlie a moment, considering the context, to realize what she was asking. "Yes," he said. "My pockets are loaded."

"Well, look no further." The girl waved him over to the shelter of a nearby hedgerow and, once they were both concealed, pulled at a hidden waistband in her gown. "Night depository box, at your service."

Charlie peered down and saw that Molly had sewn a large canvas stash bag into her dress, hidden by the enormous bell of her gown.

"No need to stare," chided Molly, causing Charlie to blush deeply as he began transferring all of his stolen items from his pockets down Molly's dress. Once he'd finished, the girl adjusted her clothing and walked away, looking not unlike someone who was recovering from some kind of pelvic surgery.

Charlie watched her leave, then turned his attention back to the dancers under the pavilion. Michiko was still matched with the older gentleman; a new song had been struck up. Charlie walked through the dance floor, excusing himself as a swaying couple swept into him and revolved away, lighter in the pockets than they'd been just moments before. It was as if Dennis himself were there on the dance floor. Approaching Michiko and her older paramour, Charlie said, "May I have this dance?"

The man acquiesced, somewhat reluctantly, and Michiko was back again in Charlie's arms.

"What took you so long?" she asked.

"I had to unload. Molly is duking."

Michiko sighed. "Let me know next time. That guy was so slick with cologne it was starting to make me gag."

Then, before the band could strike up another tune, Michiko announced, regally, that *really*, Charlie, all this dancing was quite giving her the vapors. Maybe what she needed was a glass of punch. Ever a gentleman, Charlie led her by the hand out of the pavilion and toward the Palais doors.

As they were heading up the steps, they saw Jackie being courted by four young gentlemen; she was laughing at some joke one of them had told, perhaps too loudly. "Excuse me," she said to her admirers, "I believe my date is here." With that, she spun around and threaded her hand into Charlie's free arm, saying, "How boring men can be."

And suddenly, Charlie Fisher, twelve years old and never been kissed, was accompanying two beautiful young women into a lavish soiree in an empress's former palace. What's more, they were his friends and confederates in an elaborate enterprise to shake the pillars

of society, bringing a modicum of equality to a rigged system that so clearly favored the wealthy, the moneyed and landed gentry over the working poor of the world. He was a modern-day folk hero; he was Robin Hood in a tuxedo. He'd never felt so alive.

A pair of servants stood at the door to the palace and bowed to the three of them with a deference one would expect of royal handlers; they were ushered into the magnificent ground-floor ballroom. Massive glittering chandeliers hung over the checkerboard floor like a visitation of crystalline UFOs; a crowd of impeccably dressed grown-ups milled about the parquet with champagne glasses in their hands and thousands of francs' worth of cash and jewelry littering their bodies. Several of the women wore actual crowns; some of the men wore suits draped with shining medals and badges. Servants darted here and there, handing out food and drink to partygoers.

"Incredible," whispered Charlie.

And then Sembene and Fatour were before them, their arms cradling trays of oysters, their pockets looking like overly stuffed Christmas stockings. "Where's Molly?" asked Sembene desperately.

"I feel like I've got all the hardware of a work site shoved into my underwear," said Fatour.

Charlie had to stop himself from laughing. "I saw her over by the bandstand, in the gardens," he said. "Look there."

The two boys scurried away, careful not to shake the contents of their pockets onto the floor. Another band was playing off to the side of the massive room, though no one seemed to be dancing. The crowd was intent on one another's company, on conversations that sounded as if the fate of nations were bound to them, hushed admissions and gossip that could bring down entire families. Charlie had heard such voices before, at the functions he'd been forced to attend with his father, but never in this great of a number. It was like the scions of the great families of Europe were gathered, here, in this giant glowing room, and were now deciding how the rest of the twentieth century would unfold.

The three of them walked across the floor, soaking in the aroma of this conversation, eavesdroppers to the global body politic. They found Pluto standing by an enormous crystal punch bowl set at the center of a long table that was placed against the palace's north-facing windows. The Mediterranean, bathed in the glow of the evening's twilight, could be seen just beyond; the glimmering lights of the boats in the harbor and the windows of the overlooking buildings provided a kind of winking backdrop to the party. The one-eyed boy was sipping at a glass of cordial and looking very serious.

His prats, unlike those of the rest of the pickpockets, were empty.

Jackie and Michiko let go of Charlie's arms, and the three of them backed up against the table alongside Pluto, joining him in his contemplation of the crowd.

"How goes the tip?" asked Charlie finally. He found Pluto's silence curious.

Pluto took a drink from his glass before answering, "This ain't no pea soup press, Charlie. We're not in this one for the sling and the slum."

"Oh?"

"There's a jug touch to be had, Charlie. The Big Score. And I intend to be the one to bing it."

Charlie looked over the crowd. From this casual distance, he could see many items that might, in his estimation, be considered a Big Score: he saw brooches the size of fists, medals that were so heavy in gold that they challenged the strength of whatever fastener was holding them to the fabric they'd been pinned to. He saw glittering tiaras and strings of pearls—bead rope, in the argot—that were so long and carried so many of the opaline orbs that they circled the neck of their wearer perhaps four or five times.

"Don't be so serious, Pluto," chided Jackie. "There's plenty to go around."

"Charlie and I had a lovely turn around the dance floor," said Michiko.

"It was very productive," said Charlie.

"Really, Pluto. Do try and enjoy yourself," said Jackie. She snaked her arm into Charlie's. "Come on," she said, playing the supportive party guest. "Let's take a little walk around the room, see if we know anyone."

Michiko fell in with Pluto, and the four pickpockets pushed off from their mooring at the table. They began to wander back toward

the crush of aristocracy in the center of the room. Charlie could feel the strength in Jackie's arm as they walked; she was the sort of girl who would not blithely hang on a guy's arm, that much was clear, but would actually do the leading—and Charlie found something admirable in that. He allowed her to be the captain, the navigator, of their voyage about the crowded ballroom. That way, he decided, he was better able to focus more closely on the potential bings to be had, to fan the loaded marks in the room.

This was precisely what he was doing, eyeing some general's medal of the Legion of Honor and deciding how best to undo the dipsy that was the medal's fastener, when he heard his name being said, very loudly, just behind him.

"Charlie!"

He froze. Time seemed to stop. His brain began processing the timbre of the voice that had just announced his birth-given name when it came, regretfully, again.

"Charlie Fisher!"

The added two syllables gave enough information to the flashing synapses in Charlie's mind to piece together who was saying his name. And the answer was very, very unfortunate.

It was his father.

"What are you doing here?" the voice said again as Charlie, in seeming slow motion, felt Jackie's hand guide him full circle to face the man who'd asked the question. And then Charles Fisher Sr.,

American consul general to Marseille and career diplomat, came into Charlie's vision like some great planet rounding the cosmos to eclipse the light of the sun. There he was, all five foot eleven of him, in black tie and jacket, brown, pomaded hair, graying at the temples, little mustache, Brut cologne. There was no denying it.

"I'm," said Charlie, and that was all he could manage. He tried again. "I'm." He couldn't seem to convince his mouth to provide the amount of saliva it needed to utter more than a single syllable.

And then the strangest thing happened. A smile broke across Charles Sr.'s face and he reached in with both arms, collapsing Charlie into his chest with a thundering embrace. "Well, I'm quite over the moon," said Charles after he'd stepped back from the hug and was surveying his son with a proud eye. "So you planned on coming after all!"

Charlie tried to command words, but his faculties again failed him. He hoped a simple nod would suffice.

"I really should've known it, you getting your tuxedo readied and pressed." Charles Sr. then eyed the boy's ill-fitting attire. "We will have to get you a new one, you know," he said. "This old monkey suit will simply not do. But I am so glad that you've decided to come to the party. And are these your friends? The ones I've heard so much about?"

The shock of seeing his father, the crashing of his two lives coming together like football players in a midfield collision, had all but made Charlie forget that he was standing arm in arm with Jackie and that Pluto and Michiko remained close by on either side of him.

"Very nice to meet you, sir," prompted Jackie, aware that Charlie had lost his ability to speak. "We've heard *so much* about you."

"Well, I hope all of it is good," said Charles Sr., winking gamely at his son. "And I've heard so much about you all, as well. Charlie speaks so highly of you."

"Oh, Charlie," hammed Michiko, nudging Charlie. "You're really too kind."

Charles's attention fell on Pluto. "You must be Clark," he said.

"Clark?" asked Pluto, confused.

"Clark Kent. The one who was orphaned in South Africa, raised by Pygmies, I was told," said Charles.

"Oh yes," said Pluto. "That's me. Clark. Clark Kent." He then fell into his role with command: "I thank God for those Pygmies every day, sir. Saved my life. Taught me everything I know."

Charles nodded sagely. "Yes, I can only imagine. And you ladies?"

"Aren't you going to introduce us, Charlie?" asked Michiko.

"How very rude of you, Charlie," added Jackie.

"This . . . ," Charlie managed finally. "This is Jackie and this is Michiko. This is my father, Charles Fisher Sr. And . . ." He looked at Pluto, his face feeling as if it had been sucked dry of all of its color. "And Clark you've met."

"A *pleasure*," said Michiko, extending her hand.

Charles Sr. took her palm and raised it to his lips, saying, "*Enchanté.*"

In doing so, Charles's gold Rolex watch appeared from beneath the sleeve of his jacket. Charlie let out a quiet wheeze. Before the watch could be disappeared, he abruptly grabbed Michiko's wrist and yanked it away from his father's grasp.

"Hey!" said Michiko.

"Perhaps I was being too forward," said Charlie's father, looking at his son with surprise.

"No, nothing," said Charlie. "It's just that, well, we've all met, haven't we? I don't see why we go to all the trouble of shaking hands. Seems so, you know, formal."

Michiko smiled mischievously.

"Well," Charlie said suddenly. "We were just about to be going, so . . ."

"What?" asked Jackie. "Shush, Charlie. Why, we just got here!"

"Nonsense, Charlie," said his father. He then turned to Charlie's compatriots and said, "I've been trying to get Charlie to one of these functions for months. Meet some of the movers and shakers of the European political stage, be a witness to history! But he's kept begging off, running around with you lot."

"Oh, we know, Mr. Fisher," said Jackie coyly. "Charlie can be *such* a spoilsport."

"And we're very sorry," added Michiko, "for having so comman-deered his time."

"Indeed," said Charles Sr. "Well, I don't know whose idea it was to come tonight, but I'm just gobsmacked, really. You've honestly made my night. My month! My year!"

Charlie stared at his friends pleadingly. They were offering no help. "I don't know that I feel well," he said.

"Oh, come on, Charlie," said Jackie, wrapping her arm closer around his. "The night is young! You don't want to disappoint your father, do you?"

Charlie found himself in a cul-de-sac of his own making, with no clear means of escape. "I suppose," he said, gulping loudly, "that we could stay a few minutes more."

"Fantastic," said Charles Sr. He extended his arm and took a look at his watch, which was, thankfully, still there on his wrist. "Speaking of which," he said, "I don't suppose you kids would like to see history transpire, right before your eyes?"

Before Charlie had a chance to respond, Pluto said, "We'd love to, sir."

Chapter
SEVENTEEN

"**T**his is *not* okay," hissed Charlie. Jackie was still at his side, staring straight ahead as Charles Sr. led the four well-dressed pickpockets, his son among them, across the ballroom floor.

"What's not okay, Charlie?" she asked. She was smiling ingratiatingly to the various aristocrats they were passing, shining in her role as companion to the consul general's son. "Just go with it."

"I can't go with it. The tip is off. We've given up our kissers. We've beefed the gun. It's time to nash it, Jackie, time to *get out of here*." Charlie was forced to whisper this harangue while smiling and nodding to the passersby. Their progress was agonizingly slow going across the parquet floor of the room, as Charles Sr. was intent on introducing Charlie and his charming friends to every well-heeled colleague and notable personality they passed. In turn, Charlie found himself in the awkward position of trying to thwart his friends' attempts at lifting valuables from these newfound acquaintances. "No handshakes," was Charlie's refrain. "Really not necessary. She's got a bit of a cold. Hate for you to catch it. Oh, Pluto—I mean Clark— stick with us here. No need to walk behind the gentleman there."

This charade had left him exhausted by the time they'd arrived at a pair of double doors on the far side of the ballroom, where two bulky security personnel stood guard. The two men stepped forward to stop Charles Sr. as he approached.

"It's all right," said Charlie's father. "They're with me. I'm Charles Fisher, American consul general. The queen is expecting me."

"Queen?" spouted Charlie involuntarily. By now, it seemed there was no blood left in his face. He felt like a walking bedsheet, freshly laundered.

"Queen," he heard Michiko say, just behind him.

"You know," Charlie said to his father, "we could just wait out here. We really don't want to impose."

"Nonsense," replied Charles Sr. "You shouldn't pass up an opportunity like this, Charlie. To meet royalty! I'm sure your friends would be interested."

"Oh yes," said Pluto. "We definitely are."

"See, Charlie?" said Charles, beaming at the pickpockets. "I think we have a gaggle of budding diplomats on our hands!"

And before Charlie could utter another objection, the doors had been thrown open and the five of them were ushered into the corridor beyond.

Now, the Palais du Pharo was, at this time, mostly used as a medical school—but it took very little doing to get it back to its old imperial self. The organizers of this fete were certainly keen to do just this and had brought a kind of regal glory back to the interior of the building by festooning its walls with all the trappings of royal decoration. This sensibility carried over into the receiving chamber into which Charlie and his confederates were led. A dais had been erected on one side of the room, where a princely-looking chair, painted gold for the occasion, had been placed. Tapestries showing frolicking satyrs, nymphs, and unicorns covered the walls. Ornate ceramic urns had been placed around the room, and a red carpet led to the chair in the center of the dais. Two men dressed in some kind of uncomfortable-looking traditional garb stood on either side of the chair, looking as if they had been drop-kicked from the fifteenth century. To top it off, they each held very real-looking halberds and were staring indifferently into the middle distance. An older man, dressed perhaps less anachronistically in a proper three-piece suit, approached Charles Sr., and the two of them engaged in a short, quiet conversation. The pickpockets surrounding Charlie remained ominously silent.

Charles Sr.'s conversation with the man drew to a close and the consul general turned to his son and nodded, smiling. The man with whom he'd been speaking climbed the dais and retreated through an ornate wooden door just behind the chair. Silence pervaded the room; Jackie cleared her throat, once, and apologized quietly for doing so.

Finally, the door behind the chair opened and the man in the suit reentered, taking up a position to one side of the chair. "Announcing," he said in a loud, sonorous voice, "Her Royal Highness, the Lady Nancy Drubetskaya Chertof, Exalted Queen of Lumiravia, Protector of the Fesselden Steppe, Carrier of the Flame of Krepswald." The two men in traditional garb standing to either side of the chair abruptly revealed that they had been hiding twin bugles beneath the burgundy velvet draping of their sleeves and blatted out a triumphal melody that made Charlie's stomach leap into his throat.

At that signal, an elderly woman in a jewel-bedecked gown appeared from the doorway and walked out onto the dais. She nodded perfunctorily to her announcer before sitting down in the gilded chair that served as her throne, looking relieved to be finally sitting. She was wearing an immense necklace of glittering jewels that hung down the front of her chest like a lei of bright flowers; a diamond-studded crown was perched heavily on the silver hair of her head. Rings the size of walnuts littered the frail twigs of her fingers; golden thread lined every seam of her gown.

Charlie glanced at his compatriots warily and saw they were each, to an individual, staring at the queen's adornments with the greed and excitement of a half-starved dog awaiting its dinner. Charlie's look then fell on his father, and he saw something he'd never seen before in the elder Fisher, this pillar of confidence and strength: genuine nervousness. Looking back at the Mobbies, he tried to get their attention, to whisper, "*Don't you dare*," but it was as if they were on another planet and he was earthbound, tapping out Morse code to some distant star.

Charles Fisher Sr. bowed deeply; Jackie, Pluto, Michiko, and Charlie followed his lead and bowed as well.

"Hello, Mr. Fisher," said the queen. "We are very pleased to see you well." She spoke in a deep, lilting way, filtered as it was through a kind of indistinguishable German-Slavic accent.

"Your Highness," said Charles. "It is my greatest pleasure to see you again." To the casual bystander, there might seem nothing unusual in the way the consul general spoke, but Charlie knew his father well enough to recognize that this was no typical meeting. Charlie had never heard his father speak so deferentially. There was a slight, almost imperceptible tremble in the elder Fisher's voice.

The queen then gestured to the assembled guests in the room. "Whom do we have the honor of addressing?"

"This is my son, Charlie, Your Highness," said Charles. He put his arm around Charlie's shoulder and pulled him forward. "Charlie Fisher Jr. I may have mentioned him when last we spoke."

"Oh yes," said the queen, peering down from her throne. "How do you do, Mr. Fisher?"

"Very well, thanks," said Charlie, before adding, "Your Highness."

The old woman must have been hard of hearing, as she was forced to crane her head forward to hear Charlie's words. Her jewelry jangled noisily as she did so. "Please," she said, gesturing to Charlie. "Our ears are not what they once were. All of you, please come closer."

Charlie gulped, remembering his friends. "Oh, we really shouldn't," he began to say, but stopped when he felt his father—and the pickpockets included—carry him closer to the dais.

"That's better," said the queen once they were within a few feet of her. "We have been cooped up in this room all day long, receiving visitors and well-wishers. It is a tiring business, being royalty." She allowed a sly smile.

"Not to mention that weight you're carrying," said Pluto suddenly. "I mean, the crown and the jewels and all." Charlie shot a look at him.

Every soul awaited the queen's response to this sudden, unbidden interjection; when it came, they each breathed a sigh of relief. The queen seemed amused. "Indeed," she said. "And who might you be?"

Pluto began to say his name, but Charlie interrupted. "This is Clark, Clark Kent."

"Have we met before, Mr. Kent?" asked the queen.

"I don't believe so, Your Highness," was Pluto's reply.

"Funny. The name sounds familiar."

"Well," said Charlie quickly, "it was really a tremendous honor to meet you. We shouldn't keep you any longer, Your Highness."

"But we have not yet met all the children," said the queen, ignoring Charlie's impatience. "Please, come forward and state your names."

This, Charlie could not bring himself to watch. One by one, the members of the Whiz Mob were ushered forward to stand on the dais, to bow and kiss the rings of the queen of Lumiravia. Like a man in a firing line, awaiting the countdown and the muzzle flash, Charlie stood transfixed, unable to move. He could only hope that the pickpockets' skill was honed enough for them to do their work without detection, that they might be miles from the Palais du Pharo before the alarms were rung and every policeman in Marseille had been dispatched to recover the crown jewels of the Lumiravian kingdom.

Charles Sr. stood off to one side and watched the formal introductions and the shows of deference, clearly proud to be providing these kids with this once-in-a-lifetime opportunity. When they'd finally finished, the elder Fisher was then waved forward to the dais and a short conversation transpired between him and the queen. Pluto, Jackie, and Michiko had returned to Charlie's side and were trying to hide smiles; Charlie could only imagine what they'd done.

The man in the three-piece suit, at the command of the queen, approached Charlie's father and presented him with an envelope, which Charles received with a deep bow. He opened it, surveyed its contents, and placed it in his jacket pocket with a nod. A wave of the queen's hand signaled that the visitation was over, but not before she called Charlie back over to the makeshift throne.

"Your father," said the queen, "is a very good man. He has done our country a tremendous service. You would do well to follow in his footsteps."

"Yes, Your Highness," said Charlie. Glancing up at the old woman, he made a quick inventory of the queen's adornments and was amazed to see that every jeweled ring was still there, attached to her fingers. Her baroque sash was unaltered and her crown, still perched on her head, seemed to have all of its twinkling gems accounted for. He breathed a sigh of relief; perhaps the pickpockets had read the circumstances correctly and had decided to play it safe.

With that, the queen stood. The honor guards on either side of the chair brought their bugles back to their lips and performed another loud fanfare; the queen flinched as it came to a finish. "We do so grow tired of that," Charlie heard her mutter before she shuffled off the dais and back through the door, out of the room.

Charlie could not have felt more relieved to have the whole episode over and done with, an episode that had transpired in his mind like a slow, agonizing death. His feet felt like they were floating as the visiting party exited the room and began walking down the corridor back toward the ballroom. He fell back while Pluto and Jackie talked animatedly with his father; Michiko walked in the lead of the group. Charlie was shaken to the core and decided that he would speak to his fellow Mobbies as soon as they had a private moment. He would insist that they establish some boundaries, where any kind of party or gathering that would happen to coincide with his father's line of work—or Charlie's personal life at all, for that matter—should be assiduously avoided. He felt as if he knew them well enough that they would accommodate the change.

When they arrived back at the ballroom, Charles Sr. turned around to face his son, beaming with pride.

"Well?" he asked.

"That was really neat," replied Charlie. "Thanks for inviting me. Us." Pluto, Jackie, and Michiko had gravitated away, back to the party crowds, allowing Charlie and his father to have a moment together.

"Neat doesn't half describe it," said his father. "You were just witness to one of the more seismic shifts in global politics in the last decade—scratch that, century!"

"I was?" asked Charlie. "I mean, she seemed very nice. And very, you know, royal."

Charles Sr. laughed. "What, her? She's a relic, Charlie. A figurehead. A throwback to a bygone era."

Charlie felt confused. "So," he said, "what was so"—what had his father said?—"seismic about all that?"

"Because, Charlie," began his father, now adopting a low, conspiratorial tone, "she gave me the Rosenberg Cipher."

"The what?"

Charles Sr. gestured to Charlie, indicating that he should keep his voice down. His eyes flitted about the room before returning to his son. "I should really get this off to my security detachment as soon as possible, but I did want a moment to celebrate."

"What is the Rosenberg Cipher?" pressed Charlie.

"Only the most important document to have been won in negotiation between countries, perhaps in our lifetime, itself the most powerful weapon one can have in the current global climate. Its value, immeasurable. Charlie, suffice it to say that I am speaking without hyperbole when I say that the fate of the world's superpowers currently rests in this document that is now in my possession." He took a deep breath and spoke again, quietly but firmly: "I have a feeling that once this is delivered into the hands of my betters, your father's career is all but made. French ambassador. Secretary of state. Really, I think the sky is the limit."

Something was dawning on Charlie. Something very grave. Little pieces of a puzzle tumbling together. He saw in his mind's eye the envelope being transferred from the man in the three-piece suit to his father. Charles Sr. continued speaking, rambling joyously.

"A palatial residence off the Champs-Élysées sound nice to you, Charlie? No, you're right. Perhaps we split time. Half the year in Paris, half the year in Provence. But now that you mention it, with a prominent state job, I may be back in DC, at the president's beck and call. I imagine he'll be demanding quite a bit more of my time, once it comes to light that I've managed the retrieval of the Cipher. Oh, Charlie, you don't know how long and involved these negotiations, these discussions have been. She's a funny old bird, the queen. Would only work through me. But I was the one who managed it, where so many others had failed. I was the one who got the Cipher. And now I have it, Charlie. I have it right here in my pocket."

"No, you don't," said Charlie.

Charlie spoke these words quietly, flatly. In a monotone. Words spoken in a voice completely drained of all emotion. It might've been a robot speaking them.

"What?" asked his father, suddenly shaken from his happy monologue.

"You don't have it. In your pocket."

Charlie didn't even need to stick around to see if his assumption was correct. By the time his father had reached into his inside pocket—his coat pit—and discovered that it was, in fact, completely empty, Charlie had already run to the center of the ballroom and had begun searching for the Whiz Mob. "No, no, no, no, no," dribbled from his mouth as he pushed his way through the partygoers, the princes, and the politicians. Pluto, Michiko, and Jackie, who had just been there, just beside him, were nowhere to be seen.

Vanished.

Sembene and Fatour, who, all evening long, had been shuttling between the ballroom floor and the back kitchen, were no longer visible in the phalanx of servers who plied the waters of tuxedoed and gowned aristocracy, doling champagne and oysters to willing takers.

Disappeared.

Down in the coat check, a window let onto a room full of furs and overcoats and a pair of bored, middle-aged Frenchmen sat on stools, arguing football, and did not have any idea where a large Russian boy who had been working with them might've gone, nor any clear recollection of who might've hired him or what he might've been doing there and did Charlie want to pick up his coat now or later?

Dematerialized.

He sprinted into the center of the gardens, where the music was still listing from the bandstand and couples were still squared off, shuffling blithely in the grass beneath the pavilion. Every flicker of yellow made Charlie's head whip around as he searched for that diminutive Brit euphemistically known as Mouse, called that because of her stature but also, Charlie had learned, because of her ability to slip away into the smallest cracks and evade any pursuer who should be so unfortunate as to need to pursue her.

Disparu.

The Whiz Mob had pulled a nasher. The Whiz Mob was gone.

Surrounded by cooing lovers and networking socialites on the lawn of the Palais du Pharo, Charlie stood frozen. The sun had long gone down and the stars wheeled above him, cold and indifferent.

Tears sprang unbidden to his eyes. He felt as if every brick and granite block of the Palais was unmooring itself from its mortar and collapsing onto his shoulders as he replayed every incident, every moment he'd enjoyed for the last six weeks in the company of the Whiz Mob of Marseille.

"No, no, no, no, no," he said, and he realized he'd been repeating that one, sorry syllable for the last ten minutes. As if by repeating it he could undo everything, he could spool back time and start again, spool it back to that moment in the Place Jean Jaurès when his pen had turned into a stick and he'd chased that white-shirted boy down the alleyway.

An alarm had been raised back at the ballroom; a man stopped the orchestra in the pavilion to give an urgent announcement to the crowd. Charlie did not stay to listen. He knew where he needed to go. By the time the gala function at the Palais du Pharo had been reduced to little more than a crime scene, Charlie Fisher was on his way to the Panier.

The winding streets of the ancient neighborhood were unnervingly quiet as Charlie sprinted along them. He was certainly the only individual wandering the byways of the Panier in a tuxedo, and the few fellow pedestrians he passed eyed him with suspicious glares. He hadn't bothered with the unreliable city bus, but had instead run down the hill from the Palais du Pharo. He was completely out of breath when he caught the cross-quay ferry, along with a quartet of barhopping sailors and a tipsy fisherman. His tuxedo was slicked with sweat and clung to his body like a diving suit. The bent buildings of the Panier felt particularly misshapen and looming; he felt them watching him, laughing at him for his folly.

Was this the Whiz Mob's idea of a joke? Was this some sort of hazing ritual? Would they all be waiting for him, back at the scatter, ready to laugh off the whole episode and welcome him, officially, into the gang? As much as he wanted to believe this scenario, the stakes seemed too high. Whatever it was they'd stolen—this "cipher" his father had been given—was too important. What's more, they'd stolen it from Charlie's father himself. Was there not some directive in the Whiz Mob code that forbade targeting the relatives of fellow members? He searched his memory as he walked, trying to remember what exactly the Whiz Mob code was. Certainly it was not something written down; it was not some legally binding contract. It occurred to Charlie that the Whiz Mob code was about as real and tangible as a puff of smoke. It was whatever the Whiz Mob wanted it to be. And that idea, frankly, terrified him.

His heart was racing; he could feel it beating in his skull. He ran as much as his body allowed and then was forced to walk, quickly, along the cobblestoned streets until he arrived at Rue Sainte-Françoise. He disallowed his mind to consider the implications of what had just transpired; he only wanted to find the Whiz Mob.

When he scrambled into the plaza of the Bar des 7 Coins, the address he'd searched out those many weeks ago on his search to find Amir and his comrades, he came up short.

The café was not there.

The facade of the building had been meticulously erased. Where before the sign above the doors had advertised the Bar des 7 Coins, there was now an empty space. The windows were dark; the doors were locked. Peering inside, Charlie saw only emptiness. The tables and chairs were gone. His heart sank.

One of the panes of glass in the door had been broken, and he managed to fish his hand inside it and throw the lock. The door wheezed open and Charlie wandered inside.

"Bertuccio?" he hollered. "Pluto? Jackie?"

There was no answer.

He crossed to the other side of the bar, but found that the shelves behind it had been emptied. There was no Pernod bottle to hide a mechanism to open a secret door; what's more, there was no mechanism at all. He ran his fingers along the side of mirrored wall, trying to find the edge of the door, but there did not appear to be any doorway whatsoever. It was as if the doorway, and the pathway beyond, had been somehow *erased*.

He stumbled backward, away from the bar, and tripped on an overturned chair. He went spilling to the ground comically, scraping his elbow as he did so. A fine tear appeared in the sleeve of his jacket.

He quickly clambered upright, embarrassed by his fall even though there was no one there to witness it. A feeling of dread and self-loathing was growing inside him like some diseased flower. He ran back out the door into the small square in time to see an old woman dragging a cart down the road.

"*Excusez-moi!*" he shouted. The woman stopped abruptly and turned to look at him. He struggled for the French, saying, "*Le café— le Bar des Sept Coins—vous le connaissez?*"

The woman only looked at him blankly.

Charlie pointed frantically at the empty facade of the building behind him. "*Le Bar des Sept Coins. Le café, ici!*" He found that he was now shouting. "*Où est le café?*"

The woman, seemingly unthreatened by Charlie's tone of voice, simply shook her head and continued walking down the street. Her steps echoed against the ravine of tightly knit buildings, long after she'd disappeared around a corner.

Charlie was left alone, standing in front of the empty café, with the world pressing down on him like a vise.

Chapter

EIGHTEEN

C harlie stood where he was for a long time. He stood motionless, but his interior world was churning. He had become the projectionist of his memory's penny cinema; he was watching the film of the last six weeks flicker against the screen of his mind's eye.

The first reel showed him in the Place Jean Jaurès, on the fateful Tuesday in April, writing stories in his notepad. He watched it all transpire, though now he recognized Pluto and Jackie in the crowd; he saw Molly steering the man in the fedora. He saw Michiko off to the side, and, of course, the boy Amir, sitting down next to him. He watched himself running after Amir, providing his alibi to the police officers. But now he saw Amir bow perhaps too quickly to his demand to teach him the ways of the pickpocket. Amir hadn't been threatened by Charlie's ultimatum, not in the slightest. What was stopping Amir from simply ditching this curious American boy?

No time for answers; the next reel had clicked into place. There he was, wandering the Quai des Belges with Amir, learning prats. And then Jackie appeared—it had all been orchestrated, hadn't it? The business card with the address of the Bar des 7 Coins—had it been Amir who had given it to him? Or Jackie? With each memory coming to life on the screen, the tone of the film changed from comedy to tragedy. It then occurred to Charlie that this picture he'd been living for the last several weeks had never been a lighthearted caper, but a dark and sinister documentary, totally devoid of any charm.

And he had been its biggest fool.

He'd been the perfect stall. The ultimate steer to guide the Whiz Mob to its real goal: his father. And he'd done it without even knowing it.

The reality of the situation was almost too painful to bear.

Finally, Charlie began walking. He soon found himself down by the water, hidden amid the roaring crowds of tourists and sailors, the Saturday night crowd down by the Old Port. It was getting late, but the café crowds were alive and spilling into the streets. Charlie was a funny addition to the cheery scene along the port, with his drawn face and disheveled tuxedo, torn now at the elbow. Several people made catty comments to him as he passed; he did not care, but continued walking. He didn't know where he was going; it was like he was following a *dérive*, but one that allowed his sorrow and shame to lead the way as he grappled with the barrage of emotions and questions that were assaulting his mind.

He couldn't go home to his father. Not now. Not after what had happened. He could only imagine the scene: once the Palais du Pharo had been emptied and the grounds scoured for the culprits who'd stolen this invaluable document, he imagined his father being chauffeured home. Charlie wondered if the calls from the embassy and the State Department were already flooding in, and the silence of the car ride home would be his father's last refuge for a long, long while. He imagined his father, now home, sitting in his study with his head in his hands as the three phones on his desk, each color coded by the line, were ringing unceasingly.

Perhaps he was being cowardly, but Charlie was finding the honest choice—going home straightaway and confessing to the entire debacle—nearly impossible to consider. *He*, Charlie Fisher, hadn't stolen the Cipher! He'd been tricked! He was a pawn in a ludicrously long con that had been constructed by a crew of professional criminals. Charlie was as much the victim as anyone, right?

But who would possibly believe him when he'd been running with the pickpockets for the last six weeks, engaging in the very criminal activity that he was now condemning, with no recourse for actually returning any of the stolen goods to their rightful owners. This incredible skill that Charlie had developed, this sleight of hand he'd perfected after hours and hours of practice, wasn't just some cute party trick. It was a crime! You'll be shocked to know that this was the first time the *real* implications of his decisions were dawning on poor Charlie, and they were not sitting well.

Even if he were to feign ignorance, explain that Clark Kent and his friends had been conning him, it would not take too much investigation to discover that this entire "gang" was a fiction, and one that carried no water whatsoever. Raised by Pygmies? Girls with amputated legs? The more he thought about it, the more disgusted he was with himself that his lies had been so recklessly concocted.

If only he could walk back time. If only he could redo everything.

If only he would have heeded Amir's warning, to get off the whiz. This thought made Charlie stop in his tracks (a pair of stumbling GIs ran headlong into him, shouting some deprecation that Charlie did not register). Amir hadn't been the enemy, after all. He hadn't been Charlie's lone detractor, his cruel former friend, but had actually been intent on protecting him! And Charlie had forsworn him. Instead of taking Amir's advice, he had followed the blind will of his own greed and vanity.

The night wore on. Charlie barely perceived the passage of time, so great were his troubles. Along the Can o' Beer, the café crowds had thinned, and soon it was only the diehards in the all-night cafés who remained, hunched over their drinks at the quiet bars or slouched in booths, couples fallen together, cradling each other, whispering slurred lies into each other's ears. At this hour, the streets belonged to the insomniacs and the nocturnal crowd, all scuttering like cockroaches from the light of the streetlamps.

Charlie's tired legs finally led him to the doorway of a church, where he promptly collapsed and, huddled there, fell into a fitful sleep.

When he awoke, it was to the smell of bread.

Now, some of you may be aware of the phrase "a dark night of the soul." Perhaps some of you have, in your way, experienced such a night. A night where everything looks wrong, where everything you thought was right and honorable about the world turns out to be very much the opposite. On such a night, some kind of reckoning is at hand; where the veil is torn away and you can see all your foibles and faults for what they are. You will no doubt recognize that Charlie's soul had experienced a true whopper of such a long, dark night. However, the thing to remember is that such nights tend to serve an important purpose: one is liable to wake from them (or rise from them, if sleep is elusive) with a renewed purpose and a keener sense of right and wrong. And this is precisely what happened to Charlie when his eyes peeled open to the sight of sunlight and the smell of freshly baked bread.

The smell was coming from a nearby bakery, and it brought to mind a kind of spirit of rejuvenation in Charlie. He pondered the smell for some time, sitting as he was, crouched in the alcove of the church doorway, and why it made him feel suddenly renewed.

Consider: bread, once baked, only grows more stale over time. A baguette bought in the morning, by evening inevitably becomes a mere shade of the thing it was when it was newly hatched from the oven. There's a kind of inherent tragedy to this. However, every morning, like clockwork, before anyone with any sense has left their bed, the bakers are at it again, baking fresh loaves. Renewal. Reawakening.

It was this spirit that allowed Charlie to sit up and take in the world, that morning of all mornings.

He was also reminded of something. Something very relevant to his current predicament. The smell of the freshly baked bread transported him to a place, not too far from here, where he had stood with Amir and taken in a similar aroma. There, on the rooftop of the scatter. Amir had admitted something to him, hadn't he? He had expressed a longing to remove himself from the Whiz Mob and lead a simple life—perhaps working in a kitchen somewhere. Where had it been?

The more Charlie inhaled, the more the memory came back to him.

A Lebanese restaurant. The Vallon des Auffes, below the Corniche.

That was where Amir had gone.

Just south of the Old Port, along the craggy Corniche, time and tide had cut another ancient natural port into the rocky limestone of the coast. Like its larger sibling to the north, this port was similarly cluttered with fishing boats and small yachts, crowded together like matches in a matchbox. The basilica could still be seen, some ways off, from the Vallon des Auffes; large cliffs, now supporting modern apartment complexes and houses, made two walls of a ravine that bore its way toward the chapel's hilltop. The sun was still low in the sky by the time Charlie had made his way to the Vallon and was shuffling down the steps from the bridge that crossed the inlet's mouth.

At the far end of the port, a painted sign above a squat, windowed building advertised *Abdel Wahab*, and then, in smaller letters: *Restaurant Libanais*. The restaurant's only other competition were a port-side café and a pizzeria; Charlie had found his place. He was dismayed, however, to see a sign reading *FERMÉ* hanging inside the front door as he approached. Charlie stopped abruptly and frowned. It was Sunday, after all.

But there is no one more determined, you will find, than a boy wandering Marseille in a ripped tuxedo he was still wearing from the night before, who had slept the night in a church vestibule. No "closed" sign was going to deter Charlie now. He wandered around the side of the building and found a small alleyway that led to a kind of back patio. He could hear movement, the clatter of stones. Rounding a corner, he found himself in a small brick yard. A radio was tinnily broadcasting some kind of Arabic music. A man was crouched over a basin of mortar; he was repairing a stone wall. When he saw Charlie, he gave a little shout of surprise.

"*Désolé*," said Charlie, holding out his hands. "I'm looking for someone."

Charlie must've been quite a sight, because the man didn't immediately respond. He studied the tuxedoed boy for a moment before replying, "We are closed." The man had apparently guessed Charlie's nationality, because he spoke in English.

"I know," said Charlie. "I'm looking for Amir."

"Amir? I don't know Amir."

"A boy, about my age. Maybe he didn't give his name as Amir, but that's how I knew him."

The man paused for a second, eyed Charlie warily, and then shouted something in Arabic toward the back door of the restaurant. "Maybe you mean Faruq?" he said, turning back to Charlie.

"I don't know. He would've just started, maybe a few days ago. Did you hire anyone?"

The man nodded; someone appeared at the door of the restaurant. He was wearing a stained apron. When he saw Charlie, he slowly opened the door and walked out into the patio.

"Hi, Amir," said Charlie.

"You look terrible, Charlie," said Amir.

Charlie could only nod. He felt like he could barely move. Amir didn't wait for him to speak.

"It happened, didn't it?" asked Amir.

Charlie, again, nodded.

Amir turned to the stone-laying man and spoke a few words to him in Arabic; the man looked dismayed but ultimately was appeased. Amir undid his apron and draped it over one of the chairs; he waved Charlie into the doors of the empty restaurant.

"They're a good family," Amir was explaining as they walked through the kitchen; a woman was kneading bread while two children played at her feet. He greeted her and leaned down to tousle one of the kids' heads. "I'm just doing prep work, mostly. They're letting me stay in the apartment above the restaurant. Till I can afford my boat." A large cutting board covered in vegetables had been laid on a counter, presumably Amir's station. The air smelled of garlic and thyme. In the quiet dining room, Amir led Charlie to a table and, pulling out a chair, gestured for him to sit. He then walked over to the bar and returned with two full glasses of sparkling water.

"Drink, Charlie," he said. "You're a fright."

Charlie took the glass and downed it. His hands were trembling when he set the glass back on the table. It was only then that he was able to summon words. "They took it, Amir. They used me to take it."

Amir only nodded.

"Was it—all along?" Charlie found his words coming out like water from a broken fountain: in burbles and spits. Amir, however, was more than able to fill in the missing pieces.

"Yes," he said.

"Did you . . . ?"

"Yes," said Amir.

"And the whole time . . ."

"Uh-huh," said Amir.

Something broke in Charlie, just then. Like a shock of electric current, a feeling of anger exploded inside his chest and he abruptly shot his hand across the table and grabbed Amir by the throat, upsetting the boys' glasses of water. "Why didn't you tell me?" he shouted. "Why did you do this to me?"

Amir choked out a sound of surprise. He gripped Charlie's wrist and pulled it away from his neck. He was stronger than Charlie and was able to wrestle the boy's arm to the table. The woman from the kitchen appeared at the door to the dining room. A few words in Arabic were exchanged; the woman, apparently satisfied that Amir had the situation under control and this strange guest was not ransacking the restaurant, disappeared back through the door.

"Jesus, Charlie," said Amir, his hands massaging his throat. "You're going to get me fired."

"Where are they, Amir?" asked Charlie. "I need to find them."

"Who, the Whiz Mob?"

"*Yes*, the Whiz Mob."

"Oh, Charlie," said Amir. "They're long gone."

"Long gone—as in where? Some hole in Lyon? Paris?"

Amir shook his head. "Back to the school."

"The school? The School of Seven Bells?"

This time, the boy nodded.

"In Colombia?" Charlie half shouted.

Amir held out his hand, pleading for Charlie to keep his voice down. "Yes," he said.

Charlie found he couldn't speak for a moment. Then he said, "Why didn't you tell me?"

"Charlie, what are you talking about? I did tell you! I told you to get off the whiz!"

"I was never 'on the whiz,' was I, Amir? I was the chump all along. I was the sucker. You lied to me, even when you were trying to warn me."

"You don't understand," said Amir. "You don't understand how the Whiz Mob works. I couldn't rumble you. They'd have killed me. The School of Seven Bells doesn't muck about with rats, Charlie. Believe me, I wasn't happy about it. I agonized over it. I figured you'd get the hint, yeah? That you would listen to me, me of all people, me what got you into this mess. It was the best I could do."

"Why'd you do it? I mean, why'd you even bother to tell me? Why not just leave it alone? What was I to you? I was just a mark you were hustling."

"No, Charlie," said Amir. "Listen. I have been on the whiz for so long now, so long I barely remember my life before. I ain't yellow. But I felt for you, Charlie. Suddenly, all these things I've been taught, by the Headmaster, by the mob—it suddenly don't make a lot of sense, yeah? First time I met you, Charlie, sitting there, writing your little stories. Funny stories, yeah? I think: this boy don't deserve what's about to happen."

The mention of their first meeting sent a chill down Charlie's spine.

"So," interjected Charlie, "from the very beginning."

"Oh yeah," replied Amir. "That's how it works. The long con. The only way to get to this thing—what do you call it? The Rosenberg Cipher—is through Charles Fisher Senior, American consul general, at that party. That's the weak link, yeah? When it gets passed from that bejeweled pappy to your pa. That little window. That was the banner score. And the best way to get to Charles Fisher Senior at the party is through Charles Fisher Junior. Pluto put a bee on it, you know. He had a folder going."

"It was no accident, then, you sitting next to me. In Place Jean Jaurès."

"Oh, no. But Charlie, you are in a bad place right now. You don't need to hear this."

"Yes, I do," said Charlie defiantly. "I need to hear everything."

"Everything?"

"Everything."

Amir sucked at his teeth, eyeing Charlie with the same circumspection one might use when sizing up an angry dog in one's path. "Okay," he said. "Everything."

He took a deep breath.

"It was Pluto's folder, but Jackie was going to bring you in. That was the plan from the start. She was playing victim that day, and you were gonna be her savior. I thought it was a pea soup stall, that it was no good. See, I didn't think you'd take to it. And that day, I fanned something different, sitting next to you. I saw what you were writing, saw how you thought. Took you to be the sort of kid who'd got sick of being a diplomat's son. Someone who had a kind of longing to him."

"You got that from reading my writing?" asked Charlie incredulously.

"All pieces to the puzzle, Charlie. Remember: a good pickpocket is a sort of story finder. And an unhappy person, someone who has that kind of longing, well, they're the easiest pickings." He looked at Charlie bashfully. "Sorry," he said.

"Go on," prompted Charlie.

"So I strayed from the folder. Went rogue, so to speak. Took the gamble. Pinched your pen."

"But you ran," said Charlie. "How'd you know I'd catch you?"

"The deeper the grift, Charlie, the better the score," replied Amir. "It took some doing, believe me. Had to stop a few times, let you catch up. Almost lost you, just when I got nabbed by those whiz coppers."

"Policemen—buzzers on the take, right?"

Amir let out a small laugh. "Nah, they were legit. That wasn't ever part of the plan. See, in my folder, you catch up with me, stop me, and I offer to show you the whiz. Simple. No buzzers involved. But good thing they showed, otherwise I think I'd of lost you for sure. Anyway, I was in a spot of trouble there, for real, and you bailed me out."

"Bailed you out," repeated Charlie in disbelief. "I don't know what's real and what isn't."

"First time anyone ever stood up for me like that, tell the truth," said Amir. "You were an odd one, Charlie, I'll give you that much. Threw me for a bit of a loop."

Charlie didn't say anything.

Amir continued. "From there, things just kind of tumbled into place. Few times, I thought we'd curdled you. But you never knew, you never saw what was happening. You were in, hook, line, and sinker." He stopped, suddenly embarrassed by the insult. Charlie's face fell. "Like I said, you don't need to hear this right now, Charlie."

"Keep going," was all Charlie said in reply.

The lesson at the Old Port, Charlie's steering of the lawyers in front of the courthouse, the binging of the soldier's ring—all part of the chain of events to draw Charlie further in. And when they'd run into Jackie at the end of the day—she'd been waiting to connect for hours. The slip of the business card (it had been Jackie who had managed to kick the okus to Charlie), giving away the location of the scatter—it had all been part of the mechanics of the grift. Who makes business cards for a secret hideout? Amir had just recounted their history through the racehorse tip, to the day of the *dérive* and Pluto's supposedly genuine change of heart, when Charlie waved for the pickpocket to stop speaking.

It had all been an elaborate mirage. All to get to the jug touch, the Cipher.

Amir heeded Charlie's signal to stop. They sat in silence for some time, before Amir ventured, "But I liked you, Charlie. That was one thing I did not expect. That was the one thing Pluto and the rest didn't manage to steer. You were funny and smart. And you made me feel smart, too. That wasn't supposed to happen. You're part of the sucker class—the chump world—you ain't supposed to have feelings. But I guess I never got so close to a chump, did I? I never had friends who weren't on the whiz, like me. See, on the whiz we might be family, but we ain't friends. You were my friend, Charlie."

Were those tears coming to Amir's eyes?

"Came to a point," the boy continued, sniffing, steeling himself, "you were in, you were snared—and I had to get out. I couldn't do it no more, yeah? Couldn't watch it happen to my friend. First thing I think to do was get you off the whiz. Somehow. Figured you'd listen to me, the one what turned you out in the first place, yeah? But you were too far gone. You were too deep in the grift. All that was left was for me to declare out. So I did."

Again, silence. The sound of rocks being laid, heavily, one on top of the other, could be heard from the patio. A distant radio squelching. Two children playing with cars in the kitchen.

Finally, Charlie spoke:

"I need to get it back," he said.

"You ain't getting it back, Charlie," said Amir.

It was clear Charlie wasn't listening. "And you're going to help me."

"Why am I going to do that?"

"Because you owe me," said Charlie. "Because you're my friend, and you let me down. Want to make that right? Then help me get back the Cipher."

Amir kneaded his chin absently. His palm then crept northward and began squeezing his entire face like he wanted to erase everything—himself, Charlie, the room—everything. "Charlie," he said through the cracks of his fingers, "that would mean . . ."

"I know what that means," Charlie said, interrupting. "Going to the school. And you can take me there."

"The School of Seven Bells is in South America, Charlie. You study geography with your tutor, don't you? Other side of the globe."

"I don't care if it's at the North Pole. I've got to get that envelope back."

"And what if you do manage to get there, how are you going to get this envelope? Ask nicely?"

Charlie paused. "I haven't figured that part out yet."

"This is stupid, Charlie. This is the stupidest thing I've ever heard. In a very, very long line of stupid things I have heard in my life. You never met the Headmaster. He don't take kindly to . . . Well, he don't take kindly to just about anything. I've seen him stick a kid in a windowless dungeon for two weeks, no food, for less. Much, much less. So much less that this is not even a fair comparison!"

Charlie was unmoved; he stared at Amir defiantly.

"What you're suggesting, Charlie," said Amir, rubbing his temples as he did so, "because I want to get this perfectly clear. What you're suggesting is that we find a way to Colombia, *South America*— by our own wits, I imagine, since your poor pa isn't likely to spring for plane tickets—and then somehow make our way to the school, which is a fortress, Charlie, in a secret location on top of a mountain in the middle of a jungle, and you want me to take you there, to this fortress, even though I would likely get strung up just for *telling you* that it's on a mountain in the middle of the jungle, Charlie, never mind actually *taking you there, Charlie,* and then you want to somehow confront this master thief, this master thief who turns out *other* master thieves, *Charlie,* and you expect him to just give you this thing, this piece of paper that he has sent out his most crack Whiz Mob to get for him, *Charlie,* this thing that he plans to do who-knows-what with, just because you *ask him nicely,* and you will expect to go back, unharmed, to Marseille, to return this *piece of paper* to your father. Is this what you are suggesting? *Charlie?*"

"Yes," said Charlie.

"And I am expected to do this because I am your friend and this is what friends do for other friends, yeah?"

"Yes," said Charlie.

"Okay," said Amir placidly.

Charlie was taken aback. "Okay?" he asked.

"NO, NOT OKAY," shouted Amir. He abruptly stood up, his chair sliding backward across the tile floor. He began pacing a very small circuit, like a windup toy in a shoe box. His voice was tense as he spoke. "I like you, Charlie. I like you a lot. But this is just too far. Too far." He then began speaking inwardly, as if he were addressing himself. "Come be on the whiz, they said. Enroll at the School of Seven Bells, they said. Learn a valuable trade. Travel. See the world. Reap great financial rewards." He slammed his palms down on the table, giving Charlie a jolt. "I did *not* sign up for this sort of thing."

Charlie did not reply.

"Do you *know* what they do to a cannon who throws their mob? Do you? It's not pretty. And you're talking about me throwing the whole freaking school, Charlie. I can't, like, even imagine what the punishment would be. My brain won't get that dark."

"They'd never have to know," said Charlie.

"What do you mean, they'd never have to know?"

"Just lead me to the place. And leave me. I'll figure it out from there."

Amir studied his friend closely. "I took you for a smart kid, Charlie. A kid with a lot going on up here. Private tutor. Wealthy family. Oh, how I thought that looked grand."

"Just help me get there, Amir. That's all I ask."

"And what about you? What do you think is going to happen to you when you waltz up to the gates of the school, saying, 'Hey there, can I have my daddy's envelope back? *Pretty please?*' You don't know what these people are capable of."

Charlie swallowed, hard. "That's for me to worry about."

"Oh, Charlie," said Amir. "You're crazy."

"Help me, Amir," said Charlie. "You owe me that much, at least."

Defeated, Amir slumped back down in his chair and, crossing his arms on the tabletop, proceeded to lay his head down on the backs of his wrists, like a kid playing Seven Up.

"Come on, Amir."

"I'm not talking to you," came the reply.

"You . . . ," began Charlie.

"Shhh!" shot back Amir. "I'm pretending you don't exist."

Charlie paused, scratched his cheek. He leaned forward. "You said you want a boat?"

"Mmmmm," was all that could be heard from the cocoon of Amir's arms. It sounded like the muffled cry of a dying badger.

"There'll no doubt be some kind of reward," said Charlie.

"Mmmm."

"Probably a big reward."

"Mmmm-hmm."

"Probably enough to buy a pretty nice little boat. Cozy sleeping berth. Little cookstove."

Amir's head emerged from its dugout. "AM/FM radio?"

"Every channel on the frequency," said Charlie, leaning even closer. The two boys' heads were separated by mere inches.

"Eighteen-footer? Nice wooden mast?"

"The finest Canadian pine."

Charlie was now imitating Amir's position and was cradling his chin against his knuckles. The two boys' eyes were locked together. They didn't speak for several moments. Finally, Amir said, "You're not going to let this one go, are you?"

"Not on your life," said Charlie.

Chapter
NINETEEN

And so Amir and Charlie were out on the street, walking away from the Abdel Wahab restaurant, Amir's ever-so-temporary place of employment. There had been a discussion between Amir and his employers before they'd left, but Charlie had been unable to decipher it. Amir's side of the conversation had been long and impassioned and, undoubtedly, touched a little on the nature of friendship and the kind of loyalties it engenders. It must've been persuasive, because by the time Charlie and Amir were walking out the front door, the husband-and-wife proprietors of Abdel Wahab were in the doorway to the kitchen, waving dishrags in a fond farewell. Fittingly, the couple were to receive their first Michelin star the following week. The restaurant is still there, now under the ownership of the two children we saw playing with cars in the kitchen. You should visit sometime. The *mujaddara* is delicious.

Outside, Charlie took in the scene. The boats in the port. The seagulls wheeling.

Perhaps it was because he'd slept on the streets for the first time in his life. Perhaps it was because of a sudden and overwhelming feeling of devotion to his father and to his family, or perhaps it was because of a powerful desire for revenge. Perhaps Charlie had experienced a sudden flood of civic pride and was now determined to set right what he had initially set so wrong—for whatever reason, he was transformed. Where the night before, his development as a pickpocket had only caused him pain and humiliation, he now chose to channel that self-sufficiency into a banner score of his own, to return the Rosenberg Cipher to its rightful owner. His was a noble quest. A quest for his family, his nation.

"So," said Charlie.

"So," said Amir.

"How do we get there?" asked Charlie.

Amir planted his palm against his face.

"You've been doing that a lot this morning," said Charlie.

"*How do we get there?*" parroted Amir.

"It's an innocent question," said Charlie.

"How much money do you have?"

Charlie plumbed the depths of his pockets. His hands surfaced with fifteen franc coins, a twenty-franc note, and some candy wrappers. "Not much. You?"

"What I'm carrying don't figure," said Amir. "You haven't really thought this through, have you?"

"I guess I came up with the idea on the spot."

"If you're going to folder this, Charlie, you need to put a proper bee on it. So how we are getting to South America? We are in France."

"Airport?"

"Bam. There's the Charlie I knew."

Charlie bristled. "No need to patronize."

"First off, lose the tuxedo jacket. You look like some kind of casino grifter after a bad night. That's better. And the tie." Amir scrutinized Charlie's new look. "This is never going to work."

"We don't have time," said Charlie.

Amir nodded, apparently satisfying himself. "It'll have to do."

They climbed the stairs to the Corniche; the wind whipped over the edge of the cliff side. There, in front of the great stone arch of the Monument aux Morts de l'Armée d'Orient, a wedding party was being photographed. The guests' emptied cars were lined up along the Corniche like a great procession. Charlie didn't have to be prompted.

"Can you drive?" he asked Amir.

Amir shot Charlie a disappointed look. "What do you think?"

As it turned out, Amir could only *sort of* drive. He was barely tall enough to reach the pedals, even with the seat of the convertible

MG pushed all the way forward. The basic rule of French traffic law seemed to be elusive to the young driver, and the two of them inspired a stream of protests from their fellow motorists as they sped along the Corniche, northward toward the Marseille Provence Airport. They'd "borrowed" the car from one of the wedding guests who had been so careless as to leave its keys in the ignition. Charlie had insisted on leaving a note weighted down by a rock in the car's former parking spot, declaring: *Nat'l global emergency; had to take auto. Retrieve at Mrsl/Prv Airport. C & A.* Speaking as they drove, they were forced to shout over the howl of the wind in the open-top automobile.

"I CAN GET YOU CLOSE TO THE SCHOOL," said Amir, "BUT IT'S NOT LIKE I CAN WALK YOU UP TO THE GATES. IT AIN'T SAFE FOR ME."

"HOW MUCH TIME DO WE HAVE?" asked Charlie. "DO YOU KNOW WHAT THE HEADMASTER WILL DO WITH THE CIPHER?"

"I DON'T KNOW," replied Amir. "WE WERE JUST INSTRUCTED TO GET IT, BRING IT BACK, YEAH? I THINK MAYBE HE WILL SELL IT."

"SELL IT?"

"SELL IT. SAY, YOU HAVE YOUR PASSPORT, RIGHT?"

Charlie looked at Amir blankly.

Amir slammed on the brakes.

Forty five minutes later, after a dizzying drive through the

interior avenues of Marseille, a stealthy breach of the Fisher security perimeter and the retrieval of Charlie's worn passport book from his bedroom underwear drawer, the two boys were able to resume their half-yelled conversation.

"OR HE'S GOT SOME OTHER USE FOR IT," Amir continued. "DO YOU KNOW WHAT IT IS, EVEN?"

"WHAT, THE CIPHER?"

"YEAH."

"I DON'T REALLY," said Charlie.

"WHATEVER IT IS, IT MUST BE IMPORTANT. IF YOUR PA HAD IT AND THE HEADMASTER WANTED IT, IT'S GOT TO BE BIG. WHAT HE WANTS TO DO WITH IT, THERE'S NO REAL TELLING."

"I'M NOT YELLING," said Charlie.

"WHAT?"

"YOU SAID, NO NEED YELLING. I'M JUST TRYING TO TALK OVER THE WIND."

"I SAID *NO REAL TELLING*."

"WHAT?"

Amir ignored him. "EITHER WAY, WE DO HAVE TO MOVE FAST. I THINK THE WHIZ MOB WILL JUST BE GETTING BACK TO THE SCHOOL. IF WE MOVE QUICK, YOU'LL GET TO HIM BEFORE HE'S DONE ANYTHING WITH IT."

"WATCH OUT!" shouted Charlie, even though he was already shouting. Amir had let the car drift from their lane and had encroached dangerously on the space of a neighboring Renault. He yanked hard on the steering wheel and the convertible lurched back into the right lane. The Renault let out a petulant *honk* as it sped by. When Amir and Charlie did finally arrive, some thirty minutes later, at the front curb of the Marseille Provence Airport, Charlie nearly tumbled out of the car to kiss the pavement, as if he'd survived a trip into the stratosphere.

"Look natural," was Amir's suggestion as they fell together and began walking swiftly toward the concourse.

Now, in our day and age we've become accustomed to the impenetrable gauntlet that is the modern airport security apparatus. Long lines, grumpy travelers, and grumpier airport personnel. In the spring of 1961, it was an altogether different environment. To some people's minds, this was the golden age of commercial air travel: to fly was convenient; it was comfortable and very efficient. Moreover, it was downright fashionable. A person had no more trouble boarding an airplane to some far-flung city than they would hopping on a Greyhound bus, and it was a great deal more *fabulous*. Since the Marseille Provence Airport served as the major hub for most all of the finer destinations in the south of France, the scene that greeted Amir and Charlie as they abandoned their borrowed sports car and walked through the glass doors into the airport was not unlike some kind of

Rich, Beautiful People convention. To that point: the expense of air travel in 1961 was perhaps the only resemblance to its modern-day form, and Charlie, scanning the midmorning rush, saw a decidedly moneyed crowd, one that would not miss a few one-way tickets to Colombia.

"Paris," whispered Amir, steering the tip. "We'll need to get to Paris first. There is no Colombia flight from Marseille."

"Right," said Charlie.

Together they wandered up to a small congregation of travelers who were studying a clacking timetable. There, in black-and-white tiles, were the times and gates for departures to various cities. Paris was clearly a prime destination, as there were several listings for Paris-bound flights. Charlie stood elbow to elbow with Amir, waiting for his signal. Looking over at Amir, he saw the boy was not watching the timetable, but was instead intent on the eyes of the watchers. One of the travelers, a middle-aged man in a fine blue sports coat, turned away from the board and began walking to his gate. Amir began walking in the opposite direction.

"Wait," hissed Charlie. "Where are you going?"

"I've got my ticket," said Amir.

"How did you get one?" But he knew the answer; undoubtedly the man in the blue sports coat would be arriving at his gate empty-handed. "Well, I don't."

"Well, you better get one, yeah? My flight leaves in . . ." He pulled a rectangular piece of paper from his pocket and looked at it. "Thirty minutes."

Charlie flashed a glare at Amir before returning to the departure board. He, like Amir, began illicitly watching the darting eyes of the board's captivated audience as the timetable whirred and clicked, presenting the latest times and gates. He heard one woman ask a neighbor if they knew when the next flight for Paris was; Charlie began to steer the woman but then decided that if her name was on the ticket, the likelihood of his getting caught would be greater. He needed a ticket from a man. Three fedora-wearing businessmen wielding briefcases had arrived at the board, and Charlie moved toward them. They seemed to be commuters, preparing for some sort of work trip. Since Charlie deduced that activity would likely be taking them to the commercial capital of France, he began to quietly fan them. And while their suits sported an array of potential pockets, Charlie knew just the one to reef: the coat jerve—or, in sucker's parlance, the ticket pocket.

He fanned a coat jerve on a middle-aged man. It was fastened against the fabric of the jacket by a button, and he was forced to carefully unslough the flap before he could hook his fingers into the pit. There, he quickly found gold: the feel of fresh cardstock. He stepped in, toward the man, as if he were trying to get closer to the board, which caused the man to step away. With a word of apology, Charlie allowed the motion of the man to pull the boarding pass from the man's pit, and he was away with the piece of paper. Once he'd traveled a safe distance from the scrum, he scrutinized his score.

His fanning had proved true: it was a ticket to Paris, leaving in thirty minutes.

"Nice work," said Amir.

They moved quickly toward the gate, cutting through the current of travelers like two canoes running upstream. They arrived just as the attendants began sweeping the passengers onto the plane; Charlie, upon reaching his seat, immediately asked for his seat to be changed (citing fear of air travel) in order to avoid running into any of the original ticket holder's business associates. A few more seat switches later, Charlie and Amir were sitting next to each other. When the door finally closed and the plane pushed away from the gate, they each breathed a sigh of relief. Charlie promptly fell asleep; the two hours of travel quickly passed and they were soon on the tarmac in Paris.

"Wake up," said Amir. "The tip's still on."

The Aéroport de Paris Nord resembled the Marseille Provence only in that it, too, was an airport—and that was where the similarities ended. Where a relative trickle of passengers chartered their course through the Marseille airport, a flood descended upon the Paris concourses. Amir and Charlie fell into the current and let it carry them along. While they walked, Amir gave a hushed instructional on their next moves—it was apparent that while Charlie had been sleeping, Amir had been foldering the next big bing: Paris to Bogotá.

"It ain't as simple as banging a ticket off some bates, yeah? Them commuter flight tickets are all generic. They don't put names on 'em. Not so for transatlantic flights. We got to make our own way."

"How do we do that?"

"Come on," said Amir, as they reached an intersection in the concourse. The front doors of the terminal could be seen from where they stood; a line of passengers queued, waiting to be ticketed for flights. Amir led Charlie to a desk, behind which a sign proudly displaying the logo for *AIR FRANCE* had been hung. Between the desk and the logo, a smug-looking attendant in an Air France uniform sat.

"There's our chump," said Amir quietly.

"He's not likely to have a Paris-Bogotá ticket on him," said Charlie.

Amir fixed Charlie with a glare. "Sure, but he's holding the boarding passes."

"Ah," said Charlie. "I see what you're getting at."

They briefly conferred, there in the terminal lobby, before deciding on their tack. Once they'd agreed, Charlie approached the desk.

"Hello," said Charlie to the man. "I'm traveling with my father. He's over with our luggage. He's asked me to purchase passage for two to Bogotá, Colombia."

"Certainly," said the desk clerk. Using a key attached to his belt, the clerk unlocked a drawer beneath the desk and slid it open. He pulled out a rectangular pad of paper and set it on the desktop. Charlie glanced down at it; it was a sheaf of empty boarding passes.

"The seven o'clock flight," said Charlie.

The clerk flipped open a large, spiral-bound book and began poring through it. "Ah, yes," he said. "There are still seats available."

Just then a ruckus broke out. Someone was shouting in a loud, accusatory tone. Some ten feet behind Charlie, a young Arab boy was tussling with a man in a sports coat.

"He's got it right there, on his wrist," the boy shouted. "Thief! *Voleur!*"

The Air France clerk, hearing this commotion, apologized briefly to Charlie and ran over to help mediate the confrontation that was currently taking place right in front of his counter. The pad of empty boarding passes had been left.

Charlie turned around to spectate; Amir was holding on to the man's arm, keeping him a reluctant captive while the Air France clerk waved over the airport security. "What has happened?" asked the clerk, in English.

"He stole my friend's watch," said Amir. "I saw that man bump into him. Next thing I know, I look over and he's wearing his watch!"

Charlie walked quickly to Amir's side. "What's going on?"

"Where's your watch, Charlie?" asked Amir. He reached over and pushed up the sleeve of Charlie's left arm; his wrist was bare.

"It's gone!" shouted Charlie. "My Rolex! My father gave it to me!"

"He took it," said Amir, pointing at the man. "I saw him bump up against you. I saw it happen."

"I did not," said the man, aghast. "I did no such thing."

"Show us your wrist," demanded Amir. When the man refused, he said again, "Come on, show us your wrist, then."

Sporting a look of disbelief, the man conceded and pushed back the sleeve of his jacket. There, on his wrist, was Charlie's silver watch. The man looked as surprised to see it there as anyone. The airport security pushed forward; the man quickly fumbled with the snap and dropped it to the floor as if it were a poisonous snake. "I—I . . . ," he stammered, "I have no idea how such a thing . . . I don't know how that got there."

Charlie knelt down and picked up the watch from the carpet. He flipped it over in his fingers and said, "Yep, it's mine." By this time, a policeman had arrived. Charlie brandished the back of the watch for his benefit. "It's got my name on it. Tenth birthday present."

"Arrest this man," said Amir. The policeman moved toward the accused, prepared to follow Amir's suggestion, before Charlie stopped him.

"I don't wish to press charges," said Charlie.

"You don't?" asked the policeman.

"You don't?" asked Amir.

"No," said Charlie. "He seems like a nice guy. He deserves a second chance. Besides, Amir, we have a flight to make. We can't be delayed."

Amir looked genuinely disappointed as the man was led away by the police officer, presumably to be asked a series of questions and to be released once it was clear that the man was not, in fact, a thief. The Air France clerk turned to Charlie and, ironing the front of his suit with his hands, said, "I do apologize for this, sir. Do you wish to complete your purchase?"

"I need to find my father," said Charlie. "I need to tell him what's happened."

"Understandable," said the clerk. "Please do come find me when you're prepared to finish the transaction."

The man returned to his desk; Charlie watched him greet the next customer after tidying the surface of his desk. He placed the pad of boarding passes back into its secured desk drawer, though the clerk could not have ascertained that the pad was lighter by exactly two passes. Charlie and Amir quickly walked away, into the swirling crowds.

In the men's restroom, they squeezed into a toilet stall. Charlie produced the two purloined boarding passes; Amir searched his pockets for a writing utensil.

"Shoot," he said. "You got something to write with?"

Charlie gave a sardonic smile before reaching into his pocket and pulling out the Sheaffer Imperial. They shared a look, briefly, before the pen once again traded hands.

Charlie had the necessary information written on the back of his hand; he'd gleaned it from one of the departure boards in the main concourse. "Bogotá, Colombia," he said. "Flight 458. Leaving seven thirty p.m."

"Gate?"

"Twelve. What should we put down for the seats?"

"Doesn't matter," said Amir. "Call it a clerical error if we double book. What's the flight code?"

"Ah, right. 4B22AF9."

"Got it." He handed one of the passes to Charlie. Putting the cap back on the Sheaffer Imperial, he twirled it a few times between his fingers before handing it, too, back to its rightful owner.

"No," said Charlie. "You should keep it. I did give it to you, after all."

The boy paused, holding the pen in his hand, before he flipped it into his pocket. "Thanks, Charlie." Amir then shook his sleeve aside to read the time on the watch on his wrist. "We've got an hour. Care to grab a bite?"

Charlie held out his hand.

"What?" asked Amir.

"Watch," said Charlie.

"Oh," said Amir, undoing the Rolex's clasp from his wrist and letting it fall into his opposing palm. He handed it back to Charlie sheepishly.

. . .

It was to be an eighteen-hour flight, including a planned pit stop in Senegal for refueling. Charlie and Amir quietly settled in for the ride. Thankfully, the flight had been undersold and the seats they'd chosen remained unspoken for. About an hour into the flight, a stewardess distributed postcards to each of the passengers that they might keep their loved ones at home apprised of their travels. Amir handed his to Charlie and then promptly put his chair back, nestling into the headrest to sleep. Charlie looked out the window for a time, watching the patchwork of pastoral French farmland far below with its errant tufts of cotton floating between, before setting his pen to the postcard to write.

> *Dear Father,*
> *Don't worry about me. I'm safe. I'm sorry for everything.*
> *I've got to set some things to right. Home soon.*
> *Love, Charlie*

He reread the words a few times, his eyes straying on that word *love*. It was a word he'd never used in relation to his father. He imagined his father, now, sitting in his study. He imagined the sun setting, its red glow visible through the plantation blinds of the windows. He imagined that his father hadn't turned on the lights in the room yet, and the gloom of dusk was settling on everything in the study, masking it. He imagined his father not even noticing this, sitting in his desk chair and staring out the window. He imagined the telex machine clattering away in the corner, spilling sheaves of ticker tape, unread, onto the wood-tiled floor. There was an ache in Charlie's chest, imagining the scene, an ache he was barely able to dispel in order to appear presentable to the stewardess when she arrived to take the finished postcard.

"It will arrive tomorrow," explained the stewardess. "We send them from a return flight at the stopover."

"Thanks," said Charlie. He then rested his head against the wall of the airplane and stared out the window as the ground below the plane became covered in a pinkish blanket of clouds. It soon disappeared altogether in blackness. He fell asleep.

He slept fitfully, crammed against the wall of the plane and enduring the frequent heaves of turbulence that rocked the cabin. When he finally gave in to wakefulness, it was still dark. The light was on in the seat next to him; he looked over to see Amir awake and stirring cream into a Styrofoam cup of coffee.

"Did you sleep?" asked Charlie groggily.

"A bit, yeah," said Amir. "You?"

"I think so."

Amir stirred at his coffee; the cream had long since dispersed, but still he continued stirring. He seemed to be winding something, or wishing something unwound. "Not too late to back out, you know," he said.

"It is," said Charlie.

"No one's gonna fault you for this. You're a kid, Charlie. That was part of the reason the folder was so tight—you weren't gonna be harmed. Kid chumps get forgiven; not so for grown-ups."

"I have a responsibility, Amir. I have to do it." Charlie was implacable.

Amir sighed. "Okay," he said. "Then here's the deal. We're going to catch the bus to a village called El Toro. Some ways out of town, there's a crossroads. At the crossroads, there's a shack of a shop, a little bodega. That's where I leave you, yeah? I won't be able to get any closer to the school without being spotted. If you want me to make it out of this little caper of yours—"

"I do," interrupted Charlie.

"If you want me to make it out, you don't say a word about me. I'm not even here right now. I'm rolling out dough at Abdel Wahab right now, got it? Which is what I should be doing, anyway." He lifted the coffee cup to his mouth and took a long slug.

"El Toro," prompted Charlie. "Little bodega."

"Right. Talk to the counter boy. Tell him you want a Coke and a lime in a paper cup."

"Coke and a lime . . ."

"In a paper cup. It's very important that you order this exact thing, yeah?"

"Got it. In a paper cup."

"See, the bodega is a kind of secret receiving station for the school. No one can know where the exact location of the school is, unless they're proper on the whiz, turned out, yeah? But occasionally someone from the straight world will show up, wanting to join or needing some help from the Headmaster. People travel from all over—all sorts of folks. They want something from the school; locals petition the school for this and that. The Headmaster does what he can." Amir took another sip of his coffee. "Order your Coke with lime; someone will come to take you to the school. You might want to think about what you plan to do from that point on."

"Of course," scoffed Charlie. "Already done."

Amir eyed him suspiciously.

"I know exactly what I'm doing, Amir," said Charlie, as if speaking it were enough to make it so. He turned his head and looked out into the blackness of the window. The hum of the airplane engine droned around them and the stewardesses walked the aisle, collecting empty glasses and finished postcards, as the sun rose somewhere, distantly, over the wing of the plane. The coast of Africa was below them; the whole Atlantic lay before them and their final destination.

Did he? Did he know?

Chapter
TWENTY

Colombia hove into sight below the plane; Charlie watched it appear, all dense forests of thick green, as far as the eye could see. The city of Bogotá grew out of this blanket of trees like a toy construction built inside some teeming native garden. It was early morning, though to Charlie it felt like time had stopped altogether. The last thirty-six hours had been such a blur, between sleeping in the alcove of the church, to finding Amir, to their binging two flights to Paris and Bogotá. Sleep no longer seemed like a thing he needed; he was neither hungry nor thirsty. He only wanted his revenge.

They filed off the plane, two in a long line of zombielike passengers, transformed that way by the duration of the flight and the transference of time zones. The air was thick and sodden and it enveloped Charlie like cellophane as he stepped down the gang-way onto the tarmac. A barrier of tall, crooked trees surrounded the landing strip; beyond them, a few high-rises dared breach the lowest-hanging clouds of a gray sky. Inside the terminal, women had laid out blankets and were selling handwoven baskets and cornhusk dolls. While the rest of the passengers waited for their luggage to be delivered, Charlie and Amir walked swiftly to the front doors of the airport. A brightly colored bus, looking as if it had seen action in both world wars and lived to tell the tale, was parked out front. Amir approached the driver and spoke to him in Spanish. When he'd had his answer, he turned to Charlie.

"This is our bus," said Amir.

Charlie waved him closer and said quietly, "Do you want to steer a chump for the fare?"

"Charlie," said Amir. "Look around. Who you going to bing from?"

Sure enough, a casual survey of their surroundings would be enough to quash that idea very quickly. The men and women gathering at the bus stop clearly did not have two pennies to rub together, let alone the sort of cash that would warrant them a target for two kids on the whiz. The two boys gathered the cash they had in their pockets and retreated to the currency exchange kiosk, a corrugated-tin-roofed affair, where they were given an exploitative rate on a few small stacks of pesos. Returning to the open doors of the bus, Amir paid out the full fare for the both of them.

"El Toro," the bus driver repeated to Amir, once he'd counted out the cash he'd been given and had issued two ticket stubs. *"Sí."*

The ancient, lumbering vehicle made several more stops before it hit the open road, taking on a wild cross section of this Latin American country's people: young men traveling for work, businessmen in suits they tried desperately to keep clean in the bus's down-at-heel environment, women with crying babies, women with quiet babies, old native men in colorful garb, a young married couple cradling two chickens. Charlie almost forgot the near-impossible quest before him while watching each of these fellow bus riders and imagining what fantastic story they might engender in his writing notebook.

Amir and Charlie were among the first passengers to board the bus; they were the last remaining when, some two hours later, the bus trundled into a dirt square in the middle of a few forlorn buildings and came to a wheezing stop. Charlie peered out of the mud-streaked window, marveling at the wild green jungle that rose up around the little hamlet like it was about to swallow everything whole.

"El Toro!" shouted the driver from the front of the bus.

Amir gave Charlie an elbow in the rib. "This is us," he said.

"This is El Toro?" asked Charlie, astounded that so few structures could constitute a village.

The driver must've registered the shock in Charlie's voice, because he let out a loud guffaw and said something, presumably demeaning, in Spanish. Amir didn't bother to translate it for his friend.

They stepped down into the dirt of El Toro like two astronauts newly arrived on the moon. Their Colombian surroundings enveloped them; Charlie felt as if he were hallucinating, so great were the heaviness of the humid air and the gravity of his journey bearing down on his mind. The boys' jet lag only contributed to this feeling of alienness. Before they'd barely touched down, the bus doors slammed closed behind them and the ancient vehicle lumbered away, its gears grinding audibly as it disappeared into the jungle. A spray of mud from one of the tires shellacked Charlie's left pant leg—but at this point, what did it really matter?

A flock of chickens pecked at the bare dirt of the road. A man in a cowboy hat appeared from the doorway of one of the shanties and eyed them suspiciously.

"This way," said Amir quietly. "Let's do this fast."

The road through the village jogged a few times before it branched in two just beyond the last structure; they followed the leftward tine of this Y intersection, opposite the one their bus had negotiated. A few more hovels appeared in the trees periodically, by the side of the road, but soon they were beyond all sign of human habitation. The mountains, thick with alien-looking trees, loomed about them. The gray clouds hung low. Mist clung to the topmost branches of the forest canopy. Birdsong, strange and loud, echoed through the valleys and ravines. It was an ominous scene. Charlie, for the first time in his and Amir's wild odyssey, felt something like fear and loneliness.

They walked for several miles, dodging the puddles and fallen tree limbs that made the road more like an obstacle course than any kind of usable thoroughfare. Charlie's pants had become thoroughly checkered with mud flecks and his dress shirt had become torn at the elbows. He'd begun to look like someone who'd survived a bear attack at an awards ceremony. With every mile they walked, Amir became increasingly agitated, his eyes ever straying into the dense brush on the side of the road. His pace had quickened; whenever Charlie had fallen too far behind, he would whisper some loud admonition to keep up, to keep pace. Charlie did his best to accommodate his guide.

They must've climbed in elevation, as the mist that had hovered only in the treetops had descended on the road itself, blotting out their surroundings and enveloping them in a dense, warm haze. Walking the road was not unlike navigating some thick cloud bank.

They didn't speak for some time; after a few more miles had passed, Amir said tensely, "So you're just not going to tell me, is that it?"

"What?" asked Charlie.

"Your plan."

"I wouldn't want to disappoint you," said Charlie.

"I get it."

"You do?"

"You don't actually have a plan."

Charlie didn't answer.

"Do you?" pressed Amir, his voice rising.

Charlie chose to remain silent, his eyes intent on the road in front of him. He'd had a lot of time to ponder Amir's question. In fact, he happened to share his friend's curiosity. Thing was, he was still so exhilarated by the fact that he was *doing something*, that he had, you'll perhaps be surprised to know, not entirely made up his mind as to what he was doing. You may know the feeling: when you're stuck on something or trying to take on a particularly daunting obstacle, even the illusion of progress can provide some relief. For instance: say you decided that you wanted to write a novel, but realized as you began that novel writing, despite its appearances, is no easy task. And so you press open the first blank page of your composition notebook, write *CHAPTER ONE* in your very best penmanship at the top margin, and call it good for the day, satisfied that at least *some* progress was made.

There will be people who will tell you that it is foolhardy to believe this feeling.

Those people are wrong.

And like every first-time novelist before him, Charlie had written a very large and beautiful *CHAPTER ONE* at the top of his plan to wrest the Rosenberg Cipher from its unlawful owners; he had enough faith in his storytelling ability that the rest would fall into place.

Wouldn't it?

"This is it," said Amir, stopping abruptly in the middle of the road and interrupting Charlie's brief reverie. "This is as far as I go."

Charlie looked up to see that the road had begun to widen; an intersecting road cut across the mud at a perpendicular angle. Marking one of the corners of the crossroads was a small tin shed. It seemed to almost grow out of the jungle itself, or as if the surrounding forest was intent on reclaiming it: great tree boughs and vines had wrapped themselves around the walls and roof like tentacles. Charlie looked back at Amir; Amir nodded, his face lined with worry. His feet were agitating in the dirt of the road; he was antsy to leave.

"Here?" asked Charlie.

"I gotta go, Charlie," said Amir. "I'm risking a lot just being here right now." He began to turn to leave.

"Wait," said Charlie. "I want you to have this." He undid the watchband at his wrist and dangled the silver Rolex from his fingers. "If I don't make it back."

"Oh, Charlie," said Amir. "I told you, don't do this thing."

"This'll be enough to get you started on your boat. I'm sure those nice folks at Abdel Wahab will have you back." Charlie was holding out the watch, waiting for Amir to take it.

Amir accepted the watch wordlessly. "What about you?" he said, after a beat.

"I'll work it out," said Charlie. "Don't worry about me. You shouldn't stick around."

Amir nodded. He fastened the watch at his wrist, admired it there for a moment. He then looked up at Charlie. "So long, Charlie."

"So long, Amir," said Charlie.

Amir smiled and gave a small wave. He then turned and began walking quickly the way they'd come. He soon disappeared into the mist.

Charlie took a deep, invigorating breath, coughed once, and approached the small shack. A bent tin portico hung over a porch where an old red chair stood guard. There didn't appear to be anyone occupying the building; no light shone from the single glass window next to the door. A thick layer of dirt clouded the pane, so Charlie wiped a peephole with the hem of his shirt. Inside, the shack had all the appearances of a bare-bones shop: a counter ran across the back wall, surrounded by what appeared to be empty postcard and candy racks. A refrigerator case stood by the far wall, its interior lit by a single working bulb. Charlie tried the door; it was open. He stuck his head inside and called out, "Hello?"

No one answered.

He cautiously entered the bodega. A peculiar smell of gathered dust and engine oil pervaded the interior of the shop. A noise, some creature of the jungle, far off, making its screech, gave Charlie a start. "Hello?" he repeated. Still, no answer. What was with the Whiz Mob and their uninhabited shops? It seemed to Charlie they could really stand to improve on their front operations.

He walked back out onto the road and peered in each direction.

Amir was long gone; there didn't seem to be signs of any other human in the vicinity—no truck or car that would suggest that the bodega's apparent state of abandonment was temporary. He walked back into the shop and announced, loudly, "I'd like a Coke in a paper cup, please? I mean, with a lime!" Still, no answer. He returned to the shop's front porch, where he sat down on the red chair and waited.

And waited.

Out of habit, he glanced at his wrist to read the time before remembering that he'd just given his watch away. Amir would be halfway back to El Toro by now, he figured. He hoped Amir would make it back unmolested. He could only imagine what sort of punishment would be meted out to the boy for having led him this far. A kind of dark mood fell over Charlie as he considered his predicament. He tried to sing a song to lift his spirits.

"Somewhere over the rainbow
Skies are blue
I'm in a jungle in Colombia
What, oh what did I do?"

It didn't seem to help.

Suddenly, there was movement on the road. As if materializing out of the mist, a child appeared, walking toward the shack. He was, at Charlie's best estimate, around six years old and was wearing a grubby T-shirt and jeans. He did not acknowledge Charlie's presence on the porch of the bodega, even though Charlie gave him a slight wave as he approached. He threw open the front door; it slammed closed behind him. An electronic buzz sounded and a neon sign reading *ABIERTO* flared into life in the window. It flickered noisily, as if uncertain of its own accuracy. Charlie sat for a stunned moment before standing and following the boy inside.

In the shop, the boy had taken his place behind the counter, his attention diverted to a newspaper he'd unfolded across the countertop. He appeared to be studying the results of several football matches. He still did not seem to be aware that Charlie was there.

"*Hola*," said Charlie. The boy didn't answer. Charlie cleared his throat and said, "I'd like a Coke, please. With lime."

The boy looked up from his newspaper and stared directly at Charlie.

"In a paper cup," added Charlie.

The boy calmly folded up his newspaper. He then reached his hand beneath the counter and retrieved a black Bakelite telephone, placing it on the countertop. He lifted the receiver to his ear and proceeded to input three numbers on the rotary dial. When he'd done this, he casually stared at Charlie as he waited for the other end of the line to pick up.

"*Sí*," said the boy, presumably when the call had been answered. He spoke quietly and turned his head in such a way that Charlie could not discern his speech. The conversation did not last long; in a few moments, the boy nodded twice and then hung up the receiver. He returned the phone to its place below the counter and said, in perfect English, "Wait here, please."

It appeared that Charlie would not, in fact, get his Coke with lime, which left him a little disappointed. He'd been contemplating the sad deceptiveness of the code phrase for only a few minutes when the door slammed open behind him, loudly. He began to turn around to greet the newcomers when a hood was abruptly thrown over his head and he was trundled into the seat of some kind of fitfully idling vehicle.

Charlie could smell the exhaust collecting below his hood and it made him nauseated. Two bodies bookended him into the middle of what he presumed to be the backseat of the car as the engine roared and the automobile began to move. The person to his left smelled slightly of pine needles. Neither of his escorts said a word as they traveled.

The ride lasted, to Charlie's best guess, two excruciating hours. The vehicle wound along a very snakelike road, and Charlie's shoulders ricocheted between the twin pinball cushions of his seat neighbors with every twist and turn. Not a minute passed without some kind of jarring concussion of the car as it navigated what was undoubtedly a road much in need of some basic maintenance. By the time the vehicle had grumbled to a stop, Charlie felt like he had been run through some washing machine's spin cycle, so great was his motion sickness. Plus, he desperately had to use the bathroom.

"Guys," said Charlie, "I really have to pee."

The door was thrown open and Charlie was led some feet away from the car, there to do his business. The hood was removed from his head and his vision was returned. What Charlie saw was enough to make him forget even the most insistent bladder.

It took a moment for his eyes to acclimate, but when they did, they took in one of the more spectacular vistas Charlie had witnessed in his life. He was standing, no doubt, on the top of a very large mountain—he could see several deep valley rifts opening up before him, their troughs all blanketed in fog. Only the nearby tree-strewn ridges could be seen rising above the cloud, and he towered above them all. But the thing that was most extraordinary was the solid stone edifice that stood before Charlie, just beyond the wrought-iron gate he'd been instructed to pee against.

If only the cosmos would accommodate a single thunder crack and lightning flash to starkly illuminate the building Charlie saw—but, alas, it was a moderate spring day with only a hint of cloud cover. No such revelation occurred. The pleasant weather did the monstrosity that commanded the top of the mountain a disservice. It was unlike any building Charlie had ever seen—Amir had been right to call it a fortress. It stood some ways up from the gate, across a wide lawn that had been denuded of the army of trees that lay siege to the property just beyond the fence line.

He'd arrived at the School of Seven Bells.

To Charlie's eyes, the school looked like some cobbled-together Gothic cathedral, but one that had been made by someone who had only heard descriptions of such structures and took a crack at it using whatever materials lay at hand. It had all the ornamental trappings of some dark European edifice—like a Chartres Cathedral or West-minster Abbey—but there seemed to be a strange, organic look to its construction. The stones were more rough-hewn than those in a European fortress of the same kind—their placement was less symmetrical and the size of the stones varied greatly. Some of the windows had been hung at odd angles, and none of them seemed to match their neighbors. Ornamental statues appeared occasionally in the stonework, but instead of the traditional gargoyles or angels, these monstrosities looked to be descended from some ancient native mythos, all feathered warriors in profile and towering winged giants. A central clock tower, dizzying in its height, wound up from the building like the single horn of a deranged creature. The time read four p.m.

Charlie no longer had to pee.

"You finished?" asked one of his hosts. Charlie turned around and saw that it was a boy, about Charlie's age. His skin was dark and his hair was cropped close to his head. An older girl stood next to him and was eyeing Charlie suspiciously.

"What's this about?" she asked. Apparently, she'd just joined them. She spoke with an accent Charlie couldn't ascertain— Swedish?

"He came from the forward station. Had the pass code," replied the boy. Another boy, younger than the first, walked up next to Charlie and studied him.

"Does the Headmaster expect him?" asked the girl.

"Don't know," replied the boy.

"He should," said Charlie. "Expect me, that is."

The girl, who up to this point had seemed to pretend Charlie wasn't even there, fixed him with a blinding glare. She had red hair, cut short; a scar wound its way down her left cheek. She was wearing what appeared to be the school uniform: a maroon blazer over a white shirt and a pair of trousers. An embroidered patch sporting a beetle surrounded by seven small bells had been sewn onto her coat's breast. "Who are you?" she asked. "And what do you want?"

At this moment, Charlie gathered all his courage, every last ounce. He gathered courage from places he never knew courage existed, where it had perhaps been put somewhere, long ago, and been forgotten like a set of keys or a bit of jewelry of which you had been very fond, but had given up for lost, only to be found, years later, in a place where you had thought you'd looked a thousand times but, no, there it was. And with these ounces, now amounting to pounds, Charlie spoke:

"I'm Charlie Fisher. The Headmaster has stolen something from me. I want it back."

This statement was met by complete silence. The girl looked at him in disbelief, her jaw slackened so much that Charlie could see the gold fillings in her teeth. A wind whipped over the edge of the mountain, tousling everyone's hair in a strangely jocular way.

"I'm sorry . . . ," began the girl. Charlie's response had clearly thrown her. "What did you say?"

"The Headmaster has stolen something—"

"I got that. Where did you come from? How did you get here?"

"From France. The Headmaster has stolen something from me."

"The Headmaster has."

"Yes," said Charlie. "I mean, the Whiz Mob has. For the Headmaster."

"A whiz mob stole from you."

"The Whiz Mob of Marseille, to be specific."

"How did you get here?" pressed the girl. "Who brought you here?"

"I came by my own wits. I came to see the Headmaster."

The girl continued to stare at him. Finally, she said, "Stay here." She walked away to a small booth that was set off to the side of the gate. She retrieved a radio receiver and, holding it up to her mouth and depressing the call button, began relaying this information to some unseen person on the other end.

The younger boy on Charlie's left side, standing close by, said, "You came from France?"

Charlie nodded, still watching the girl in the booth.

"To get something that a whiz mob stole from you," repeated the boy. He began laughing until the other boy shot him a glare, and he hastily put on a straight face.

The red-haired girl in the booth stuck her head out and called out to Charlie, "Sorry, what's your name again? The Headmaster wants to know."

"Tell him," began Charlie. He paused, feeling suddenly emboldened. "Tell him it's the Grenadine Kid."

The girl raised an eyebrow and related this information into the receiver. The boy on Charlie's left said, "The Grenadine Kid?"

"It's my nickname, from the mob," said Charlie proudly.

"That's a dumb name," said the boy, before he was again reproached by his partner.

The girl returned from the booth, a bemused look on her face.

"Take him to the office," she said. She looked squarely at Charlie. "The Headmaster will decide what to do with you, *Grenadine Kid*."

The gate was thrown open and Charlie was marched onto the campus of the School of Seven Bells.

The grounds of the school, through which Charlie was rudely escorted, bore an eerie resemblance to your typical American East Coast private or Ivy League school—the grass seemed recently shorn to a comfortable picnic-outing length, and there were enough manicured trees and shrubs scattered across the great lawn to satisfy the most demanding landscape designer's eye. Here and there, groups of students were gathered, lying about on blankets or sitting in circles, no doubt discussing some new and high-minded approach to binging a souper off a fat pappy. They all wore identical maroon blazers over crisp white shirts. An older man wearing a corduroy jacket with leather elbows addressed a small crowd of younger students, evidently having taken advantage of the fine weather to host the lecture alfresco. He flipped a coin between his fingers while he spoke. As Charlie and his captors walked past, Charlie saw the professor slip the coin into a pocket of his blazer and then invite a student to attempt the prat. Charlie didn't get a chance to see the test resolved before he was navigating the stone steps to the front doors of the school.

The massive oaken doors—ancient, mottled things—were so large as to require, Charlie imagined, some sort of mechanical device to open them. For more casual use, a smaller entry had been cut into the center of the doors, and it was through this opening that Charlie was ushered. They walked into an enormous foyer, its floor made of weathered granite flagstones, its ceiling a splendor of decorated arches and vaults; there they were greeted by a guard in a red blazer, a pin on his chest indicating his station. When he was told of Charlie's provenance, the guard looked at him aghast.

"France," he said.

"Yes, France," said the girl.

He waved them through a set of double doors on the far side of the foyer, which let into a room that Charlie judged to be about half the length of an American football field. The walls on all sides were lined with tall shelves filled with books. Light poured in from the arched windows on either side of the room, windows that were so tall as to nearly touch the wooden beamed ceiling, some sixty feet above Charlie's head. Along the floor of the giant room had been placed dozens of practice dummies, much like the one Charlie had cobbled together in his room back home, dressed in a costume shop's variety of clothing. They were all currently being set upon by cannons-to-be, each eagerly practicing new and better ways of removing coins from unseen places. Instructors hovered around the would-be thieves and their silent marks, shouting commands—"Left hip! Keister! Coat pit!"—as the students tried to manage each pinch. A few onlookers stopped to stare at Charlie as he was paraded by; some appeared to size him up as a chump, their faces contorting as if they'd caught a whiff of some terrible smell.

A staircase wound up beyond the glass doors at the end of the room; Charlie and his entourage climbed these stairs several floors to a long hallway, this one lined with dark wooden wainscoting. At the end of the hall was a glass-paned door. On the glass, in plain type, had been painted a single word:

HEADMASTER.

Arriving at the door, the girl rapped her knuckles against the glass. A moment passed before a voice from within called out, "Enter!"

The girl gave Charlie a look that he could not decipher—was it pity? Or annoyance? Perhaps he sensed a flicker of resentment that he, a mere chump, would be seeing the Headmaster, the mysterious figurehead propped at the helm of this strange ship. In any case, he didn't have time to ponder it, as the door was swung open and there, in the center of a very well-appointed room, was a large desk, and behind the desk sat a large man. A crossword puzzle, cut from a newspaper page, was laid out in front of him, something the man's attention remained fixed upon even as Charlie and his escorts entered the room.

"Charlie Fisher," said the man, etching letters into the white boxes of his puzzle with a ballpoint pen. Studiously, he read what he'd written and tapped the tip of the pen against the paper. "Welcome to the School of Seven Bells."

Chapter
TWENTY-ONE

The Headmaster was not the leering, medieval monster Charlie had envisaged. Instead, he had all the bearing of a dowdy English schoolmaster in his rumpled three-piece suit, spotted on the lapels with what could only be mustard, his oversized glasses, which hung askew on his face, and his disheveled gray laurel of hair around a liver-spotted bald head. He even spoke in such a manner, like someone who'd devoted his life to the poetries of Dante and Virgil only to find himself, year after year, teaching the same rudimentary arithmetic to an ever-revolving gang of unruly pupils. There was a sort of tired resignation to his plummy King's English accent. His diet had obviously overstepped the bounds of his suit, as the buttons on his vest seemed near to bursting, barely able to keep the fleshy shape of the Headmaster contained within its fabric.

Charlie, seizing the initiative, began to speak. "My name is Charlie Fisher. My father is——"

"Charlie, Charlie, Charlie," said the man as he flattened out the crossword puzzle against the desktop. "How was your travel? Comfortable, I hope?"

Charlie was thrown by the question. He had no answer readily available. His words seemed to catch in his throat.

"I'll take that as a yes. What a very long way to go, what. Didn't get a chance to pack a valise, I see. Five-letter word for 'oceangoing vessel.'"

"Excuse me?"

The Headmaster seemed to answer his own question. "Yacht, yes." He picked up his pen and scribbled the answer into the boxes on his puzzle. He began to read another clue, his eyes scanning the page lazily. Charlie tried again:

"My name is Charlie Fisher. My father is Charles Fisher Senior. You stole something from me. From my father. The Rosenberg Cipher. I'd like it back."

The man looked up from the puzzle and studied Charlie with something approaching fascination, like a wildlife biologist observing the social habits of some rare species. "Have a seat, please," he said.

"I'd rather stand, thanks," said Charlie.

The Headmaster waved his hand impatiently at one of the boys behind Charlie; the boy gripped Charlie by the shoulders and guided him to the chair that sat opposite the Headmaster. Once Charlie had been seated, the man continued, "Yes, yes, I know. The Rosenberg Cipher. Yes, I stole it. No, you can't have it back."

Charlie couldn't say anything in response. Admittedly, the Headmaster's reply was the most obvious of all the answers he was bound to receive. But Charlie had been living under the spell of a kind of magical thinking—it was as if he hadn't dared consider this most elementary response. To be fair, he'd never have made it this far if he'd considered anything other than full cooperation on the Headmaster's part. This was a fault of Charlie's, and it was something with which he was just now forced to reckon.

The Headmaster smiled at Charlie, perhaps guessing his feelings. His teeth seemed abnormally long and yellowed. They hung in his gums like weathered siding on an old barn. "Charlie Fisher. Junior. Son of Charles and Sieglinde. I do confess: I've admired your family from afar. Career diplomats, to a man. Did you know your grandfather was instrumental in bringing about the Russian Revolution? Idealistic fellow. A close friend of Lenin's. Ilya was rumored to refer to him as his 'little sparrow.' You didn't know that, did you? Not many do. Powerful piece of information, what. But, like your father, he was a man dedicated to a global vision. Not one of these dilettante ambassadors, propped up by some president or other because they happened to give enough money to the winning side, their little gamble having paid off. No, the Fishers stand alone. Men and women of cordiality and curiosity, education and strength."

The man paused, then, taking a deep breath. He lifted a pipe from the desk, packed it with tobacco, placed its stem in his mouth. "Which makes it all the more perplexing as to why you, a boy of good upbringing and education, should make as rash a decision as this." He lit the bowl, puffed at it a few times, whipped the match extinguished, placed it in an ashtray, removed the pipe, studied the ember, and, placing it back in his lips, happily smoked away. "What on earth were you thinking?"

"I thought—"

"You thought I'd just give it back to you, just like that?"

"I'm a cannon. I'm on the whiz," said Charlie. "I ran duke, I hooked. I did all the stuff. And—"

"And it's in with the pinches, in with the pokes, right?" the Headmaster said, finishing Charlie's thought.

"Yes," answered Charlie warily.

The Headmaster let out a laugh. Smoke puffed from the side of his mouth. "They really did a fine job on you, I must say. Extra plaudits, all around, for the Whiz Mob *de Marseille*. Rarely has a chump been so taken in by the grift." He chortled around the stem of his pipe as he took another long draw. "Tell me," he said, pulling the pipe from his lips. "Tell me . . . What *is* the Rosenberg Cipher, hmm?"

Charlie searched for an answer that might satisfy his questioner. In fact, he did not have one.

"You don't know, do you?" said the Headmaster, "This thing for which you have traveled so far. This piece of paper you've risked life and limb for. How can you want something *so much* and yet not have the faintest clue what it is?"

Again, Charlie had no answer.

The Headmaster continued, "Have you taken even a moment, Mr. Fisher, to ponder what sort of power this piece of paper has—or, indeed, if it has any at all? What if it were a kind of poison, hmmm? A sort of evil charm that bedeviled the man who took possession of it. Shouldn't, in that case, you want it *out* of your family's care? Have you even stopped to consider this possibility?

"Well, let me tell you one thing, Mr. Fisher. The Cipher, in all its traveling, in all the various hands through which it has been traded, is now safe. It is finally home, what. I would say that we did not as such steal the Cipher as *save* it. We saved it from its abuse in the hands of the too powerful. In the hands of America, the Cipher would be a cudgel, clouting and disfiguring the countries and kingdoms that did not come to heel. The powerless. Do you wish to have the powerless *cudgeled*?"

Charlie sat silently, assuming the question had been rhetorical. When a few seconds passed, he realized it hadn't. "Uh, no?"

"I would think not," replied the Headmaster. "I. Would. Think. Not. Rachel." Here he spoke to the girl behind Charlie, his red-haired escort. "A cup of tea, please. Boiling hot. No milk."

"Yes, sir," said Rachel. She shot Charlie an annoyed glance, the sort of glance that might suggest that she blamed him for having to fetch tea when there were other things she could be doing, before turning around and walking briskly down the hallway. The two other boys who had accompanied them sidled in nearer to their captive.

The Headmaster continued, "Consider, Charlie: the Rosenberg Cipher has arrived in my possession the way that it has, since its creation, always transferred ownership. By theft. Ergo, it has come to me in a perfectly lawful way. Think on this, Charlie: the dozens and dozens of hands the simple piece of paper has passed through—the transference carried out always by sleight of hand, by the play of wits. Don't think your father accepted this without some pound of flesh being paid, Charlie. No, no one is untouched by the stain of the Cipher."

Charlie smarted at the idea that his father had worked in any kind of extralegal way—it seemed impossible. "That's not true," he said. "My father—"

"Your father is a good man, Charlie, yes. But perhaps you don't understand the adult world as well as you claim—one must always be prepared to bend the rules to achieve justice, what. Your father knows this as well as anyone. It is a principle we share."

"So why do you want it? What are you going to do with it?" asked Charlie.

"I suppose I should use it in whichever manner I choose," responded the Headmaster. "Whether to wield its great power in the service of the powerless or to assay its value on the common market and reap whatever financial rewards it can fetch. This is my prerogative. Surely you must understand this, one criminal to another."

"I'm not a criminal," said Charlie.

"Oh, but you are, Charlie," said the Headmaster. "You've said it yourself. In with the pinches, what? That ship has sailed, my boy. You are forever tainted by your association. This is not something the straight world will likely forget. Oh, you poor boy. Look at your hangdog face. You hadn't really thought that far, had you? No, you were too intent on somehow convincing me to give you back this thing. You're checkered, Charlie. You're 'the Grenadine Kid'—isn't that right? How does it feel?"

"I—I made a mistake," said Charlie. "I can make it right. I know it."

"You've got a gifted imagination, I'll give you that much. Thing is, Charlie, you have no *network*. That's really what separates us, you and me. See, when you've got a network, a community of your own, a state, a nation, you can do whatever you like. You can decide what's true and false, what's right and wrong. When you're on your own, you've got nothing. You're in a den of thieves, Charlie, and yet you are the trespasser. You are the transgressor. Isn't that strange?"

The Headmaster did not wait for a response, but continued his hammering: "No, you'll return to the straight world, branded a criminal. That's what you get for straddling the two worlds, Charlie, living your two lives—you suffer the worst consequences of both and reap the benefit of neither."

Charlie felt like he'd arrived at some sort of virtual dead end, where no direction was the correct one. The Headmaster was right: he could visualize himself sprawled, facedown, across a chasm. On one side was himself, Charlie Fisher, and on the other was this *thing* called the Grenadine Kid. The chasm was very wide; as wide as his life. Having never truly chosen one side or the other, he was fated to bridge that gap until the inevitable moment that his arms gave out and he fell, spinning, into his doom.

At this moment, Rachel returned. She placed the Headmaster's tea on the desk. It arrived in a ceramic mug that read *#1 TEACHER!* He thanked the girl and gingerly took a sip. Giving a satisfied sigh, he placed it on the desk next to the crossword puzzle.

"TARE," exclaimed the Headmaster abruptly, for no particular reason. Everyone in the room gave a little jump, including Charlie.

"E-excuse me?" asked Charlie.

"Four-letter word for 'biblical weed,' what," said the Headmaster, his attention again diverted to the crossword puzzle on his desk. He inscribed the answer into the puzzle, giving the final letter of the word a little celebratory flourish. Having done this, he looked back at Charlie. "Credit where credit is due, Charlie," he said. "I'm rather impressed you made it this far. You may be the first chump to have

the courage, much less the gall, to come all this way and by whatever means arrive here, at my desk. It truly is unprecedented."

"Thank you," said Charlie uncertainly.

"All for this single thing. Quite remarkable." He began to shuffle through some papers that had been stacked on his desk. "Now, where did I put it?" he muttered to himself. He stood up slowly from his desk chair and walked over to a filing cabinet, where he began thumbing through the contents of the top drawer. He paused for a moment, noticing that one of the many framed pictures—a collection of photographs, awards, and citations not dissimilar to the decorations that festooned Charlie's father's walls—had gone crooked. In the process of straightening it, he noticed something on top of a particularly untidy stack of papers atop the cabinet. "Oh. Here it is," he said, brandishing a white envelope.

Returning to the desk, he waved it in the air in front of him. "I'm inclined to just give you the Cipher, in recognition of your stick-to-it-iveness. Your gumption."

Charlie stared at the envelope. There hung the thing he'd traveled all this way to reclaim. He swallowed hard before saying, "You are?"

"Of course not," said the Headmaster, rolling his eyes. He removed the document from the envelope and studied it closely, as if it were a wasp or a fly he'd caught. He wore a look that came close to disgust.

"Look at it," he said. "This one sheet of paper. A bit of pulp, really, covered in tiny figures and symbols. It's almost *vulgar* in its simplicity. And yet entire societies hang in its power—entire so-called 'advanced' societies. I wonder: If such a thing can topple a regime or bring down a political party, this simple piece of paper, what good is that regime? What *real* power does that party have, what?"

His rumination came to an end when he abruptly returned the Cipher to its envelope and slid it into the interior pocket of his suit coat. "No, Charlie, I will be keeping this with me. And you will be heading back to your father and the rest of the straight-world chumps. Is that clear?"

Charlie felt his hackles rise. He sensed his time was running short. "I'm not a chump, *sir*," he said.

"There you go again," said the Headmaster. "Which is it? Are you a criminal? Or are you straight? You don't seem to be able to make up your mind."

"It was just a . . . a . . ." Charlie searched for the word. "A lark. A sort of game. I didn't know . . ."

"But you see, my boy, you are right on one front. The whiz is a kind of game. A puzzle in which everything in the world is its pieces. It is decidedly not for the faint of heart, this game. Perhaps you should've chosen a different one."

"It wasn't my choice," said Charlie. "I was taken in."

"I needn't give you a lecture on free will, Charlie?"

"Let me ask you this," said Charlie. "If I was a graduate. Of the

School of Seven Bells. Would you have still stolen from me or my father?"

"I'm not interested in answering hypotheticals," said the Headmaster testily.

"But if I was. You wouldn't, would you." Charlie gestured to the kids planted behind him, the two boys and the girl named Rachel. "What about them? Their parents? Would you steal from them? Would they be considered chumps, suckers? Where do you draw the line?"

The Headmaster shifted in his chair. His eyes strayed warily to the kids behind Charlie. "Well, now," he began, "there are considerations . . ."

Charlie turned and looked at the boy to his left. He was a few years younger than Charlie; he was staring uncertainly at his captive. "You," said Charlie. "You think your parents are safe from this man? Do you think *you're* safe?"

"Mr. Fisher . . . ," interjected the Headmaster.

"What about you, Rachel?" asked Charlie, swiveling to face the redheaded girl. "How can you be sure you're not the mark in some long con, huh?"

The girl gave no response; she shot a confused look at the Headmaster.

"I don't know what you're getting at, Charlie, but it's a dangerous game you're playing," said the Headmaster. His voice then changed;

his tone became almost assuaging as he addressed the kids behind Charlie as much as Charlie himself. "Of course there are protections in place. That is to say, there is an accepted immunity. For students, alumni, and various associates. We're not Neanderthals, after all—" He interrupted himself, saying gruffly, "But this is a fool's line of questioning. You are not a graduate of the School of Seven Bells."

"But I was conscripted—I was an equal to everyone in the mob. I worked for you. I made money for you."

The Headmaster tittered. "I think it's a *bit of a* stretch to say you worked for me. Not in the way you think, leastways. See, in this arrangement, you were the chump. The sucker."

"I told you, I'm no sucker."

"Yes, yes," said the Headmaster, his voice now showing his impatience. "We've argued this point. Now, if you don't mind, I do have a school to run. So long, Charlie. Best of luck." He gave a look to Charlie's captors; Charlie felt the familiar grip of their hands at his elbows.

"I've got the know. The whiz know," said Charlie defiantly, louder now. "I'm a turned-out cannon."

"Thanks for your interest in the School of Seven Bells, but we're not looking to fill any vacancies in the student rolls at present," said the Headmaster. "Don't call us. We'll call you, what," he said. He'd returned to his crossword, was filling in the boxes. Charlie felt himself pulled from his chair.

"Let me take the test," Charlie said suddenly.

Many things can happen in a very small amount of time. Your eyelid will rise and fall in three hundred to four hundred milliseconds; a hummingbird will beat its wings ten to fifteen times in the span of a single second. It takes just about half a second for a fifty-pound weight to fall five feet, perhaps even onto the toe of the person who dropped that weight; it will take even less time for that fact to register, via expedited telegraph through the nervous system, from the foot to the brain of this unfortunate soul. It could be said that Charlie, in a similarly expeditious amount of time, made a very complex decision in the dispute between the warring twins inside him.

And you may be pleased to know that the Grenadine Kid won out.

"Pardon?" asked the Headmaster.

"The Test of the Seven Bells," said Charlie. "Let me take it."

The finger grips on Charlie's elbows had not slackened. Indeed, the kids were still intent on leading him out of the room. Charlie had to set his feet squarely to resist their force.

"You," said the Headmaster. "You want to take the test."

Charlie nodded, his eyes fixed on the Headmaster's.

"That is impossible," said the Headmaster.

"It's not. I can do it."

The man seemed flustered by Charlie's insistence. "I mean to say it's impossible for you to pass it, Charlie, no matter how highly you esteem your supposed whiz know. It denigrates the school itself to even suggest such a thing."

"You're afraid," said Charlie. "You're afraid I can do it. You're afraid I'm right, that I'm a cannon."

"Nothing could be further from the truth, my boy, it's just that—"

"Then let me take it."

The Headmaster was annoyed; Charlie was getting under his skin. "Gifted students, scholars of the whiz, have failed this test. Many on several occasions. Whatever you were told about the Test of the Seven Bells, you should know it is not some cursory entrance exam. It is the true and final test of a learned cannon's skill. No chump has ever taken the test, let alone passed it. This is folly." He then addressed the kids at Charlie's elbow. "Please, take him back to El Toro. I'm weary of this."

"Come on, let's go," said one of the boys behind Charlie. He grabbed at Charlie's shoulder, his fingers digging into his collarbone. Charlie jerked free and slammed his palms down on the desktop before him. Stacks of paper scattered across the surface; the Headmaster's teacup nearly toppled, but the man's agile fingers managed to stop the accident before it occurred. Charlie's captors tried to grab him again, but he swung around, his back to the Headmaster, and shot them a defiant glare.

"Please, Charlie. Don't embarrass yourself," said the Headmaster. "I granted you this meeting out of consideration for your audacity, to let you speak your piece. You've now really overstayed your welcome. Don't make me regret the invitation."

"Let me prove it," said Charlie, turning back to face the man. "Let me take the test. Let me prove to everyone that I'm a class cannon."

The Headmaster cast a look over Charlie's shoulder at Rachel and the two boys. They acquiesced to the man's silent command and backed away. He stared back at Charlie and said, "And what, pray tell, would that achieve?"

"If I can pass the test, I'm as good as any graduate."

"It stands to reason," responded the Headmaster.

"In which case, the Cipher will have been unlawfully stolen from a proper, turned-out member of the Whiz Mob of Marseille."

"And . . . ," prompted the Headmaster, beginning to see Charlie's line of argument.

"And so," said Charlie, "I'm granted immunity. You will have to give it back to me, to return it to its rightful owner."

There was a long breath of absolute silence in the room. Nobody moved or said a word. It was as if the occupants of the Headmaster's office had all been struck by some supervillain's freeze ray and were only waiting for the antidote to come along and unstick them. The antidote, in this case, happened to be a long and wheezing laugh from the Headmaster himself. The laugh poured out of his lungs like so much pipe smoke, and he doubled over from the effort of it. The rest of the occupants of the room squirmed uncomfortably to witness this uncharacteristic behavior from their principal. All, that is, except for Charlie.

Apparently the kids behind Charlie read the Headmaster's mirth as his last straw. "We'll get him out of here, sir," said Rachel testily. "He won't trouble you anymore."

The Headmaster, still laughing, waved a hand and shook his head. He steadied himself on his desk. He removed the glasses from his face and studied the lenses through the ceiling light, then pulled a hand-kerchief from his coat pocket to wipe them clean. He was chortling the whole while, as if some funny film was being played through the lenses of his glasses. He then rubbed his eyes and placed the frames back on his face.

"It would," he said, regaining his composure, "be fitting."

"Sir?" Rachel asked from over Charlie's shoulder.

Charlie did not share the girl's surprise; the Headmaster's response was the one he'd anticipated, the one he'd most hoped for.

"A genius gamble, really," said the Headmaster. "One perfectly suiting the transference of the Cipher. To think: of all the hands it has passed through, the dozens of clutching, greedy fingers—has its ownership ever faced such a dubious gambit?"

He placed his hands in his pockets and turned to face the wall of photographs behind him—a mosaic of student body portraits over the years, a gradient of color changing from stark black and white to bright color from framed picture to framed picture. Valedicto-rian graduates glad-handing their headmaster on a beribboned dais; signed headshots of particularly beloved pupils, having achieved some special notoriety in the real world. The Headmaster seemed to take them all in. "Everyone on this wall has passed the Test of the Seven Bells," he said. "Look at them all. Most failed their first and second attempts. What you don't see are the faces of those who never passed, whose skills were never up to the challenge of the test. Those who never quite fulfilled their promise and were sent back, thrown down to the straight world from whence they came. They far outnumber the ones you see here." The Headmaster turned back to Charlie and, frowning, said, "I will agree to your little proposition. You will have one chance. If you fail, you leave this place immediately."

"Agreed," said Charlie.

"You will return to your home by whatever means you arrived here. You will not speak a word of what you have seen on your little adventure. Is that clear?"

"Yes, sir," said Charlie. "But if I pass."

"You will not pass."

"If I pass, you give me the Cipher."

The Headmaster took a long look at Charlie, as if seeing him for the first time. He raised an eyebrow, adjusted the rims of his glasses, took a long sip from his teacup and, setting it down, said, "Agreed." He turned to the kids behind Charlie and said, "Very well then, children. Let us prepare the exam room."

Chapter
TWENTY-TWO

Don't be fooled: Charlie was terrified. In fact, he'd never been so terrified in his life. For all the braggadocio of his performance in the Headmaster's office, he was still Charlie Fisher, son of Charles, recently of Marseille, France, writer in training, serial lumberjack impersonator. He had not yet shed that persona completely. Thing was, he'd discovered a little depth to his second persona, the one named the Grenadine Kid. The Grenadine Kid was not daunted in the face of danger. The Grenadine Kid did not shy from adventure, and the Grenadine Kid did not—most certainly—talk into his chin. Charlie was trying his very darnedest to channel the voice of the Grenadine Kid while he was led back down the stained wood-paneled hallway of the School of Seven Bells.

By this time, enough commotion had transpired in the Headmaster's study that it had attracted interest from the student body; many of the doors along the hallway that had previously been closed when Charlie had first been marched past them were now cracked open—prying eyes were peering out from the jambs. One such door flew open when Charlie walked by, revealing a stunned Michiko staring into the hallway. Charlie gave her a little wave before she disappeared from view.

The Headmaster had apparently decided to make Charlie's test a public affair, because as they were walking, the PA system squawked into life, broadcasting a short announcement to the student body: "ALL STUDENTS ARE ASKED TO REPORT TO THE EXAM ARENA—REPEAT, ALL STUDENTS, REPORT TO THE EXAM ARENA FOR A SPECIAL ASSEMBLY BY INSTRUCTION OF THE HEADMASTER." Following this announcement, there came a murmuring of excitement from the classrooms Charlie passed. Clearly, pickpocket students were no different from your traditional schoolkid—they all enjoyed any excuse to get out of class early.

It was a strange parade: Charlie and the two boys flanking him, his arms restrained by their steady grips, with Rachel following close behind. The Headmaster played the drum major of this particular marching band, walking with all the swagger of a man in his position some ten feet ahead of the procession. Children, abandoning their classrooms and study groups, fell in line. As they walked through the giant dummy-dotted room that Charlie had crossed earlier, Charlie felt a tug at his sleeve. He looked over to see Molly the Mouse in the place of his right-hand guard. She'd shed her Marseille attire for the de rigueur maroon school uniform and had pinned back the scant bangs of her short brown hair with a barrette.

"What are you doing here, Charlie?" she hissed.

"Molly!" Charlie exclaimed. He had to bat away his first instinct, which was to be genuinely enthused to see his former comrade at arms. His tone changed quickly. "What does it look like?" he asked, with as much venom as he could muster.

"Um, you're about to be publically executed?"

"No," Charlie shot back, blanching. "I'm getting the Cipher back. The thing you guys stole."

Molly's eyes widened at the thought of it. "How you gonna do that, Charlie?"

"I'm taking the test."

"*The* test?"

"Is there another?"

Molly puffed out her cheeks and made an expressive exhale. "Is there a pool going? What are the odds?"

"Mouse," said Rachel, from behind them. "Leave him be."

"Right, right," said Molly. "Well, good luck, Charlie."

"Whatever," said Charlie.

"C'mon, Charlie, don't be mad. It's all part of the whiz. No hard feelings and all that."

"Just leave me alone."

Molly shot a glance at Rachel before grabbing Charlie by the shoulder and hopping up to put her mouth to his ear. "Second prat's a dipsy," she whispered. And then she was gone.

A crowd of kids had amassed in the foyer, the vaulted entry chamber that had been so placid and empty when Charlie had first arrived. They were queuing up to enter a pair of double doors that had been swung open to one side of the room. When they saw the Headmaster arrive, the crowd immediately hushed and parted, leaving a wide channel of tiled floor for the procession to follow. The students stared at Charlie as he passed, as if he were some bizarre creature; they whispered quiet observations to one another, their eyes never leaving the specimen. Charlie tried to stare some of them down, but they appeared unashamed of their gawking.

A dark passageway, lined with the same aged wooden paneling that had covered the walls of the upstairs hallway, opened up just beyond the foyer. This hall ended in another set of doors, these ones much larger than any Charlie had seen on the premises—massive, iron-banded things. A shiny placard above the doors read *EXAM ARENA* in utilitarian type. The Headmaster pulled the doors open with something approaching flamboyance, holding his hands aloft while they swung out on their large brass hinges. He then disappeared, descending into the gloom beyond.

When Charlie and his cohorts arrived at the doorway, he could now see the reason for the Headmaster's dramatic reveal: they were standing on a short balcony overlooking a huge, circular room. Above the darkened floor loomed three tiers of galleries; they began to be filled with eager students, wandering silhouettes against the lamplight inside the galleries' arcades. Every surface seemed to be carved from the same amber mahogany that appeared elsewhere in the school's design. The room struck Charlie as an odd collision between a university lecture theater and a Roman coliseum.

A loud noise sounded, a kind of reverberant *clunk*, and a cone of light suddenly shot down from a massive spotlight hanging from the domed ceiling. Charlie gawped to see what it illuminated.

Was it a person?

No, it had no head. It was a dummy, a mannequin.

The floor of the arena was empty save for this single, headless mannequin dressed in a strange uniform. The overhead spotlight threw a perfect white circle around the dummy and cast the contours of its clothing in eerie shadow. Charlie did not have time to savor the view before the kids at his elbow rushed him down a set of stairs to the arena floor. There, he was left alone. Alone with the dummy.

The encircling arcades above him rumbled with activity—the hum of hundreds of voices busily chattering to one another as they assumed their places. Charlie took in his surrounding audience but found that the dizzying height of the galleries gave him a brief fit of vertigo—he returned his attention to the mannequin in the center of the room.

It was somewhat taller than Dennis, his practice dummy back home. It also wore a more complete outfit, as if it were readying itself to walk out onto the streets of Manhattan in December—an overcoat, or benny in the argot, hung over a three-piece suit. The lower half of a pair of tapered trousers could be seen from beneath the hem of the benny. However, what really distinguished the mannequin from poor Marseille Dennis was the fact that the pockets visible to Charlie were each labeled with an embroidered number. Charlie, from his distance, could see the numerals 1 and 2 stitched into the fabric of the topcoat's left and right tog pits. But that was not all.

A bit of shiny chrome, just at the opening of the pits, glinted in the glow of the spotlight—Charlie had to squint in the low light to see that a single silver bell hung from each of the visible pockets.

Seven pockets. Seven bells.

Somewhere, a speaker gave a burst of feedback and squawked to life—the Headmaster's voice was broadcast inside the cavernous room: "Welcome, Charlie," he said. "Welcome to the Exam Arena. You have volunteered to take the Test of the Seven Bells."

The room was silenced by this announcement. All the murmuring and laughing—the persistent buzz of the spectating students—came to an abrupt halt.

"The exam will measure your level of expertise in the field of pickpocketing, it will examine your understanding of the whiz and the breadth of knowledge you have accumulated as a matriculating student. . . ." The Headmaster's voice trailed off. "Well, that part doesn't apply to you, does it?" He cleared his throat and continued, the PA system clicking in and out between each sentence the man spoke. "Seven coins have been seeded into seven pockets on the dummy. Each of these pockets is numbered. Each of these pockets is rigged with a bell. You must retrieve the coin from each pocket, in the correct numerical order, without ringing the bell. If a single bell is rung, the exam is considered a fail. Are the rules understood?"

Charlie looked out into the open air of the arena and said, "Yes."

"You may begin," came the Headmaster's disembodied voice.

"And if I pass, you give me the Cipher," said Charlie loudly. "Right? I want everyone to witness this."

There was a pause before the reply arrived: "Yes, Charlie. That was the arrangement."

The audience gave a kind of collective, anticipatory murmur as Charlie approached the dummy, sizing up the two visible tog pits. They were uptown britches—the openings were cut diagonally—which was of some relief. He'd always had better luck with the diagonal-cut prats; he found them easier to navigate. He squeezed his hands into a fist, calming the quaver in his fingers, before raising the breast of the benny—*carefully*—with his index and middle fingers so that it was lifted a mere inch from the mannequin's suit coat. In the light, he clearly saw the numeral 4 stitched on the hem of the right jerve of the jacket; next to it was a silver bell, a small yellow thread connecting it to the fabric.

Where was pocket number three?

Just then a flash of light caught his eye and he craned his neck to see a bell dangling from the tog pit—the inside pocket—of the topcoat. He caught his breath in his throat; the bell dangled dangerously from the fabric, its small clapper threatening to strike against the bell's sloping waist at the smallest provocation. The numeral 3 was embroidered on this pocket. No other labeled pockets were visible.

Right tog tail. Left tog tail. Tog pit. Coat pit.

He decided to focus on the first four before fanning the fifth, sixth, and seventh pockets. He stepped back a few feet, steeling himself.

"Come on, Charlie," came the Headmaster's voice through the PA. "Make your frame. We're waiting."

Charlie ceremonially cracked his knuckles and got to work.

He homed in on the first pocket—the right tog tail of the topcoat. Using his thumb and forefinger in a reverse pinch, he eased open the hem of the pocket. The fabric moved, carrying its bell along with it. The clapper swung slightly, but made no contact. Transferring the weight of the pocket opening to his index finger, Charlie first hooked his middle finger into the interior of the pocket before slowly moving the rest of his hand into the prat's now open mouth. His eyes remained fixed on the little silver bell, hung by the thread from the hem of the pocket.

Inside the prat, his fingers felt cool metal; a coin.

Carefully, without so much as moving the heavier fabric of the pocket's hem, his index finger stationary, Charlie managed to pinch the coin between the second knuckles of his index and middle fingers. The coin safely lodged there, he removed his hand in an exact reversal of its initial descent into the pocket. The prat slowly closed as the tips of his fingers emerged; the silver bell returned to its initial position without a noise.

Charlie stepped back. He let the coin fall into his palm.

"One!" he said loudly, triumphantly. He held up the coin, briefly, before letting it fall to the stone floor. It made a noisy clatter. The audience in the galleries hummed their approval.

"Well done," came the Headmaster's voice, after a short squeal of feedback from the PA system. "Very well done. Rudimentary, how-ever. A palate cleanser. The real test begins now."

Charlie did his best to ignore the insinuations of the voice. He remembered the Whiz Mob's description of the test, those many weeks ago in the catacomb below Marseille: the Test of the Seven Bells grew more difficult as it went on, not merely because of each pocket's increasing difficulty, but because of the Headmaster's mind games, his seedings of self-doubt into the exam. Charlie breathed in the challenge; he welcomed it. In fact, he was counting on it. He moved forward, fanning the next pinch.

It seemed innocuous enough: the left tog tail—a mirror image of the first bing. As he began to reach for the pocket, however, he remembered Molly's whisper in the hallway—something about the second pocket. What had she said? Charlie realized he'd been so overcome by his gamble at the time that he hadn't entirely registered her words.

Best to play it safe, he decided. His caution was rewarded when he probed the lining of the pocket to discover that a safety pin, a dipsy, had been carefully threaded between the opposing fabrics of the pocket's opening, effectively fastening it closed. It had been placed in such a way as to escape casual detection. Had Charlie simply moved in to reef the kick, he would've snagged the dipsy and sent the bell swinging.

Charlie let a puff of air escape his pursed lips. He inwardly thanked the Mouse for her guidance. He then glanced up at the galleries, the faceless audience above him. He could hear them chatter quietly to one another.

This time, he worked with his left hand. It was Sembene who had taught him that much. When fronting the mark, you're better off if you can work ambidextrously; you'll avoid having to unnecessarily crook your wrist in order to handle some basic pinch. With his left index, he felt along the cool metal of the pin to where it was held closed in its hasp. Bracing the front of the prat with his thumb, he pinched at the hasp, breathing a quick sigh of relief when he felt the pin give way. As he moved his fingers back into position, however, he felt the point of the dipsy stick him. A sharp pain shot through his middle finger, and he let out a cry that was as much of surprise as it was anguish.

He felt his finger flinch.

The audience in the galleries gasped; they listened for a ring.

The ring did not come.

With a quick swipe of his index finger, he slid the safety pin from the fabric. He pinched it between his index and middle finger before it fell too deep into the pit, pulled it from the pocket, and let it fall to the ground. From there, it was a basic prat dig. In the span of a few seconds, he had the coin in his hand and was holding it up for his audience to witness.

"Two," came the Headmaster's voice. "Very good, Charlie. Very good. You've passed your first major hurdle, what. The first pocket of the test acts as a kind of bait. Gets the student's confidence up, only to be thwarted by something as simple as a dipsy. I have to say, this is proving to be quite the show, after all."

Charlie inspected his left middle finger: a small bulb of blood emerged from where the dipsy had stuck him. He jammed the fingertip into his mouth and sucked it clean. "Glad you're so entertained," he murmured. He shook out the pain in his finger and reoriented his concentration back on the dummy.

Number three was where things would get tricky, Charlie knew. The tog pit. Having learned his trade in Marseille in the springtime months, Charlie hadn't had much practice on heavy coats. Most of the pockets he'd emptied during his time on the Marseille whiz had been sewn into linen jackets and loose-fitting chinos: fabric that was light and manipulatable, not so beholden to the constraints of gravity. This benny was an altogether different story: a heavy wool topcoat, the sort of thing a Chicagoan might spend entire months swaddled inside during the worst of a midwestern winter.

His focus was shattered when the Headmaster spoke again. "I see your hesitation, Charlie. Right tog pit. A simple pinch, really, though it can be disastrous for the unprepared. Are you prepared, Charlie? Are you up to the challenge?"

It became clear that now, having arrived at this chapter of the gambit, the Headmaster intended to talk through the entire pinch. Charlie tried to block out the noise as he moved in on the dummy.

"You finessed the dipsy in the tog tail quite well, I must say," came the man's voice. "But you'll not have as much leeway with the pit. Remember, should *any* bell ring, you fail the exam. Upon which, you will be leaving immediately, never to bother me again."

Charlie felt beads of sweat appear on his brow. He wiped them away with the sleeve of his shirt. He faced up to the dummy, chest to chest, trying to determine how to best position his body.

"You'll be interested to know," came the Headmaster's voice after another squelch of feedback, "that a full quarter of our students fail on the third pit. So, should you fail, you will not be alone. You might take that as some consolation."

Charlie squeezed his eyes tight, willing the words away. He envisaged himself on a Marseillais tram, trundling down the tracks toward the Old Port. He envisioned Amir sitting off to his side, watching him work. His pounding heart seemed to quiet at this sudden transposition. He was facing his chump; he was fronting the mark—some oblivious bates with cash to burn. In his mind, he looked to Amir. In his mind, Amir frowned and shook his head.

Of course. Tog pit. Don't front the mark.

Like a dancer orbiting his partner, Charlie abruptly rounded the left shoulder of the dummy, placing himself directly *behind* the mannequin. From that angle, his left hand easily wound its way into the coat, pushing the heavy wool of the benny from the inner jacket like he was parting a curtain.

"Careful now, Charlie," came the voice archly, though to Charlie's mind it might as well have been the tram conductor, calling out the next stop on the line. "Working behind, you're working blind, what."

It was true; he was working blind. But having the back of his wrist against the heaviness of the coat allowed him more control of its movement. The bell remained unstruck. Soon, his fingers were delving into the interior of the satin-lined pocket, the coat open only as much as his small wrist would allow. His fingers found the smash and retrieved it. With a cascade of relief, he pulled away from the dummy and fell backward, the coin in his hand.

A few of the onlookers allowed a hoot of congratulation and a smattering of applause, all of which were quickly hushed by the squeal of the PA.

"SILENCE!" shouted the Headmaster.

The crowd immediately followed his command. Apparently, the button on the PA microphone had become stuck; a stream of frustrated dialogue, unexpurgated, was broadcast into the arena as the Headmaster struggled with some unseen obstacle. "Rachel," sounded the voice after a time. "How do you . . . I can't seem to . . . Oh, just turn the whole thing off!" A crackling noise followed and the PA system was suddenly dead.

Moments later, a door opened in the far end of the arena. A shadowy figure appeared and began walking across the chalky ground. When the figure came within the throw of the spotlight's circle, Charlie could see it was the Headmaster. The man crossed his arms and looked squarely at Charlie. He glanced at the coins Charlie had thrown to the floor and frowned.

"Well done," he said. "But you still have four more to go."

Chapter
TWENTY-THREE

The Headmaster, as if mindful of Charlie's working space, remained just on the edge of the spotlight's throw. He had his hands firmly placed in his pockets as he studied Charlie. The buzzing of the crowd above them was a murmur of white noise, spectators between acts of a gripping drama, discussing pivotal moves and rehashing what had already transpired. Charlie glanced into the upper galleries; a large figure caught his attention—was that Borra? And that girl, just next to him, had the dusty blond hair of Jackie. It was no time to speculate; the Headmaster cleared his throat and said, "Please, if the student . . ." He stopped himself before saying, "If you will continue the exam, Mr. Fisher."

Charlie returned his attention to the dummy. He approached it, letting his eyes stray over the lines and seams of the topcoat, the way the interior opening of the jacket could be seen beneath. The line of the trousers, sprouting out from beneath the jacket's hemline, held firmly to the mannequin's waist by a leather belt. He knew from his earlier reconnaissance that the fourth pocket of the test was the coat jerve—the ticket pocket—of the jacket. Beyond that, he couldn't be sure. He decided to bing the fourth pocket and then worry about the fifth.

"I can see promise," said the Headmaster abruptly, as Charlie reached for the opening of the topcoat. The suddenness made Charlie's fingers briefly recoil. "A student such as yourself. Sloppy, inelegant, yes—a far sight from a proper cannon. But still, a diamond in the rough, perhaps. I'm surprised our agents hadn't reported on your abilities."

"Now's your chance, I guess," said Charlie, feeling annoyed as he situated himself again for his pinch. He carefully pulled back the front of the topcoat, mindful of the bell hanging from pocket two, and revealed the coat jerve labeled 4. The jerve was mid-waist on the jacket, and its interior was protected by a wide flap over the opening. The pocket's bell hung from the flap. The challenge here was to unslough the pocket flap without ringing the bell, no matter what sort of okus might be awaiting his fingers. He peered more closely at the pocket; a rectangular expression in the fabric gave away the presence of a skin, a wallet.

"Yes, Charlie," said the Headmaster, confirming his suspicion, "pocket four. This particular poke wants only the coin, not the dead skin. The student is required to kick the okus back, emptied." Charlie moved to attempt the poke, but the Headmaster, timing his commentary, said, "All without ringing the bell, of course."

"Are you going to talk through this whole thing?" asked Charlie, having removed his hand.

The Headmaster gave a little laugh. "A cannon should not expect to make his pinches in a vacuum. Working inside the noise is part of the exam. Pray, continue."

Charlie glared at the man before returning his attention to the coat jerve. First, he needed to mind the topcoat, the benny, before he could even think about the ticket pocket. He did so by finessing his right hand between the inner fabric of the benny and the jacket—now his wrist was acting as a bridge between the two coats. Flipping his hand palm up, he lifted—ever so carefully—the pocket flap with his middle finger, his eyes riveted to the silver bell as it ascended. Once the flap had been fully opened, he flipped his palm back over and transferred the weight of the flap to his thumb, neatly pinning the flap to the suit jacket. This way, the bell was effectively muted against the fabric of the jacket. His other four fingers now free to work, he let his middle and ring fingers move into the interior of the prat until they'd touched the leather of the okus.

"So much effort," said the Headmaster suddenly. "Really, a

tremendous amount of effort. To retrieve this thing, this Cipher. Tell me, what *truly* is your motivation? Is it *saving the world*? From a *monster* such as myself?"

Charlie frowned and tried to remain focused on the pocket.

"Or," continued the Headmaster, "is it a boy's desperate need for love and approval from his father?"

Charlie felt his fingers flinch. The bell shifted, but did not sound. The tell was all the Headmaster needed to continue: "That's it, isn't it? *Fascinating*. So much effort. It's a wonder that such approval should be lacking in the first place, what. Leaves a boy somewhat vulnerable. He begins looking for approval elsewhere, I daresay." He pointed at the dummy. "Careful there. Wouldn't want to rumble your mark. You will soon be, as they say, in flagrante delicto."

Having practiced binging an okus on his dummy back home, Charlie knew that the position of the wallet was crucial to the job. He let his fingers probe, found that it was *lying down*—it was sitting in such a way that the fold was perpendicular to the pocket opening. Carefully, he topped it up—manipulating it so that the fold was, instead, in line with the pocket hem. Then, with his fingers locked on the wallet, Charlie swiveled his wrist so that he managed to lift the okus from the interior of the pocket. His thumb remained fixed to the pocket flap, he let his hand pivot until the wallet was free of its hold. He manipulated the skin between his free fingers, and once it had been upended, he deftly swung it with his index and middle fingers.

The coin fell from the wallet into his left hand. He then reversed the motion: dropped the wallet into the pocket, carefully lowered the pocket flap, and stepped back from the dummy.

"Four," he said triumphantly. He threw the coin to the ground in front of the Headmaster.

The galleries were immediately awash in chatter. A few spectators let out cheers but were quickly hushed by their neighbors.

The Headmaster began pacing at the threshold of the spotlight's shine. "Very good, Charlie, very good. A remarkable stretch of luck for an unlearned chump. A chump and a mark. Does that not rankle you, Charlie? That you were the mark all along?"

Charlie felt the anger seethe in his chest. He tried to stamp it down, to push it further away, reminding himself that this was merely another tack the Headmaster was using to distract him—and yet it continued to steam like a kettle in his heart. He moved forward, fanning the mannequin for its fifth pocket. It took him a few moments of carefully shifting the layers of wool and rayon that made up the dummy's outfit before he saw it: the vest jerve. Inside the protection of the jacket, the dummy was wearing a buttoned vest. The left front pocket of the vest was clearly marked 5, and a bell clung to the seam of the pocket like a barnacle. However, what really caught Charlie's eye was the long gold chain that fed out of the pocket's opening, dangled low to the hem of the vest, and ended, high, pinned to the vest's opening, just above the second button.

"A souper," he muttered.

The Headmaster apparently heard him, because he said, "Yes, very good. You didn't think you'd just be binging coins like you were some carnival louse, did you? This coin, coin five, is, for all practical purposes, a bit of block and tackle. A coin nonetheless, but one attached to the chain. This is one mark who keeps his ridge under high security, what."

"All the easier," said Charlie, attempting defiance. His voice cracked slightly, somewhat undercutting the effect.

Smiling with his stained teeth, the Headmaster said, "Then don't let me keep you."

A souper was an easy bing—Charlie'd done it on no lesser mark than his own father—but he knew not to be overly confident. There was no margin for error. The trick was to unpin the chain; the rest was a cakewalk. The chain would act as a line to the coin, and Charlie need only reel it in. He began by slowly opening the top buttons of the vest, so as to better study the way the chain was being attached. The Headmaster spoke while he did this.

"Of course, the hallmark of a true sucker is having the illusion of security. I'll repeat that: the *illusion* of security. It lets down the mark's guard. It blinds his eyes to the real gaps in his defenses. It leads him to do things for which he wouldn't otherwise bear the risk."

Charlie allowed the words to become ambience in his head. His fingers worked their way up the opening of the vest, looking for the pin holding the chain in place.

"For example, it might influence a chump to lead the cannon to the very place where the true score is. The illusion of security. Or, in your case, the illusion of friendship. The thing that made you give up the Cipher."

Just then, a series of events occurred within a very small fraction of time: the Headmaster's words materialized from the ambience and struck him at the heart, his fingers moved a little too quickly, the pin holding the chain in place turned out not to be a pin after all, but a mere clasp. The clasp came abruptly loose, the chain fell.

Charlie saw it fall. Its swing, in this merest portion of a second, fell swiftly toward the bell. The metal of the chain came within centimeters of its target.

Charlie caught it.

The bell remained unstruck.

Charlie let out an exasperated sigh, pausing in his work before coiling the gold chain around his finger until the coin to which it was attached tumbled from the pocket and swung freely in the air.

He turned and dangled the coin from its chain before him, looking at the Headmaster. "Five," he said.

The students in the gallery resumed their excited conversation. Someone shouted, "Go, Charlie!" Did he recognize the voice? Was it Pluto, of all people?

"Quiet!" shouted the Headmaster. "This sort of behavior during an exam is strictly verboten, students! I'll not have you all hooting like a bunch of urchins at a panto!"

Charlie's eyes strayed to the crowds in the galleries above the arena. He was sure now. He saw them all: Molly, Borra, Michiko, and Pluto. They'd all crowded to the front of the press, their arms hanging over the stone guardrail. And there, just to the side of them, were Sembene and Fatour. They were unmistakable in the audience. Behind the twins was a tall blond girl: Jackie. Was she smiling at him? The light was too dim to tell.

He suddenly knew that this was the vengeance he was seeking. It wasn't retrieving the Rosenberg Cipher, not any longer. It wasn't just righting the wrong that the School of Seven Bells had done to him and his family, to his country's interests. It wasn't proving himself to his father. No, it was this. It was showing the Whiz Mob that he would beat them at their own game. He was a class cannon. They were the chumps.

He was the Grenadine Kid.

With this newfound fire burning in his gut, he stepped forward to the mannequin. He was so confident, in fact, that he didn't care that the Headmaster had now borne down on him and was standing directly behind him—so close that Charlie could smell the sweet putrefaction of his breath as he spoke.

"Five pockets. Five coins. You've shown some spunk, I'll give you that, Charlie Fisher," said the Headmaster, leering over Charlie's shoulder. "I'm prepared to chalk it up to luck. However, this is the point that separates the touts from the mere prat diggers. The sixth and seventh pockets of the Test of the Seven Bells are the most challenging of the exam, the ones that require the most acuity and presence of the know in a student."

The man spoke while Charlie rounded the mannequin, surveying the various pockets for clues as to which one he was expected to empty. There were three more pockets on the jacket, two more on the vest—but none wore a bell or were graffitied with an embroidered number. It wasn't until he'd faced the mannequin and gently lifted the front of the dummy's benny that he saw, just below the bottom hem of the inner jacket, a number 6 sewn into the fabric above the right front hip pocket of the dummy's pants—a top britch, in the argot, with an opening cut parallel to the waistband. Just above the number was a little silver bell.

"Ah yes," said the Headmaster, his body still nearly pressing against Charlie's back. "You've found it. Number six. Britch kick."

Charlie moved to begin his poke, but the Headmaster spoke again: "Notice anything strange?"

The man's breath was clammy and warm; his clothing, evidently having been last laundered in the 1930s, gave off a peculiar scent, like a damp rag that had been left too long by the sink. Charlie tried his best to shake off the halo of unpleasant aroma surrounding him as he knelt down to examine the kick.

Sure enough, he could see what was different about this pocket: a large bulge at the bottom of the pit suggested that this dummy had been collecting change—the pocket was heavy with smash.

"One coin," said the Headmaster. "For one pocket."

"How am I—"

"How are you supposed to know which coin? Oh, Charlie. This is where your lack of education is made painfully obvious. Had you matriculated as a student of the School of Seven Bells, you would've spent an entire semester learning the relative weights of every currency in the world—their size and heft, the pattern of their edges. By the end of your second year, you would've been able to, blindfolded, properly distinguish a centime from a drachma, a forint from a nickel—by the weight alone." The Headmaster heaved a satisfied sigh. "Our mannequin, here, is quite the worldly gentleman, what. There is a global community of change in his pocket. Alas, you must find the coin that matches the ones you've already pinched."

Charlie looked down at the coins that lay scattered on the clay floor. He picked one up and studied it. It was a simple peso, nondescript in size and weight. Had he not read the legend, set in relief on the coin face, he would not know from which country it had hailed.

The Headmaster drew even closer. Charlie could feel the man's balloonlike belly press against the small of his back. His rasp rang in Charlie's ear: "Best not rummage about too long in there. That bell will be going ding-a-ling."

Beads of sweat broke out anew on Charlie's brow. He stared at the coin in his hand. He stared at the bulging pocket on the mannequin.

"Ding-a-ling," whispered the Headmaster.

Charlie had had enough. Throwing the coin to the ground, he spun around and faced the Headmaster, allowing his chest to press against the man's bulbous gut. He fixed his eyes boldly on the Headmaster's; the two remained there for a time before Charlie said, "You gonna let me work?"

"This is part of the test, chump," said the Headmaster. "You must work under duress."

"I think you're trying to put your thumb on the scales."

"Why on earth would I want to do that?"

"Because you know you're wrong."

"And what, pray tell, could I possibly be wrong about?"

"That I'm a cannon," said Charlie, pushing himself even closer to the Headmaster's body, if such a thing was possible. "And I didn't even need your dumb school to become one. That's why you're afraid."

"Nonsense," huffed the Headmaster.

Charlie gestured to the silent mass of kids who hung in the galleries, watching their stare-down. The Headmaster's gaze followed his arm. "If I pass," said Charlie, "it makes their 'education' meaningless. It makes the Test of the Seven Bells mean nothing."

The Headmaster laughed. "Nothing could be further from the truth. The Test of the Seven Bells speaks for itself. It is an exam that has lasted centuries. It is the Rubicon that separates the straight world from the touts. You might ask yourself: Are you prepared to cross that river?"

Charlie didn't answer. He turned and faced the mannequin. He adjusted the waist of his trousers. He could still feel the Headmaster's close presence, hear his breath. Charlie recalibrated his attention; he returned to the task at hand. He was to remove a single coin from the right hip pocket of the dummy, one amid a large collection, all without seeing the coin—or ringing the bell attached to the pocket. The Headmaster had been right: he did not have the education or experience required to identify the coin blindly. He could imagine getting to that point, with time, but now his deficits were showing.

An idea occurred to him.

The coin on the ground. The one that he'd had in his hand.

"A curious approach," said the Headmaster, as Charlie stooped and picked up the coin he'd just thrown to the floor. "Bus fare for the ride home?"

Charlie shot him a glare as he approached the dummy. The Headmaster shadowed him closely. Charlie could feel the rustle in the Headmaster's suit as Charlie's hand went for the pocket. His opposing hand delicately held back the hem of the topcoat and the jacket, allowing safe passage for the hand holding the coin.

"What's your plan, here? Are we kicking the ridge back? Watch that bell. I've just had the bells redone, you know. They'd grown a little dull over the years, with the amount of ringing they'd done. Something about the crispness of the silver—the ring didn't quite have the sparkle it once did. I loved that sparkle. The sudden chiming of the bell, sounding as if it were pealing from some steeple tower, over a wide valley. That's what it sounds like, Charlie. It rings into your very soul."

Charlie moved his hand into the britch kick, the coin pinched between his thumb and index finger. He snaked his hand down into the pocket until his fingertips rested at the top of the pile of coins amassed at the bottom.

"Your very soul, what," repeated the Headmaster, now transfixed on Charlie's attempt on the pocket. "But they'd lost that chime, you know. Such a shame. Now they're back to ringing like the bells of heaven, believe me. What are you doing?"

With his middle finger, Charlie was now patiently dragging individual coins from the pile to be pancaked against the one pinched between his thumb and finger. It was tedious work, and his eyes remained steadily affixed to the bell at the opening of the pocket . . .

The Headmaster continued his harangue: "Careful now, Mr. Fisher. No time to second-guess. The mark's attentions are unpredictable."

. . . but eventually he found a coin that seemed to match the size and heft of the one in his hand.

"His movements are fluid. Capricious. Are you watching? Are you aware?"

Charlie took an extra moment to rub the two coins together before he determined that they were one and the same. Armed thus, he removed his hand from the pocket with the confidence and surety of a proper class cannon.

DING.

At first, it didn't make sense to Charlie. At first, it didn't seem to even come from his current plane of existence, but there it was. The Headmaster had been right: the bell rang with the clarity and resonance of crystal shattering.

DING.

The crowd let out a collective groan of disappointment.

The Headmaster seemed as surprised by the sudden chime of the bell as Charlie had been. They stared at each other in a kind of matching disbelief before a smile broke across the Headmaster's face. He grabbed Charlie's wrist and yanked it up to his face.

"Nice work, Charlie," he said. "Very close. Can I?" He pulled the two coins from Charlie's fingers and studied them. They were matching.

Charlie had, after all, managed to nick the right coin. But in his zealousness to retrieve the coin and verify his success, he'd lost track of the higher goal—to make the prat without ringing the bell.

The Headmaster threw the coins to the ground with something approaching glee. He looked at Charlie. He clapped his hands five times, slowly, applauding. "Very good," he said. "But, alas, not good enough. The Cipher remains, as it should, in my possession." He reached into his coat pit and retrieved the stuffed white envelope, studying it in the glow of the spotlight. "Do not despair, Charlie. Consider this a victory for the downtrodden. A stunning win for the disrupters against the greedy sheep of Western civilization." Slipping the Cipher back into his pocket, he looked at Charlie thoughtfully and said, "To which do you belong?"

"I don't know," said Charlie despondently. He stared at the coins on the ground, willing them all to disappear, to erase the memory of his failure.

The galleries were already emptying; the students began to file out of the arena, back to their classrooms and lecture halls. An air of disappointment hung over them, a mass of circus-goers somehow denied the moment when the tiger jumps through the fiery hoop. What's more, the supremacy of the Test of the Seven Bells had been upheld—it was and would remain that ultimate barrier between novice and cannon. The structures and strata of the school were intact. There were no easy bings to be had here.

"You have promise, you know," said the Headmaster to Charlie. "Brilliant trick there at the end. Perhaps a hint of the know was in there, after all. I'd have to see what our current enrollment is, but perhaps, in a year or two, with some improvements, we could see to your being wait-listed."

"No, thank you," said Charlie.

"Suit yourself," said the Headmaster. "Rachel! Zephyr!"

Two figures approached from the stairs leading down to the arena floor.

"Kindly show Mr. Fisher to the gates," said the Headmaster. He turned to Charlie. "Per our agreement, you'll be hooded and returned to the crossroads at El Toro. Apologies for the crudeness of your transport, but precautions must be taken. This is the School of Seven Bells, after all. Secrecy is king. Good-bye, Charlie. It's been . . . *enlightening*."

The man in the rumpled gray suit walked away across the arena floor and up the stairs toward the balcony and the double doors. He stopped, briefly, at the first tier of the galleries and turned to Charlie, saying, "One more thing. It might be best if you didn't show your face here again, Charlie. I think next time we will not be so accommodating."

And with that, the Headmaster was gone.

"Hey, Charlie," came a voice from the galleries. A few of the students had lingered, hanging at the first tier's balcony rail. Charlie immediately recognized the voice; it was Michiko's. "Nice try," she continued. "You're a real bang-up operator, you are. I was rooting for you."

"Nearly did it," came another voice—the Mouse. "I put you at fifteen to one to bing a single coin. You beat the odds there, mate."

"I make thirty dollars off you, Charlie," came a voice awash in a

Slavic accent. "You make up for bad tip at racecourse."

"Thanks, but no thanks, Borra," replied Charlie.

"I thought you were gonna do it, to be honest." In the dim light, Charlie recognized Pluto, eye patch and all, as he sat down at the edge of the balcony, his legs straddling one of the columnar supports of the guardrail and dangling over the edge. "When I took the test, I failed it three times before I even made it past the fourth pocket."

Jackie stood behind him. "You put up a good fight."

"Go away," said Charlie. "All of you."

"Is that how you talk to your friends?" asked Pluto archly.

Molly gave him a little kick. "Shut up, Pluto," she said.

Sembene appeared at the rail, his head just peeking over the top. "See you around, Charlie."

"Yeah, see ya," said Fatour, standing next to him.

The Whiz Mob of Marseille, hangers-on at a cinema, watching till the last of the credits scrolled up the screen, saw that the show had truly come to an end and began, collectively, to move their way toward the exit. Charlie was silent as he watched them leave. Only Molly hung back, waiting till the rest of the mob had left and the galleries were empty before she, too, headed for the exit. Just as she was about to disappear, though, she turned and said, "I say you're a cannon, Charlie. A real class one. Don't let no one tell you different."

And then she, too, was gone.

Charlie was escorted down the hall, through the foyer, and across the campus of the School of Seven Bells. Several groups of students loitered on the lawn and, wordlessly, they watched him go by. A black sedan awaited him just beyond the grille of the iron gate. He nodded to the driver before taking in a last glimpse of the gargantuan structure that sat atop the slope above him, the rolling lawn, the idling students.

"Ready?" asked the driver.

A hood was placed over Charlie's head, and he was ushered into the backseat of the car.

He arrived, two hours later, at the crossroads outside El Toro. His hood was removed and he was ushered from the vehicle. His captors said nothing as they closed the door behind him, revved the engine, and disappeared back along the dirt road. The kiosk's door swung open, blown by the wind. The *ABIERTO* sign was off, though Charlie could not tell if it was a mere malfunction. He breathed a sigh and began walking down the road toward El Toro.

He hadn't walked long before he heard an approaching motor. The mist had cleared; the sun was just beginning to set. From around a bend came a dilapidated truck, its fenders and hood wearing bright stains of rust where the paint had been scraped away. It came to a squealing stop just alongside Charlie; the passenger door was thrown open.

"Get in," said the driver. Charlie looked up to see it was Amir.

"How did you—" began Charlie, gesturing to the truck.

"You'd be surprised what a silver Rolex will fetch in pesos." He revved the engine ostentatiously. "C'mon," he said. "Before the touts catch wind."

Charlie climbed aboard and threw himself into the seat alongside his friend. Amir wrestled the truck into gear and they headed off down the road.

"So . . . ," began Amir, glancing over at Charlie. "What happened? How'd it go?"

"Just drive," said Charlie.

And so Amir did.

THE END

Chapter
TWENTY-FOUR

Y ou didn't think the story was going to end there, did you?
Of course it doesn't.

Of course there's more.

But first, let's leave our two heroes as they navigate the potholed road through El Toro and out of the jungle interior of Colombia, winding their way toward Cartagena, which, they'd decided, would be the quickest and best route home, there to catch the first steamer leaving the port. Let's leave them, for now, to their journey. They have a long way to go, and Charlie could no doubt use what little rest is afforded him in the cab of the truck as it bumps along the country road toward the coast.

It'd be better not to disturb them.

Let's instead return to the School of Seven Bells. Let's watch the Headmaster.

The Headmaster was tired. He'd had plenty on his plate before the disruption of the impromptu exam had occurred—he still had applications to review, the senior class's thesis papers to grade, graduation ceremonies to prepare—all with an entirely new freshman class arriving within a few months. What's more, he'd only just left the arena when he was collared by the Okus Technologies professor, wanting to know the status of his tenure application. He'd scarcely finished the tedious conversation (this particular professor, while talented, was a bit of an irritant) when a group of students had mobbed him, wanting to show a new stall they'd developed. And so it was some relief when he finally, after what seemed like an eternity, was heading toward his office.

It was evening and the classrooms were emptying. The halls were beginning to come alive with students heading to dinner—all happily chattering about the exam they'd witnessed that afternoon. As often happens when a school year is winding down, the smallest bits of drama tend to take on an otherworldly aspect, and Charlie's exam was the only thing anyone was talking about. To the Headmaster's mind, he'd given them a bit of a show, putting Charlie up to the exam—a kind of reward for their dutiful hard work that year. Before long, most of them would be off to faraway destinations all over the globe, fully on the whiz for the first time in their lives.

This thought made the Headmaster smile. On the whiz for the first time—think of it. He almost envied those kids, those newly anointed cannons, all wondering at their deployment and what the future would hold for them. Who would they be matched with? What would be their role in the mob, their position? What strange and beautiful city would they be sent to? Oslo? Berlin? Shanghai? Each city filled with its own particular brand of wonder and mystery, each filled with crushes of easy marks, just waiting to be systematically lightened of their wealth. It put him in mind of his first assignment, in '22. Nearly forty years ago now.

The thought made him chuckle in surprise. Had it been that long? Yes, forty years. Cairo, Egypt. That ancient city on the Nile. He'd arrived a fresh-faced graduate of the school, tasked with foldering for a mob he'd not yet even met. The air had been so dry and clear, he'd breathed it in like it was a tonic—could any place have been more different from that gray, embattled industrial town his parents had raised him in? Manchester might've existed on a different planet altogether than Cairo, with its swarming avenues and braying street vendors, the air scented everywhere with safflower and rose. The first day of his arrival, he'd arranged transport to visit the pyramids at Giza. He'd made a mint that day, fleecing the tourists. Oh, and the pyramids had been lovely too. He allowed himself another laugh.

Which reminded him: fifteen across! "Head of a pyramid scheme." It had been a stumper, for some reason, and he'd spent all afternoon hammering himself, trying to unlock the answer. The question had been a dark cloud over the lower right corner of the crossword puzzle—but he'd been going about it all wrong, trying to think of famous grifters (and he happened to know a few), bilking money from chumps in an investment scheme.

"Pharaoh!" he said suddenly, and very loudly.

A student, passing him in the hall, said, "Excuse me, sir?"

"Nothing, Lucy," he said. "Just thinking aloud, what."

He quickened his step. In no time at all, he was back in his office, giddy with the anticipation of cracking open a puzzle that had been bothering him for well-nigh twenty-four hours. He whistled to himself as he whipped off his jacket and hung it on a hook by the door. He then rolled up his shirtsleeves (was that a tattoo of a pincer-mandibled beetle on his forearm?) in an almost ceremonial fashion before taking a moment to pick the very best pen for the job from his desk drawer. After inspecting the tip, he reached for the crossword puzzle he'd left on the top of his desk.

It was not there.

"Strange," he said to himself.

He searched through the papers, the essays, and the applications that were piled neatly on his desk. He opened each drawer and searched its contents. The puzzle was not in any of these places. He walked around the desk, looking for the folded piece of newsprint; he searched the wastebaskets. He got on all fours and crawled, somewhat awkwardly, under the desk. And this happened to be the unflattering position he was in when a thought occurred to him, one that drained the blood from his cheeks and caused him to freeze in place.

"No," he whispered.

He carefully extracted himself from beneath the desk and walked over to the coatrack by the door. Folding back one of the lapels of his jacket, he reached into his coat pit, his fingers alighting on the familiar heft of a white envelope, the very white envelope that held the Rosenberg Cipher. Pulling it from the pocket, he could barely bring himself to lift the flap and see what it contained.

Inside was the crossword puzzle.

BWAAARRRNNN.

The steamship made another loud pronouncement, heralding its farewell to the Colombian shoreline, and the cries of seagulls seemed to respond testily to the near-deafening noise. Charlie was standing at the handrail of the upper deck, watching the lights of the quay recede in the distance behind them as the boat plied its way out into the Caribbean Sea. He'd taken this position as soon as they'd boarded and had refused to leave it; he'd insisted on keeping his eyes fixed on the coastline, his mind busy willing the boat into motion. Now that they'd pushed off and several hundred yards separated the boat from the busy port, only now did a feeling of relief wash over Charlie.

"Relax, Charlie," someone said. It might as well have been his interior voice, but it was, in fact, Amir, who was sitting in a lounge chair on the deck behind him. "You're not going to stand there the whole trip, are you?"

They'd used their fleeting moments in Cartagena to purchase entirely new outfits—Charlie, you might be happy to know, had given his war-scarred tuxedo a proper send-off into a street-side garbage can; Amir had even said a few words in memoriam. Amir was wearing a fresh pair of khaki shorts, a pink collared shirt, and some knockoff Ray-Bans. Charlie, freshly showered, in his brand-new jeans and blue gingham shirt, would not have been recognizable in comparison to his sullied former self. Even after the expense of these purchases, they'd had enough money left over to book first-class passage on the SS *Excalibur*, bound that evening for Lisbon.

The ship was picking up speed; the wind whipped at their hair and clothing. Great ribbons of white water splashed away from the hull of the boat, some fifty feet below them. Seabirds wheeled and glided above the decks. The skyline of Cartagena, painted gloriously pink by a setting sun, receded farther and farther into the distance.

"I guess not," said Charlie. He walked over to his friend and sat down on the side of a neighboring sun chair. "Just feeling a bit stirred up still."

Amir shook his head disdainfully, saying, "That's your problem, Charlie. You can't relax. What's done is done, yeah?" He waved his hand in the air, signaling to a nearby waitress. When she arrived, he

asked for a Coca-Cola and then nodded to Charlie.

"Grenadine and milk, please," Charlie said.

The waitress looked at him quizzically.

"*Granadina con leche,*" translated Amir.

The waitress's look of confusion did not much alter. "*¿Sí?*" she asked Charlie, as if verifying that this was, indeed, what he intended to order. Amir nodded to Charlie.

"*Sí, por favor,*" said Charlie.

"The Grenadine Kid," said Amir, once the waitress had left.

"Quite a mantle," said Charlie self-seriously. "But one I will endeavor to live up to." He smiled, something he hadn't been able to do since they'd arrived in Cartagena.

"There we go, Charlie," said Amir.

A moment passed; a comfortable silence situated itself between the two comrades. Finally, Amir spoke up: "So . . ."

"So?"

"Can I see it?"

Charlie looked around hesitantly. "You think it's safe?"

"Charlie," said Amir, "you have *got* to lighten up a bit. You're going to give yourself an ulcer. Look at us—we're safe as kelsey. I mean, a bit of precaution is good—but at some point you have to peek the knockup, yeah?"

"Okay," said Charlie. He reached down into the pocket of his trousers to retrieve a folded-up piece of paper, gone slightly bent and crumpled from its traveling situation. He flattened it out and handed it to Amir.

Amir sat up straight while Charlie presented it, as if he were being handed some delicate heirloom. He unfolded the page and looked at its contents greedily. After having studied it, however, his first response was: "Any idea what this all means?" He flipped the piece of paper upside down; it still appeared inscrutable to his eye.

"No clue," said Charlie.

Amir gave a little whistle. "All this, for a piece of paper."

"Pretty incredible, huh?"

"I'd say so. You've got to wonder what the Headmaster wanted with it."

Charlie furrowed his brow. "I don't think he knew, to be honest. He did say something about it being able to 'bring countries to heel,' or something to that effect."

"This?" asked Amir, in disbelief.

Charlie nodded. "Makes you wonder, doesn't it? I mean, he was making it out to be this horrible, powerful thing. If that's the case, what does my father want with it?"

"To bring some country to heel, probably."

The boys sat in silence for a moment, each considering the implications of their conversation.

Just then, the waitress returned, and Amir hastily pressed the paper against his chest. The girl laid out two cocktail napkins on the table between their chairs. On one, she placed Amir's bottle of Coke; on the other a glass of an indeterminate pink liquid. Dropping a fiery-red cherry into the concoction, she said, somewhat triumphantly, "*Granadina con leche.*"

Looking up at the girl, Charlie blushed, saying, "*Gracias.*"

"*De nada.* It's nothing," said the girl. She then screwed up her face at the beverage as Charlie took his first gulp. "Weird drink," she said.

"All in a day's work for the Grenadine Kid," said Amir, laughing.

She gave a little curtsy and walked away; other passengers, ambling along the deck, were needing her attention. Amir began to give the piece of paper back to Charlie when he paused and said, "You know, Charlie . . ."

"What, Amir?"

"You've got to wonder what this would fetch on the black market. A couple of touts like yourself and me—just think what we could do with that kind of money. Who knows, we could even put together our own whiz mob; you could stall, I'd hook. . . ."

Charlie shot him a look and held out his open palm.

"Right," said Amir, crestfallen. "Off the whiz." He returned the Rosenberg Cipher to Charlie, who, in turn, slipped it back into the depths of his pants pocket.

Amir reclined back in his chair and took a long slug of his Coke before saying, in a somewhat offhand manner, "You knew you couldn't pass the test, huh?"

"Was there any doubt?" Charlie said, laughing. "I'm amazed I got as far as I did."

"Five pockets," said Amir. "Really, that's not bad. I didn't get to the fifth till my second try. And I graduated magna cum laude."

"Thing is," continued Charlie, "I didn't think I'd *need* to get that far. I thought he started hazing you, all up close, on the third pocket."

Amir shrugged. "Sometimes he does, sometimes he waits. It was always a risky tip, Charlie. But a brilliant, brilliant stall. And to think that was your plan all along."

Charlie didn't say anything; a smile crept across his face.

"That *was* your plan all along, wasn't it?" Amir asked, peering at his friend over the top of his sunglasses.

The white noise of the ocean waves crashing against the ship colored the air; an older couple took up a game of shuffleboard, just down the deck. A band had set up in the bandstand, not too far away, and had just struck into some swingy Spanish melody. Instead of answering Amir's question, Charlie raised the candy-stripe straw of his glass to his lips and took a long, languorous pull.

Amir smiled, interpreting his friend's silence as best he could. He began to say something but stopped himself, watching Charlie's beatific composure with something close to admiration. He reclined in his chair, stretching out his legs. Charlie did likewise and the two boys sat this way, their backs pressed to the slats of their deck chairs, their fingers laced behind their heads, watching as the rosy sky faded to blue and the moon crawled its way above the distant horizon.

And you there, enjoying this same view. Yes, you, sitting quietly in a neighboring deck chair. How have you come to be here? Have you escaped the suffocating company of your parents, just for a moment, to drink in a bit of quiet solitude? Or have you, like Charlie and Amir, been traveling alone and, having come to the end of an incredible adventure, are surprised that something new and very exciting is just beginning?

What would you make of the two boys sitting next to you?

What kind of story would you write for them?

THE END

(REALLY.)

GLOSSARY

banged. stolen (also *binged*)

banner score. biggest touch of the day, trip, or season

bates. mark approximately forty years old

bead rope. pearl necklace

beef the gun. announce publicly that one has been robbed

benny. overcoat

binged. stolen (also *banged*)

block and tackle. watch and chain

blow one's moxie. abandon a job out of fear

blute. rolled-up newspaper used for shading the duke

britch kicks. side pants pockets (left britch and right britch)

cannon. pickpocket

carnival lice. road mob that travels with a circus or carnival

center field, playing or working. along for the ride, not working

chump. mark or victim

class cannon. highly skilled pickpocket

class mob. skilled group

clout and lam. hit and run

coat jerve. ticket pocket

coat pit. inside breast pocket

coat tail. side pockets of a suit coat

cordeen. accordion billfold

crush. crowd (also *tip, press, push*)

curdled. lose a mark's trust

dead ones. empty wallets (or *dead skins*)

declare oneself out. bow out of a job

ding the dead ones. get rid of empty wallets

dipsy. safety pin put through pocket from inside of coat as deterrent

down on the knuckle. poor

egg. mark under thirty years old

fanning. locating the wallet or money

fat mark. moneyed target

flat jointer. con man working the gambling rackets

folder man. whiz mob member who organizes a job (also *steer man*)

fuzz. the police (also *whiskers*)

fronting the mark. working in front of the victim

giving up your kisser. allowing the mark to see your face

goulash joint. café

grift know. natural skill at the pickpocket trade (or *grift sense*)

grift racket. skilled, specialized illegal schemes

hanger. wallet sticking out of a pocket (or *pop up* or *kick out*)

hangout. hideout

heavy rackets. using violence or threat of violence

hook. a tool who specializes in hooking his finger onto a poke

hustling (or working) three-handed. mob with two stalls and a tool (one stall being a steer)

ice. diamonds

in with the pinches, in with the pokes. if a pickpocket is committed, he gets his share

jerve. pocket

jug touch. victim with a large amount of money in his wallet (or *set up*)

keister kicks. back pockets (also *prat kicks*)

kick. pocket

kick the okus back. return the score to the victim

knockup. the day's take

know, the. a fundamental understanding of the whiz rackets

layoff spot. hideaway, where one does not pickpocket

leather. wallet

lone wolves. pickpockets who work alone

make the frame. organize in the moment to pickpocket

make the meet. prearranged time to connect for a job

nash. to flee

nasher. flight from the scene of the crime

off the whiz. no longer a pickpocket

okus. proceeds of a crime (also *touch* or *score*)

pappy. elderly mark (or *pap*)

patch pockets. side pockets of a sweater

pea soup. cheap, not worth working

pinch. steal, pickpocket

poke. single score off a pocket

prat. pocket

prat digger. tool who just works pockets

prat kicks. back pockets (also *keister kicks*)

press. crowd (also *tip, crush, push*)

punching gun. talking shop, reminiscing about old jobs

push. crowd (also *tip, press, crush*)

put the bee on. identify a victim and plan a theft

putting up your hump. stalling for someone

racket. the pickpocket's way of life

reefing a kick. making pleats in a pocket lining with your fingers, bringing up the leather from the bottom of a pit

ridge. metal coins (also *smash*)

rumbled. victim is alerted to the theft

safe as kelsey. conservative or careful tool

scatter. hangout

score. proceeds of a crime (also *touch* or *okus*)

shade the duke. cover the hand of the tool with a newspaper or such device

shag. cheap jewelry (or *crow*)

skin the poke. empty the wallet, usually in safety

slum. any type of jewelry

smash. metal coins (also *ridge*)

sneak job. successful robbery without victim knowing it

souper. watch

stall. distraction member; also the act of distracting the victim

steer man. plans the mob's itinerary (also *folder man*)

swing with it. to successfully pickpocket an item

throw your mob. turn your confederates over to authorities

ticker score. watch theft

tip. crowd (also *press*, *crush*, *push*)

tog pit. inside breast pocket of a topcoat

tog tail. outside topcoat pocket

tool. a pickpocket; a whiz mob member

top britch. front pocket cut parallel to waistband

touch. proceeds of a crime (also *score* or *okus*)

turned out. a pickpocket who is taught and sent out into the world or coached and used as a partner

tweezer. billfold with small clasps

two-handed mob. two pickpockets working together

unslough. undo a pocket button (rhymes with *plow*)

uptown britch. britch pocket cut diagonally

vest jerves. vest pockets

whiskers. the police (also *fuzz*)

whiz. a pickpocket's line of work; his way of life

whiz copper. a policeman or detective specializing in collaring pickpockets (or *whiz dick*)

whiz moll. girl pickpocket

working rough. robbing while armed

Acknowledgments

This book wouldn't exist without the work of David W. Maurer and his incredible book *Whiz Mob: A Correlation of the Technical Argot of Pickpockets with Their Behavior Pattern*. If you'd like to dig further into the language and organization of the Whiz, I highly recommend it—what I cribbed for Charlie and his crew was a mere skimming of the surface. I'd learned about the book from reading Adam Green's excellent profile of Apollo Robbins, a professional tout himself, in the *New Yorker* magazine in January 2013—almost exactly four years ago. I set that piece down and immediately began forming the events that would lead Charlie Fisher into the waiting arms of his Whiz Mob. I had the good fortune to have a plot that could take place in virtually any city environment; I landed on Marseille because of its reputation, as Charlie puts it, as a thieves' paradise—and because I'd really wanted an excuse to hang out in Provence for a few weeks. Of course, Marseille's infamy is ill-warranted—it is a gorgeous and welcoming city, its people are charming and accommodating. Having spent time there, I'm inclined to think its reputation is all part of a conspiracy on the part of the French to keep unwanted tourists away from this incredible Mediterranean paradise. Carson did get pickpocketed, but it must've been a greenhorn on the clout-and-lam circuit—she managed to grab him by the collar and demand the return of the stolen goods (her phone) before punching him in the shoulder, hard, and letting him run off to his friend. Guy clearly did not have the whiz know.

Thanks are due to Mac Barnett for being a helpful plot-wrangler and early reader; likewise to Steve Malk, my agent, for his support. Many thanks to my editor, Donna Bray, for her keen eye and helpful insights and for her belief in the project from the get-go. Augustin Brajeux, my brother-in-law, aided in much of the French language that appears in the book (*merci!*) and was an excellent source on French living. I'm also very thankful to former ambassador to Bulgaria Avis Bohlen, daughter of the United States ambassador to France, Charles "Chip" Bohlen ('62–'68), for being gracious with her time and allowing me to ask her dumb questions about growing up in an ambassador's family in the 1960s. Many thanks to the office of the Honorable Jane D. Hartley, former ambassador to France, for setting up that interview.

Since I do not have a time machine, I was reliant on existing documentation of 1960s France (and Marseille in particular) to flesh out Charlie and Amir's world—of which there is, thankfully, plenty. The French New Wave era of filmmaking did a pretty great job capturing the vibe of this time period, in particular the films *Rififi*, *Mon Oncle*, *Pickpocket*, *The Umbrellas of Cherbourg*—the list could go on. And no research on the Marseille of old is complete without a healthy immersion in Marcel Pagnol's Marseille trilogy: *Marius*, *César*, and *Fanny*. Of course, the literature of 1950s–1960s France is very rich and I owe a great deal to Raymond Queneau's fabulously surreal *Zazie dans le Métro* and its anarchistic titular character. Everyone, even the grown-ups, drinks grenadine and milk in Queneau's Paris. (Our son, Hank, began drinking them at my suggestion—to the great curiosity of the waitstaff at our local restaurants. So much so that our friend Laura Park, while visiting, began calling him the Grenadine Kid—credit where credit is due.) *The Black Docker* by Ousmane Sembène was a terrific resource for painting the Marseille landscape of 1961; Daniel Anselme's novel *On Leave* provided helpful background to the political topic of that day: the Algerian War.

The *dérive* is not a pickpocket's scheme; I borrowed it from the Letterists, a midcentury Parisian artist collective led by Guy Debord. The mob must've picked it up from him. There are still *dérives* being followed today—perhaps you should start your own group of psychogeographers and drift your city or town. . . .

As always, I'm forever indebted to Carson Ellis, my wife and collaborator, for supporting me while I wrote this thing, for wrangling our children when I couldn't, for being a great reader and listener, and, last but not least, providing the beautiful, evocative illustrations you see accompanying the story.

Merci! Au revoir!